The
Rebel's Mark

The
Rebel's Mark

GIVEN HOFFMAN

PRESS ON
PUBLISHING

Copyright ©2021 Given Hoffman. All rights reserved. No part of this publication may be reproduced, distributed, or transmitted in any form or by any means, including photocopying, recording, or other electronic or mechanical methods, without the prior written permission of the author except in the case of a brief quotation embodied in critical reviews and certain other noncommercial uses permitted by copyright law.

Map ©2020 created by BriAnn Beck and Given Hoffman.

Cover ©2021 designed by Elena Karoumpali

This is a work of fiction. Names, characters, businesses, places, events, locales, and incidents are either the products of the author's imagination or used in a fictitious manner. Any resemblance to actual persons, living or dead, or actual events is purely coincidental.

Scripture taken from the New King James Version. Copyright ©1982 by Thomas Nelson, Inc. Used by permission. All rights reserved.

ISBN: 979-8-98522-440-5 (print)

ISBN: 979-8-98522-441-2 (eBook)

To Noah, who was not afraid to remind me
how much a person's past impacts their view of God.

Author's Note

There is something continually intriguing about the medieval time period. I'm still not sure what it is exactly that draws so many of us to the tales of knights and nobility. Perhaps it's the battles, weapons, castles, honor, and bravery. I personally dove deeper into medieval research several years ago because I knew Gage belonged in a medieval setting.

Accuracy in historical fiction has always mattered a great deal to me, and the fear that I might possibly misrepresent real people and times in history is why I have never dared traverse into writing historical fiction. In creating Gage's story, I allowed myself several concessions, which shifted this novel's genre instead to medieval action/adventure.

1. I chose to make the setting medieval but still fictitious.

2. I chose no particular historical dates but rather used details and research from the medieval age as a whole.

3. I took liberties within my fictitious setting and altered what would have been the typical religious styles, governments, laws, etc.

These decisions gave me the freedom to write Gage's story with many of the fascinating factors of the medieval time period but without the restrictions or fear of having to hold perfectly to history.

I hope you enjoy the medieval flavor and setting of this story.

Glossary of Terms

Aye – "Yes"

Bailey – The inner walled enclosure located at the heart of a medieval castle

Barbican – A fortified defense over a castle gateway

Caltrop – A spiked metal device with four or more spines used to cripple mounts

Caparisoned – A covering, often displaying a coat-of-arms, designed for a horse

Couched – When a lance is held tucked against the body in a lowered position of attack

Curtain Wall – A fortified wall surrounding a castle or fortress

Destrier – A valuable war horse

Gauntlet – Armored gloves or thick leather gloves

Gittern – A gut-strung round-backed instrument, usually played with a quill

Hay Wain – A large open wagon, drawn by horses, used to carry loads of hay

Infirmarer – A person in charge of the infirmary in a medieval monastery

Keep – A fortified tower, typically within a castle or fortress

Matins – At or around midnight, approximately 12:00 p.m.

Mayhap – "Perhaps"

Nay – "No"

None – Midafternoon, approximately 3:00 p.m.

Parapet – A protective wall around the edge of a roof, bridge, balcony, or walkway

Palfrey – A smooth-gaited, quality riding horse

Parlour – A room where the monks conducted business with outsiders

Pommel – A round knob on the end of the handle of a sword or dagger

Prithee – "Please"

Refectory – A room used for communal meals

Shawm – A wind instrument with a double reed and a penetrating tone

Solar – An upper chamber in a medieval house and the family's private living area

Surcoat – A loose, sleeveless robe that bears an insignia and is worn over a knight's armor

Tabard – Similar to a surcoat but often shorter with open sides and made of a rougher material

Terce – Later morning, approximately 9:00 a.m.

Tonsure – The shaving of the top of the head as a symbol of religious devotion

Vambrace – Armor for the forearm

Character List

King Axel – King of Edelmar

Queen Irena – Queen of Edelmar

Prince Haaken – Firstborn son of King Axel and Queen Irena

    Joel – Haaken's squire

    Sir Renner – Haaken's right-hand knight

    Sir Holbird – Haaken's knight and brother to Lady Cathleen

    Sir Jocelyn – Haaken's knight and the most athletic of the group

    Sir Adrian – Haaken's knight

Prince Gage – Second-born son of King Axel and Queen Irena

    Allard – Gage's deceased squire, son of Baron Roger of Ulbin

    Sir Wick – Gage's youngest knight, son of Lord Clement

Brother Sholan – Infirmarer at Saint Jerome's Abbey

Father Thomas – Abbot at Saint Jerome's Abbey

Brother Ephraim – Monk at Saint Jerome's Abbey

King Bryant – King of Keric

Queen Vivian – Second-wife of King Bryant

Princess Rhonalyn – Acting Queen of Keric, only child of King Bryant

Lady Aisley – Young lady-in-waiting to Princess Rhonalyn

Baron Philip – Commander of Keric's Royal Guard

Sir Nolan – Second-in-Command of Keric's Royal Guard and Rhonalyn's cousin

Sir Erwyn – (Wyn) a member of Keric's Royal Guard and Rhonalyn's cousin

King Maurice – Deceased king of Delkara

King Strephon – King of Delkara, firstborn son of deceased King Maurice

Prince Thayer – Deceased second-born son of King Maurice

Lord Gregory – Baron of Veiroot, traitor to Edelmar, and father of Lady Natriece

Lady Natriece – Daughter of Lord Gregory of Veiroot

Felix – A man who betrayed Gage and his retinue to the Blue Crow

The Blue Crow – A deceased thief who ambushed Gage on the road to Aro

Manton – Gage's previous traveling companion

Sir Jarret – The knight who branded Gage

Prior Joseph – Manton's friend, the prior of a monastery in Burnel

Sir Hedrick – Commander of the White Fortress outside Clement in Edelmar

Lord Hadrian – Lord of Delipp, where there is the artesian well

Baron Bertram – Baron of Lyster, whose coat-of-arms is a dog with a ring of keys

Baron Elmon – Baron of Awnquera and Gage's uncle on his mother's side

Baron Roger – Gage's previous instructor and the baron of Ulbin

Lady Novia – A friend of Gage's and Haaken's who drowned as a child

Baron Selwin – Baron of Nikledon, son of the deceased Lord Terryn

Baroness Juliana – Wife of Baron Selwin and Baroness of Nikledon

Baron Hewitt – Baron of Duvall, firstborn son of the deceased Baron Lucas

Evan & Tilda – Chandlers from Delipp

Moses – The mystery play performer who is hauled off by Baron Sewin's soldiers

Arron & Michael – Manton's friends from Dinslage, whom Gage meets at Nikledon

1

Pain found Gage in the endless darkness. Like an arrow hitting its mark, it pierced deep into his chest and shoulder, decimating the calm in which his mind had been floating.

He cried out and tried to struggle away from whatever was causing the excruciating pain, but hands gripped his arms, holding him in place, and a male voice spoke sharply. Gage's muddled mind could not put meaning to the words, nor could he draw himself out of the darkness to resist the man's hold. The pain increased and was forced deeper into his chest.

Unable to escape the overwhelming agony, he screamed, and then his mind mercifully drew him back into unconsciousness.

⁂

When Gage could next perceive anything, the intense agony had settled to a heavy ache in his chest and shoulder while other pain drifted to his attention. His wrists throbbed, his body burned, and his pounding head assaulted him in waves.

He tried to recall what had happened to him, but no matter where he searched in his mind there were no answers. He encountered only a suffocating heat from which he could not escape. Why was he so hot? And why couldn't he remember or wake up?

Fatigue and a frightening sense of vulnerability overwhelmed him. He fought to recall any memory that would explain his current state, but no matter how hard he tried to seize what he knew was there, the memories slipped from his grasp.

Days or perhaps weeks later with the inferno still burning inside him, Gage heard the distant glory of angelic singing. He wondered if perhaps he was dying or dead. But if he was in heaven, why was he trapped in the fires of hell? And if he was in hell, why were angels singing?

Fresh heat shredded his thoughts. An urgent sense of fear and the need to escape remained, but he could not recall from what or why. He tried to compel his mind to remember, but focusing on anything beyond his boiling exhaustion proved too grueling a task. Swept away again and again, he wandered in distorted dreams and disjointed thoughts.

Eventually, the stifling heat diminished in waves, and his ability to think returned. But weariness still weighed on him. Worn out by the continual struggle, part of him longed to embrace the cooling emptiness and simply let his mind drift, but another part of him screamed in stubborn anger every time a memory came and then slipped from his grasp.

The knowledge of needing to warn someone stayed, but he could not remember whom he needed to warn. Then he saw Haaken and heard his brother's teasing voice. *"Or you can send chestnuts and a croissant."*

Warmth threatened to carry the thought away, but Gage seized the recollection and zealously guarded its ragged edges. He repeated the words in his mind, and slowly the memory of the conversations he'd had with Haaken and his parents before leaving Edelmar became fuller and more defined. His memories spread out from there, swiftly regaining ground across Delkara.

He broke free of the steamy fog in his mind like a traveler bursting from a hot dell to a mountain's crest where the air is cold and the view stretches to the horizon, but the sight he encountered made him wish he'd stayed in the dell.

He remembered traveling with Manton across Delkara, buying and selling mounts at the fair in Nikledon, spotting his stolen brooch, talking with Lady Natriece, finding out Manton was a rebel smuggler, having Sir Jarret discover stolen gold in his saddlebags, and being branded a thief by the knight. The permanence and judgment of what Sir Jarret had done brought the anger, fear, and humiliation back to the surface of Gage's mind. He was a marked man, and there was nothing he could do to change that.

Somehow he knew that wasn't the only thing he had to fear though. Sir Jarret had put him in a wagon to be taken to his master, and their wagons had been attacked on the road. But what had happened after that? Who had brought him to wherever he was now? The rebels or the soldiers?

Forcing his thoughts past the heat lingering in his body, Gage pushed his senses beyond the chaos of his mind to what he could glean of his surroundings.

He was lying on what had to be straw. A thin material separated him from it, but the chaff pricked through to his skin and did little to pad the hard surface beneath. It smelled dank, like moldy grass. Drawing a full breath, he became aware again of pain throughout his body. He also realized he was shirtless, but a strip of something was wrapped tightly over his chest, and he felt pressure around his wrists. His heart beat faster. He wanted to move his arms to discover how firmly he was tethered, but just then a sound like cloth fluttering in the wind filled his ears. It was followed by a scuffing sound. Then a young male voice close beside him snapped Gage's mind into focus. "You see? He doesn't seem to burn as hot with fever as he did before."

A cool hand touched Gage's forehead, making his insides jump. "You're right," a quieter male voice said.

"Is it certain then that he will live?"

"Only God knows who will live and who will die. Now, get on with you. I will keep the next watch."

Gage wanted to stir to prove he was alive, but then he realized that maybe he didn't want to reveal his awareness to them. His bound wrists and the excruciating pain he remembered from earlier made him wonder if perhaps they valued his well-being not for his sake but for their own.

Were they servants of his new master, told to report if he survived? Or were they soldiers needing him alive, so they could put him back in a wagon and deliver him to their master? Or were they rebels hoping he lived, so they could use him in their war against the nobles?

Their war against the nobles! The urgency Gage had felt to warn someone flickered back to life again inside him. Haaken and his father needed to be told about Lord Gregory and the additional rebels headed for Edelmar. He needed to get word to them, but how?

If his captors were servants to a lord, would they let him send a message to Edelmar? He doubted they'd believe that he was trying to help the nobility, but he had to try. What if his captors were rebels though?

His insides shuddered. If they were rebels, he needed to find a way to escape. But where was he? He tried to recall where in Delkara he could possibly be. Weakness and exhaustion crippled his thoughts though, and his weariness dragged him back into slumber.

2

Beyond the clash of swords, Princess Rhonalyn heard the unexpected thunder of hooves crossing the drawbridge from the city into Arcis Castle. Seizing her smooth green-gold skirt, she hurried out onto the wide terrace where its curving stone steps descended to the castle's bailey.

Sweaty castle swordsmen in the middle of training pages and squires paused their mock battles and bowed to the arriving lords.

The two barons pulled their mounts to a stop while their combined retinues spilled into the paved courtyard behind them. Sunlight glinted off the companies' weapons and armor. Rhonalyn lifted her hand to block the glare. By the looks on the barons' faces, their trip to Arcis had not been a pleasant one.

Rhonalyn shoved aside her annoyance and forced her lips into a smile. Nothing a good meal and some entertainment could not solve, or so she hoped. She had spent the better part of the morning detailing exactly what food was to be prepared for them, the specific chambers they were to be given, and which castle servants would be devoted to the barons upon their arrival. She had arranged it all to be ready for that evening because that was when they were supposed to have arrived.

Instead the infernal sun was directly overhead, the castle's wash was still on the drying lines, the yard was full of half-dressed guards and ill-trained youth, and her selected servants were nowhere to be seen, though there were plenty of others about.

Rhonalyn set her shoulders and lifted her chin. At least she had already had her chambermaid entwine her dark brown hair around her diadem and exchanged her everyday dress for a flattering gown of gold and emerald.

She lowered her hands to the cloth, letting the sunlight blaze across her face and shoulders. Attendants would see to the lord's mounts, and her father's marshal had assured her that morning there was space enough and hay ready in the stable for both barons' retinues. She needed only to confirm that same state of readiness was true of their accommodations.

She snapped her fingers at a pair of servants who had followed her out onto the steps. "You two," she said in the commoners' tongue, "make sure the lords' rooms are as I requested—supplied with clean linens and fresh basins of water. And you three, see to it the barons and their men's saddlebags are delivered to their chambers."

"Yes, Your Royal Highness." Both groups bowed and hurried off.

Rhonalyn looked to their castle's steward, Baron Hughart, who stood removed from the remaining servants, and addressed him in the noblemen's tongue, "Hugh, prithee, will you see to it refreshments are brought to the great hall?"

The wiry man dipped his head and departed for the castle's interior in quick, easy strides.

Sending a sharp glance over the rest of her servants to make sure they were properly positioned and attired, Rhonalyn strode to the edge of the terrace steps. A shuffle and a small nervous inhale of breath followed her.

Having forgotten about her recently added shadow, she turned to find the ten-year-old directly behind her. The child's blond hair fell in lush waves beneath a twisted maroon hairpiece. Her round face and anxious brown-eyes were thus framed by a cloud of gold that Rhonalyn, with her hazelnut tresses, could only dream of possessing. It was a beauty she hoped to teach the child to embrace, if only she could first succeed in teaching her to stop hiding behind everything in sight.

"Aisley." She gestured forcefully for the girl to stand beside her. The girl stepped that way, revealing her bare feet beneath her dress as she did. Mortified, Rhonalyn glanced at her dismounting guests, then back at the child. "Where are your shoes?" she hissed.

Aisley shrank. "I took 'em off, Your Royal Highness, when you told me to sit 'n work on my stitchin'."

Rhonalyn cringed at the girl's lapse into her old horrid speech, but she set aside addressing that, along with her desire to know why the girl had not bothered to slip her shoes back on when she had finished stitching. "Go fetch them, and put them on immediately. A proper lady never goes barefoot."

Chin trembling, the young girl curtsied haphazardly, then scurried back inside.

Rhonalyn looked back at her guests, disregarding the twinge of guilt she felt for snapping at the girl. Aisley needed to learn that, as a woman, if she was to gain any respect or control in life, she must value her appearance and poise above her comfort. Besides, reprimanding her in front of the servants was far kinder than letting her embarrass them both in front of the barons.

The two men ascended the steps with their knights. Gracing them with a warm smile, Rhonalyn welcomed them into the royal castle of Keric.

Rhonalyn's guests consumed food and drink in the cool interior of the castle's great hall. Sunlight poured down through the balconies, crowned with shields, and shone on portions of the columns and walls that displayed banners and tapestries depicting Keric's legacy and Rhonalyn's lineage. A portion of the hall's floor was furnished with benches and tables. Her guests were happily settled around them.

Hosting was something Rhonalyn's royal household knew well and did with relative ease. Two of her more vivacious ladies-in-waiting conversed merrily with several handsome knights from Tenebris. Rhonalyn focused her attention dutifully on the knights' older lord. She motioned for a servant to refill his cup. "How is your wife, Baron Tenebris?" she asked in the noblemen's tongue.

The oval-faced, dark-haired baron nodded soberly as he accepted the cup. "She is well but still nervous about having anyone ride out, even with a guard. It will take time before she does not fear for our safety. But eventually I hope things will be as they were before. She appreciated your letter of condolence."

Rhonalyn nodded. She had written the letter to Lady Tenebris out of obligation. That her expression of remorse over the loss of Tenebris's knights and soldiers had meant something to the woman gave her a feeling of accomplishment. She turned her attention to the second somewhat younger baron. "How is your new bride faring, Baron Durum?"

The man's broad face blushed to his auburn hairline. "She is well, Your Royal Highness. She misses being a lady-in-waiting to yourself, but I think she is finding Durum to her liking."

Rhonalyn raised her chalice. "With the sun-lit western mountains a curtain wall to your manor and the waterfalls a serenade to the valley, I imagine she would indeed."

"Aye, this was my sincere hope," the baron said, "but Durum is a fair bit different from here at Arcis or her past home at Caterva."

Seeing in her mind the flat grasslands of Caterva's manor speckled as they always were with horned goats and scruffy sheep, Rhonalyn disguised her scorn and laughed softly. "Indeed, Baron Durum."

In her opinion, Lady Theda had done quite well marrying the baron. He was a bit obvious, what with his face displaying every feeling he felt, but Theda had only ever taken people at face value anyway, so in the end the Baron Durum's genuine regard and his easygoing nature fit well and overlooked much in regard to Theda's ill confidence in managing her own domain.

Rhonalyn swished the liquid in her goblet, watching its rich color swirl. "The fields grow tall this year. I presume the crops around Tenebris are doing well?"

Baron Tenebris glanced her way but seemed distracted. "Aye, we hope for a good harvest this year, unlike last year." His gaze shifted across the board.

Rhonalyn followed his gaze to her steward, Baron Hughart. The two men exchanged looks. She frowned inwardly but disguised her annoyance and her curiosity by raising her voice. "And how has fishing been, Baron Durum?"

Nestled between the eastern base of the mountains and the western end of the cliffs of Nikor, which created their border with Delkara, the city of Durum was Keric's only foothold beyond its highlands and the closest Keric stronghold to Delkara's harbor. The city sat near fish-filled mountain water, unlike the city of Tenebris, which stood as Keric's sentinel on flat rich soil at the top of the pass cutting through the cliffs of Nikor.

"Fishing has been excellent, Your Royal Highness."

Rhonalyn raised her glass to him and again shifted her attention. "And Baron Tenebris, have you hunted many deer this year?"

The baron's serious gaze returned to her. "Nay, Your Royal Highness. I am afraid what hunting my men and I have done of late has not been for game." Setting aside his cup, he cleared his throat. "Forgive my impatience, but when might we expect King Bryant?"

Rhonalyn lifted her eyebrows. The baron's question mixed with what seemed displeasure stirred anger inside her, particularly since they were the ones to have arrived early. But she kept her response pleasant. "Their majesties are due to return today before the evening meal. Two new shafts were opened at the mines in the mountains this month, and my father, King Bryant, went to see their progress."

"Her Majesty, Queen Vivian traveled with His Majesty to the mines?" Baron Durum asked, surprise in his voice.

"Aye, my stepmother enjoys traveling."

She saw Hughart's eyebrows arch and his lips pressed together. Rhonalyn swept her goblet to her mouth and drank. So what if it was a lie? Of course it was ridiculous that Vivian would go along to the mines, but so was the woman's refusal to stay five days alone with Rhonalyn in the castle. She would rather ride to the mines—a trip Vivian described as a mind-numbing trek across endless fields to the mountains—and stay in a small village where her only control was in what horse she rode and what clothes she wore. But as Vivian had said when she left, "At least there I won't have to stand aside for you."

Rhonalyn's father had married Vivian out of loneliness and supposedly love. Vivian, on the other hand, had married him simply to possess the title of Queen of Keric, or so Rhonalyn was convinced. No doubt Vivian had hoped to gain all that she assumed went with that title. But Rhonalyn, starting at age fifteen, had been performing the duties of Keric's queen since her mother's death three years earlier, and by Keric law she would take the throne upon her father's death. Thus she had appealed to her father to allow her to retain the full duties of queenship. He had agreed. Therefore, she maintained the castle's keys and purse and when he was away had full authority over Arcis.

Despite Vivian's obvious ambitions, the woman had eventually, though grudgingly, settled for the notoriety of being a king's wife and gave up striving for the power Rhonalyn would have fought her for to her last breath.

"Do you like to travel, Your Royal Highness?" Baron Durum asked.

Rhonalyn gave him a swift smile. "I am not disinclined to travel, though duty often keeps me busy here in Arcis."

"Best not to be out traveling these days if one can help it," Baron Tenebris said. "At least not until these murderous outlaws are caught. Attackers who kill knights and steal His Royal Majesty's coin are not likely to stay their hand for a lady."

Rhonalyn stiffened. "His Majesty's coin? My father had money stolen in the attack on your men?"

Baron Tenebris looked exceedingly uncomfortable at her sharp tone. "Aye, your father sent with my men the toll to pay King Strephon for Keric's use of Nikor Harbor. I assumed the loss of it was why my presence was requested here at Arcis."

Confusion stirred within Rhonalyn. The last she had heard, they didn't have the quantity of coin needed to pay for their use of Delkara's harbor. She had thought that was why her father had gone to the mines. How then was it that almost a fortnight ago he had sent the money for the toll? Where had he gotten the funds? And why had he not told her about it?

"If I assumed wrongly, Your Royal Highness, I apologize. I meant no disrespect."

Rhonalyn ignored him, for it had suddenly occurred to her exactly where her father might have gotten the coin to pay King Strephon. Clawing her fingernails into her cup, she drew air. "Excuse me." Turning, she set her goblet on the board and hurried for the nearest stairwell. It did not take her long to reach the castle's treasury and unlock it.

Shoving aside a rolled tapestry stored in the depths of the room, Rhonalyn coughed and squinted. She stared at the flickering outline of a large gold-painted trunk that once belonged to her mother. Seizing the candlestick she had grabbed on her way to the storeroom, she thrust its flame closer. Lines of dust on the trunk's embellished lid showed where a smaller chest had sat atop it. A shriek of fury rose inside Rhonalyn.

She would have released it too if she had not heard footsteps in the corridor behind her. Someone entered and paused inside the treasury. Rhonalyn spun around to find Hughart behind her. His shadow stretched his thin form upward like a ghost amid the chamber of treasures. He bowed. "Your Royal Highness, may I be of assistance?"

Stabbing a finger toward the empty space atop the trunk, Rhonalyn let her voice display her indignation. "Where is it?"

He glanced at where she pointed. "Where is what?"

"My mother's coin chest!" Hughart cringed, and it took all Rhonalyn's willpower to not seize one of the ornate daggers laying in a bundle beside her and hurl it at him. "You knew!"

"Forgive me, Your Royal Highness," he said with fortitude despite the uncertainty in his gaze. "His Majesty requested you not be told."

"Not be told! Not be told he was using my mother's coin! To pay some stupid toll!" Her words echoed in the small chamber at a painful volume, but she did not lower her voice. "Where is the rest of it?"

He looked genuinely alarmed at the question. "I do not know, Your Royal Highness."

Unsure whether or not to believe him and too furious at the loss of the treasure to care, Rhonalyn pointed to the door. "Get out! Get out of my sight!"

He bowed and retreated.

She gripped the candlestick in her hand as if it alone might save her from the darkness and rage coiling about her body. How could he? How could he use the gold for something so menial when her mother had had such dreams for it?

3

Rhonalyn sat through the evening meal, stewing. She had managed to bury her fury before returning to the castle's guests, but it still boiled beneath the surface. Her father had arrived back from the mines distracted and in his own foul mood, not so obviously that either of the two visiting barons would have noticed though.

Her father had greeted them with all the pomp and civility expected of royalty, but Rhonalyn could tell something was wrong by the way her father pushed past his beloved hunting hounds and took to the table without changing his clothes or tying back his long brown hair. He conversed smoothly with the barons but watched the evening's entertainment, which Rhonalyn had painstakingly acquired, as if he were blind and deaf.

The only upside to the evening was that Vivian, after traveling all day, chose to retire for the night rather than join them. But the empty chair only served to reinforce Rhonalyn's thoughts about her mother and the missing gold coins. She had known well her mother's ambitions for the money and had always promised herself that she would see her mother's desires for it fulfilled.

She engaged with the others politely throughout the meal, but all she really wanted to do was rid the castle of guests and unleash her fury upon her father.

By the end of the meal, she was still feeding her ill will. As often occurred when barons visited, her father departed with the two men to a smaller private hall. Rhonalyn usually wasn't concerned by these meetings or even at all interested in what was discussed during them, but this time her distrust ran rampant. Her ladies-in-waiting mingled with the others, including the visiting knights and men-at-arms. They talked and laughed, but Rhonalyn slipped away.

She knew her father would at some point send out Hughart to speak with the butler about having beverages brought from the cellar. So, she waited at the base of the hall's northwest stairwell. It wasn't long before the steward came. She stepped from the shadows. "Hugh."

He stepped back, startled. "Your Royal Highness."

"Tell my father I need to speak with him in the old solar, now."

"He's in the middle of—" She lifted her eyebrows, daring him to continue. Hughart bowed. "I will tell him."

"Do so. And make sure that is all you tell him."

※

THE DOOR TO the old solar slammed against the wall, chipping more stone from its dented surface. "Rhonalyn! What is so urgent it could not wait until morning?"

Seated on a cushion-covered window seat far to the left of the door, Rhonalyn set aside the leather-bound book she'd been turning in her hands. She was beyond the light of the candelabra she'd left lit on the table in the solar's center.

"Where are you, girl?" Her father turned amid the room's walls of books and artwork. Rhonalyn took satisfaction in that he now shared her anger. Rising behind him, she cleared her throat. He spun around and glared. "Well? What is it?"

Rhonalyn stepped forward. Had Vivian not insisted on having a new and more elaborate great chamber constructed for herself and Rhonalyn's father, the solar where they stood would likely have been stripped and redecorated. As it was, it remained a living memory of Rhonalyn's mother and a room Vivian never visited, thus it was Rhonalyn's favorite spot. But tonight the room of memories offered her no comfort.

Her mother's collection of books and art only made Rhonalyn that much more outraged by her father's actions. She glided past him and thrust the door closed. Running her hand along the hard edge of the hinges that spread across the door like tree roots, she drew her anger into sharp focus and faced him. "Verily, the coins Mother was saving?"

Her father straightened to his full height, which was only a half head taller than her. "The toll to Strephon had to be paid."

"With Mother's coin?"

Her father eyed her with a stubborn resolve she knew well, for it too ran in her blood. "It was the only logical choice."

"The only choice!" Rhonalyn's anger burst forth. "Her long-saved treasure? And you sent it to gain what? Access to Nikor Harbor? And now where are those coins, hmm? Where are her dreams for that money, Father?"

His voice sharpened to match hers. "Your mother stored away that chest of gold in a time of abundance, Rhonalyn, to someday accomplish her dream. But it never happened. And that time is gone. Our mines have not been yielding, and new shafts won't solve this year's problems. We need access to Delkara's harbor. We have shipments to claim and trade that must take place. This year's crops are good, but unless we have somewhere to sell them, we will make little profit."

Her father's words about the mines hit Rhonalyn hard. He had acted as if the new shafts would be more than enough to solve their problems. His deception, along with his words about the harbor, brought a new layer of her anger to the surface. "I understand the harbor's significance, Father." She tossed up her hand. "How could I not? Every year Delkara's toll for us to use their harbor is a bane upon our kingdom. Yet always you refuse to renegotiate with Strephon, and we are stuck paying it year after year. And now a priceless treasure is sent as a toll, and it is lost! Can we not even defend ourselves against common thieves now?"

"Silence, girl! What do you know? Was it you who first negotiated to use Delkara's harbor? Was it you who haggled to get the deal we currently have? You think it's a simple matter, one king negotiating for the use of a harbor that another king owns?"

Rhonalyn clenched her fists. The fact that Delkara had been allowed to maintain their ownership of Nikor Harbor was a point of deep contention between them, but that was an argument for another day. She raised her chin sharply. "Nay, but finding murderous thieves within our own kingdom and getting back our gold should be."

Her father slammed his fist on the table. "I agree."

Jumping, Rhonalyn snapped back, "Then why have they not been found?"

"Because..." Her father huffed and leaned against the table. "Their trail was lost in the cliffs of Nikor."

"Oh," Rhonalyn breathed.

The cliffs, though a clear border between them and Delkara, were also a sprawling no-man's land. Numerous caves and watercourses cut through the area's jagged gorges, steep crags, and tightly bound forests, making it a maze of game trails and narrow ledges that led anywhere and nowhere. With isolated valleys and pitch-black caverns, the cliffs were made even more treacherous by frequent rockslides, flash floods from the mountains, and aggressive wildlife. Every year at least one poor soul, usually someone determined to retrieve lost livestock or hunt game, went missing in the cliffs. Kalev, an old sheepherder who lived near the cliff's rim, claimed that at night one could hear the haunted cries of lost souls forever stuck wandering the crags.

Rhonalyn shuddered. "What is to be done then? How is the money to be recovered?"

"If the thieves survive the cliffs, they will likely escape to Delkara and either begin using the coins one piece at a time or else melt them down to sell. Regardless, I am afraid the money is lost to us, along with our access to Nikor Harbor."

The defeat in her father's voice drew Rhonalyn from her rampant anger to a frustrated but logical assessment of their situation. "Is there truly no other means by which we might yet pay Delkara's toll?"

He shook his head. "There are only a few coins left from your mother's treasure and little else. There is nothing coming out of the mines currently, and we've already collected and used the taxes owed us. The excess goods we were to sell through the harbor this harvest were meant to refill our coffers."

At his words, cold dread crept through Rhonalyn. Apparently, more was at risk in the kingdom than she realized. She had been so focused on her duties at the castle, she hadn't sought to know what was happening abroad and hadn't noticed that he'd stopped telling her. "Then we cannot afford to simply leave the toll unpaid."

Her father dropped onto a wooden bench by the solar's empty fireplace. "Nay, and our barons expect to have access to Nikor Harbor. If that is denied them, they will begin to question why, and if they discover their king is penniless…" He trailed off, but Rhonalyn understood his meaning.

"Strephon will also expect to get his toll."

"Aye." Her father looked up at her. "There may be a means, at least where Strephon is concerned. I could issue another tax in the kingdom. If collected in the next week, the toll to Strephon could yet be paid."

Rhonalyn quickly calculated the risk of his proposal and shook her head. "The people would despise you for what they would consider an unwarranted tax, as would the barons. Why avoid disgrace with Strephon if only to destroy the trust of our own people? Nay, a tax is not the answer." Rhonalyn began to pace while her mind delved into other options. "Could we not provide goods to Strephon for the toll rather than paying it in coin?"

"Such is not the agreement."

"Aye, but is such outside the agreement?"

Her father sighed. "What would we offer him? Goats? Wool? Turnips? Strephon is no fool. He won't take goods. It would be an insult to his pride as well as mine."

Rhonalyn returned to pacing. He was probably right. They had nothing to barter with that would appeal to Strephon more than money and nothing that wouldn't blatantly display their current disadvantage. She turned back toward her father. "Do we not have items of gold or silver we could melt down and turn into coin?"

"I considered that as well. But you know how Vivian and her maids are. If anything outside the treasury went missing, less than an hour later it would be rumored around all of Arcis that we were stripping down our own castle. And Vivian has placed on display almost everything we own of gold and silver. I searched our treasury thoroughly. There is nothing of sufficient quantity to melt down and pay the toll. And if we sent gemstones or anything else mixed in, Strephon would know our metal mines are not yielding and that we have no other means by which to gain money than his port." Her father's tone darkened. "And that is a knowledge I would rather he not have."

Rhonalyn frowned. "Nor our own barons."

Her father exhaled irritably. "Baron Tenebris already suspects as much, but I prefer not to prove his suspicions. And there is still this band of outlaws running rampant. According to Baron Tenebris, they are commoners, though well armed and skilled enough to take on soldiers."

Rhonalyn drew a breath. Over the years her father had done well maintaining Keric as a kingdom, but that was the problem. All he had ever attempted to do was maintain what was. He had never endeavored to strive for more. Thus, it seemed he had simply plodded along despite the old ways failing before his eyes. As he had said though, what was, was no more. Where he had failed to do anything different in response, she would not. But would she have the chance? If drastic actions were not taken now, what glory remained of her kingdom would be lost before she ever officially became its queen. Having long dreamed of the day she truly possessed the power to bring about Keric's full potential, she would not let all her patience be for nothing. If playing to Strephon's pride was the only solution, so be it. She lifted her chin. "Let me negotiate with Strephon over the toll."

Her father eyed her, then grunted. "It is kings' business."

Rhonalyn softened her bearing and turned her voice to silk. "You said yourself that two kings negotiating is no simple matter. But where two men come to an impasse, a woman might yet find a way to disarm a man's pride."

He squinted at her. "You think you can successfully negotiate with Strephon?"

"Father, I am the future queen of Keric. I am more than capable of maintaining our kingdom's best interest while at the same time bartering to save it."

He scoffed. "You are still so young. How can you even know what you are proposing?"

Shoving down the rush of irritation she felt over his lack of confidence in her, let alone his lack of appreciation for the years she had spent haggling over everything from baronesses' wedding gifts to oxen for field work, Rhonalyn carefully controlled her tone. "Consider it this way, Father. Allow me the opportunity to negotiate with Strephon, and even if he refuses me, at the very least, I will have bought us time."

He frowned for a moment, then nodded. "Very well."

4

Low voices tugged Gage from the haze of his slumber. He dragged open his eyelids. His eyes stung with grit. Blinking several times, he managed to clear them enough to see his surroundings.

A plank ceiling and walls of masoned stone flickered in a shadowy light. He turned his head to try to locate the source of the voices. Across the room, two brown-cloaked figures holding lamps stood talking in a doorway that gaped into darkness. From the angle at which he could see them, Gage realized he was not on the ground, as he had supposed, but on some sort of raised board. He breathed in the room's dry, smoky air.

While he had the chance, he carefully slid his wrists toward himself to see how tightly he was bound. Nothing tugged his arms to a stop. Confused but keeping his focus on the men at the door, he brushed his right wrist against his side. He felt only cloth, nothing hard. No ropes or chains were holding him down. He was free to move, which made him that much more curious to know in whose keeping he was.

He attempted to lift his head to better see his surroundings. Pain ripped across his chest and shoulder. He hissed in a breath, and his eyes blurred with tears.

The voices ceased. A swift scuffing followed. The brightness of a candle filled Gage's vision, and a hand touched his arm. Flinching, he blinked and squinted past the flame to stare up at the anxious, round face of a man with tonsured gray hair. A second younger monk leaned in beside the first. "He's awake! Should I fetch Br—"

"Shhh!" the older monk reprimanded. "Speak softly. But yes, by all means, go."

The younger monk rushed away, and the older brother sat down beside Gage. His brown eyes regarded Gage with concern. "You have slept a long time. How do you feel?"

Gage tried to swallow, but his tongue and mouth felt like dry clay. "Wh…whe…er…?" His throat constricted, and he coughed. Pain splintered through his chest and shoulder. Gasping air, he tried not to cry out.

The monk laid a warm, broad hand on Gage's bare arm. "Easy. Let me get you something to drink." The monk turned and poured liquid. He lifted the cup in one hand while deftly tucking his other hand behind Gage's neck to raise his head.

Startled by the man's thick fingers in his long, tangled hair and the rough sleeve brushing his ear, Gage stared at the liquid in the cup and then into the monk's eyes. The monk was focused on holding the cup for him.

Caught between embarrassment and fear, Gage hesitated to accept its contents. The monk's gaze shifted to meet his. "It's alright, lad," he said gently. "Drink." Gage parted his lips and let the monk pour a small slosh into his mouth. His tongue soaked up what was simply water. Relieved, he swallowed it greedily, trying not to choke.

"Easy. There is plenty more to be had." The monk continued to cradle Gage's head while tipping swallow after swallow into his mouth.

Feeling as helpless as a baby bird yet desperate for the water, Gage endured the tedious process in painful silence. With his head raised, he noticed that the cloth bound around his wrists and upper body were not restraints but bandages. He could smell a poultice soaking through the one encircling his chest and shoulder.

Clearly, these monks had aided him, but under whose orders? He swallowed another mouthful and then paused to catch his breath. Exhausted, he gasped air as if he were fighting in a battle, not simply getting a drink.

When the cup was empty, the monk lowered Gage's head and eased his fingers out from beneath his neck. "Now, you had something you wished to ask?"

The reality that so minimal an effort had so thoroughly stripped his strength frightened Gage even more than the question he struggled to produce. "Where...where am I?"

The monk smiled. "Saint Jerome's Abbey."

An abbey? Had the soldiers brought him there for help? Or was this where they had been headed all along? Gage searched the monk's eyes. "Why? Why am I here?"

The monk's broad lips and graying eyebrows lifted in compassionate amusement. "Because it would seem God wishes you yet alive."

Frustration stirred within Gage. Of course a monk would see it that way. He tried once more, hoping to gain the information he wanted to know yet dreaded to hear. "How...did I come? Who...who brought me here?"

"We did."

Weariness ground over Gage. "Who...is we?"

"Ah. Right. I suppose you would not remember much of your journey here." The monk eyed him seriously. "Truly, it is a miracle you were found at all. During early morning prayer, Brother Matthew received a vision of someone lost in the woods. Confident he was supposed to go out looking for this person, he requested permission from our prior to leave the abbey. Father Philip granted it, and Brother

Matthew searched the woods all day. He had found no one and was just returning when he stumbled across you.

"You were barely alive and badly injured. Even once he'd fetched us to help him, it took time to get past your horse, so we could get close enough to see to you and carry you back here to Saint Jerome's Abbey. Since then our infirmarer, Brother Sholan, has been carefully tending to your wounds while others of us have traded off sitting with you and praying for you."

Gage heard the monk's words, but no memories came to fill in the gaps. He had no recollection of leaving the soldiers, being injured, or entering the woods.

He could only assume the horse the monk spoke of was Athalos, but how had he gone from being chained in a wagon to being alone in the woods with his horse?

"God indeed has a purpose for your life, for without a doubt it is only by His grace that you live," the monk continued. "When we got you here, Brother Sholan and I cleaned and bound the long slash across your chest and shoulder as well as we could, along with your other injuries, but they had been dirty and uncovered too long before we found you. You burned hot with fever for days. We worried we would lose you. Only upon your fever breaking did we know God had once more intervened to save you."

The monk's words explained his means of coming to the abbey and the grueling heat he had endured, but it did not explain who they were or what they would do with him. Lying there as weak as he was, Gage still felt like a prisoner. He couldn't even lift his head, let alone stand, and he wasn't at all sure a lord's shackle wouldn't be locked once more around his wrists before he could rise. He looked at the man and parted his lips.

The monk patted his hand. "Rest now. There will be plenty of time to talk more later."

Gage couldn't help but fear that "later" would be after they had informed a lord that he, a marked man, yet lived. This could be his only chance to explain. The monk shifted to rise. Gage attempted to grab his arm but caught only the monk's brown sleeve. "I'm not…who you think…I am."

The monk met his gaze. "You are a soul in need of rest and healing. For now that is all that matters. Who you are and how you have come to us can wait for another day. Now, be at peace and rest."

Seeing sincerity in the monk's eyes, Gage released his sleeve. "Thank you." He was asleep again before the younger monk returned with whomever he had gone to fetch.

5

Movement close beside Gage drew him awake with a start. A lightweight wool blanket had been placed over him, and daylight poured from a slatted window above him. He turned his head toward movement to his right. A tall middle-aged monk with a thin face and intelligent eyes stood beside him stirring a steaming mug. "Ah, you are awake again. I am Brother Sholan, head of the infirmary here at Saint Jerome's. How are you feeling?"

Gage took a moment to answer. He could still feel pain in his wrists, his knee, and most intensely in the wound across his chest and shoulder, but nothing like he remembered from before. "Better... thanks to you, I hear."

"I did what I could, but truly it was God who saved you. You were beyond my reach." The monk's words sent a twinge through Gage. How close had he come to dying? He shoved the thought away. He was alive, and being alive had enough questions of its own. Brother Sholan raised the mug he held. "I made you some tea. Will you drink some?"

Finding his throat dry again, Gage nodded. The monk slid his hand under Gage's neck to lift his head just as the older brother had done and held the cup to his lips. Gage swallowed a mouthful of the liquid and nearly choked on it. The hot tea tasted awful despite the honey obviously mixed into it. "Careful! Drink it slowly," the monk said. "The last thing your wound needs is you coughing."

Gage sipped the tea more cautiously. He was grateful for the beverage's soothing effect on his throat and the bit of strength it gave him. The thought of healing though caused his heartbeat to quicken. No matter which way he looked at his situation, the results were not favorable. He met the monk's gaze. "What will be done with me?"

His forehead furrowing, Brother Sholan set aside the mug. "To be sure you will be fed and cared for until you are on your feet again."

Gage began to sweat. "And what about after that?"

"After you're well? I don't know."

Though both his wrists were wrapped, Gage raised his right hand. "Were you not the one to bandage this?"

Lips pressing together, Brother Sholan nodded. "It was only after we had brought you here and Brother John and I were tending to you that it was even noticed. You were half dead at the time, so its presence mattered little. It was a recent branding, yes?"

Gage felt both angry and ashamed. "Yes."

"It looked to be." The monk's eyes took on a sad reflection. "Even now it is still healing."

"I was marked unjustly," Gage said. "The knight who arrested me didn't give me the chance to speak before a court or to a lord. He condemned me without even listening to anything I had to say. I didn't do what he thought I'd done."

Rising, Brother Sholan diverted his gaze and paced across the room. "I think it's best if you wait and discuss this with our abbot, Father Thomas. He returns in two days' time."

"No, you don't understand," Gage said. "It's not just the injustice of the mark that causes me to speak; it is also news I carry that needs to be delivered to the noblemen of Edelmar. News that could save lives if it reaches them in time. Please, if you assist me, I know—"

"Stop." Brother Sholan held up his hand. "I cannot help you with what you are asking. You will have to wait and speak with Father Thomas. In fact, he is the only one you should speak to about any of this."

Gage felt as if every bit of the strength he'd gained since waking had just been kicked out of him. "If that is how it must be, I will honor your request." He spoke calmly, but inside he was reeling. He was being silenced, and he couldn't help but wonder where Father Thomas had gone and to what purpose. He pictured the abbot bringing Sir Jarret back with him and leading the knight to where he lay. Gage's stomach rolled. What if no one listened to him or believed him?

Thoughts of escaping before the abbot returned filled his mind, but as weak as he was, he'd be lucky to make it three steps. He wouldn't get away or get word to his father in time, not without help. But there was no help to be had. Frustration and desperation churned within him.

"I should see to your wounds," Brother Sholan said.

Gage wanted so badly to let his anger and fear erupt at the man, but his desire to explode was restrained by Sholan's position as a monk, his own fatigue, and the fact that none of his problems were Brother Sholan's fault.

The monk moved around the bed and set about unbinding Gage's left wrist. "The scrapes here from whatever bound you are almost completely healed, though the bruising will likely remain for some time," the monk said. Untying the cloth wrapped about Gage's chest and then the one about his shoulder, the monk lifted a poultice-soaked material out from beneath each and gave a satisfied nod. "These appear to be finally healing well." Taking up a nearby bowl, Brother Sholan applied a fresh poultice that smelled strongly of staunchgrass.

Gage cringed at the pain and wrinkled his nose. He'd never liked the smell of the plant, but he knew enough of its medicinal properties not to complain about its presence.

"You are fortunate that whoever struck you didn't cut you any deeper," the monk commented as he worked. "As it is, it's a long, nasty-looking blade wound, but most of it is fairly shallow. The worst of the damage is here at the edge of your chest and across the front of your shoulder." The monk finished and covered the wounds once more. "It'll be painful for a while, but provided you keep still for the next couple of days, it should heal well."

The monk circled then to Gage's marked wrist and began to unwrap its bandage. The last layer of the fabric stuck. The monk slowly peeled it loose, causing the cloth to tug at the burnt flesh. Gage hissed air. Brother Sholan winced as if he too felt the pain. "Forgive me. It's free now." Cradling Gage's wrist in his hand, the monk drew a small clay jar from his robe. "This should help the burn heal and keep it from binding again to the cloth." He tipped the jar over Gage's exposed wrist. A thick golden liquid rolled out.

"What is it?" Gage flinched when it settled in a swirl in the middle of the branded flail-and-crossbow seared in an X above his hand.

"Honey." Setting aside the jar, the monk used the cloth to spread the thick substance.

Realizing he was holding his breath, Gage slowly exhaled. He was unnerved by the thought that the monk had done all of this before without him even being aware of it. He also felt ashamed of his distrust now, considering the monk had been seeing to his wounds for days, even when it was uncertain if he would live. "Thank you for tending to me."

Brother Sholan met his gaze. "You're welcome. Are you hungry?"

Gage smiled weakly. "Starving."

GAGE HAD FALLEN asleep before Brother Sholan returned with the food, but when he woke again, the monk fetched the vegetable and beef broth.

Propping a blanket beneath Gage's head, Brother Sholan settled beside him with a bowl and spoon in hand. He scooped the broth and held it out to Gage as if he were feeding a baby.

Realizing he'd have to swallow his pride with every mouthful, Gage was half inclined to tell the monk he was no longer interested. But the smell of the food filled his nose, and his stomach growled noisily. He parted his lips, and the monk tipped the spoonful of broth into his mouth. The rich liquid flowed over Gage's tongue. Immediately forgetting his objections, he opened his mouth for more.

"You know, you have challenged my faith and cost me a fair bit of sleep," Brother Sholan commented as he methodically delivered the bowl's contents.

Gage wasn't sure how to respond to this, but apparently a response wasn't needed. The monk tipped the next spoonful into his mouth and continued. "You see, I've always believed in visions and healings in Scripture, but when Brother Matthew said he'd had a vision about someone lost in the woods, God forgive me, I figured he'd just fallen asleep at prayer. Then he returned, having found you, and I watched you recover from a fever that should've killed you. So, you see, because of you, twice I've had to repent for my lack of faith." Chuckling softly, Brother Sholan held out another spoonful of broth.

To Gage, the monk's words were far from amusing. Staring at the spoon in front of him, he thought of the moments in his life when he'd come far too close to death. He could have drowned with Novia. Had that branch not come along when it did, probably no one would've ever even found their bodies. They'd have simply gone missing, lost forever to the river's cold current. And at the ambush, when the archer across the mire had drawn an arrow on him. Had Sir Brent not had a blade, he'd have been killed. Or when the Blue Crow had stood over him, ready to run him through. Air stuck in Gage's lungs, and his head ached.

Could there be a God who had influenced each of those moments? If there was, why had that God not save Allard? Or Bardon? Or Novia? He swallowed another spoonful of the broth but no longer tasted it. A God present and capable of saving him but who'd let Novia drown in his grasp and Allard die beside him wasn't the kind of God he wanted. He'd rather believe, like he had since Novia's death, that events were simply what they were and that there was no God alive to alter them.

"Are you alright?" Brother Sholan asked.

Gage silenced his thoughts. "Just tired." It was true, for even eating seemed to take too much effort.

Brother Sholan fed him the last two scoops of the broth, then stood with the empty bowl. "You should rest. I will look in on you later."

The monk departed, and Gage lay staring up at the ceiling. He still couldn't remember how he'd gone from a lord's supply wagon to being found half dead in the woods. Yet he remembered other things clearly, like his conversation with Lady Natriece at the fair.

Suddenly, he wondered how long it had been since the fair. What if it was already too late to warn his father about Felix's additional men? Even if the news came after the new rebels' arrival, his father still needed to know about the rebels at Veiroot and Lord Gregory's betrayal. Gage had to speak to Father Thomas, but would the abbot allow him, a marked man, to send a message to Edelmar, or would he tell him to take the matter up with his new master? His insides shuddered at the question.

Lady Natriece's words about marching upon Veiroot to stop Felix and his men surfaced in Gage's mind. *"At your command, it would be a simple matter."* At his command. He recalled as well Haaken's words at Nardell. *"I do not think your judgment is what has you questioning yourself. Rather, I believe it's your own leadership in the making that intimidates you."* Gage's stomach twisted. If only he'd been intimidated enough to never leave Ulbin, or if he'd actually questioned his own judgment before traveling with Manton. Perhaps then he wouldn't be in this mess.

He'd failed every element of his family's hopes for him, and now because of Manton, the rebels, and what Sir Jarret had done, there was no going back to either life he'd had before.

His father's warning before he'd left for Delkara echoed in his mind. *"If you choose to travel as a commoner, the responsibility of that choice is yours and yours alone."* Never would he have thought agreeing to those words would mean dealing with being unjustly marked a rebel thief.

Perhaps he deserved to deal with it alone though. For despite all he'd learned from Manton about other people's deception, Manton had been the most thorough liar of them all. And he hadn't seen it. Worst of all, he didn't even have an explanation for how he'd been so stupidly blind and self-absorbed to not realize he was again traveling with his enemy.

Now he could spot the moments where he should have seen Manton's alliance with the rebels. But he would never have thought him capable of being part of the Blue Crow's cause. The only thing he was grateful for was that at least this time the consequences of his naivete had cost no one else their life. This time the price was his and his alone.

Gage bit his cheek until he tasted blood. The debt of the stolen gold Sir Jarret had found in his saddlebags could potentially take a lifetime to repay. He'd live enslaved to a lord, possibly never again free to return to Edelmar or his family.

Bitter grief seeped from every hollow place inside him, pooling in his chest and at the back of his eyes. Even if he toiled faithfully and eventually gained the required restitution to pay for his freedom, what then? What kind of existence would be left to him? Even set free, the disgrace he bore would remain. For once a marked individual's service was fulfilled, their release came only by the means of two additional brands—a freedom brand from the lord they'd owed and a brand of pardon from the king. The three marks always told the same dishonorable story.

Anger mixed with his misery. His brand was evidence of his supposed irrefutable guilt and his inability to pay restitution. That would not change, not even if he was able to tell the lord who had owned the stolen gold that he had coin enough buried outside of Aro to pay for his freedom. The lord likely wouldn't believe that the money existed, let alone that it truly belonged to him. It might be different if he could prove he was a king's son, but even the thought of trying to claim his title for that purpose made his heart beat faster and his stomach knot in humiliation.

He recalled his father's words. *"Understand this as well. If you travel as a commoner, the laws of the land will apply to you as if you are truly a commoner. And we will respect your choice by treating you not as royalty but as a commoner."*

He'd promised his father he would be solely responsible for his choices. If he sought now to be identified as a king's son in order to save himself from his own stupidity, the shame would be unbearable. He would not and could not ask his father to attempt to come to his rescue or bear the dishonor of his mistakes.

Better that as a marked man he never uttered a word about who he really was and not risk dragging his family's name through the mud trying to dispute a claim that, at present, he had no way of proving to be false.

Gage considered the possibility of running away and burning over the brand to hide it, but even the thought made him queasy. Such a scar—unless extensive enough not to look like an intentional concealment of a marking—would still bring suspicion. And in addition to being horribly painful, broad burns could be deadly.

His stomach churning, he thought about what it would be like belonging to a master and of Sir Jarret's threat, *"A whip will take from your back retribution and from your mouth the true names of those rebels who assisted you."* Gage shuddered and took solace that he might prevent at least this. For no whip would be needed to gain his assistance against the rebels. The moment he stood in the presence of any lord, he would willingly speak of every person he knew who was possibly associated with the rebellion and the theft of the lord's gold.

After all, the rebels were ultimately the ones responsible for all that had befallen him. Yes, a lord's knight had unjustly branded him as part of their rebellion, but no matter what anyone said, did, or thought, he would never be a rebel.

He would help the Delkaran lords catch the rebels slipping past them and hope his aid led to the dismantling of the rebellion. He wished he could believe that in doing so he also might regain his freedom, but he doubted it. Even if, through his help, the true thieves of the gold were discovered, the Delkaran lords would probably assume he'd simply betrayed his rebel companions to save himself from further judgment. He might stop the likes of Felix and Manton, but there was no undoing what they had done to him.

His life as he'd known it was over. Gage squeezed his eyes shut. Hot tears seeped from under his eyelashes and trailed down his cheeks.

6

GAGE NEVER THOUGHT he'd be grateful for an exhaustion that brought frequent slumber, but sleep offered him at least some reprieve from fretting about Father Thomas's return. He wanted to believe the abbot would listen to him and aid him at least in his request to send word to Edelmar. But what if he waited only to have the monk refuse to hear him and instead turn him over to his new master?

He wanted so badly to speak of it with Brother Sholan, but the monk's instruction to wait and discuss the matter only with Father Thomas rang clearly in his mind. He didn't know what response would be made if he violated the request. They were monks, after all. But if he tread upon their generosity, he didn't doubt them capable of forcing him into silence either by restriction or further isolation. So, he guarded his tongue and bided his time, desperately hoping the abbot might still help him and that what he knew might yet reach Edelmar in time to prevent further rebel attacks.

Each new day seemed to last forever. Twice daily Brother Sholan checked on him, and the older monk, Brother John, who had first greeted him upon his waking, brought him food.

Gage had little strength, was often lightheaded, and any attempt he made even to shift his position caused the pain in his chest and shoulder to flare so badly it made him nauseated and forced him to lie still. Thus bound by his own body, his only means of passing the time were his brief conversations with the monks and what was in his own mind.

He was sick of his own thoughts and desperately wished he could be about some activity, or else at the very least have someone, anyone, to talk to. Lying trapped, alone, and hurting was a miserable existence.

Eventually, bored beyond measure and so tired of being in pain, he distracted himself by searching his mind to fill in the gap in his memory. The last thing he could recall was being in the wagon and ducking behind barrels as the rebels attacked. He knew there had to be more, for he'd obviously encountered someone with a blade.

Suddenly, he felt the cold depths of a knife's edge slice his skin and the panic of knowing how badly he'd been wounded. His chest tightened. Vulnerability like he'd felt with the Blue Crow standing over him flooded through him. He remembered pressing his fingers to the painful wound and then trying to pick up a sword with his bloody hand, but by then the fight had been over.

Why though? Why had it ended? A memory surfaced of being surrounded by soldiers. Strangely, Gage recalled feeling less afraid of them than someone else with them. Who else had been there? He'd been seated on the ground, and he'd turned and seen…Felix! Felix had been there, riding with the soldiers.

"You think I helped plan today's ambush?" He heard again Felix's words and his baffled scorn. *"You still don't know. You've tracked me halfway across Delkara and gotten yourself captured and branded a rebel thief, but still you don't know."*

Gage's heart wrenched anew at Felix's words. The rest of their encounter rushed through his mind—his and Felix's fight, Felix's attempt to flee on Athalos, and the man's fall off the edge of the ravine. Felix was dead.

Gage re-experienced everything that came with that knowledge. He was glad but also angry because Felix had taken a secret with him. *"You still don't know."* What didn't he know? It had to be something significant about Felix or the rebellion. Otherwise, why would Felix have been so shocked that he didn't know it? But what was it?

Gage ransacked his mind for the answer. He ceased a moment later when he realized how pointless it was to think he could make his mind produce something it didn't know. Still, the knowledge that he had somehow missed something hounded him. Maybe Natriece could shed light on Felix's words.

That thought brought back to him the abrupt realization that he'd likely never get the chance to ask her. Sighing, Gage returned to retracing his journey to the abbey. Free but injured, he remembered fleeing into the woods on Athalos to avoid the soldiers.

He recalled it all now. He'd ridden for what felt like hours, getting weaker and weaker as he went. He'd known he wouldn't survive without help, but the forest had been empty and endless. He'd thought for sure he was going to die, and he'd—

Remembering what he'd done, he clenched his jaw.

He'd prayed. He'd begged God for help.

Gage scowled. Why had he done that? He didn't believe God existed. Why then ask Him for help? Gage swallowed. Every bit of him wanted to flee from the question and its answer. But where normally there was someplace else he could go or some activity he could throw himself into as a distraction, this time he was stuck with nothing but his thoughts.

Brother Sholan's words played through his mind. *"Brother Matthew had a vision about someone lost in the woods....I watched you recover from a fever that should have killed you....Truly it was God who saved you."*

Gage's stomach twisted. Had Brother Matthew really gone out searching the woods because of a vision from God? Couldn't there have been some other explanation for his search?

A fever breaking of its own accord could easily be claimed as an act of God, but Brother Matthew knowing to search the woods for him was not so simple to explain away. There were other possibilities beyond divine intervention, but none of them made sense.

Had the account of a God-given vision been told to him by ale-drinking louts in a tavern, he'd have easily chalked up the story to a cleverly devised afterthought to explain two unrelated events. Something like someone out past curfew stumbling upon an injured person in the woods and then inventing a story about how "God directed me there" in order to turn a late-night venture into an act of godly heroism rather than a punishable infraction would have made sense.

But unlike louts in a tavern, monks dedicated themselves to living out scriptural principles, which included telling no lies. And according to Brother Sholan, Brother Matthew had reported the vision before leaving to search the woods. So, either the monks of Saint Jerome's Abbey were all lying, which as far as Gage could tell they had no reason to, or his being sought and found really had happened just as they'd claimed.

Logic said he should still be alone in the forest and probably dead, but he wasn't. A monk he didn't know had come looking for him because God had supposedly told him to do so. So, either they were all crazy, or God existed.

The straw poking through the bed's linen sheet suddenly became overwhelmingly itchy and irritating. Gage wanted to scream, to rise, to flee and do anything other than lie there thinking about God truly existing.

Long ago he'd concluded that Scripture was no more true than the made-up tales spun by troubadours. He'd listened for years to his family and friends uphold the presence of an eternal, almighty, and all-seeing God, and he'd kept his mouth shut about his rejection of that belief. He did so to avoid offending or disappointing his family and because he understood that the teachings of Christianity and the fear of an all-seeing God motivated integrity and justice in people's lives. Thus, though he rejected God, he accepted that religion was a helpful means of maintaining Edelmar's moral structure.

The thought now of it possibly being more than that stuck in his mind like a caltrop. What if an eternal, almighty, and all-seeing God did exist? What if all the things God had done in Scripture were real? Gage clenched his teeth.

The idea was ludicrous and infuriating to him. Wasn't it ridiculous to think such a being as God existed? Ridiculous to believe in events like seas parting, city walls falling, impossible battles succeeding, men walking unharmed out of fires, and people being raised from the dead? Weren't they just tales of what people wished could happen?

He stared at the ceiling, wondering about this. When he actually followed through with that thought, it didn't make sense. If the stories in Scripture were simply what people wished for, why include as well the accounts of humanity's defeats in battle, lives lost to plagues, idol worship, cities destroyed, rebellious sons, enemies' successes, and so much more that one wouldn't include if the stories were what the writers wished to be? And why bother with pointless facts like births, deaths, and genealogies? If they were just tales, were not these the tedious details no one would bother to write?

By the same reasoning, if the stories were meant to teach people morality, why include the impossible victories and the acts of God that simply clouded the realities of life?

The more he thought about all of this the more deeply unsettled he felt. The feeling reminded him of the night he'd been questioned by Prior Joseph. *"What of you, Manton's traveling companion? Do you too say, 'I'll believe when I see?' Or do you believe without having first seen?"*

Gage had spent years telling himself he didn't believe in God, but when asked, he'd told Prior Joseph he didn't know. And now one thought screamed louder than all others. He had prayed. He had prayed to God, and a monk who claimed to be sent by God had shown up.

"Scripture is being silenced," Prior Joseph had said to Manton, *"and you know it's not because it lacks power but because it has it. God does exist, and He is at work."*

Gage hated that thought. He hated it because he didn't want it to be true. He didn't want an all-powerful God to exist. Because if a God existed who could have saved the people he cared about but who had chosen not to, then he would hate that God more than he hated anyone or anything.

But no matter how much he loathed what was before him, there was no getting around it. An all-seeing God had answered his prayer and aided him. But why would a God, who had rejected his prayers in the past and let so many others die, keep him alive? His conclusion was that God must want something from him.

Gage ground his teeth. If that was the case, he was now indebted to a Delkaran lord and to a God he despised.

7

Gage woke in the gray light of what he could only assume was morning. He shifted and groaned. His back and hips were bruised from being in the same position, and his head and wounds ached. Sighing, he listened to the distant sound of the monks singing.

Sometime after they'd finished, he heard a shuffle at his room's door. He turned his head without moving his shoulders. The door swung open on well-oiled hinges, and Brother Sholan entered, followed by a stooped, older monk wearing a cross over his monastic robes. Far shorter than Brother Sholan and almost completely bald, the older monk motioned for Brother Sholan to close the door behind them.

Though the abbot's narrow shoulders were boney and bent, he moved like someone accustomed to accomplishing endeavors no matter how arduous a hindrance lay in his path. Craggy gray eyebrows overshadowed his deep-set eyes, and crow's feet trailed into his cheeks toward his large ears. An expression of welcome warmed his gaze. But at the same time, saddened curiosity furrowed his forehead and deepened the lines bordering his thin lips. Gage hadn't seen any soldiers or knights beyond the room, but that didn't mean they weren't there.

"Father Thomas," Gage said respectfully.

The abbot tucked his closed hands into his long sleeves. "I am indeed, and you are the guest, who I've been told was found by the grace of our good Lord. I understand you've been recovering here at Saint Jerome's Abbey for almost as long as I have been away."

"Yes." Feeling awkward and oddly inferior lying on his back staring up at the monk, Gage realized his discomfort in this regard came from being unprepared to address the abbot. It occurred to him that in being marked he had also forfeited his right to accept or reject the means and timing of a person's arrival into his presence.

Without his title, he held no position of significance; therefore, his desires were not sought, let alone carried out. And as a marked man, he could not have even required that his requests be obeyed, nor could he bestow any honor upon anyone for doing so. Instead he was at the monks' mercy.

He slowly inhaled a fortifying breath. "Father, I'm humbly grateful for the care and hospitality of the monks of Saint Jerome's Abbey. And I know I've no right to ask this, but I beg your help to send a message to Edelmar by the hand of one of your monks, for I carry news that could spare the lives of noblemen and commoners alike if it's received in time."

Stepping close to where he lay, the abbot peered down at him. Gage would have stood superior to him in height and unintimidated by the man's presence, but flat on his back, he felt like a wayward child found wanting. "This message you are asking me to send for you would bear your name, I'd presume, yet no one here knows what that is. By what are you called?"

It was a simple question, but with the abbot looming over him and so many memories bearing down upon him, it drove the air from Gage's lungs. His heart began to pound. A year ago, announcing who he was would not have caused him pause, let alone panic, but so much had changed since he'd stood happily hailed before a hall.

The Blue Crow had placed a sword's tip to his chest because of who he was. Sir Jarret had branded him a thief regardless of who he was. And now he lay at the mercy of an abbot who doubtless knew him to be a marked man but still sought to know who he was. Gage tried to tell himself all this didn't matter, but it did.

At the look in the monk's eyes, he knew he couldn't just remain silent. He swallowed. Father Thomas had asked what he was called, not who he was. His heart slowed its frantic pace. He only had to give a name. But dare he give even that?

Pinned under Father Thomas's steady scrutiny, he felt like he was being taken apart by the abbot's gaze. He clenched his teeth and curled his toes. "I've been called both Gage and Gabe."

"Which, if either name, were you given at birth?"

Gage's stomach churned and his heart raced. He wanted to tell the monk to back off and leave him be, but he couldn't. He needed their help. "Gage is the name I was given at birth."

"And where are you from, Gage?"

Other than his family, no one had ever addressed him as just Gage. Hearing the abbot do so felt like being stripped of any shred of control or dignity he had left. Meanwhile, the pain in his wounds tugged at his awareness like a petulant child calling for his attention. He wished he could shut it all out and sink through the prickly straw mattress, but there was no escape, and people needed the information he carried. "I'm from Edelmar."

"Edelmar. What brought you to Delkara?"

Apparently, the abbot had a list of questions he wanted answered before he'd allow Gage to make his own request. Gage resigned himself to this. "I came to buy and sell mounts."

Father Thomas's eyebrows lifted, then drew together. "Why were you marked?"

Anger shoved past Gage's pain. He yearned to rise to his feet and boldly defend himself, but words were all he had left to him, which increased his anger and his self-loathing. "I was marked because I neglected to realize soon enough that my traveling companion was a smuggler and a liar." His heart pounding, Gage forced his voice to remain under control. "As soon as I discovered this, I parted ways with him. I didn't know that he'd stolen what he was smuggling or that he'd placed some of those items in my saddlebags.

"Shortly after separating from him, I was stopped on the road and searched by Delkaran soldiers. They found his stolen items in my bags and assumed that I was guilty of theft. I tried to tell them they had the wrong person, but they wouldn't listen to me. I was branded a thief the following morning. No witnesses were called, and I wasn't allowed to speak before a court."

Neither monks' expression changed, but Brother Sholan glanced at Father Thomas. The abbot lifted his chin. "What proof do you have that such events happened as you say they did and that you are indeed innocent of thievery?"

Gage clenched his teeth, the pain of his wounds wearing on him. "None but my own word."

"It's your word that is in question."

Gage bit his tongue. The abbot's insinuation that he really could be a liar and a thief carved away his remaining patience. Wanting to let his emotions loose yet knowing he needed their help, he forced himself to reason his way back to their perspective. For why wouldn't they think him a liar and a thief? Proof against his own words was seared into his wrist. Of course they'd believe him to be the common thief Sir Jarret had branded him. But where did that leave him? Weariness entangled him like a weighted net. Was there no path left to address the injustice of what had taken place or to seek their aid to help Edelmar?

"Are you a baron's son or a baron?" Father Thomas asked.

Startled by the question, Gage searched the abbot's gaze. "No."

"Then are you a steward," the abbot asked, "an emissary, or the right-hand knight of a lord?"

Did they think him a spy? Was that the reason for these questions?

"I am none of these things. I was not sent by anyone to Delkara. I came here, as I said, to buy and sell mounts. The news I encountered while traveling here I intended to take back to Edelmar myself for the sake of justice."

"As a marked man?"

"No!" Gage closed his eyes. His fatigue and pain were growing incessant, and concentrating and controlling his emotions was becoming increasingly difficult. Opening his eyes, he met Father Thomas's gaze. "I learned the information moments before I discovered my traveling companion was a smuggler. I immediately left his company and started for Edelmar. That is when I was stopped and searched by Delkaran soldiers and falsely branded a thief."

"You are lying," Father Thomas said in the noblemen's tongue.

"I am not lying! Why would I—" Gage swallowed his next words. His stomach sank against his spine, and his heart pounded. The abbot had just shown that he understood the noblemen's tongue, which meant he was either of noble birth or a commoner who knew a language that was forbidden for him to learn.

The abbot's craggy eyebrows were raised, and the man switched back to the commoners' tongue. "Now that we clearly understand each other, would you like to begin again?"

His chest tightening, Gage embraced the pain of his wound. The sensation melded with his anger and humiliation. "How did you know I spoke the noblemen's tongue?"

"When you were hot with fever," Brother Sholan answered quietly, "you used it several times."

Gage's skin prickled. How much had he said? Was Brother Sholan from a noble family? Could he understand the noblemen's tongue or just identify it? What did they know about him? Clearly not everything, otherwise why ask him these questions? Or were they just waiting for him to confirm what they already knew?

Unsure how to proceed, he closed his mouth and felt what little was left of his strength begin to slip away. Even breathing felt like it required an act of will. Lying there, he wished he could simply deny himself air and end this whole miserable mess.

The thought reminded him of the day Allard had died, and a realization twisted hard inside him. If he did not get the news he carried back to Edelmar, the sacrifice Allard had made to stop the Blue Crow would be for nothing. A rush of determination expanded Gage's lungs. He would not let that happen. "Please, Father Thomas, regardless of whatever you think of me, the news I carry must reach Edelmar."

"It is obvious to me that God has spared your life and brought you to us for a reason," Father Thomas said. "But as to sending word on your behalf, I'll consider no request until you tell me the truth." He nodded to Gage's wrist. "You're already a marked man. There's no need for you to lie to seek our help."

"I've not lied to you!" Gage immediately regretted making the forceful declaration. Not only because the action spread pain across his body but also because if all his words were true, it meant there had to be more to his story.

The abbot's skepticism rang out harshly. "You claim you are neither a liar nor a thief. You say as well that you are a seller of mounts, yet you speak the noblemen's tongue. How do you explain that, if truly none of it is a lie?"

It took a moment, but the answer flowed off Gage's tongue because it was the truth—or at least another part of it. "I'm not a baron's child, but I grew up in a baron's home with his sons and was treated as family. Almost a year ago, I left his household and began to travel and sell mounts to make a living." Gage regretted the impression his words left of Baron Roger, but shedding light any other way would've led to the one fact he didn't want revealed.

"I see," Father Thomas said, "and this baron, did he bestow the privileges of a son upon you? Do you carry proof with you of the authority you possess from your connection to him?"

Even the thought of receiving any such honor from Baron Roger after what had happened to Allard made Gage's skin crawl with shame. "No."

"Then you are still lying. For either you're not who you say you are, or you are a thief. Because items such as these do not belong to a commoner." Withdrawing his hands from his sleeves, the abbot opened his fingers to reveal in one hand Gage's signet ring and in the other the gold brooch with its four blood-red rubies.

Gage drew a sharp breath. Pain made his vision waver. He had completely forgotten about the brooch he'd pinned under his belt and the signet ring he'd last had concealed within Athalos's saddle.

"From what I know for certain," the abbot said, "you have recently been shackled, heavily abused, marked, and badly injured by what appears to be a sword blade. You were found half dead beside a partially tacked horse nowhere near a manor, and you had a nobleman's signet ring on your finger and tucked beneath your commoner's clothes a brooch worth a small fortune. Would you believe you if all this was your evidence?"

Frustration and despair crawled through Gage's exhausted body. Maybe the monk was right. Perhaps there was no point in continuing to dispute the claim, for what good would it do? The ceiling above him blurred, and he wished he could somehow just make all of this go away.

The full truth would explain all the inconsistencies in his story, but it would also introduce a whole new problem. He was, after all, an Edelmarian prince whose only reason for being in Delkara was an explanation no nobleman would believe. And the only person who could verify his innocent intentions *was* a liar and a thief. He had not come to Delkara as a spy, but at this point if he was known to be a prince, he could easily be accused of being one.

By all considerations it was safer to accept the accusation of being a common thief. At least then the trouble would stay with him alone, and he might yet persuade the monks to believe enough of his story to send word to Edelmar.

He swallowed and turned the words over inside him. He had been charged with stealing from a nobleman. If what had been stolen was altered from a thing to a person, then perhaps he was a thief. For had not his actions stolen Allard from his family? And had not Allard's older brother basically accused him of such?

He blinked to keep at bay the burning in the back of his eyes. "I have done much that I regret, Father Thomas."

The abbot's expression softened for the first time since the start of their conversation. "We all have, my son. But as long as you live, you have the chance to confess it and set things right."

The words offered a strange balm to Gage's soul but also a sharp conviction, for his statement was truthful but resided in deception. Frightened by that thought, he discarded all but a genuine request. "Will you help me set things right?"

"I will." Father Thomas displayed the ring and brooch in his hand. "But only if you tell me honestly where you got these items."

Every muscle in Gage's body trembled as he tried to weather the emotional strain of the conversation and keep himself from tumbling backward into his pain. "They belong to an Edelmarian nobleman. And if I could go back to the day I took them, believe me, I'd make a different decision." He held the abbot's gaze. "Please return them to Edelmar for me, and send with them my message of aid. Let me express within it my regret for my actions." He struggled to keep the full extent of his emotions from spilling into his voice and down his face, for he was sorry for his decisions, sorrier than anyone would ever know.

"I will indeed arrange for their return." Father Thomas tucked the ring and brooch away in his robe. "Now, what of the lord whose mark you bear? Has all that was taken been returned to him?"

Gage drew a sharp breath, his body quivering. "I told you! I didn't steal what the soldiers found in my bags. I don't even know what lord it belonged to."

"If you were not brought before the lord, then how and by whom were you judged?"

"Father Thomas," Brother Sholan interrupted, "I think it might be wise to resume this conversation later. He is still recovering, and this is clearly taxing him."

Gage couldn't bear the thought of retreating now. "No, please, let me answer." He fought through his fatigue. "It was a knight with no displayed coat-of-arms who beat me, chained me, and had me branded. He placed me with soldiers who were to take me to the lord from whom I supposedly stole. The soldiers were attacked by rebels on the road. I was wounded in the chaos and fled into the woods on my horse." Struggling for air, Gage continued. "That is the truth. Now please, Father Thomas, I beg you, grant the Edelmarian lords the news I carry. It is the hiding place of a group long sought by the nobles of

Edelmar. The group has committed grievous crimes, most significantly the murders of a faithful servant and a lord's son. Allow the noblemen to use the information to protect the people and to bring about justice on behalf of the innocent." Allard's young face and dead eyes surfaced in Gage's mind. Emotion caught in his throat. "The lord's son was but a squire. He was too young to die."

"You knew him?" Father Thomas said.

"Yes." With his sight blurring and his body weary beyond measure, Gage met the abbot's gaze. "And I have made no decent decision since his death. So please let me at least do one thing right. Let me honor him by stopping these murderers." The words flowed out of him like those of a dying man, for he was too weak and desperate to be cautious.

Silence settled over the room. Fear that he would simply be called a liar again tightened like scar tissue around Gage's aching chest. Heat spread down his body, and darkness edged into his vision.

"Tell me where and to whom you would have this message sent."

Gage heard the abbot's words and felt hope flutter back to life inside him, but he had pushed himself too far. His weary body was beyond reclaiming. He wanted to respond, but numbness had already wrapped itself around him. Enveloped within it, he fell backward into darkness.

8

Rhonalyn dipped her quill in the gallnut ink in a horn beside her desk. A knife in one hand and a feather in the other, she held the parchment flat with her blade and wrote carefully. At a second desk against the adjacent wall, Aisley used her own knife to scratch away an error. "Gently, Aisley." Rhonalyn glanced over to make sure the child wasn't ruining the skin. "Good. Now mind your lines, and do not angle them."

"Aye, I will do my best." Aisley said the words like a sigh and held the quill more evenly while copying the lyrical verse Rhonalyn had given her as a writing assignment.

It was clear to Rhonalyn that Aisley disliked the task, but the skill of writing was one that she insisted the girl master. After all, one never knew how important it might be. She returned her focus to her own work.

Carefully forming the next curled word, she continued writing her letter to King Strephon. It had been tedious finding the perfect way to request to renegotiate the harbor toll. Particularly difficult was finding a means of payment that would hopefully please him as well as be acceptable to her, but slowly she had devised exactly the message she wished to send. Typically, the castle's scribe would write royal correspondence, but scribing this letter herself was her only way to be sure its content would remain confidential and not spread about Arcis Castle or to the streets beyond.

She'd learned the hard way, at about Aisley's age, that secrets, particularly those involving royalty, carried their own currency in the kingdom. As royalty, if you didn't want anyone using your information for their own gain and possibly to your detriment, then you kept to yourself whatever you didn't want shared. For even those you thought to be your most loyal friends would tell your deepest desires and intimate words in trade for some undivided attention and a bit of fame at the local market or a neighboring manor. At the memory, Rhonalyn's face flamed once more, and her blood boiled. She had wanted to have the lord's daughter publicly flogged, but her mother had suggested quietly sending the girl away rather than openly punishing her, which would've only confirmed the gossip.

Her mother had been the only person Rhonalyn could tell anything to without fear of where it would go and to whom it would be repeated. They had agreed to always guard each other's secrets, and her mother had honored her by sharing many of her private thoughts. Thus, Rhonalyn knew the ambition her mother had had for Keric and its people, and she had sworn at her mother's grave to see those dreams fulfilled.

A mostly passive and quiet soul, her mother had been the kind of queen who stated her desires and then waited patiently for her husband to approve of them. The results spoke for themselves. Their coffers were empty. Her mother was dead. And the only dream her father sought was that of survival.

Unlike her father, Rhonalyn wasn't satisfied with scraping the bottom of the barrel year after year. And unlike her mother, she wasn't a quiet or tolerant soul. She wanted to do more, not just dream about it. She wanted to see her kingdom flourish, and she would do whatever it took to get there. Renegotiating their rights to the harbor was just the beginning of that process.

She finished the final letters in the paragraph of text she'd been working on and shifted to start the next line. The scratching of the nib of Aisley's quill stopped. Rhonalyn glanced over at her, then she too heard it. The sound of flustered voices coming from the chamber beyond.

Rhonalyn motioned to the female servant standing by the room's door. "Tess," she commanded in the commoners' tongue, "go see what all the fuss is about."

"Yes, Your Royal Highness." The young woman curtsied and headed for the door. It opened before she could reach it. Two of Rhonalyn's ladies-in-waiting swept inside and bowed.

"Princess Rhonalyn." Lady Amanda, the shorter of the two with black hair, striking blue eyes, and a pleasant voice, spoke in the noblemen's tongue. "There is a messenger here from Asper."

Rhonalyn set aside her quill pen. "A messenger?"

"Aye, he seeks an audience with the king. His news is apparently urgent. King Bryant is being sought. I assumed you would wish to know."

"You did well." Rhonalyn placed the letter inside her desk, closed the desk's lid, and locked it using one of the many keys hanging from her belt. She had no idea how any news from Asper could possibly be urgent, but urgent news was usually bad news. "Aisley, stay here and continue your writing. Lady Pricilla will remain to instruct you."

A tall girl with a lively personality and pleasant looks, Lady Pricilla bowed and stepped further into the room while Lady Amanda returned to the passage to await Rhonalyn. Though curiosity and concern burned within her, Rhonalyn kept her bearing relaxed as she headed for the door. In her mind, she could hear her mother's voice. *"The secret to being a good ruler is to act like nothing in the world can shake you. So, regardless of how uncertain you feel, do not ask questions like a frightened child or run to the scene of an incident like an uninformed commoner. You are a royal, so present yourself as such, and proceed as if you know a secret everyone else does not. For if this is how you respond, you always will possess a secret."*

The other day, Rhonalyn had been caught off guard by Baron Tenebris, and it had shown. She did not intend to let that happen again. "Where is the messenger now?"

Lady Amanda fell into step behind her. "He is still in the great hall."

"Very well. Send a servant to the kitchen to tell the chief cook and butler I wish food and drink brought to the smaller private hall."

"I will see to it." Lady Amanda continued toward the stairs that led to the lower levels of the castle. Pausing, Rhonalyn unlocked a side door. She slipped through it, descended a set of steps, and moved along a narrow passage. A dozen or so openings led off from it, some to arrow loops, others to storage chambers, and one to the balcony crowning the great hall.

She turned down the last opening, reached the door at its end, and used a key to open it. Stepping out of the passage, she stood on the balcony behind one of the massive tapestries that graced the upper portion of the hall. She could hear the voice of their usher, Stevens, below. "Sir Martin, if you'll follow me, His Royal Majesty, King Bryant will receive you in a private hall."

Rhonalyn smiled. Her ability to predict people's actions around the castle was a useful skill and one she prided herself on using well. She swept along the balcony and glided down the northwest spiral stairs. She matched her pace to the sound of the two men crossing the great hall so that she arrived beside the smaller hall's door just as they reached it.

"Princess Rhonalyn." Stevens bowed. Sir Martin, a young knight, who looked agitated, quickly did the same. When he straightened, unlike most men, his gaze did not linger to consider her looks. Instead, he glanced toward the hall's door.

His news had to be dire indeed. Rhonalyn gestured for him to proceed. "My father is likely already awaiting us within, and I am sure you are eager to give him the news you carry." She pushed open the door and preceded the knight into the private hall. Her father and Baron Hughart were just entering the chamber from the opposite direction. Hughart caught Rhonalyn's gaze with a look of vexed admiration.

She acted like she didn't notice and glided into the room as if she'd been invited.

Regardless of how often he left her uninformed of what he concluded to be exclusively the king's business, she always managed to sweep into whatever meetings she chose to attend at the ideal moment to be included. It was a challenge she enjoyed winning, and thus a game she allowed him to play.

Unbeknownst to her father though, Hughart walked a thin edge between them. Were he ever to outright speak against her authority rather than just leaving her uninformed, she'd have instantly banished him from the castle. He had his position, and she had hers, and they maintained an understanding between them, particularly when it came to royal business.

Her father, on the other hand, accepted her presence as if she'd been expected to attend. He glanced at the knight, who bowed with the usher while his hands clenched and unclenched.

"Your Royal Majesty, Sir Martin from Asper," Stevens announced.

"Thank you. You may leave us, Stevens," King Bryant said in the commoners' tongue. Stevens backed out of the room, closing the hall's door as he went. Rhonalyn's father switched to the noblemen's tongue. "Sir Martin, what is this news you bring from Asper?"

Rhonalyn steeled herself for Sir Martin's answer.

"Your Majesty, yesterday morning my lord's sheriff was collecting taxes and making his inspections of several outlying manors. We—I was riding with them—were passing between villages when we were ambushed by a group of armed commoners."

For a moment Rhonalyn felt a flutter of hope that perhaps Asper's sheriff had caught the men responsible for the first attack, but the knight's unease told her there was no happy ending to his story.

"We were taken by surprise," Sir Martin said, "but being well-armed we were able to fend off their attack. We even captured one of them and interrogated him on the spot. He said he was from outside Caterva and was one of many commoners across Keric seeking to balance the scales of justice. He claimed they are tired of being dominated by lords who have lied to them and cheated them and a king who…" The knight cleared his throat. "The man's words, not mine, Your Majesty, 'a king who seeks only to fill his own coffers while treating his people like simpleminded slaves.' He also said that for every one of them we kill or capture, another will rise to take their place."

Dread settled over Rhonalyn. This was not the news she wanted to hear, not after the first attack and not when they were already on the brink of being questioned by their lords.

"Did he indeed," her father said, "and where is this impudent fool now?"

Rhonalyn glanced at Sir Martin. Yes, where was he? For the man was guilty of treason.

The knight cringed and looked to the floor. "I regret to say, he escaped, Your Majesty. His fellow thieves were apparently not as routed as we thought. They…they struck a second time, injuring five of ours and killing a sixth. They freed their companion, stole the bag of tax money we had collected, and fled toward the cliffs of Nikor. We gave chase and cut down four of theirs, but the other half dozen or so of them eluded us in the crags."

Rhonalyn's hands went cold. They had lost more men and money and had let the murderous commoners escape! Commoners who claimed to have an abundance of companions and clearly were not easily deterred. She reminded herself of her mother's words to never look shaken. Swallowing, she drew a slow breath. She could appear calm, but what good did it do her when her kingdom was tearing itself apart at the seams?

The more she thought about the situation though, the more her fear turned to anger. She forced herself to stay still, but inside she was screaming and throwing things. How had a sheriff, of all people, managed to lose these men? Why hadn't they continued after them and tracked them down? These commoners and their lies had to be stopped.

The cost of the first two attacks was bad enough. If there was a third attack, she had no doubt the price would not just be in men and money but also in the dismantling of the barons' confidence in the crown and the asking of questions to which they had no answers.

It was one thing to be unsuccessful in stopping something none of them knew was coming, but if, after a second assault, decisive action was not taken, Rhonalyn feared the people and nobles alike would see it as the exposure and exploitation of a weakness in Keric's crown. And rulers had been overthrown for far less.

Her father needed to take a clear stand. If a large number of commoners felt as these thieves did, any report of hesitation on the king's part could be disastrous, particularly in their current financial crisis. Her father's continued silence stirred her to action. If he would not save them, she would. For there was more than one way to express power.

"I am sure what my father is too stunned to ask, Sir Martin, is why the sheriff of Asper, of all people, failed in catching these commoners. Does he not have a decent tracker within his men? These thieves are not ghosts, are they? Therefore, explain to us how a freshly made trail could be so completely lost by a man whose very job it is to find such criminals."

The knight stared at the floor and swallowed. "We did not have a tracker with us, Your Royal Highness. But the sheriff, with his best tracker, was returning to the place where we lost their trail at the time I was sent here."

"How many men did he take with him?" her father asked, finally breaking his silence.

"Twenty-five men, Your Majesty."

Rhonalyn could tell her father was considering leaving the situation in the clearly incompetent hands of Asper's sheriff. She lifted her chin. "These commoners' treachery is an offense against every honorable soul in Keric. They should be ridden into the ground by twice that number of men as a response to their arrogance in thinking to stand against the lords and king of Keric." She met her father's gaze challengingly.

He held her stare for a moment, then responded with kingly authority. "Her Royal Highness is right. They and their words are an offense against all of Keric. Baron Hughart, tell my captains to assemble their men, and tell the marshal to see to it my horse is readied. I myself will ride to Asper."

Rhonalyn stood at a tower window and watched her father ride out under the castle's barbican followed by a stream of mounted knights, spearmen, and archers.

A momentary twinge of doubt crept through her. She had not expected her father to go to Asper himself. What if his presence did not bring the desired results? Questions could be raised, confidences might still be lost, and they might end up in exactly the position she had hoped to avoid.

She set the thought aside. A strong response from the king to these commoners' actions had been needed. If it turned out the men could not be tracked, blame could easily be placed on the sheriff for letting the trail go cold. The lack of results would be his, not the king's. Of course, if they succeeded in tracking the commoners, and the king's guard helped bring them to justice, her father could claim that triumph.

But what if other commoners really were ready to rise up in their place? Could so many of their subjects be willing to commit such treason? If so, why rise up now and in this way? The fields looked good, and harvest was coming. Food was in no shortage. No one else knew of the issues with the harbor. As far as the commoners of Keric knew, the year held the promise of prosperity. And considering their accusations about the king's coffers, clearly, they had no idea of the crown's financial state. For that she was grateful.

The thought of her father being what they claimed—a greedy oppressor—made her shake her head and almost wish it were true. For if he were a greedy king, he'd have announced new taxation years ago, which would have solved the issue of the harbor toll, among other things. But such was not the case. The crown of Keric did not oppress its people. Yet this was the thanks they received.

Rhonalyn turned away from the window. Such was the life of royalty. Not the ease and comfort those looking on believed it to be. Rather, it was the constant striving to keep the people happy enough to partner with you, productive enough to support you, loyal enough to serve you, and ambitious enough to join you in new endeavors, all while keeping them satisfied enough not to supplant you. It was a challenge Rhonalyn intended to master.

9

Gage came awake with a jerk that set his wounds instantly aching. He grimaced in the candlelit room.

"Awake again, I see," a reproving voice said. "You gave Father Thomas and Brother Sholan quite the scare."

Gage turned his head to find Brother John seated beside him.

The monk closed his prayer book with his thick hands. "I've known Brother Sholan since we were both novices. He's not usually one to get angry, but he lectured you up and down for not listening to him and resting when you should have."

Gage frowned. "He lectured, I don't recall—"

"No, of course you don't. You weren't conscious at the time, but that didn't stop him." The monk wagged a finger at him. "You deserved every word of it too. Here he spent days tending you back to health, and what do you do the first chance you get? You go and nearly undo it all in the course of one conversation."

"It wasn't that bad," Gage said. "Besides what was I supposed to do, admit I was too weak to talk?"

"Man's pride," Brother John shook his head, "to great glory and great folly it doth lead."

Gage glanced up at the window. The folly it had led him into was indeed a concern. No light came in from outside, and he could hear crickets. It had to be night, which meant most of a day had slipped away. His stomach grumbled. At least he hoped it had been just a day. "Brother John, how long ago did Father Thomas and I speak?"

The monk's gentle demeanor returned. "Just this morning."

Gage exhaled in relief. "Where's Father Thomas now? I need to finish talking with him."

"No, you don't. You need to rest."

"Rest? What do you think I've been doing all day? Please, Brother John, you must fetch him. I have requested something of him that I must see completed. Otherwise it may fail to profit anyone."

Brother John's fingers tapped his book. "I will see what I can do. But I make no promises." Rising, the monk left the room.

Gage clung to the hope that he had not dreamed Father Thomas's last words and that the abbot had not changed his mind since then, though the thought of composing a message stirred its own concerns. He'd been so focused on trying to persuade them to help him that he hadn't considered what he would say in a message. How was he to include the information required without causing Father Thomas to ask more questions? And where and to whom should it be sent?

He would prefer the message be delivered to Haaken, but he had no idea where Haaken was and thought it unwise to ask for a letter to be taken directly to Einhart Castle. That would doubtless stir unwanted questions on both sides. No, he needed it delivered to someone who could be located easily, who knew the issues, and who would understand the meaning of his words even if they were veiled. He thought of a person who fit all three requirements.

The latch on the door lifted, and Brother Sholan entered with a tray of food. "Brother John told me you were awake again. Perhaps next time you will heed my warning before pushing yourself beyond your abilities." Gage opened his mouth, but the monk cut him off by clunking down the tray. "And before you ask, no, Brother John is not fetching Father Thomas. The abbot is asleep, and I won't have him awakened just so you can exhaust him and yourself some more."

The scent of the food drifted to Gage's nose, causing his stomach to clench. He met Brother Sholan's gaze and tried to keep his annoyance and hunger from making his words sound angry. "Too much time has already passed. Other people could be killed because these murderers were not stopped as soon as they could have been. Do you want that on yours or your abbot's hands?"

Brother Sholan frowned at him. "Threats are a poor way to gain an ally. And before you continue spouting them, you should know I won't wake Father Thomas because he has already granted your request. Though perhaps you were already too far gone to remember it."

Gage took a deep breath. "I thought it might have been a dream."

The monk shook his head. "It wasn't. Your message will be sent. But first you must eat to regain enough strength to tell it to me. I will write it for you, and one of our brothers will leave with it at dawn tomorrow."

※

IT WAS TWO days later before Gage had the chance to express his gratitude to Father Thomas. This time he was propped up against a blanket, so he wasn't flat on his back as they talked.

The abbot's craggy eyebrows met. "I am sure those who receive your letter in Edelmar will be grateful, but gratitude is not all you and I have to discuss. Good deeds do not remove guilt. You are still a marked man."

Gage had known this reality would eventually resurface, and now that it had, it felt like a behemoth had come to devour him.

"We've encountered no one looking for you," the abbot said, "though I suspect this is because you have been assumed dead. I am unfamiliar with the mark you bear, but the lord of Legan would no doubt know to whom…it belongs."

Desperation tightened around Gage's chest. He wanted so badly to argue his innocence and that he should not belong to anyone, but how could he when he'd as much as admitted he'd stolen a nobleman's ring and brooch? He had done what he had to and paid one debt by locking himself into another. He didn't much like the results, but it was a decision he couldn't undo. Struggling to breathe, he met Father Thomas's gaze and silently begged for mercy, even as he said, "You must do what you have to."

"We here at Saint Jerome's Abbey are men of God, not lords' men, Gage."

He studied the abbot's face. "I'm not sure I understand."

"We're not required by law to turn you over to a lord," Father Thomas explained. "I have the choice to inform a lord of your presence here and let him decide what to do with you. I also have the choice to grant you a claim of sanctuary within our walls. You have expressed your regret for your actions and have acted upon your desire to make amends, and I believe here you could learn to continue to bear fruit worthy of that repentance. For the time allotted, you will be provided refuge here at Saint Jerome's Abbey, if you so wish."

"Refuge," Gage replied with a frown, "you mean as long as I remain within the abbey's walls."

Father Thomas nodded. "If you step beyond our walls you will forfeit the church's protection, and any lords' man can seize you and take you to the owner of the mark you bear."

Gage closed his eyes. So much for getting the abbot's help in gaining a fair hearing for the injustice he had endured. He supposed the offer was generous in light of his confession of thievery. He opened his eyes and considered his two options—live trapped within the abbey's walls or enslaved to a lord.

Inside him, his fury flared anew at Manton, the rebels, and every person who had ever aided them. No matter which direction he turned, he remained tangled amid their treason. They had taken everything from him, and because of being marked he couldn't even go after them himself.

If he ever managed to lay his hands on Manton, he'd beat him senseless, then hand him over to Sir Jarret's lord. Ultimately, though, he wanted every last rebel caught and punished.

At least because of what he knew, Edelmar's lords would soon know where to start finding the rebels.

What if telling those in Edelmar wasn't enough though? Communicating what he knew to the lords of Delkara could lead to a faster dismantling of the rebellion. He frowned. But could he safely tell them? He considered the abbot's offer of sanctuary. It might give him a way to speak to the Delkaran lords without the risk of being seized. Or would it?

The monks knew him to be marked as a thief. If they were aware he was also thought to be a rebel would they still protect him? What if there were brothers among them who sympathized with the rebels' cause? Any rebels who heard of his intentions to reveal what he knew would not likely sit by while he divulged names and locations to the Delkaran lords.

And those weren't his only concerns. Revealing his allegiances by taking his knowledge to a lord also presented risks, what with Lord Gregory being loyal to the rebels and Baron Bertram willingly defiling church tradition to capture them. Gage shuddered thinking as well of Sir Jarret's response to him. *"Your guilt is indisputable. If there is any injustice, it is that you were not caught and punished sooner."*

Even among the lords he had no way of knowing whom he could trust. "Father Thomas." Gage's voice paused the monk at the door. "You offer me sanctuary here, but what if I claim it, and it is not honored by those who seek me?"

"No one would dare dishonor the right of sanctuary." Father Thomas sounded absolutely convinced of this, but Gage knew better.

He desperately wanted to see every last rebel brought to justice, but he didn't want to end up in some dark hole with them. Claiming sanctuary seemed his only possible means of staying safe, but it could simply make him an easier target for both sides.

10

"Watch you head, Sir Wick."

Deep in the White Fortress in Edelmar, Wick ducked to clear the cellar's low door and nodded to the fortress's butler. "I'll inform the commander that you were right. The man definitely shorted us a barrel."

The butler hung his lantern on a peg beside the cellar's door and began to lock up. Wick brushed a loose lock of his straight, dark hair out of his eyes and held up his light to navigate his way out of the underbelly of the White Fortress.

"On time! You want them on time?" The angry voice of the fortress's chief cook echoed down the underground passage. "Then you can just come make the garrison's meals yourself!"

Wick exchanged looks with the butler. By the sound of things in the kitchen, a missing barrel wasn't the only problem in the bowels of the fortress.

"I'm simply suggesting," the loud voice of Charles, the commander's personal attendant, replied, "that preparations should perhaps be started earlier. That way meals can again be served when they are supposed to be."

Wick winced. Charles was as hardworking as anyone in the fortress, but he was too much like the commander and quite tactless in his approach to problem solving.

"That's it!" Metal hit stone with a resounding clang. "Get out of my kitchen!"

Wick and the butler both jumped.

"How dare—" Another clang reverberated, and Charles's fleeing form came into sight at the end of the passage. "I tell you, the commander will hear of this!" the man called over his shoulder. Cupping the flame of his lamp, Charles lunged beyond the reach of a third hurled item. The iron skillet ricocheted off the wall and settled with a long, resounding clatter on the corridor's stone floor behind him. Charles huffed past Wick, his face livid. "I tell you, that man is out of control and dangerous."

The butler snorted as Charles stormed off. "Dangerous my eye." He glanced at Wick. "If Osbert were truly out of control and dangerous he'd be throwing knives not pans. And believe me, were his intentions malicious, he'd not miss with either."

Wick remembered as a page how he'd witnessed the cook arrange a knife-throwing contest after one of the soldiers had foolishly made a remark about Osbert being just a cook. Wick agreed with the butler's assessment. If Osbert had wished Charles harm, he'd have easily done some.

Many of the men who served in the fortress had been there most of their lives. Wick glanced after Charles. Unfortunately, that didn't mean they'd all actually learned how to get along with one another. And in such close quarters, it often took only one person having a bad day for everyone to know about it and respond in kind.

Another crash came from the kitchen, followed by a pottery dish shattering. "That's it! I quit!"

The butler eyed Wick. "Sounds to me like we'll be making our own midday meal if someone doesn't do something about that."

Wick had long been known among the garrison to be someone who could stay calm, solve people problems, and coax even some of the most belligerent people into doing their jobs. They were skills he'd developed out of necessity, and they'd served him well at the fortress, along with his skill at lock picking, since misplaced keys were also a frequent issue. More than anything though he wished he could be back riding in Prince Gage's retinue.

When he had returned unexpectedly to the White Fortress over a month ago, no one beyond the commander had asked him why he'd been sent back. Instead, a rumor had spread that Prince Gage had dismissed him because of something he'd done. He didn't dare inform the gossipers that King Axel had returned every member of Prince Gage's retinue to their previous places of service. It was, after all, still his duty to protect His Highness, and such information would only reveal that wherever Prince Gage was now, he was without his former guard.

Wick often wondered what King Axel had meant when he'd said that Prince Gage was content with his current existence and no longer in need of his knights. Could it be His Highness had settled at some little-known manor with local knights as his protectors? Since no one besides Prince Gage's family had seen him since Aro, him living quietly somewhere off Edelmar's beaten paths seemed logical. Maybe he'd even found himself a wife and planned to raise a family.

Such a happy possibility added weight to Wick's silence. Some would have shared whatever tidbits they knew about the royal family, but he kept his mouth shut about even the most mundane details he'd learned while riding with Prince Gage, for despite what anyone said, he was an honorable knight and was good at his job.

Upon his return, he'd spent almost all of his time at the fortress, in Clement doing tasks for the commander, or serving beside the ford.

He had visited his parents twice but had avoided any interaction with his six older brothers, several of whom had their own manors nearby. He knew they'd offer the worst criticism of him being sent back to his previous posting. In their eyes, as the youngest he'd never been expected to amount to much. He had done his best to prove them wrong, pouring every bit of himself into weapons training, into his service at the fortress, and into becoming a valuable knight.

None of that had made any difference though, not until the day Prince Gage had requested that he join his royal retinue. Such an honor had changed everyone's perspective. His brothers had finally shown him some respect, and people everywhere had begun to interact with him like he actually had something to offer.

In truth, he'd been as astonished as anyone that Prince Gage had chosen him for his retinue. It was a position he had worked hard to remain worthy of keeping. Him being younger than all Prince Gage's other knights and older than Prince Gage was a dynamic he'd been afraid would be impossible to navigate. But the other knights had treated him like an equal, and Prince Gage's age had never seemed to hinder His Highness's leadership, though it had made each of his knights that much more protective of him. Wick had even begun to dare to hope that among Prince Gage's retinue he had found a place where he could truly belong.

Then the ambush had happened, and he'd encountered the very painful truth that when such a great honor is given and then revoked, the disgrace it brings is ten times worse than if the honor had never been bestowed in the first place. He was now not just Baron Jacob's youngest son who served at the White Fortress. He was, according to the gossipers, the royally rejected and disgraced youngest son of the baron of Clement.

Had it not been for King Axel's letter he was sure Sir Hedrick would have hesitated to accept him back. That stung the most since he had trained under the commander. But having done so, he knew Sir Hedrick to be more practical than empathetic. He also knew if he wasn't careful the rumors surrounding his return could still impact his post at the fortress.

Thus, in the weeks since being back, he'd worked harder than ever to stay in everyone's good graces and willingly assisted anyone in anything they needed, all in a strident effort to regain something close to his previous standing. He'd made some progress, but the few friends he had in the White Fortress and Clement told him that speculations continued to abound about what he'd done wrong while in Prince Gage's service. Even in the garrison his position felt fragile, like everyone was waiting and watching for his unforgivable flaw to emerge.

So, here he was counting barrels and striving to be as useful as possible. Would he risk Osbert throwing a pan at him in order to try to help solve whatever was the matter in the kitchen? Indeed, because that was what he did now. He strove daily to prove to everyone around him that he was still a worthwhile knight.

He'd spent quite a while when he'd first come back telling God how unfair it was that this was what he'd earned after all his faithful efforts. The following Sunday the priest had preached about doing service as to the Lord and not to men and being willing to be humbled that Christ's name might be lifted up. Wick had tried taking the words to heart, and now it was even a joke within the fortress, *"If you need something done, ask Sir Wick. He won't refuse you."*

Wick sighed. He supposed there were worse things to be known for. Heading for the kitchen, he scooped up the skillet from the stone floor and trekked around the corner into the hot, high-ceilinged room with long open fireplaces and enclosed bread ovens.

The kitchen had three large tables covered in all kinds of half-prepared food. The air smelled of onions, apples, and yeast. Searching the cavernous space, Wick spotted Osbert kneeling beside the second of the kitchen's heavily used boards. The cook was in the middle of vegetables strewn from an overturned basket and was tossing wet, sticky pieces of a jar into a wooden bowl while muttering to himself. Meanwhile, the other cook, the spit boys, and three scullions kept warily to the room's edges.

Wick knew from his experiences with his older brothers that being called out in front of others did little to improve one's attitude. So, instead of reprimanding the cook, he tried a more subtle approach in the commoners' tongue. "Osbert, may I seek your advice about something?"

Pausing in his muttering, the cook looked up at him with annoyance.

"If you're busy, I can come back later." Wick set the skillet on the nearest board.

Eyeing the skillet as he climbed to his feet, Osbert wiped his hands on his apron and cleared his throat. "I, um, can take a moment."

"I'd appreciate it." Wick motioned to the corner of the kitchen. Osbert joined him there, and one of the scullions quickly took over cleaning up the vegetables and broken jar. Wick respectfully met Osbert's gaze, though the cook struggled to return the courtesy. "I'd like to seek your advice as to who I should talk to about helping to solve whatever is causing tension in the kitchen."

"Well, you can start with the commander," the cook huffed.

"Pardon me?" Wick had thought Osbert would say himself.

"It's the commander who caused the problem." The cook looked him full in the face, his tone weary. "I mean no disrespect in saying it. It's just a fact. I'm the one responsible for feeding every person in this place, but he goes and lets two of my scullions go. He's clearly not going to bother replacing them, but I'm left four hands light, and still everyone expects all the meals to end up where they're supposed to, exactly when they're supposed to. I tell you, it wouldn't matter how early we got up. We simply can't keep up with it all."

"Wait, no one told you what happened with your two scullions?"

Osbert frowned in anger. "When I asked about them not showing up for work, I was told, 'Manage without them.'"

Wick blinked. How had that been all that was passed along? No wonder Osbert was upset. Marveling anew at people's knack for failing to communicate what actually mattered and for other people's ability to not ask more questions, Wick shook his head. "Osbert, those two scullions were caught fighting in Clement with the tavern boys. They were sentenced to four days in the stocks. They'll be back tomorrow."

The cook's forehead wrinkled. "Then…they're not gone for good?"

"No." Wick chuckled at the cook's savage look of relief. "I promise, you'll have your two workers back in your kitchen no later than tomorrow night. They'll doubtless be a little worse for the wear but hopefully a bit wiser."

Osbert ran his hand down his face, looking more human. "Ah, and here I've gone accusing the commander of—"

Wick held up his hand. "Of nothing that wasn't warranted. You should have been told more than you were." He eyed Osbert anew. "And now that you know that they'll return, can I assume the extra work in the kitchen will be managed with a bit more grace until then?"

Osbert gave him a sheepish look. "If you're asking if there'll be any more pan throwing, I think I can restrain myself. As long as Charles doesn't come back, that is."

Wick chuckled. "Good enough for me." Departing the kitchen, he ascended through several passages to reach the large room where the garrison soldiers ate and could assemble or train when the weather was foul. The space was directly adjacent to Sir Hedrick's study and personal chambers. The layout had at first seemed like an odd choice to Wick, due to the noise level often created within the hall, but as a squire he'd noticed that unless the soldiers were absolutely sure the commander was not present within the fortress, the layout resulted in more controlled interactions among the men. When soldiers knew their commander might walk in at any moment, they did not start fights about someone receiving the best portion of meat or getting cheated at dice, particularly not when that commander was Sir Hedrick.

Wick was halfway through the room's empty trestle tables when Charles stepped out of the study's door. No doubt the man had come to report Osbert's behavior to the commander. Wick caught Charles's gaze and was about to mention what he'd learned from Osbert and that the problem was resolved, but Charles spoke before he could. "If you're hoping to speak with the commander, you should return later. He's currently meeting with a baron who would like his son to join the garrison's ranks. The commander will not want to be disturbed."

Wick paused mid-stride and wondered which baron might be seeking a position for his son at the fortress. By the time his attention returned to matters at hand, Charles was already gone. Frowning, Wick looked toward the study's closed door. It would likely be over an hour before he could report his findings to the commander. Thus it would probably be late in the day before he was sent to speak with the seller in Clement. The issue with the barrel would get solved, just not any time soon. He turned from the door and considered what other tasks to pursue in the meantime, for there was always more to do.

The fortress's porter, a short, paunchy man, hurried into the large chamber. His determined expression brightened. "Sir Wick, there you are. I was just coming to see if the commander knew where I might find you." The porter held out a sealed letter and a small leather pouch. "These were just delivered for you. He said it was imperative Sir Wick of the White Fortress receive them as soon as possible. I thought it best to place them directly into your hands myself."

11

Wick took the letter the porter held out to him and frowned at its unfamiliar seal. Why would someone he didn't know be sending him an urgent message? He looked at the porter. "Did the man who delivered this mention who sent it?"

"It was a monk who brought it. Said they were from a guest of Saint Jerome's Abbey."

Wick had never heard of Saint Jerome's Abbey, and he found it odd an abbey guest would ask a monk to deliver a message for him. He wondered if the abbey was nearby since the guest knew his name. He broke the seal and unfolded the letter. It was written in a flowing script on quality parchment.

To the honorable Sir Wick, Knight of the White Fortress and Son of Baron Jacob of Clement, I send you this letter in hopes that the information it contains might be able to be used to bring about justice.

In my recent travels, I happened upon Lady Natriece of Veiroot. She had, through no intention of her own, come in contact with the man responsible for the murders of Squire Allard and Bardon of Weldon. Threatened to silence by this man, her ladyship had not before dared speak of what she knew of him or of the evidence she carried against him, but knowing my connection to the two she revealed both to me.

The letter's writer had to be speaking of Felix. Hundreds of Edelmarian knights had, on King Axel's orders, tried and failed to track down Felix after the ambush. The Blue Crow had been questioned but had revealed nothing, and eventually the search had been abandoned. Yet Lady Natriece had come upon him? Had Felix fled into the mountains near Veiroot? Was that how she had encountered him? Wick returned his focus to the letter.

According to Lady Natriece's testimony, this man has collected anew others loyal to his cause, and even now additional men are traveling to join them.

Wick's stomach lurched. The one satisfaction he'd felt watching the Blue Crow and his men hang was in knowing their murderous ways were over. The thought that Felix was reviving their cause was enough to make him ill. He kept reading.

Lives could be saved if action is taken before those loyal to him depart their current location. A position where their capture, according to Lady Natriece, could be accomplished without bloodshed if done correctly.

This exact location can be gained by sending a well-armed company to Lady Natriece's father, Lord Gregory, at Veiroot, and asking after Felix, his long-term guest. Between Felix and Lady Natriece, all that needs be told shall be revealed.

Felix! A chill crawled over Wick. A long-term guest? Could Lord Gregory of Edelmar truly have hidden a man who had attacked the king's son and murdered another lord's son? Fury filled him. If it was true, Lord Gregory deserved worse than hanging. But who dared accuse him? He scanned swiftly to the bottom of the letter and read the name written there. *Humbly, Gage.*

Gage? Wick blinked. As in, His Highness, Prince Gage? He knew no other Gage. But if Prince Gage had sent the letter, why was it not sealed with his seal? And why sign it in such an informal way? Or send it through a monk? And for that matter, why deliver it to him and not to Einhart? Perhaps there was an explanation in the rest of the letter. He continued reading.

Additionally, there is another person I encountered in my journeys who would no doubt prove useful in this endeavor of justice. He is a traveler by the name of Manton, son of Brit. He sells carven goods at inns and taverns and connects with and aids people, similar to how Fran and Wes of the woods help people. Every few months Manton returns to restock his goods from his father's shop in Dulcis, and I have it on good authority he will circle back there soon. It may be that you could yet find him there and utilize his connections in this regard.

Anger coursed through Wick. Oh, they would indeed utilize this Manton's connections, and this time they'd be the ones with surprise on their side. They'd seize every last person involved, because there was no way he was going to let Felix gather another group of traitorous peasants. Exhaling, Wick purged enough of his emotions to finish the letter.

All of this information I impart to you desiring only to see these murderers brought to justice. I know I have made mistakes and am thus aware my words may not carry the weight they once did. I hope, though, that the items returned with this letter will bear earnest proof of my deep regret for my actions and my integrity in this regard. And I trust that you, Sir Wick, will see them and this letter placed in the right hands.

Humbly, Gage

Wick stared at the letter and frowned. The details and names matched what Prince Gage would know, and the ardent desire for justice in bringing down Felix and those gathering to him was that of someone familiar with their cause, but the way the letter was written bothered him. It was like it had been composed to conceal what it was revealing. But why?

Everything about it stirred questions. He looked at the porter, who stood waiting. "You said a monk delivered this letter?"

"Yes, it and this." The porter handed him a small yet surprisingly weighty leather pouch.

Frowning further, Wick worked to untie the bag's laces. "Is the monk still here?"

"When I came to find you, he was refilling his waterskins at our well. I don't know if he still remains within the fortress's walls."

His mind churning over the monk's involvement and the quandaries surrounding the letter, Wick splayed open the small leather pouch and absently dumped what was in it into his hand. Two solid gold items of unequal weight landed on his palm with a loud clank.

Air left Wick's lungs. To see the ruby brooch was shocking enough. Seeing it beside Prince Gage's signet ring reawakened all the angst he'd felt during the months no one had known where Prince Gage was or what had happened to him.

The ring was proof Prince Gage was undoubtedly involved with the letter's creation, but under what circumstances? "Porter, find the monk who brought this. Immediately! And heaven help you, do not let him leave until I have spoken with him." Wick wanted to know everything the monk knew about how the items had ended up in his possession and who exactly had told him to bring them to him.

Confusion and concern crossed the porter's face. "Yes, sir." As the man hurried off, Wick strode to the door of the commander's study, knocked twice, and did something he'd never done before. He entered without waiting for permission.

Seated opposite a well-dressed baron, the commander glanced up in annoyance. "Sir Wick, I am in the middle of an important meeting. What—"

"Forgive me, sir. This cannot wait." Even as the words left his mouth, Wick swallowed. He'd just dared to presume what he had to say was more important than whatever was being said. He took a fortifying breath. It wasn't his words though he was deeming important; it was the arrival of a prince's signet ring absent its owner.

Sir Hedrick bowed to the baron. "Give me a moment, your lordship?" The baron nodded, and the commander stood and tromped to where Wick waited at the door. Sir Hedrick motioned for him to precede him out into the hall. Wick obeyed, and the commander shut the door behind him but continued in the noblemen's tongue. "What is it, Sir Wick?" His voice was stern, but his gaze was expectant.

Wick opened his mouth to answer. But it occurred to him just then that if the letter was true, and Lord Gregory was a traitor, others in Edelmar's ranks could be as well. He hesitated. Perhaps it was best to share the particulars of the letter only with Prince Gage's own family.

"Sir, I have just received urgent news for Edelmar's crown. It must be delivered immediately. I seek your permission to depart and send word ahead by pigeon to Einhart Castle to tell them I am coming."

"You have an urgent message for the crown. By all means, go."

Wick nodded. "Yes, sir. Thank you, sir."

12

Hurrying through the White Fortress, Wick sent one servant to have a horse prepared and another to ask Osbert to pack him food for his journey, a task the cook would no doubt be thrilled to fit into his busy schedule. Unfortunately, the timing couldn't be helped. Wick gathered his belongings from the chamber he shared with three of the fortress's other knights. Having spent a lot of time coming and going to tournaments with Prince Gage, he'd learned to keep his personal possessions to a minimum and his saddlebags close at hand.

Since his current mission was official Edelmarian business, he remained in his White Fortress armor and surcoat and headed to request the master of the dovecote send his message to Einhart.

The note had to be short, and if the information in the letter about the seller Manton returning to his father's shop was true, time was of the essence. Which meant it would be foolish to travel first to Einhart just to explain where they needed to go, so he sent to Einhart Castle the following message: "Urgent! Heard from Prince Gage. Meet me at Dulcis. Sir Wick."

Part of him felt awkward acting like the situation was dire when he knew so little, but another part of him was certain the two items and the letter's content made urgency absolutely warranted.

He watched the dovecote master tediously write the words on a small slip of linen and then carefully secure the cloth around a pigeon's leg. Then the man stepped to the door and released the bird. With a fluttering burst of its wings, the creature flew for the sky. It banked on the breeze a moment later and headed for Einhart.

Pigeons from all the major Edelmarian cities were kept at the fortress so that important news could be sent by the fastest means possible. Whoever was at Einhart Castle would get Wick's message before he'd even made it a quarter of the way to Luert. Wick hoped that meant King Axel or Prince Haaken would receive it and meet him in Dulcis.

He headed for the stable wondering if the porter had succeeded in finding the monk from Saint Jerome's Abbey. A groom handed him the reins of a bay mount. Wick secured his sword and personal saddlebags alongside the supplies already tied between the animal's black mane and tail. Then he turned toward the fortress's gate.

He feared the monk would have disappeared like Felix, but there beside the porter and a soldier was a brown-robed stranger with a mule. The monk looked young, possibly not even as old as Prince Gage.

Wick evaluated him as he approached. Was the brother really who he said he was? Or was he one of Felix's men? The monk's only visible weapon was a small traveler's knife. His blond hair was tonsured short, his robe was tied up to allow for easier movement, and his expression held a wariness that increased as Wick drew near.

Grappling with the desire to straight up interrogate him, Wick reminded himself that he knew nothing for certain about how the monk had gotten the items he'd delivered. So, despite his misgivings, he kept a calm tone. "I'm the one who asked our porter to delay you," he said in the commoners' tongue. "I'm Sir Wick. I have some questions I'm hoping you can answer for me about the letter and items you delivered."

The monk's gaze and posture relaxed. "Sir Wick, you are the knight he asked the letter to be given to. I'm Brother Ephraim. I will help you any way I can. Our abbot wasn't sure if our guest spoke truthfully or not, but since he claimed his information could save lives, we did what we could to deliver it into your hands."

Wick motioned for the monk to walk with him and nodded for the soldier and porter to return to their tasks. Once he and Brother Ephraim were in relative privacy, he paused and met the monk's gaze, searching for any hint of deception. "This guest of your abbey, he wrote the letter himself that you brought here?"

"I believe one of our brothers scribed it for him, but the words and information came from him."

"I see." Wick kept his questions casual despite his suspicions. "Did he say why he wanted the letter and items delivered here and not to Einhart?"

Brother Ephraim looked worried. "I was told it was because he believed you were someone who would know what to do with them."

Wick hoped he did, but that didn't staunch his fears. "Why did this guest not deliver the message himself?"

"From what I was told, he believed having it arrive sooner rather than later was important, and he was not yet well enough to stand, let alone ride."

Wick stiffened. "What do you mean? What happened to him?"

Brother Ephraim looked taken aback. "Well, he, um, was badly injured by a blade. One of our brothers found him that way, half dead in the woods. We brought him back to our infirmarer, who has been looking after him ever since. He burned with a fever for several days, but he's recovered now and healing. The first thing he asked when he was better was that we carry this message for him."

Wick heard the words "recovered" and "healing" following the descriptions "badly injured" and "half dead." Still, worry tightened in his chest. "Where is this abbey?"

"Saint Jerome's? It's a bit west of Legan."

"Legan!" That was halfway across Delkara. A jumble of emotions crashed around inside Wick. He felt relieved Prince Gage was alive, outraged he'd forsaken his retinue to apparently travel alone in Delkara, and burdened with concern over his well-being. Though at the center of it all, he felt a renewed respect for Prince Gage in that he had insisted word be sent about Felix, the additional men, and the traveler, Manton.

Was seeking Felix why Prince Gage had traveled into Delkara? And what about the monks? So far, no part of what he'd heard accounted for the strange way the information in the letter had been worded, nor the fact that Prince Gage would send his signet ring with the letter. He studied Brother Ephraim's face. "Did His Highness say why he'd traveled to Delkara?"

"His Highness?" Brother Ephraim shook his head as if he didn't understand what Wick was asking.

Wick clenched his fingers into fists. "Yes. Your guest, Prince Gage. The one whose signet ring you just delivered to me. Did he say why he'd traveled to Delkara?"

The monk blinked and stepped back. "Our guest is a commoner, not a prince."

Wick felt as if the earth were tipping out from under him. Reaching to his waist, he clenched his fingers around the small pouch containing the ring and brooch. "If that is true, then tell me swiftly where you got the items in this pouch. For I know for a fact they belong to His Highness, Prince Gage of Edelmar."

Brother Ephraim looked genuinely alarmed. "I don't know. I wasn't shown what was placed in that pouch. Nor did I read the letter. I was simply told by Father Thomas to deliver both here to you."

"You *never* saw what was placed in the pouch?"

"No."

"Did you actually see this guest you speak of?" Wick demanded.

"Of course. I helped fetch him out of the woods and bring him to the abbey." Brother Ephraim shuddered. "Though I wish I hadn't. The sight of his injury is still in my head. I thought for sure he was dead, but Brother Matthew was positive he was alive. And I promise you, his clothes were that of a commoner."

"Describe him to me."

"He's got long dark hair, like yours but curly. At least, once it was clean it was. Standing, he'd maybe be a bit shorter than you and definitely broader in his build. He's got a roundish face and a dark beard."

Despite being confused over why Prince Gage would be alone and dressed as a commoner, Wick found some small measure of relief in hearing Brother Ephraim's description. Glancing up at the sun, he frowned. He dared not delay his departure any longer. He scrubbed his hand down his face. He knew he must deliver to Dulcis the information Prince Gage had passed along, but that didn't keep him from also wishing he could first charge into Delkara and make sure Prince Gage was truly safe.

There was still so much he wanted to know from Brother Ephraim. And though irrational, he felt like if he let the monk out of his sight, he might never see Prince Gage again. "Will you ride with me to the royal family, Brother Ephraim? They too will wish to hear your account of all of this."

Brother Ephraim hesitated.

Wick knew asking was better than forcing, and he hoped the monk would agree. Because regardless of his answer, Brother Ephraim was coming with him. "You said you'd assist me in any way you could."

"Yes, I did. I will come."

***

WITH THE DAY's sun already descending, Wick pushed hard on the road and was thankful when they made it to Luert late that night.

They slept a few hours and then headed on to Dulcis early the following day. Along the way he further questioned Brother Ephraim.

The monk's account of the miraculous events of His Highness's arrival at Saint Jerome's Abbey were as startling to Wick as Prince Gage's presence in Delkara, but beyond the brothers' efforts to restore His Highness's health, there was little more to glean. Therefore, why Prince Gage was in Delkara and what had happened to him remained mysteries yet to be solved.

"I'm sorry I'm not more help to you," Brother Ephraim said. "Like I said, Brother John, Brother Sholan, and Father Thomas are the only ones who spoke directly with him."

Wick nodded. "It's likely that Prince Gage asked them to keep it that way for the sake of his safety." The letter's content stirred Wick's thoughts. He mulled over as well what it would mean to try to take into custody those associated with Felix. Fear mingled with his thoughts. Defeating the Blue Crow had cost the lives of two good men. If the lord of Veiroot was truly involved, how many more good men would be killed trying to bring an end to such treachery?

How did a group like Felix's even come to exist? The Blue Crow had spoken blatant lies about the plight of the common people, so why follow him? Wick recalled the money the Blue Crow had offered Emerett and Bardon. He supposed that was the answer. Their cause was not on behalf of poor, wrongfully treated commoners but that of greedy cowards.

Abuse of any person was not something Prince Gage or his family would have ignored or allowed. In fact, Wick was fairly certain Prince Gage would've even heard the boy Wes's complaints that day in the mud had the others not attacked, though he was also sure Wes had possessed no legitimate grievance, only those contrived by the group as an excuse and distraction.

If somewhere in Edelmar people were being cheated and stolen from, all they had to do was bring their case to King Axel. But regardless, no amount of stolen goods or mistreatment could justify what the Blue Crow's group had done. And evidently, leaving even one person willing to hawk their lies was one person too many.

13

Trotting his mount to the top of a hill, Wick finally had a clear line of sight to Dulcis. Built amid knolls and large fields, the city was situated on the trade road leading from Einhart to Edelmar's southern cities. Thus, despite its less than impressive size, Dulcis bustled with travelers. Squinting, Wick spotted outside the city's gate two knights whose mounts were caparisoned in the blue and white overlaid by the royal gold and purple belonging to His Majesty, King Axel.

"Thank God." Wick turned back to Brother Ephraim. "My message was received! Someone from the royal house is in Dulcis." He couldn't make out if there were additional markings on the flags or the knights' coat-of-arms. Therefore, he wasn't sure who of the royal house had come, but regardless, his relief was enough to restore his energy. "Come on, Brother Ephraim."

The monk called to him while steering around a peasant trudging toward the city carrying a bundle of furs. "Your eagerness is admirable, but I've spent several more days in the saddle than you. I'm afraid at this point, speed would be more of a hazard on my part than an accomplishment. But don't delay on my account, please. I will follow as quickly as I can."

Wick slowed his horse. He'd come this far without letting the monk out of his sight. He wasn't about to rush ahead now and risk losing him. "No, we'll arrive together." He glanced back toward the gate and noted that he wasn't the only one feeling impatient. One of the knights was galloping toward them.

Thundering past an ox cart, a man herding geese, and a group of serfs, the knight drew back his horse's reins. His mount threw its head and slid to a stop.

Wick noted the symbol on the horse's saddle cloth and recognized the knight's face from when they had crossed paths serving the princes of Edelmar. "Sir Renner."

"Sir Wick, it is good to see you. His Royal Highness, Prince Haaken, is awaiting your arrival in Dulcis," the knight said in the noblemen's tongue as he drew his mount around and beside Wick's horse. He nodded to the monk. "Who is this?"

"Brother Ephraim of Saint Jerome's Abbey. It was he who brought the news of Prince Gage. I believe His Royal Highness will wish to speak to him."

Sir Renner looked like he wished to inquire further, but he merely nodded. "Follow me." He preceded them along the busy road to the city's gate where they were joined by his companion, Sir Adrian.

The gatemen exchanged nods with the two knights and allowed the four of them through the city's fortified entrance. Sir Renner turned right and led them along Dulcis's thick city wall to where it merged with a round guard tower. Outside the tower were attendants, horses, and more knights wearing the colors of Edelmar's royal family.

Sir Renner dismounted at the tower's door. Wick did the same and motioned for Brother Ephraim to do likewise. In anticipation of speaking to Edelmar's future king, Wick's heart beat faster and fresh sweat dampened his tunic. It didn't help that he had no idea how Prince Haaken would react to the news he brought. Swallowing hard, he followed Sir Renner through the tower's low doorway and into a large, musty stone room.

Two more of Prince Haaken's knights, Prince Haaken's squire, and Prince Haaken himself awaited him within. Lighted by five bracketed candles, the round chamber held a board and benches at its center, a small fireplace, a well-kept collection of weaponry stored against the walls, and a second door that probably led to spiral stairs.

The two knights already in the room flanked the fireplace while Prince Haaken paced near his squire on the opposite side of the room. Sword belted over a richly embellished tunic and crown glinting in the candlelight, Prince Haaken paused mid-stride as they entered.

Wick dropped his gaze and bowed, his heartbeat reverberating in his ears. "Your Royal Highness."

"Good," Prince Haaken said in the noblemen's tongue, "you are here at last. I was beginning to wonder how much longer it might be. Between yours and Gage's cryptic messages, I have spent more time than I care to admit puzzling over mysteries. So, tell me, Sir Wick, what have you heard from my brother?"

Keeping his expression blank, a skill he'd learned serving the commander, Wick sent a quick glance at Prince Haaken's face. Despite his calm, half-joking tone, concern furrowed Prince Haaken's forehead. Wick swallowed to moisten his mouth and answered in the noblemen's tongue. "Two days ago I received a letter at the White Fortress with news from Prince Gage—at least I am fairly certain it was sent by him. This was delivered with it." He fumbled for a moment trying to untie the small pouch at his belt and withdraw its contents. With his fingers finally closed around the ring and brooch, he leaned across the table to lay them on the board.

Prince Haaken strode forward and picked each one up. He shook his head at the signet ring, but he paused on the ruby brooch. "Is this not what my brother received as tournament victor at Nardell?"

Feeling his nervous heartbeat shift to the steady pound of anger, Wick nodded. "It is, and that which was stolen by Felix during the ambush."

Every knight present stiffened at the name, and Prince Haaken's gaze snapped to Wick's. "He found Felix?"

Wick shifted on his feet. He had no desire to be the one to tell Prince Haaken about Felix's connection to Lord Gregory. "You had best read the letter." He pulled it from his satchel and handed it across the board.

Frowning at him, Prince Haaken unfolded the letter. As he read, his expression darkened from impatient curiosity to tightly controlled anger. He looked beyond Wick. "Sir Holbird, find me the location of a carver's shop here in Dulcis owned by a man named Brit."

"Aye, Your Royal Highness." The tower's door creaked, then thudded closed.

"Who else has read this, Sir Wick?"

"As far as I know, Your Royal Highness, only you and me."

Prince Haaken set the letter on the board and tapped a finger on it. "The handwriting is not my brother's. Nor is the seal one I know. Where did this come from?"

"From what I have been told the letter was scribed for His Highness at Saint Jerome's Abbey just outside of Legan in Delkara."

"An abbey in Delkara?" Prince Haaken flattened his hands on either side of the letter and stared down at it. He shook his head. "Gage learns this kind of news in Delkara, and he sends a letter? Nay, it is not like him." Prince Haaken straightened. "There is something amiss here. I might disagree with my brother's recent decision making, but I know him well enough to be sure he would never send this sort of news by such a means."

"That was my thought as well," Wick said, "but it would seem bringing it himself was not a possibility available to him." He motioned then to Brother Ephraim, whose confused expression indicated he hadn't understood anything they had just said. Wick switched to the commoners' tongue. "Brother Ephraim, will you please tell His Royal Highness how Prince Gage came to be a guest at Saint Jerome's Abbey and why he requested a letter be delivered on his behalf?"

Stuffing his arms into his brown sleeves, Brother Ephraim cleared his throat. "Well…Your Royal Highness, we, um…we didn't know he was a prince. You see, when Brother Matthew found him in the woods injured and unconscious beside his horse, he was dressed as a commoner. His mount, a faithful creature, had no saddle to identify him either. We actually had to drive off the animal in order to get to where His Highness lay.

"He'd been badly cut by a blade. We brought him back to our abbey's infirmary. After several days, thanks be to God, he recovered enough to converse briefly with two of our brothers. A few days after that, he asked our abbot if one of us would carry a letter for him. Thus, I was sent while he remained at Saint Jerome's Abbey to recover fully."

Prince Haaken had stood perfectly still, displaying no emotions during Brother Ephraim's explanation. The moment the monk was through though, he began pacing the length of the board, his expression concerned and stormy. He balled one hand into a fist and clenched the other around his sword's hilt. "Sir Wick," he said in the noblemen's tongue, "what I am about to tell you has been kept secret from those not involved for many of the same reasons the activities of the Blue Crow were initially concealed."

Wick held his breath, not sure he wanted to know whatever Prince Haaken was about to tell him.

"Due to events following the Blue Crow's execution, we have for some time now known there were others like him still in Edelmar. But until now we have not known where to look for them, let alone who was supporting and concealing them.

"Tales of the Blue Crow's exploits spread during his trial, and less than a month after his execution, offenses and crimes began to be committed against lords. They were perpetrated by men reportedly acting in service to other lords, some even bearing their coat-of-arms. The result was the questioning of the integrity of those on both sides, creating a rising animosity among the nobles.

"In hopes of identifying those behind these incidents, a portion of the time at the Noblemen's Feast was utilized as a court of inquiry. But despite my father's best efforts and the apparent cooperation of all parties present, no clear perpetrators were discovered. A decision was made then that any interaction between two lords' men unfamiliar with each other would be verified beforehand and confirmed at the encounter. Anyone unable to be identified in this manner would be taken into custody and held until a lord could either verify or deny their claim.

"Of course, at that point the perpetrators changed their tactics. From then on they began to more closely resemble the tactics of the Blue Crow, attacking at night, stealing from storerooms and treasuries, and killing anyone in their way. Not long ago, Baron James's knights cornered one of their men. He spouted the Blue Crows cry of injustice and claimed the common people had the right to take back what had been stolen from them. Then he killed himself with his own dagger before he could be detained and questioned further."

Wick shuddered. "Then it's true. What happened with the Blue Crow is not over."

"Nay, it is not." Prince Haaken tapped Prince Gage's letter. "And this explains why they have avoided our nets. We will go after Lord Gregory. But first, we will find this Manton. Will you ride with us?"

Determination surged through Wick. "Aye, Your Royal Highness."

14

Riding beside Prince Haaken toward Brit Carver's shop, Wick was tempted to let himself experience all the emotions of being part of a royal retinue again, but under the circumstances he held himself to one emotion only: gratitude. Prince Haaken could have simply sent him back to the White Fortress, but he'd brought him along. The problem was, Wick had no idea what Prince Haaken expected of him. In fact, even just passing through Dulcis with Prince Haaken was so different from anything he'd experienced with Prince Gage.

Regardless of the purpose of his journey, Prince Gage had always seemed in a hurry to get through a city and back to the countryside, whereas Prince Haaken even now rode at a painfully leisurely pace that, from Wick's perspective, made no sense considering their urgent business.

And unlike Prince Gage's polite yet removed interactions with people, Prince Haaken responded to everyone along the street with an amiability that slowed their progress even further. His Highness addressed all those who greeted him in a way that took the attention directed toward him and returned it to them with equal or greater reward. Shopkeepers bowed and greeted him, travelers smiled and happily made way for him, and small children called out and waved to him.

Any other day, Wick would have found it admirable, but he kept biting his tongue and tightening his fingers on his reins to keep his impatience at bay. Knowing what he now knew of the rebels, he had no idea how Prince Haaken could travel so calmly through a crowd when anyone around him could be one of Felix's men.

Busy considering all of this and looking for concealed archers, Wick was startled when Prince Haaken steered his mount close and spoke quietly in the noblemen's tongue. "Sir Wick, this traveler and seller that we seek, do you supposed his father knows of his dealings with the likes of Felix, or do you think it possible he is unaware of his son's alliances?"

Taken aback that Prince Haaken was asking for his opinion, it took Wick a moment to evaluate and answer the question. "I think it could be either, Your Royal Highness. Fathers and sons sometimes do lean quite differently in their mindsets." He thought of his own family.

"Best then I suppose to have my visit to the father's shop appear as nothing more than any other stop I might make in Dulcis. And may God help us discern which side the father is on."

Wick hoped the same and realized Prince Haaken had just explained why they weren't hurrying through the city. No one observing them would know that anything out of the ordinary was taking place. Instead, it was simply a pleasant day, which Prince Haaken was choosing to spend in the city. Loosening his hands on his reins, Wick let his body relax and tried to embrace this mindset as they continued onward.

"Your Royal Highness," Sir Holbird said quietly, "the shop you seek is the last one on the street ahead."

"Then we shall dismount here." Prince Haaken pulled his horse to a stop. "You, Sir Wick, and Sir Renner shall accompany me. Sir Jocelyn and Sir Adrian, circle around the back of the shop. If anyone associated with the place leaves that direction, bring them to me. The rest of you stay here."

The knights Prince Haaken had named dismounted and handed their reins to attendants. Wick did likewise and glanced back at Brother Ephraim. "Wait here," he instructed in the commoners' tongue before following Prince Haaken and his two knights.

Prince Haaken viewed the goods in windows along the street and interacted with shopkeepers and buyers in his pleasant and seemingly carefree manner. His knights also appeared at ease yet vigilant to the movement around them. Meanwhile, Wick let his gaze wander to the shop where they were headed.

A canopy of bright striped cloth shaded its large window where lifelike carvings of fox, deer, and other forest creatures were on display. The shop's door stood open. Thankfully, it didn't take long to reach it. Sir Renner walked in first, Prince Haaken entered next, and Sir Holbird followed. Wick trailed behind them all.

Inside were shelves upon shelves of carven items, everything from plain wood bowls to elegant hair combs. Wick swept his gaze over the skillfully crafted woodwork of varying colors and locked onto movement at the back of the shop. Beside a closed door, a burly man sat on a stool absorbed in working on a piece of dark wood. He had a double chin, thinning hair, and hands so large they nearly engulfed the tool and the chunk of wood he held. Beyond the door a woman could be heard calling directions to someone. She was probably the man's wife, busily preparing an evening meal.

"Are you the owner of this shop?" Prince Haaken asked.

The man glanced up. His eyes widened, and in his haste to rise and bow, he lost hold of his chunk of wood. "Your Royal Highness! Beggin' your pardon."

"No, forgive me," Prince Haaken said. "I seem to have the terrible habit of startling people. My knight's say I should let them announce my presence at the door, but that often has the same effect." Prince Haaken stooped and gathered from the floor the wood chunk, which had rolled toward him, and held it out to the man. "Here. You were hard at work at something? What are you making?"

Taking the wood, the man brushed shavings off himself. "Um. Making? Me? I, um, just a spoon, Your Royal Highness." He distractedly set the tool and half-finished carving on a nearby shelf. "Is there, um, anything I can do for you or help you find? I can make a vast variety of things."

"All this is yours? You do beautiful work," Prince Haaken said. "I take it then you are Brit Carver, craftsman and owner of this shop?"

"I am." The man looked both embarrassed and pleased at Prince Haaken's compliment.

"Do you travel and sell your woodwork in other places?"

"Me? Travel? No." Brit shook his head and pointed down at the floor. "Here's where I sell my goods. I don't pack up my wares and trek them to fairs and the like. Plenty others do, but I've kept my own shop here now for a good number of years. I've no need to sell elsewhere. Got an apprentice and plenty to do."

"I suppose it's nice then that your son, Manton, helps sell for you?"

Brit eyed Prince Haaken sharply. "My son, Manton?" He frowned. "Yes, I suppose one could say he's helpful in selling. Nothing wrong with that, is there?" Fear and a defensiveness trailed through the man's voice. "Has someone complained about him?"

Wick's heart rate quickened. Maybe Manton's activities were known by his father.

"Is there a reason someone might have complained about him?" Prince Haaken sounded confused rather than caught by the man's question.

"No." Brit huffed. "Not that I know of. He's a good boy. Smart with coin and respectful. I can't see why anyone would have any problem with him."

"Do you know the company he keeps these days?" Prince Haaken asked.

The man looked dumbfounded. "The company he keeps?" He ran his hand through his thinning hair. "Well, there's the wheelwright's sons down the street and the saddler's daughter, but other than them, I don't know anyone else he spends time with. Why do you ask? Has something happened involving my son?" Though Brit's tone was respectful, his suspicions were as taut as a bowstring, and his patience seemed to be wearing thin. "Please, what is this about, Your Royal Highness? For clearly you've come here about my boy."

"The truth is your son may know several people I wish to find and speak to. Do you know where Manton is now or when he might next return home?"

"Where is he now? Well, he's currently in the kitchen helping his mother."

Wick stiffened and watched in amazement as Prince Haaken continued as if not at all surprised by this news. "Then it would seem my timing is perfect. Would you ask him to join us, so I can speak with him?"

His forehead furrowed, Brit eyed them all. Clearly still confused but not about to object, he unlatched the door beside him. "Manton, will you come here?"

There was a patter of footsteps, and a young, plump boy with tawny brown hair twisted through the door. "Papa, what is it?" Spotting the four of them, the boy grabbed Brit's arm, his eyes wide. "Papa, is that the king?" the boy whispered loudly. "Should I bow?"

Looking embarrassed, Brit murmured to his son, "He's the Crown Prince. And yes, you should bow."

The boy did so, and Prince Haaken smiled. "I've come to see your brother Manton."

The boy tipped his head sideways. "I'm Manton. Why have you come to see me?"

Wick blinked. Was this boy really who Prince Gage had meant when he'd written about someone traveling to inns and taverns and helping the likes of Felix? It seemed unlikely, but then again he had compared him to Wes and Fran, so maybe he was.

"You're Manton?" Prince Haaken shook his head. "That can't be."

"Well, he's my only son, and I assure you his name is Manton," Brit said defensively.

"No, of course," Prince Haaken said. "I didn't mean to imply otherwise. It's just, I was told that Manton, son of Brit, travels with carven goods from his father's shop and that he sells those goods at taverns and inns across Edelmar."

Brit's face brightened. "Ah, well, your information's mostly right. It's just the names you've gotten told a bit wrong. There *is* a Manton who sells carven goods that he's bought from my shop, but he's not my Manton, son of Brit Carver. That would be this fella here." Brit laid his big hand on his son's head. "You know, we joked when Manton bought his first load of goods from me that someone who'd never met him and my son might confuse the two. I never thought it'd actually happen though."

Wick looked at Prince Haaken and wondered if he too was thinking that Manton the traveler had probably shrewdly taken that idea and utilized it to misdirect people. For it had been the same with

Felix. He had claimed to be a tanner's apprentice from Decoro, but that had proven just as false as the traveler they now sought being the son of Brit Carver of Dulcis.

"This other Manton, have you seen him recently?" Prince Haaken asked.

Wick followed His Royal Highness's line of thought. Brit had said when Manton bought his first load, which implied the information Prince Gage had provided about him returning to buy again from the shop may still be accurate.

"No, unfortunately not," Brit said. "Usually every few months or so, he or someone he knows picks up what he's commissioned me to make. He was supposed to come five days ago, but neither he nor anyone else has shown."

"Has he ever been late before?"

"Never," Brit said. "I figured I'd keep the items a day or two more, then put them out for sale."

Wick frowned. So the man had intended to return to Dulcis but had abandoned that plan. Had he known Prince Gage was aware of his connections? Was that why he hadn't returned?

"What sorts of items did he commission you to make?" Prince Haaken asked.

"All kinds of things but mostly chess pieces and boards. He requests some sets to be normal and some to have pieces with hollowed-out interiors that leave a secret space inside."

Prince Haaken's surprised expression mirrored what Wick felt. "Do you currently have such a set? May I see it?"

"I do." Brit touched his son's shoulder. "Bring me the last chess set I finished for him."

"Yes, Papa." The boy disappeared through the door and returned a moment later with a chessboard tucked under his arm and its pieces gathered in his tunic.

"See here?" Brit collected one of the bishops and showed them how its lower half turned and popped open, revealing a hollow inside. "Many of the pieces are carved out like this," Brit said as he handed a knight to Prince Haaken to open. "I guess the uniqueness of it appeals to people."

Wick's stomach twisted. He was pretty sure the uniqueness wasn't the appeal. Prince Gage's letter had said Manton aided people like Felix. Perhaps this was how, by providing them a means at inns and taverns to pass messages without even having to be at the same location at the same time. All someone would need to know is which tavern or inn to go to and what chess piece to search. Dozens of messages could be passed along without anyone else knowing.

Prince Haaken twisted the knight closed. "May I purchase this set?"

"Of course, Your Royal Highness. Manton, fetch a bag for the pieces."

"Is there anything else that you know about this man that might help me find him?" Prince Haaken asked. "Because, as I said, I'd very much like to speak with him."

Brit scratched his head. "Manton's always been a talkative one, but now that I think about it, he's never said much of any consequence about himself."

"Well, thank you anyway." Prince Haaken paid Brit, received the board and bag, and headed out of the shop. Wick trailed behind them as they made their way back to their horses.

Prince Haaken passed his purchase to one of his attendants. "I do not think I will ever be able to look at chess pieces the same way again," he commented soberly in the noblemen's tongue.

Sir Holbird nodded. "Indeed."

"What is the plan now, Your Royal Highness?" Sir Renner asked.

"Well, I doubt our traveler will show himself again here in Dulcis. If we are to find him, I think it will be elsewhere. Meanwhile, I am sorely tempted to command that every chessboard in Edelmar with hollow interiors be confiscated and destroyed, but that might be a bit rash." Prince Haaken smiled. "My father has two sayings that are mayhap relevant here: 'Do not punish everyone for the actions of a few people' and 'Do not destroy what might be utilized.' We might yet find this Manton by using his own game against him."

Wick wondered if any of the taverns and inns in the mountain city of Veiroot had such chess sets. Perhaps they should start there.

15

With an abundance of time on his hands, Gage couldn't help but think about what it would mean if he attempted to claim sanctuary at Saint Jerome's. Baron Bertram's actions and threats against the church and townspeople of Delipp played through his mind, and he kept seeing the monk who'd played Moses in Nikledon's mystery play be struck down in front of him.

Claiming sanctuary may not keep him safe, and if the monks tried to uphold his right of sanctuary, he feared they too might be treated like the townspeople of Delipp had been.

With these thoughts churning in his head, he had waited in dread for a lord to come for him. But days passed, and it seemed the abbot must not have brought his presence at the abbey to a lord's attention. That gave life to a new thought. If he recovered enough to travel, he could perhaps slip away from the abbey before a lord was ever informed, and if he was careful he could journey back to Edelmar where he was not sought as a marked man.

He'd need provisions to travel, an opportunity to leave the abbey without being seen, and a means to avoid encountering any lords' men on the road, which meant finding a way across the border that didn't involve a town. Once in Edelmar though, he could retake his authority as a prince, and as long as no one else found out about his mark, he would be free to use his knowledge to help fight the rebels.

He'd hidden his royalty while traveling as a commoner. Keeping his mark a secret while being a royal couldn't be that much harder, could it? His experiences when last in Einhart sat in the back of his mind. It burdened his thoughts, along with the daunting nature of acquiring all he would need to escape Delkara, but it was better than thinking about the alternative.

Still, it didn't offer much of a diversion.

More and more, the walls of his small room felt like they were closing in on him. Restless, he eventually attempted going after the one goal within his grasp: to stand. His body and head protested viciously against his efforts, and he came close to blacking out the first several times he managed to struggle upright.

Despite his pounding head and the continual risk of ending up on the floor, he kept at it. Slowly, his body yielded to his will, and soon he could rise and cross the room without holding on to anything.

He was still far from fully healed though. The blade wound across his chest and shoulder was still such that any use of his left arm caused him a good deal of pain. It ached even if he just sat down hard or shifted too fast. Thus, he was limited to slow, steady movements and using his right arm only.

That didn't stop him from climbing onto the bed to peer out the room's slatted window though. The opening overlooked a garden of herbs and flowers backed by a stone wall. Since his door was locked, the window was his only view. He visited it dozens of times throughout the day. Once while staring out, he spotted two monks working in the garden. The younger of the two brothers he recognized as the youth who had rushed off to fetch someone the first night he woke. Watching them at work made Gage long to put his own hands to a task.

He was able now to keep track of the day's hours by the bells and the monks' routines. He could recognize which monk was arriving with his food by the sound of their footsteps. He'd also counted the number of stones making up his room's walls. He'd traced every crack in the mortar, followed every line in the floor, memorized the location of each knothole in the ceiling, and watched the wax of one too many candles melt away.

So it was that when Brother Sholan came to check his wounds one morning, Gage used his right arm to push himself upright, and without the monk's assistance, he carefully stripped off the loose tunic he'd been given.

"You seem to be doing better," Brother Sholan commented as he untied the bandages wrapped across Gage's chest and shoulder.

Sitting with his left arm tucked against his side, Gage snorted. "Better? I'm going mad being cooped up in here."

Brother Sholan simply grunted and tended to his wounds.

Once the monk was finished, Gage pulled his tunic back on. "Please, Brother Sholan, is there not a task I might do? Surely there's something I could help with around the abbey, even with one arm. Perhaps weed a garden or collect eggs?" He desperately needed to get out of the confines of the room. Not to mention that figuring out the lay of the land would be useful.

Brother Sholan chuckled. "A while ago several of us monks discussed how long it'd take before you begged for something to do. Most of us figured you'd respond like a novice and seek relief from boredom within a day or two. Father Thomas was the only one who thought you'd last longer. He told us you'd make your request when you were ready. I'm fairly certain though that weeding was not what he had in mind. At least not in the physical sense." The monk's amused and reflective expression drifted into a frown. "Though as to the physical, perhaps you could offer some advice. When we brought you back from the woods, your mount followed. It has been wandering about the abbey ever since, causing trouble."

Gage felt a surge of joy. Athalos! He had assumed the horse had been lost to him, like everything else.

"At first several of our brothers tried to catch the animal. The creature bit one of them and nearly kicked another. So, they gave up their efforts to contain it and drove the beast away, but it keeps returning. It was in our grain fields for a while. Then it was grazing by the abbey's main gate, terrorizing our guests and pilgrims, and yesterday evening it was pulling hay from one of our storehouses.

"Last night a novice got close enough to seize its reins and foolishly tried to lead it in with our mules. The animal bolted and dragged him. I spent a quarter hour cleaning up the lad's scraped knees and elbows. Since the animal was covered in your blood and standing guard over you, I assume it is rideable and able to be caught and contained. Is there a safe way to do so?"

Gage's heart raced at the thought of how the monks might yet respond to Athalos's aggression and what the horse's next rampage could cause. "Yes, but don't let anyone else attempt it." Determined to save them and his horse, Gage swung his legs off the edge of the bed and shot to his feet. He became instantly lightheaded.

"Easy!" Brother Sholan caught him as he wavered. "What do you think you're doing? And don't tell me you're going to go catch that crazy beast. You may be bored out of your mind, but surely you recognize that you can barely stand."

Gage pushed free and righted himself. "I can stand well enough." He tried to look authoritative as he said it, but he found himself staring up at Brother Sholan, who to his surprise was half a head taller than him. The monk frowned sternly at him. Figuring he'd have to argue his case, Gage drew a deep breath. The action pulled at his injury, and he grimaced and pressed his hand to his chest.

"Exactly," Brother Sholan said. "You aren't yet healed. You shouldn't be trying to catch any horse, let alone that horse."

Breathing shallowly, Gage grunted. "My wounds hurt regardless of whether I'm lying down or standing up. Besides, Athalos is terrorizing people. You said it yourself. He cannot remain loose. And believe me when I say I'm probably the only person who can deal with him safely."

He didn't dare mention that he'd actually watched the horse kill someone. Though really, that hadn't been Athalos's fault. The animal had simply fought to rid himself of an abusive rider and would no doubt do so again, which made Athalos dangerous but not malicious. "Please, let me help with him so that he causes no more harm. I can take him wherever you want him contained."

"And you plan to do this how exactly?" Brother Sholan asked. "No matter your resolve, you're in no condition to struggle to control a horse."

"Take me to where I can call to him," Gage said. "He will come to me. You have already seen that he will follow me anywhere. He won't resist me leading him."

Brother Sholan remained skeptical. "You're sure?"

"Yes." Gage met the monk's gaze. He wasn't some inexperienced youth asking to ride a war horse, though it certainly felt like it with how the monk eyed him. Brother Sholan knew he bought and sold mounts and had sought his advice about Athalos, so obviously the monk held some respect for him. Still, the question showed Gage just how far removed he was from being known and praised as a renowned jouster who could not just handle a horse but also stay on one even when a lance was rammed against him.

"I'll let you try." Brother Sholan pointed a finger at him. "But if anything goes wrong, you do not risk injury. Do we understand each other?"

Gage nodded. Eager to see Athalos and the outdoors, he cautiously followed the monk out of the room. Brother Sholan led him along a narrow stone hall, through a door, and out into daylight. Squinting, Gage took in the new sights. The building they'd just exited occupied one outer edge of a walled, grassy enclosure that butted up against a partition of stone buildings, two of which rose high overhead. The spires of one structure indicated it was likely the abbey's church. The other Gage wasn't sure about but thought perhaps it was a dormitory or chapter house.

He embraced the sunlight and inhaled the fresh air. His shoulder twinged. Wincing, Gage pretended he didn't see Brother Sholan's concerned look and focused on keeping his balance as they strode slowly across the enclosure.

The narrow walled yard they were in had at its end two other small buildings along with the garden he'd seen from his window. They crossed its lush sliver of ground and traveled along a stone path through an ornate arched passage. It cut through the center of a low building connecting the two larger buildings. Gage admired the tunnel's detailed masonry as they walked through it.

The passage came out into a cloister. The pillars of the covered walkway framed a carefully maintained central garden that was canopied by trees and graced with hewn benches. Two monks strode the far side of the area, and another monk sat reading within the garden.

Relieved not to see Athalos tearing about the colonnades, Gage was thankful when Brother Sholan paused there for a moment to let him catch his breath. The monk shifted back into motion a moment later, and Gage trailed beside him along the cloister for a short distance.

Brother Sholan then made a right turn and led him down yet another passage that cut through a building and dumped back into sunlight.

From the look of the area, Gage figured they were on the backside of the abbey. The large, beautiful buildings were behind them while a massive vegetable garden, full drying lines, extensive animal pens, and numerous outbuildings cluttered the walled, rolling ground before them. Monks and lay brothers were everywhere doing various tasks, from making clay pots to unloading hay wagons pulled by mule teams.

Brother Sholan pointed. "There. Next to the refectory."

Large trees shaded the back doorway of a building incorporated into the core of the abbey. Beyond the trees a circle of flagstones surrounded a well. Past the well beside the building was Athalos, still bridled, grazing a patch of grass between the well and the vegetable garden. A monk going to draw water gave the animal a wide berth, but still Athalos's ears laid back.

Never had Gage thought he'd be so happy to own such a disreputable yet loyal creature. But own him he still did, and for that he was abundantly grateful.

He wet his lips and whistled. Athalos's head popped up. Gage grinned and whistled again. This time the horse spotted him, nickered, and trotted toward him. Then Athalos paused and stared. Gage laughed. "Yes, Athalos, it's really me."

The horse threw its head, sending broken reins flying, and galloped to him. Sliding to a stop in front of him, Athalos stretched out his neck and huffed. Gage laughed and stroked the horse's dark face. "Yeah, I've missed you too."

Sniffing at his chest, Athalos nudged him. Gage grunted in pain. "I know it smells strange, but don't touch it." Placing his hand on Athalos's nose, he pushed. "Back up." Athalos stepped backward.

Gage gazed into the horse's big brown eyes. "I hear you've been terrorizing our hosts." He ran his right hand along the horse's cheek and then down his sleek dark brown neck. "Not exactly a good way to make friends, you know." He stroked his way around Athalos's body to evaluate the animal's condition. The horse had a few more cuts and scrapes atop his previous scars but otherwise appeared well, even a bit fat.

"No more free access to grainfields for you, my friend." Keeping his left arm against his side, Gage gathered Athalos's reins. One rein was still decently long, but the other wasn't even the length of his forearm. So much for owning tack. Gage glanced at Brother Sholan. "Where do you want me to take him?"

"He's like a completely different animal." Sounding amazed, Brother Sholan stepped toward Athalos. The horse instantly flattened its ears. "But only for you, I see."

Feeling accused and a bit like a spectacle, Gage's discomfort heightened further when he discovered other monks about the abbey grounds were also staring at him and Athalos. He wanted to be rid of their prying eyes. Grateful that at least his mark was still covered, he tucked himself beside Athalos. "Where should I take him?"

"Will he stay tied in a barn?" the monk asked. "Or will he tear the place to pieces to come after you when you leave?"

"Once he is tied, he will stay. Though whoever feeds him will need to stay clear of his hooves and teeth."

"Bring him this way then." Brother Sholan turned between two outbuildings and headed along a path that curved down a hill. The path led around a pond to a broad building encircled by fences.

Clutching Athalos's broken reins and following slowly, Gage realized having a horse meant he was one step closer to being able to slip away. He still needed supplies though, like food and tack, and he had no means to purchase or trade for them.

The abbot's words played through his mind like a suggestion, *"You're already a marked man."* Gage knew acting upon his assumed guilt was not the application Father Thomas had intended in his comment, but the thought grew in Gage's mind regardless. He'd always been taught stealing was wrong, but he had also been taught that injustice was wrong. If a lord and his knight could violate the law, why couldn't he? The thought stirred a powerful suggestion of disregard for authority, but it also left him feeling gutted and honorless, like he'd lost something vital even in considering it.

The energy he'd felt upon seeing Athalos waned abruptly into a tiredness he couldn't shake. Upon his next step, his legs felt unsteady. Breathing became a struggle. Weariness wrapped itself around him in thickening layers like a wet cloak. He tried to continue forward but couldn't take another step. Even standing felt too arduous. He dropped Athalos's reins and clutched the horse's neck to keep himself upright. Lightheaded again, he feared he might collapse.

He fought the sensation for the sake of practicality and pride. Sweat dampened his chest and pooled under his arms. Thankfully, Brother Sholan hadn't yet noticed his delay. Gage swallowed and focused on the barn at the bottom of the hill. All he had to do was make it to where he could tie up Athalos. Then he could sit down. Clinging to Athalos, he urged the horse forward and forced his own body to follow. Every trembling step screamed how feeble his strength was, but his legs obeyed and carried him.

Brother Sholan reached the barn and turned to look for him. Gage tried to appear steady on his feet, but he could tell by the monk's apprehensive and angered expression that he'd failed. "For heaven sake, Gage! You're as pale as bleached linen. Leave the horse. He can be contained another day."

"I can manage." Gage drew a breath. "Just show me where you want him tied."

Brother Sholan scowled and glanced about. "Here. Just put him in here." He drew open the gate to a fenced enclosure probably meant for their mules. "Then sit and rest, do you hear me?"

"I can take him all the way inside."

"No, you can't!"

At the monk's strident tone, Athalos raised his head and laid back his ears. Panic shot through Gage's body. He grabbed for the horse's reins. "Easy, Athalos."

16

Gage clung to Athalos's reins with his good arm, fearing the animal would bolt and prove Brother Sholan's concerns all too legitimate. Athalos's head remained high and his body stiff. "Easy." Gage forced a calmness into his voice. "You're alright, Athalos." The horse's ears twisted toward him. "That's right. Just walk on, boy."

Athalos stepped forward. Relieved, Gage maneuvered the horse into the pen, and Brother Sholan swung the gate closed behind them. Gage stopped in the churned up ground inside the fence. The coursing panic that had rushed through him swiftly dissipated from his body, taking with it the burst of energy it had given him. Teetering once more on his feet, Gage reached up to try to remove Athalos's bridle but his hand was shaking so badly he couldn't unbuckle it.

"Leave it," Brother Sholan said.

Knowing Athalos had survived this long with the bridle on, Gage obeyed and thrust his quivering body toward the gate. The monk stepped in and hooked an arm around his waist, drawing him out of the pen.

"Sit." Pushing Gage toward the ground, Brother Sholan secured the gate.

Gage willingly sank to the grass and breathed slowly. The moment his concentration was no longer on staying upright, a deep aching pain in his shoulder and chest hit his senses like the stinging recoil of a tree branch. He dropped to his back with a groan and lay staring at the clear sky. Apparently, he wasn't as ready to be on his feet as he'd thought.

Cringing through the pain, he turned his head to watch Athalos wander about the pen. The horse searched for grass, but there was none to be found. Gage already felt sorry for the animal. "He will be fed, yes?"

"Will we feed your horse?" Brother Sholan stared at him incredulously, then sat down beside him. "Tell me, will you bother letting yourself heal, hmm? Or are you going to keep pushing yourself to extreme feats of stupidity?"

Gage frowned. "Here I thought monks were supposed to be kind, patient souls."

"Before I met you, I was." Brother Sholan eyed him, then shook his head in amusement.

Gage chuckled too, then groaned and pressed his hand to his chest. He lay breathing for a few moments, then spoke. "I don't mean to be so much trouble, you know." He closed his eyes and let his body relax in the sunlight.

"No," Brother Sholan said, "I don't suppose you do. But whether it's to be intentionally less troublesome or simply to help yourself, you need to stop trying to live beyond your limits. You were badly injured, Gage. God miraculously saved you from death, but you must do your part to heal. From what I can tell though, perhaps it is not just your body that needs healing."

Gage opened his eyes to glare at the monk. "What's that supposed to mean?"

"Simply that spiritual health, or lack thereof, impacts all areas of one's life."

Taken aback, Gage wanted to object to the monk's claim but couldn't find the words. "I'm not a bad person," he muttered. As he said it, he was reminded that he was talking to a monk who thought him a thief.

"When you view your actions within a hierarchy, you can perhaps come to that conclusion, but every last one of us is a sinful, lost soul." Brother Sholan glanced sideways at him. "What's strange about you though is that typically when someone is convicted of a crime, they're willing to acknowledge their sin and their need for God's mercy and forgiveness. You've been rescued from death by God and offered sanctuary from your crimes within His church, but you make no thanks to God as a believer. Nor have you responded like a non-believer by asking who this God is or why He would give you such grace. Why is that?"

Silence stretched between them for a long moment. Finally, Gage answered as he watched his trapped horse pace. "Perhaps because I am neither of the two."

"That's odd," Brother Sholan said. "In my experience people are either one or the other."

"Well, there's a third option." Using his good arm, Gage pushed himself to a seated position. "It's where someone believes God exists but gives no thanks to Him for who He is or what He does."

Brother Sholan's expression turned angry, as if Gage's words were offensive to him. "Why disregard God when you know He exists?"

"Because." Gage glared at the monk. "Everyone like you talks about Him being such a good, gracious, loving God, but it's not true. God chose to intervene and save my life, but meanwhile He lets other people nicer and better than me die all the time. How is that right or good? How is that gracious or acceptable? How is that just?"

Brother Sholan looked out across the abbey's grounds for a long moment. Finally he answered, "Death is hard for all of us to accept. I've seen that often as an infirmarer. It does feel unfair. But we have no right to judge whether or not it was someone else's time to depart this earth. Our time here belongs to Him." Brother Sholan glanced back at Gage. "We belong to Him. And truly, for someone who is devoted to God, it is more of a mercy to leave this existence than to stay in it. But I admit that doesn't mend the hole their absence leaves for those who remain behind."

Gage's eyes burned while indignation tightened in his chest. "So why does God do it then? Why does He let some people die and save others? Why doesn't He answer our prayers for someone to live? Does He just not care? Or is it His way of punishing us?"

The monk squinted in the sunlight. "I suppose there are times that a person's death could be a punishment toward someone else. In the Scripture we read that the Lord God took the life of King David's newborn child because of David's sin. But we also read that King Jeroboam's son was taken to the grave as a mercy because something good was found in the child toward the Lord. So clearly, both can be true."

Gage clenched his right hand into a fist. "Why? Why would God punish a person for someone else's mistakes? Can't He have the decency to deal with us directly?"

"Oh, He does deal with us directly." Brother Sholan nodded confidently. "God brings our sin right to our door. Make no mistake about that. He does not punish others unjustly because of us nor does He punish us while we are in ignorance of how we have acted against Him. No, He shows us or tells us our wrongs because His goal is to turn us back to Him, through His punishment, not to harm us for some unknown reason. That's not His nature. He's not underhanded, vindictive, or cruel. He is good and honorable. So, if it is God who is taking action against you, and not Satan or the natural consequences of your own sin, I promise you there is a reason.

"And even when it's not Him taking action against us because of our sin, there is always a reason for what He allows. Sometimes it's about letting events happen which He in His foreknowledge knows are needed to bring about a greater purpose. Being able to discern the difference is significant because one requires a change in the direction we are going while the other requires a steadfast continuation on the path already before us. But you seem to think God is punishing you. Why? Did you ignore something He told you to do?"

"No," Gage said swiftly but then thought about his long-term rejection of God. "Maybe. I don't know." He ripped up a handful of clover and threw it. "How exactly are we supposed to know what He wants from us?" Brother Sholan's expression turned to sympathy and concern, which irritated Gage even more. He didn't want to be pitied or treated like a child who needed teaching. "Never mind. It doesn't matter." He shifted to rise.

Brother Sholan touched his arm. "Do you truly want to know? Because you can."

Biting his cheek, Gage considered the question. Did he really want to know what God desired from him? He'd spent years trying not to think about God because endeavoring to understand why and how God had stood by and let Novia die had led to the very hatred he felt. He'd gotten past it only by deciding it was stupid to harbor such hurt and rage at someone who wasn't there. Because clearly if there had been a good and honorable God present, He would have done something to save her.

But now there was no doubt in his mind that God existed and had been there, watching and doing nothing, and all the anger he had thrust aside back then had returned. His stomach tightened with it. He didn't want that God in his life, not then and not now. God had lied to him and betrayed him.

As an eight-year-old who'd wholeheartedly believed God cared and would always be there for him, he had begged God for help that day. But God's answer had been to do nothing. Gage gritted his teeth. So, why had God suddenly bothered to answer his prayer in the woods and save him? Why hadn't God just stepped back and done nothing like He'd always done?

He pictured himself like a pawn kept on a chessboard to be utilized and then discarded. He looked at Brother Sholan with cold determination. "Yes, I want to know what God wants from me."

17

"Princess Rhonalyn, this just arrived for you." The maidservant curtsied and held out a sealed letter. Rhonalyn motioned for Aisley and her other ladies-in-waiting to continue their needlework. Standing, she took the letter and headed to the privacy of a curtained alcove with a window.

Ignoring the cushioned seats on either side of her, Rhonalyn paused at the stone windowsill and drew a breath to fortify herself. She worked her fingers under the royal seal of Delkara—a crowned lion with one paw resting upon the top edge of a shield and the other paw resting upon the hilt of a sword. She broke the red wax seal but hesitated to open the letter. What if King Strephon had refused her offer?

Neither Asper's sheriff nor her father's men had managed to track down the attackers and regain their stolen money. The men and the gold were gone. Her father had returned from Asper in an even fouler mood than when he'd returned from the mines. Knowing there was little she could do to help with that, Rhonalyn had focused her efforts on solving the problem of the port.

She had spent the better part of the last week collecting as many rare goods unique to Keric's land and people as she could. Intricate tapestries, beautiful wool cloaks, copper ornaments, magnificent paintings, elegant pottery, embellished weapons, armor, and even a king's destrier, trained by one of their finest horsemen.

A number of the items she had found in their own treasury, but others she had obtained by trading harvested produce for the items. The destrier was one of many horses her father kept for his own use and would not be missed by Vivian because the woman never visited the castle's stable.

Rhonalyn had already arranged with her father for him and Vivian to be traveling elsewhere over the time that the negotiations were to take place. She had persuaded him that to avoid the pride of two kings becoming part of the discussion it was best not to have two kings present. He had agreed to her request, which would also provide her the opportunity to discuss renegotiating their current toll and actually offer King Strephon an entirely new deal in exchange for their use of Nikor Harbor. But all of this would be for nothing if Strephon had refused her offer. Rhonalyn unfolded the letter and began to read.

> *To Her Royal Highness, Princess Rhonalyn of Keric, your request to meet, to offer trade, and to renegotiate the harbor agreement made in years past by my late father, King Maurice, and your father, King Bryant, is a proposition I, King Strephon, find most intriguing. Your father has sought little from Delkara beyond access to Nikor Harbor, yet you speak of the advantages we might offer each other.*
>
> *As the future Queen of Keric, your recognition of new ways being significant to continued prosperity is of particular interest to me. After my father's untimely death, I too have found old ways less than ideal. Change and growth is required if we are to see our kingdoms thrive.*

I believe a new partnership between Delkara and Keric may serve this purpose well and raise both our kingdoms to new heights.

I am therefore, most grateful for your generous offer to host a meeting between us at Arcis Castle. Regretfully, I am currently unable to spare the time away from my people to travel into Keric. Thus, instead, I invite you, Princess Rhonalyn, to be my guest and that of the Baron Selwin's at Nikledon Manor on the same dates for the same purpose.

With highest regard, His Royal Majesty, King Strephon of Delkara

Rhonalyn breathed in relief. Then she read the letter once more. Tendrils of fear played through her stomach. Strephon was willing to hear her offer, but what if he was not interested in any of the goods she had gathered? What if all her efforts to dazzle and intrigue him proved futile? When she reconsidered what he'd said in the letter though, her confidence returned.

King Strephon was already intrigued. He would not reject her offer completely because her father had been right. They had nothing to barter with that would appeal to Strephon's pride more than money, except their stance on trade. And that was exactly what had seized his interest.

She swallowed at this thought though because for Keric to officially negotiate trade with Delkara was indeed a change. Out of necessity they paid for the use of Nikor Harbor, but for as long as she could remember they had shunned Delkara as a trading partner. This was due to a short yet bloody battle their two kingdoms had once fought over who had the right to the harbor.

For Keric, maintaining this strident yet peaceful trade restriction had been a matter of pride and tradition, both of which she would be defying.

Her heartbeat quickened at the thought of how her father would likely respond when he discovered she'd offered trade to Strephon. But he'd been the one who'd said the old ways were gone. She shrugged off her concerns and embraced her plan. After all, it was her father's doing that got them into this situation, and it would be her doing that got them out of it. Because it was true, neither king would set aside his pride, but she was no king.

The old ways had failed. Traditions would not sustain them, and she would not stand by and watch her kingdom shrivel away behind the cliffs of Nikor, penniless and powerless. Not when she could still save it. Better to sacrifice a position they had chosen in the abundance of their past and see to it their access to Nikor Harbor refilled their coffers for the future.

She would offer King Strephon trade and flaunt doing so as if the old traditions mattered nothing to her. Like an exalted empress, she would present to him each treasure she'd collected as if it were one of hundreds filling her treasury. She'd answer any question regarding her motives as if she were simply seeking to expand her reach, and she'd respond to any pressure he applied as if any decision he made was entirely inconsequential to her kingdom's well-being. And, as if she were not risking an endeavor as perilous as the cliffs, she would do so while bartering for the best deal she could get.

The boldness of it exhilarated her, and for a moment she gloried in the feeling. Then she thought of what else was now required in order to meet with King Strephon, and she shuddered. To negotiate with him, she would have to travel across Keric and into Delkara to Nikledon.

She had journeyed long distances very little in the last five years, and to consider taking such a trip while random attacks were still occurring made her skin crawl. Dare she travel all that way without her father? King Strephon's letter seemed to imply he expected only her, which had been as she'd wished. She didn't want to appear now like some scared, needy child. Plus, she hated the thought of Vivian reigning in Arcis while they were both away.

She heaved a sigh. There was also the huge inconvenience of getting everything to Nikledon. It would mean packing all the items she intended to display to King Strephon. She would also have to figure out ahead of time what she planned to wear, decide by what means she would travel to Nikledon, what sort of guard to take, which of her ladies-in-waiting to bring with her, and so many other details.

Rhonalyn set down the letter and rubbed her temples. Why couldn't Strephon have just come to Arcis?

The only pleasing element to the meeting being in Nikledon instead of Arcis Castle was that she didn't have to host. That removed the burden of needing to impress King Strephon through the meals, accommodations, and entertainment she chose. But that was the only advantage she could see. Otherwise the change just created numerous things she would need to decide and learn, all in the next few days. Like how was she supposed to present herself to King Strephon?

Other than her father, she'd only ever addressed people of lower rank than herself, which meant they were required to bow to her. Since King Strephon outranked her, she would need to bow to him, but would he also bow to her? She was a princess and he a king. Therefore, it was possible he would not. That thought annoyed her. She was as much Queen of Keric as Vivian was.

Still, until her title actually reflected that, she'd have to find a way to deal with the possibility of being greeted as inferior while still making sure she was treated as an equal. To hold her ground in negotiations, she would need to possess equivalent authority. Her father had given that to her by agreeing to let her handle the negotiation, but many people disagreed with a woman holding such a position. She was also younger than King Strephon by almost eight years.

No one in Keric dared disrespect her to her face, but she could picture Baron Hughart in a position above her rather than below her and knew it was possible she'd face issues over her age and gender. She curled her fingers into claws. Would King Strephon give her the respect due her for who she was and what she represented, or would he treat her like a neighbor's willful daughter?

She considered his letter once more and reread his words: *"As the future Queen of Keric, your recognition of new ways being significant to continued prosperity is of particular interest to me."*

Rhonalyn's concern faded, and her fingers relaxed. He had already recognized her position. He and she were not at odds. Their kingdoms may have once strongly disagreed, but that did not mean they could not form a new and profitable alliance.

It was time to set aside the past and forge a new future.

18

Seated in the hot sunlight beside the abbey's mule barn, Gage scooped up another piece of harness to wipe down. He was abundantly happy to be outside working rather than sitting in the chapel listening to lectures or recitations or in his cell reading Scripture. What felt like a month ago Brother Sholan had told him that he would in these ways find his answers. He remained unconvinced. All the brothers were required to attend services and spend hours in prayer and study along with seeing to their daily work duties, and Father Thomas had also strongly suggested Gage do likewise. Thus, he spent his days following the abbey's routines. Few of the activities were to his liking, but they did keep him busy.

Many of the scriptural passages were as curious and engaging to him as he remembered from childhood. Others he found confusing or infuriating. The general requirements of Christianity were nothing new to him. They were the same standards he had been taught by his father and Baron Roger, and for the most part he already followed them. He'd never done so as strictly as he might have though, and definitely not as faithfully as the monks did. He had also never done so for God.

Aligning his life and actions to the standards of Scripture in order to appease God turned Gage's stomach. Not only did he have no desire to do so, he also knew he wasn't capable of it. The passage read that very morning by one of the brothers was a perfect example: *"You shall not steal, nor deal falsely, nor lie one to another."* Ever since Novia's death, in one way or another, the way he lived had been based in deception. That hadn't changed in the last weeks, nor did he want it to. He scrubbed the cloth he held back and forth on the mule harness trying to remove a particularly dirty patch in the leather. Athalos pawed at the nearby pen's gate and snorted at him. Gage sighed. "I know, you and me both."

He glanced out across the hills visible beyond the abbey's walls. He longed to go racing across them, but he didn't dare leave the abbey. He was also trying hard for the sake of his recovery to live within his current limits as Brother Sholan had instructed. He felt stifled by the lack of freedom, but his body was healing. Each day he felt his wounds getting better and his strength returning.

Clutching the dirty rag in his fist, Gage rubbed his arm across his damp forehead.

So far no master had come to claim him. Part of him still held out hope that maybe Father Thomas hadn't said and wouldn't say anything to a lord about his presence at the abbey, but he knew he couldn't count on that. He'd been saving what he could from his food and collecting things he would need for travel, like the leftover end of a candle, a discarded length of rope to replace Athalos's snapped rein, and a broken-handled water jug. It was a start, but it wasn't everything he needed, nor was it his biggest concern.

He glanced down at the dirt-smeared bandage wrapped around his right wrist. The brand was definitely healed enough to be uncovered, but Brother Sholan had left it wrapped. Gage didn't know how many of the other brothers knew what the cloth concealed. But, like his disgust for God, he was happy to leave the brand hidden from the others.

At the same time, he did what was required to appease Brother Sholan and Father Thomas's desires for him to love and serve God. After all, he was good at pretending he was something he wasn't.

But regardless of how much Scripture the monks gave him to read or how much time he spent listening to them lecture, he knew what they didn't. It was just as impossible for him to love God as it was for him to be happy about the mark he bore.

God had walked out on him. He should have had the right to do the same. Anger twisted in his chest. He had tried walking out too, but it hadn't kept God from showing up and demanding he serve Him. If there had ever been a choice in the matter, it wasn't much of one.

Finishing with the tack, Gage gathered the pieces of harness into his arms and took them into the barn. His shoulder bore the weight without pain, though he was careful to not load his left arm too heavily. In the barn's shadowy interior, he hung the tack, then returned outside to give Athalos a final pat before heading to his next chore across the abbey.

An hour later in the narrow yard near his cell, Gage was plucking weeds from between the plants of the infirmary's herb garden when he was approached by a monk who delivered messages for the abbot. "Father Thomas requests your presence in the outer parlour."

Brushing dirt from his hands, Gage frowned at the request. The outer parlour was where communication and business was done with outsiders. "Do you know why, Brother Simon?"

"There is a knight there who has come seeking you."

Gage's heart plummeted, then pounded. "A knight?"

"Yes, and you'd best not delay. He appears ready to search every bit of the place if you don't quickly make your presence known."

Every fear Gage had had since being marked swept back through him. He wanted to bolt from the abbey, but he was surrounded by walls with no nearby gates. Had he been beside the barn still, he'd have leapt upon Athalos and ridden as fast and as far as he could away from the abbey, but he was without his horse, with no weapon in sight, and nowhere to go.

All too clearly he remembered the treatment he'd received at Sir Jarret's hand. He thought about hiding in the abbey, but he recalled as well the soldiers' search of Delipp for the rebels. They'd been thorough and ruthless, finding and taking every last person they had come for. He swallowed hard, panic crashing through him.

"Are you coming or not?" Brother Simon asked. "Because if you delay any longer you'll get an earful from Father Thomas."

Gage wished a lecture was his only concern and that the abbot's position was one to be feared. But if it was a knight like Sir Jarret who had come, he was positive it wouldn't matter what cries of sanctuary or leniency were made on his behalf or by him; he would be taken from the abbey and probably beaten for having escaped on the road.

He glanced toward the tunnel leading to the cloister. If he ran, maybe he could still make it to Athalos and escape. With Brother Simon beside him though, he knew it was a useless thought. The monk would doubtless prevent him from going, and the knight probably already had soldiers placed at every one of the abbey's gates. But that didn't stop Gage's mind from desperately spitting out ideas, even as he stepped from the garden to go with Brother Simon.

Gage knew claiming sanctuary would possibly put the monks at risk, but everything in him screamed for him to seize any possible protection. Fear surged inside him with a feverish heat. All he had was his own life. It was his right to seek safety and save himself from an unjust fate.

In his mind he saw the man in Delipp who had claimed sanctuary but had been dragged down the steps of the church regardless. Gage's hopes folded in on themselves. What if there was no way to save himself?

He wondered then if perhaps it would be better for him to turn himself over and maybe at least spare himself some of the knight's wrath. But the very thought of willingly handing himself over to the likes of Sir Jarret produced such an intense fear inside him that he couldn't draw breath. He stopped midway to the buildings, his heart pounding so hard that he wavered on his feet.

Brother Simon glared at him. "What now?"

Gage bent over and pressed his hand to his chest. His knees trembled, and his palms were slick with sweat.

Brother Simon's annoyed tone shifted to concern. "Are you alright? Should I get Brother Sholan?"

His heart racing, Gage continued to struggle to draw air. Unable to answer or stay upright, he sat down hard in the grass.

"I'll fetch Brother Sholan."

Gage could only watch as Brother Simon hurried for the infirmary. Clearly, the monk thought his collapse was connected to his recent injuries, but Gage knew it was no physical wound that was stripping his body of strength.

As the monk disappeared into the infirmary, Gage fought to regain control of his mind and body. He couldn't be found like this, gasping like some helpless fool. Nor could he neglect the opportunity suddenly before him. Breathing in sharp painful bursts, he struggled to his feet. With Brother Simon no longer beside him, he had a chance to get down the tunnel to the cloister and find some means of escape.

Gage took two steps in that direction but, to his horror, spotted the forms of a knight and a short monk coming through the dark tunnel toward him. He knew it was a knight by the silhouette of a sword at his side and figured the monk was Father Thomas. In the tunnel's shadows, he couldn't make out the knight's identity, but then the man's armor and surcoat became visible in the sunlight, along with his face.

19

Gage's heart skipped a beat as the knight hurried toward him and bowed. "Prince Gage, I cannot begin to tell you how relieved I am to see you."

Stunned, Gage stared at Sir Wick. He couldn't believe his fortune, to face a friend and not Sir Jarret, but then it occurred to him what Sir Wick had just said. Mortified, he glanced at Father Thomas. The abbot seemed not at all surprised by the way the knight had just addressed him. Realizing Sir Wick must have already told the monk who he was, Gage inhaled a shuddering breath. What all had been said between the two of them? He cringed as he spoke in the commoners' tongue. "Sir Wick, why have you come here?"

The knight's expression was a combination of respect, surprise, and something Gage couldn't identify. "I was sent here by His Royal Highness, Prince Haaken, to see you safely to Edelmar."

"Safely to Edelmar?" Gage shook his head. Though grateful that he faced a knight who possessed honor rather than the likes of Sir Jarret, it didn't change the positions they both held. He was a marked man, and unlike the monks, by law Sir Wick, as a lord's man, was required to turn him over to the mark's owner. If the knight didn't do so, and it was discovered that he had helped a marked man flee over the border by means of Prince Haaken's orders, Sir Wick could be arrested and possibly Haaken along with him.

"Is something amiss, Your Highness?" Sir Wick asked in the noblemen's tongue. "You are well, are you not?" The knight's forehead furrowed. "Brother Ephraim told us you were badly injured and ill for a time, but he said you were recovering. The porter too, just a moment ago, said you were indeed doing better. Is that not true?" Sir Wick's gaze shifted down Gage as if evaluating all of him to make sure he hadn't missed something. The knight's eyes paused on Gage's cloth-wrapped wrist, then returned to his face. A deeper, unreadable frown filled the knight's face. "Your Highness?"

Gage couldn't find words. Considering that Sir Wick's intention was to see him back to Edelmar, it had to be that the knight knew nothing about his mark. But why had the monks not told him?

The flapping of sandals preceded Brother Sholan's voice calling to him from across the yard. "Gage, Brother Simon said you were in need of me. Are you alright?" The monk hurried forward, eyeing him with concern and confusion.

Agitated by the attention, Gage answered all of them in the commoners' tongue. "I'm fine."

"Oh, yes. I can see that," Brother Sholan said with the same annoyance he'd exhibited on numerous other occasions when Gage had refused to acknowledge pain. "You're completely fine, but Brother Simon saw you—"

"I just needed to catch my breath. That is all. As I said, I'm fine now."

Brother Sholan gave him a look that said he didn't believe him and then scowled forcefully in Sir Wick's direction. "What is going on? Father, I thought we promised him sanctuary within our walls? Why is—"

Father Thomas silenced him with a raised hand. "This is Sir Wick of the White Fortress of Edelmar. Sir Wick, Brother Sholan, our infirmarer here at Saint Jerome's Abbey."

Brother Sholan looked at Gage in surprise. "This is the knight you addressed in your letter?"

"Yes," Gage answered, "but he shouldn't have been sent here to find me."

Sir Wick stiffened. "You were reported injured," he said in the commoners' tongue. "Did you really expect His Royal Highness to ignore that and send no one?"

Gage clenched his teeth. Sir Wick was right. He should have guessed whoever delivered his letter might pass along information about him. He'd been so focused on the letter itself, it had never occurred to him that by sending it he might inadvertently put into motion exactly what he did not want and had promised his father he wouldn't do. His stomach churned. "Sir Wick, I didn't send what I did in order to receive aid. I sent it only so that Allard's and Bardon's murderers could be found and stopped."

"Well, God be thanked then that your intentions do not decide Prince Haaken's actions," Sir Wick said, anger in his voice. "For whether appreciated or not, your well-being was His Royal Highness's foremost concern. Regardless, it's not the only reason he sent me. He wishes to know all you learned about those involved with Felix."

Gage blinked and opened his mouth, but Sir Wick wasn't finished.

"His Royal Highness also wanted to make sure you receive back that which belongs to you." The knight dug into the pouch at his belt, stepped forward, and thrust out his closed hand.

By his words, Gage knew exactly what it was Sir Wick carried. No matter how many times he took it off, he had a feeling his family would always insist it stay with him. Arguing was pointless. He held his hand under Sir Wick's fist and felt his signet ring drop into his palm. He closed his fingers around it and stood, his heart hammering, wondering where a marked man was supposed to keep such an item.

"Prince Haaken said to tell you as well that next time he expects you to use it for its intended purpose. And that if he ever sees it without you again or has to decipher one more cryptic message without a seal, he'll do what he said he'd do to you the night he rescued you from the night patrol."

Gage recalled Haaken's words about pummeling him until he could not stand upright. He pictured Haaken trying to look excessively angry as he said it but in reality just looking annoyed, protective, and worried.

Sir Wick retrieved one more thing from his purse. "He wished this returned to you as well."

Gage cringed at the sight of the brooch with its four rubies. It reminded him only of a man whose life had done nothing but plague him and whose death had not appeased his losses. He refused to touch it. "Give it to Father Thomas, Sir Wick, as a thanks for all that has been done for me by the monks of Saint Jerome's Abbey."

The moment the words were out of his mouth he regretted them, for the brooch was the one thing of value yet within his reach. He'd have done better to sell it and divide the money between himself and the monks. But what was done was done, and he was glad to be rid of it.

The abbot took the brooch with a nod of gratitude.

"Father Thomas?" Brother Sholan looked disturbed.

"It's alright, Brother Sholan," Father Thomas said. "Things are not as we thought them to be. The items found upon our guest do belong to a nobleman, a nobleman who is truly not a baron or a baron's son. No, instead, unbeknownst to us, we have been hosting royalty. This is His Highness, Prince Gage of Edelmar."

Brother Sholan turned to Gage, his expression astonished and his voice accusatory. "A prince of Edelmar? And you did not bother to mention this? You've been here among us all this time and said nothing. Why didn't you reveal your title?"

Gage glanced between Brother Sholan and Father Thomas. "You had proof of my title in hand and thought me a liar and a thief. I doubted mentioning I was a prince would clear up the matter, particularly considering the other false accusations made against me."

Brother Sholan's gaze flicked down to Gage's wrist, then back to his face.

"We misjudged each other," Father Thomas said.

Gage swallowed. "Yes, we did." Still, he was unsure where the monk might yet take the matter.

"The reason that God brought you here to us was made clear to me when your knight explained your story," Father Thomas said in the noblemen's tongue while holding Gage's gaze. "God's desire is for justice and righteousness to prevail. Therefore your title and the condition in which you came to us will remain known as it is currently only by me, Brother Sholan, and Brother John. For I trust, in light of who you are and what has been done to you, that you will depart from here and seek an accurate reckoning of justice for yourself and for those yet in need of it."

Gage exhaled in relief that Father Thomas was letting him go and not insisting the matter of his mark and title be taken to a Delkaran authority. He was marveling at this when it occurred to him that it wasn't as if Father Thomas was actually setting him free. Rather, it was kind of the other way around. Since he was still marked, the only actual change was that the monks of Saint Jerome's Abbey were no longer the ones responsible for him.

Still, their silence and permission for him to depart were a help that he was more than willing to accept. As far as the rest of Father Thomas's commission, he was pretty sure he wasn't going to risk trying to convince a Delkaran lord of his innocence. Then again, he had plenty of reasons for wanting to find the true thieves. He turned to Sir Wick. "You said Haaken needed more information about those involved with Felix," he said in the noblemen's tongue. "Did he go to Veiroot? Were Felix's men there?"

"He has not yet gone to Veiroot. There are questions he wants answered before then."

Gage's stomach clenched. "What about Manton? Was he sought?"

"We were not able to find him. He did not return to Dulcis, and he is not the son of Brit Carver. Brit has a son named Manton, but he is a child. The Manton you sent us after lied and is as much of a ghost as Felix has been. Hence the reason His Royal Highness seeks to know more about what Lady Natriece revealed to you and how sure you are that she has not lied as well."

Gage dug his fingernails into his palms. Of course Manton had lied about his family's shop. Could Lady Natriece be lying too? Gage had no idea. He swallowed hard, his mind spiraling. He hadn't realized until then that part of him had been holding onto some insane hope that Haaken would find Manton and somehow unravel the whole mess surrounding the rebels, and in so doing help set him free.

Gage wished now that he'd taken Manton into custody at the fair or, if nothing else, chained Felix to a tree and gotten as much information as he could out of him before trying to take him to a lord. As it was, he felt as much at a loss to answer Haaken's questions as he felt trying to answer his own. Because of traveling with Manton though, he did know things about the rebels, things he had not dared put in his letter.

"Prince Haaken awaits your aid at Awnquera," Sir Wick said. "If you are capable of riding, we should leave as soon as possible."

There were so many reasons going back to Edelmar with Sir Wick was a bad idea, not the least of which was the fact that he was a marked man. "I will not travel back with you to Edelmar, Sir Wick. But I will tell you all I know about those at Veiroot. Then you can deliver the information to Haaken in Awnquera."

"No!" Blanching immediately as if embarrassed by his outburst, Sir Wick continued more calmly but just as firmly. "I do not currently answer to you. I answer to His Royal Highness, Prince Haaken, and his orders are for me to return with you to Edelmar." His jawline tightening, Sir Wick looked straight into Gage's eyes. "And as you know, I follow my orders."

The hardness in Sir Wick's expression was something Gage hadn't encountered before. It was clear the knight's mind wouldn't be changed.

The only solution, it seemed, was to go with him.

It was neither ideal nor safe, but going with him would at least allow Gage the chance to communicate everything he knew about the rebels to Sir Wick before parting ways with him for both their sakes. He nodded to the knight. "Then we shall leave within the hour."

20

Gage's saddle, gifted to him by Father Thomas, creaked loudly under him as he and Sir Wick rode from the abbey. The abbot had also provided a waterskin, a cloak, and a bag of supplies, and strapped about Gage's wrists were plain leather vambraces given to him by Brother Sholan. "May they safeguard you on your journey," the monk had said with a knowing look.

Departing the abbey reminded Gage of riding from Einhart. At the time he'd had plenty and was blessed by the extra his parents had given him, a sharp contrast to his current state. If not for the monks' generosity, likely due to his title, he'd have wanted for the simplest things, like food and clothes.

The abhorrent reality of this reawakened his anger at the rebels and Sir Jarret. They had stripped him of everything he had rightfully gained even as a commoner. He especially resented not having any weapons, but at least he had Athalos.

The horse snorted in the afternoon heat and surged along the trail. Sir Wick led the way since, unlike Gage, he knew how to get from the abbey to Legan. Gage viewed the thick undergrowth around them and shuddered. He had thought he'd feel relieved leaving the abbey, but nothing about traveling as a commoner or a nobleman felt safe anymore.

Their mounts forged their way along the wooded trail, snapping twigs, crunching pinecones, and stirring up wildlife. A rabbit bolted away from them through the underbrush, and Gage frowned at a squirrel that fussed and threw acorns at them. He was mentally telling them all to be quiet when Sir Wick called back loudly in the noblemen's tongue, "In Legan we can mayhap find clothes more befitting your station."

Gage bit his cheek to keep from shushing Sir Wick and instead answered quietly in the commoners' tongue. "No need. It's better if we travel as we are. A knight with a servant will attract less attention crossing Delkara, and it will be safer for us both than riding as two nobles."

Sir Wick twisted in his saddle to look back at him. "What do you mean 'safer'?" he asked in the commoners' tongue.

"The rebels who ambushed us outside of Aro and those gathering at Lord Gregory's stronghold aren't just a few disgruntled men in Edelmar," Gage explained, keeping an eye on the woods. "And we didn't catch and hang the group's leader. We hanged a leader and not even the one we should have." He thought of Felix. "I think their defiance against the nobles started here in Delkara, and it's still spreading. Like the Blue Crow, they reject the authority of the lords and justify their actions by any means necessary. And the likelihood is, the more successful they are in their efforts, the more others will join their cause, and the more ambushes will take place.

"They routinely plunder the noblemen here in Delkara, attacking their supply caravans and entourages at whim, and the Delkaran lords are going mad trying to stop them. It's no wonder though, for they are attempting to stop a force that is everywhere and anyone. A fletcher dutifully making arrows for his lord is at the same time secretly passing arrows to a smuggler, who in the next town hands them off to a peasant, who then uses them to attack the wagons of a different lord."

Gage shook his head at the dilemma and became lost in thought. Even if the lords could tell who was loyal and who was a rebel, they needed to discover all three—supplier, smuggler, and attacker. Otherwise, they would never truly defeat the rebels.

It was little wonder why the Delkaran lords' men approached commoners with suspicion and why they treated everyone they thought to be a rebel with harsh judgment. Considering this, for a moment Gage questioned his abhorrence for Sir Jarret. But then he felt again the chains digging into his skin and the brand searing into his flesh. He clenched his jaw. No, there was no excuse for Sir Jarret's actions. A knight's duty was to uphold the laws of justice regardless of his fear or anger. Sir Jarret had used his own judgment and willfully bent the law. That made him just as much of a threat to justice as the rebels.

"Is that why you came here to Delkara," Sir Wick asked, "to track down those involved in Allard's death?"

The knight's question reminded Gage of all the reasons he had left Edelmar. In many ways his fears back then seemed like good company compared to the burdens he now carried. He swallowed and overrode the temptation to lie. "No, I didn't come here to track down the likes of Felix. It was only after I was across the border that I learned that there were commoners here in Delkara who were attacking lords and spouting the same accusations and justifications for their crimes as the Blue Crow."

Thinking of Manton smuggling weapons, the rebels who had raided Lord Bertram's wagons, and the ambush on the soldiers that he had witnessed, he swallowed hard. "I wasn't tracking the rebels, but the moment I learned of their location in Edelmar, I knew I had to get word to my father. If they are left unchecked and manage to grow their ranks in Edelmar, as they have in Delkara, Allard and Bardon's deaths will only be the beginning of what is coming."

Sir Wick slowed his horse so that they rode side by side. "And you believe it is indeed Lord Gregory who has aided them in Edelmar by providing them concealment?"

"What I know," Gage said bitterly, "is that Lord Gregory and Lady Natriece have done far more than just cross paths with Felix. Do you remember the Blue Crow's boast that day, about how the lords of Edelmar had failed to find him? And that they would continue to fail because they were blind to their own weakness?"

Sir Wick nodded. "I do."

"Well, Natriece said for a large sum her father agreed to provide a place to stay and provisions for the Blue Crow and his men. That fits with the Blue Crow's boast, for what lord would think to search another lord's home?"

"None," Sir Wick replied, "we assume the loyalty of our own."

"Exactly, blind to our own weakness." Gage thought again about what Felix had said to him: *"You think I helped plan today's ambush? You still don't know."* Gage tightened his fingers on Athalos's reins. Had he overestimated Felix's importance to the rebellion or underestimated it? Who had Felix actually been? Gage's memories drifted through his and Felix's encounter and abruptly led to him reliving their fight on the road. His wound began to ache. Switching his reins to his left hand, he pressed his right hand to his chest, willing the pain away.

"Does it still ail you?" Sir Wick asked in the noblemen's tongue.

"Don't address me anymore in the noblemen's tongue, Sir Wick," Gage said in the commoners' tongue. "Haven't you heard a word I've said? The rebels won't hesitate to kill two noblemen riding alone on the road. The lords also won't think twice before seizing suspicious commoners. So, while we are in Delkara, you must treat me like a servant. That way, as nobleman and commoner, we will hopefully protect each other until we are back in Edelmar." His voice trailed off on the last word because he remembered he had no intention of going all the way back to Edelmar with Sir Wick. He shifted in his saddle and found himself considering when he should break company with the knight.

Sir Wick interrupted his thoughts. "If I'm to treat you like a servant, how should I address you?"

"Call me Gabe or Gabriel."

Sir Wick's expression held curiosity and a deeper, unidentifiable emotion. "I take it this isn't your first time doing something like this?"

Unsure whether to feel accused or complimented, Gage shook his head. "No, it isn't."

"Is that how you disappeared after Aro and how you found out so much about these rebels? By pretending to be a commoner?"

Gage urged Athalos into a faster pace. "There are many different circumstances, Sir Wick, where blending in as a commoner is safer than traveling as a nobleman."

"Right, just not when monks find you half dead in the woods and assume you've stolen your own possessions." This time there was no mistaking the accusation in Sir Wick's voice.

Gage glared back at him. "I didn't ask you to come rescue me, and I certainly don't owe you an explanation for my decisions." He faced forward again in his saddle and decided leaving the knight's company would be good for more than one reason.

"No, of course you don't owe me anything," Sir Wick replied angrily, "because you're a prince, and you have the right to do whatever you please, regardless of how…" Wick stopped himself. Clearly, he had more to say, but apparently he had thought better of saying it.

Gage wished Sir Wick was right and that a prince really could do whatever he pleased, but he couldn't. And he'd grown exceedingly tired of people's dumb assumptions. "You have no idea what it's like to be a prince." He meant the statement as a reprimand and a final word on the subject.

"No, I don't," Sir Wick responded, his voice hard. "But I do know what it's like to be deceived by one. I saw the same look on your face a moment ago that I saw in Aro when you told me you would return with Sir Reid and Sir Brent. If you're planning to disappear on me again, know this: I won't let it happen. You want to be treated like a servant? Good. Then let me make myself perfectly clear, Gabriel. My orders from Crown Prince Haaken are to see you safely to Edelmar. Therefore, I'll do whatever is necessary to make sure you and I cross that border together. Even bind you to bring you with me if I have to."

※

It took past their arrival in Legan before Gage could even look at Sir Wick, let alone speak to him. Thankfully, their entrance into Legan was a quiet one. The city's guardsmen noted him trailing behind the knight but treated him as completely inconsequential. They asked all their questions of Sir Wick, who answered and was waved on with Gage in tow.

Gage's hope had been that taking a servant's role under Sir Wick would remove any inquiry into his status, and his direct subjugation to the knight had indeed accomplished that. A little too well really. Even commoners steered clear of him, and with Sir Wick's threats, he truly felt like a runaway servant being fetched home.

They dismounted at the inn Sir Wick had chosen, and Gage broke his icy silence only to play his part as an obedient servant. He saw to their horses, carried the knight's saddlebags, and slept on the floor along with the other commoners staying at the inn.

He wasn't afraid of Sir Wick, but he couldn't help being angry at him and fearing what would happen if the knight discovered he was marked. At the moment they were safe from any legal ultimatum between them, but that would last only as long as Sir Wick didn't know about his brand. For the same honor that had bound Sir Wick to obey him at Aro and motivated the knight to follow Haaken's orders would also drive Sir Wick to obey the law requiring him to deliver a marked man to his master.

Sir Wick was unlikely to carry out his threat of binding him, but Gage wasn't about to test that theory. He'd choose a moment to slip away when he was absolutely certain he could do so without getting caught.

21

Wick's journey with Prince Gage the following day took place in loud silence. While the hours passed, Wick thought of numerous ways to try to fix the discord between them. Offering an apology came to mind more than once. Every time he decided on something to say though, he would fail to persuade himself to open his mouth and actually say it. He knew he had crossed a line and would probably be stripped of his knighthood the moment Prince Gage told Prince Haaken what he'd said, but he also knew his reputation as a knight wouldn't survive returning to Edelmar without Prince Gage. So really, what was there to say?

Eventually he gave up trying to find anything to say and let the silence reign. They traveled through small towns and safely crossed paths with peasants, merchants, and pilgrims. The rest of the day, they spent alone on the road.

It was a relief finally seeing Nikledon's extensive walls bright in the rays of the setting sun. They were a day closer to Edelmar and could sleep within Nikledon. Built on either side of the Plene River, the city was divided by water. Despite being a relatively quiet waterway with little depths to its banks, the Plene River had no nearby ferries. The only way across was to travel through Nikledon and over one of its bridges.

Wick's plan was for them to spend the night at an inn in the city. He dreaded this process though, particularly with the way things were between him and Prince Gage. It was awkward enough being at odds with His Highness. Having to watch Prince Gage make a show of serving him made him squirm all the more.

He'd left Edelmar for Saint Jerome's Abbey assuming Prince Gage would be grateful to him for coming and would appreciate his aid and protection on the way back to Edelmar. Instead it was like he had intruded into something he wasn't part of and was now an unwanted and despised overseer forcing His Highness to go somewhere he didn't want to go.

Twisting around in his saddle, Wick squinted in the last of the day's sunlight and tried to spot Prince Gage. Annoyingly, His Highness had taken to trailing a good ten horse-lengths behind him. At first Wick had worked to adjust his speed and keep the gap between them to a minimum, but his efforts never lasted long. Halfway through the day he'd given up and simply began checking in on Prince Gage at intervals.

The nearer they came to the city, the more people there were on the road around them. Everyone was headed toward the raised gate embedded between the city's duel towers. Flags with the baron of Nikledon's shield—half blue with a gold upright lion and the other half green with a black eagle—flew from the top of the towers. With commoners all around them, Wick once more slowed his horse to ride just in front of Prince Gage's mount and said, "Stay close." He meant it as a means of assuring His Highness's safety, but judging by the look Prince Gage sent him, it apparently got lumped in as a continuation of his threat from the day before.

Groaning inwardly, Wick wanted so badly to switch to the noblemen's tongue and clarify his words. He also wished he could ask why, despite having chosen him as the recipient of his letter, Prince Gage now seemed to want nothing to do with him. According to His Highness though, he wasn't owed an explanation nor any appreciation for how hard he was trying to do his job.

Part of Wick wanted to scream like Osbert, "I quit!" Because maybe then someone would explain why Prince Gage now felt like a total stranger to him. The rational part of Wick's mind said it didn't matter what he felt. His duty was to his orders, regardless of his desires. Besides, what else could he do? As the seventh son of the lord of Clement, commitment to his duty was all he had to his name.

Weaving his mount toward Nikledon's gate, he focused his attention on those around them. Knowing any of them could be rebels, he evaluated everyone he passed: a thin man steering a vegetable cart, a weary-looking herdsman driving several cows, a barefoot youth with a donkey laden with firewood, and a homely maiden carrying crated chickens. Every last one of them kept their gazes averted from him, much like Prince Gage had done for the majority of the day. They all seemed to hate him, but at least none of them looked capable of trying to kill him or Prince Gage.

※

BY THE TIME he and Prince Gage reached the base of the bridge-like ramp up to Nikledon's gate, the brightness of the setting sun was being pushed away by shadows creeping up the city's walls. The foremost gateman's patience seemed to have departed with the sunlight. "What is your business in Nikledon, peasant?" the bulky man asked of a traveler just ahead of them.

From atop his horse, Wick observed the commoner who'd gained the guard's scrutiny. He noted as well the additional armored gatemen positioned inside the entrance along with those on the gate's ramp. The traveler being questioned appeared to Wick to be nothing but a simple fieldworker, but from what Prince Gage had said about the rebels, who could be sure?

Glancing up between the towers, Wick spotted four more soldiers atop the wall. They carried crossbows and patrolled the gate's fortified barbican. The guards' numbers seemed excessive considering a city's gate was easily closed and defended by only a few men, but Wick supposed in a kingdom where armed rebels might at any time set their sights beyond an entourage, there was perhaps wisdom in such caution.

"Visiting a cousin, is it? Let me see your bags." The bulky guard drew the traveler's satchel off his shoulder and handed it behind him to a blond, bearded guard who began to dig through it.

The peasant's annoyed expression was one Wick knew well. He'd seen the same look on many a face at the ford when he or another guard investigated someone's goods or personal belongings. Smart travelers endured the intrusion without complaint. Others spit protests as if believing they could actually stop the search.

Usually, such belligerence just caused the guards to search all the more carefully because those with something to hide often objected the loudest. Occasionally, it turned out though that someone's dogged complaints were simply them voicing their protests of what they considered an unnecessary inconvenience, in which case everyone suffered. The guardsmen's job was made twice as difficult and miserable due to the person's badgering, and the person was delayed twice as long because of the guards' attentive search.

Thankfully the commoner ahead of them was a smart traveler and was quickly handed back his satchel. He was tying it closed when the guard motioned brusquely. "Get going." Leaving his bag untied, the peasant hurried up the ramp. The bulky guard turned to Wick, a look of amusement on his face. "You must be newly knighted."

Wick frowned at the strange comment. "Excuse me?"

"You're standing in line," the guard said. "Clearly waiting on others hasn't worn off you yet." The other guardsmen snickered. "What's your business in Nikledon?"

"I've no business here," Wick replied, annoyed by the commentary on his age and the insult to his manners. "We're simply after a night's rest and a way across the river."

"We?"

Wick inwardly berated himself for the slip but embraced the error. "Yes, me and my servant." He turned in his saddle to gesture at Prince Gage. What he saw made his insides lurch. Prince Gage's face had drained of color, and he gripped his saddle as if struggling to stay upright.

Concern coursed through Wick. His Highness had been fine just a moment ago. What had happened? Was it his wound, or was there something else ailing him?

"Where're you coming from and where are you going?"

Wick focused on the guard and prioritized getting through the gate first, then figuring out in private what was wrong with Prince Gage. "I come from Edelmar and am returning there."

"Ah, you're Edelmarian then. I thought it odd I didn't recognize your emblem. What brought you to Delkara?"

Still annoyed and now impatient as well, Wick responded as truthfully and concisely as he could. "I was sent here to retrieve this servant. He fell ill on a journey and needed time to recover at an abbey."

"You're sure he's recovered?" one of the guards asked half-jokingly.

Not at all sure, Wick wished he could abandon all pretenses, announce Prince Gage as royalty, and demand the guards clear the way for them. Instead he forced himself to feign indifference. "We've had a long day of riding."

The bulky guard backed away. "Get into the city then before your servant keels over in our gate." Meanwhile the blond, bearded guard eyed Prince Gage as if trying to decide whether or not he wanted a sick person entering Nikledon.

More than happy to follow the first guard's instructions, Wick urged his mount up the ramp. Prince Gage followed close behind. Their horses' hoofbeats thudded loudly on the wooden beams and echoed against the ground below. At the top of the ramp, Wick paused to ask one of the soldiers there. "Is there an inn nearby where we might find lodging for the night?" With the way Prince Gage looked he didn't want to go any farther than necessary.

The man pointed into the city. "One street past the glover's shop, turn left. Three streets down from there, go right and all the way to the bridge crossing. Pay the toll, and follow that same street until you spot Bottoms Up alehouse. Turn right after it, and a few doors down you'll see a sign for the Weary Wanderer."

"Thanks." Wick glanced over his shoulder at Prince Gage while they rode down the gate's second ramp and into a street, which was still bustling with people, animals, and carts. The moment they were out of sight of the gatemen, Wick pulled his horse as close as he dared to Prince Gage's temperamental mount and asked, "Are you alright?"

"I'm fine. It was nothing," Prince Gage said, a shudder in his voice.

It hadn't been nothing, of that Wick was certain. The color was returning to Prince Gage's face though. And since His Highness claimed he was fine, there wasn't much point arguing about it.

22

Following the guard's instructions over a bridge and into the second half of the city, Wick found the street they sought. They wove through the overflowing patrons of the alehouse with its upside down tankard and found the whitewashed inn beyond it. It was a three-story building with half a dozen windows, a collection of potted plants out front, and two chimneys. A sheltered alley alongside it seemed to serve as its stable. A wood manger had been built under tie rings, and a cart of fodder was at the alley's end. Above the shelter's thatched roof, large sections of colored cloth hung on drying lines between windows. The colorful fabric of the dyer's shop drifted in a twisting breeze that carried with it the city's noise, the scent of ale, and the smell of weedy river water.

It wasn't an ideal location for sleep, particularly not with the alehouse's boisterous occupants spilling out onto the street, but it would do. Collecting his sword, Wick swung off his horse. He was about to lead the animal to the manger when a hand touched his arm. "I'll see to him."

Wick reluctantly gave his reins to Prince Gage. The insanity of His Highness untacking their horses felt even more potent considering Prince Gage's questionable health. Miraculously, Prince Gage did seem fine though. He went about the task as if nothing had happened and like it was perfectly logical for him to be working as a servant.

Standing there, Wick wanted to grab him by his tunic, shake him, and demand answers for all the strange inconsistencies of his choices and the actions that violated everything he'd thought he'd known about him. A king's son and an accomplished jouster, Prince Gage had had every advantage anyone could've asked for, but instead of valuing the people and opportunities that power gave him, what had Prince Gage done with it? He'd dumped it all to travel as some commoner.

Other people spent their whole lives trying to attain the sort of privilege and position Prince Gage had been born into and then disregarded, all before he'd even turned twenty-one. Wick had been convinced in reading Prince Gage's letter that His Highness had deserted his place in Edelmar out of some zealous desire to find Felix. But Prince Gage had said himself, he hadn't traveled to Delkara to look for Felix, and clearly he hadn't done so to attend to any royal matter either. Whatever the reason for how Prince Gage had traveled and where, Wick now realized that it hadn't been on behalf of Edelmar's people or out of any obligation to his title.

Arguing with Prince Gage and ultimately threatening him hadn't been how Wick had planned on responding to that realization. In fact, despite being told he should never have been sent to the abbey, that he should go back to Edelmar alone, and that he had no right to ask for an explanation, he still intended to peaceably carry out his orders.

But knowing it was a calculated betrayal Prince Gage had made in Aro and was again planning to make was more than he could stomach. Particularly since, once upon a time, he'd been inspired by a young prince who had led his men with consideration, teased and joked with them like old friends, reprimanded those in error with compassion, and gave a voice to all those around him. With an abundance of possibilities open to him, Prince Gage had been headed places Wick had only dreamed of going. By inviting them into his retinue, His Highness had promised each of them a place beside him on that journey. And Wick would have heartily seconded Allard's declaration that Prince Gage was a good man, worth following anywhere.

Even after the ambush, they had all been more than willing to stand with him, but Prince Gage had not been willing to let them. Coming to him at the abbey, Wick had hoped maybe that had changed, but Prince Gage's words clearly expressed that it hadn't.

Wick angrily watched His Highness finish untacking their horses and gather their belongings. Lifting the saddlebags, Prince Gage paused and pressed his hand to his shoulder. Wick frowned and wondered again how healed his injuries really were. He recalled what Saint Jerome's abbot had said when he'd spoken with him about Prince Gage. *"More befell him than just a sword wound. He's..."* The abbot had hesitated, then shook his head. *"No. If what you say of his identity is true, it is best if I allow him to choose when and how he reveals what happened to him. Such is not required of my position, nor would I consider it any longer my concern to do so, particularly in light of his lineage. No, you must learn of it yourself or wait for him to reveal it to you. I will tell you this though: whatever his intended path, events took place beyond his control."*

Wick had only briefly considered the abbot's words at the time because he'd been too busy trying to confirm that their guest really was Prince Gage. He'd also assumed His Highness would tell him whatever he needed to know about what had happened. But the way things were now, he wished he'd pushed harder to get answers from Father Thomas.

Prince Gage approached with his arms full of their belongings and his gaze submissively downcast. "Do you wish me to bring all the bags inside?"

Standing there, Wick wanted to snatch the bags from his hands and use them to knock some sense into Prince Gage. Instead, he turned his back and headed for the inn's door. If His Highness wanted so badly to take on the role of a servant, then let him be a servant. "Yes, carry them all in."

23

Wick woke the next morning to find Prince Gage gone. The blankets he'd used were folded on a bench, and his bags of provisions were no longer on the floor by the door. Wick flung off his own blanket and hurriedly attempted to dress and put on his armor, not exactly an easy endeavor without assistance. He was halfway through doing so when there was a knock at the door. "Who is it?" he called out angrily.

"It's Latham," the innkeeper answered. "Your servant said you'd wish to be awakened in time to break your fast before departing. He's currently saddling your horses."

Taking a breath, Wick calmed himself. "Thank you. I'll be down shortly." He wasn't sure if Prince Gage had arisen early to truly be helpful or to show him he could have left but hadn't. Regardless, Wick was irate and relieved. Finishing with his armor he strapped on his belt and dagger, then grabbed up his saddlebags and his sheathed sword.

He trudged down the stairs, past the front door, and into the inn's main room. It was clean swept, well lit, and had four tables, a fireplace with a low bench beside it, a line of pegs above a bench for cloaks, and a shelf in the far corner that held several games. Wick had checked the collection the night before for a chessboard but had found none.

The innkeeper—a slim man with an oval face and brown hair—stood chatting with the two other guests currently occupying the space. A silver-haired old man dressed like a craftsman sat eating with a woman, who was either his daughter or his wife. Wick couldn't tell which.

At Wick's approach, Latham turned toward him. "Ah, did you rest well?"

"Well enough," Wick answered. In truth, the alehouse's occupants had kept him awake until what felt like matins, and the bed had been excessively lumpy, but somewhere in there he had actually gotten some rest.

"Food is what you need now then." Latham yelled toward a door at the back of the room. "Estella! Bring out food for the knight and his servant."

"Yes, Father!" a female voice called back.

Latham gestured to him. "Sit, please. She'll have your food and drink out shortly."

Wanting to check on Prince Gage, Wick glanced toward the inn's door, but he figured if His Highness had left he'd still need to eat before going after him. He chose a table at the front of the inn and on the opposite end of the room from the other guests. Swinging one leg over the bench farthest from the door, he dropped his weight onto the seat sideways so that he faced the room and could see the door while leaning against the wall.

He deposited his saddlebags on the floor beside him and placed his sword on the table. Latham returned to chatting. The inn's door opened, and Prince Gage entered, wiping his hands on his tunic. Lowering his eyes to the floor, he headed past Wick to the low bench beside the fireplace under the line of pegs. He settled onto the bench and didn't glance up even when Wick stared long and hard at him.

Apparently, as far as Prince Gage was concerned they weren't going to talk. Wick pressed his lips together and was about to address him anyway when a young woman carrying a tray of food and drinks pushed through the door at the back of the room. She crossed to Wick and placed a tankard, a small jar of butter, bread, a soft-boiled egg, and a chunk of salt pork on the table.

He inhaled the smell of it all and had already taken his first bite of meat before he realized Estella had handed Prince Gage a bowl of barley gruel and nothing else. The girl checked with the other two guests, who seemed to have been fed similarly to Wick, and then disappeared back into the kitchen.

Wick frowned. Had servants at inns always been fed less than their masters? He'd never thought before to pay attention. Rising, he brought his bread to where His Highness sat and held it out to him. Surprise, and something akin to embarrassment, flashed in Prince Gage's eyes. Taking the extra food, he murmured his thanks and then ducked his head once more.

As His Highness spooned the gruel from the bowl he held propped between his knees, Wick returned to his own food. Watching His Highness and wondering what it had been like for him living as a commoner, Wick suddenly noticed how much Prince Gage's loose tunic and thick belt had disguised the leanness of his body and how well his dark beard hid the thinning of his face.

Wondering what else he'd failed to observe, he viewed Prince Gage more closely. His Highness's hunched form was absent of more than just the evidence of feasts. Not only had the liveliness and audacity in his face been replaced by weariness, submission, and a flinch of fear, he also made no claim to his place in a room or really expressed his existence in it at all. It was like everything that had made him who he was had been stripped out of him.

Wick was still lost in thought over this when Estella came and took away his empty dishes. As she moved across the room, Wick heard the inn's door open, followed by the scuffing of heavy boots. He glanced up, expecting to find travelers seeking a place to stay, though it was an odd time of day to arrive at an inn.

Three soldiers wearing the blue-and-green tabards of Nikledon over their armor paused just inside the inn's door. The first soldier was the blond, bearded guard who had stood behind the bulky gateman at Nikledon's entrance the night before. The second was a tall, solid man with brown hair, a square face, and a neatly trimmed beard. The third was a shorter, muscular soldier with green eyes and a long nose. The blond guard pointed toward Prince Gage and murmured to his tall companion, "There. It's him. Took me all night to remember where I'd seen him before. It was on the road with Sir Jarret on the last day of the fair. Radnor here was at the manor later and can verify my words."

The tall soldier looked at the shorter, muscular guard. "Well, Radnor?"

"It's him."

Set on edge by their expressions and the way they gripped their weapons as they spoke, Wick wondered what they were doing there and why they were so interested in Prince Gage. Did they know who he was, or had he attracted their attention for some other reason? He glanced at Prince Gage. His Highness had once again gone chalk white and sat frozen in place like a creature cornered by wolves.

Whatever their interest, it wasn't good. The taller soldier, who seemed to be in charge, approached Wick. "You're the knight of Edelmar who was sent to retrieve this commoner?"

Wick felt his stomach clench. "I am. What's it to you?" Everything about the soldier's bearing told him Prince Gage was in trouble, but he had no idea why. He breathed slowly and reminded himself he outranked them.

The soldier leaned forward and pinned Wick's sword to the board with his left hand. "We're here to seize him, and you're to come with us as well to answer some questions." The man motioned with his chin. His two companions drew their weapons and headed for Prince Gage, who scrambled to his feet, his eyes wide with fear.

A protective indignation and years of being harassed at meals by older brothers and older knights instinctively coiled Wick's fingers. He slammed a fist down on the soldier's hand, leaped to his feet, and grabbed the soldier's tabard. Yelping in pain, the man yanked up his hand. Wick seized the hilt of his freed sword and unsheathed the weapon in one swift motion, bringing its naked edge to bear against the soldier's throat. "You or your men touch him or me, and I swear I'll draw blood."

The man's companions paused their advance on Prince Gage. "Drake?" The blond guard questioned the soldier, who flexed the fingers Wick had smashed and looked impressively calm despite having a blade at his throat. At the same time, the muscular soldier, Radnor, growled and took a step forward.

Wick shifted his grip. "I don't make idle threats."

"Stand fast, Radnor," Drake commanded. His attention returned to Wick. "If you are truly a knight, I exhort you as a fellow lord's man to do your duty. Let me go, and let us take him." He jutted his chin toward Prince Gage.

Latham, Estella, and the inn's two guests remained silent and motionless beyond where Prince Gage stood. Wick sympathized with their shock, but he wasn't about to back down. "Why should I? You've no right to seize him."

"If you think that," the blond soldier said, "then you don't know who he is."

"Oh, I think I know who he is a whole lot better than you do."

"Sir Wick, don't," Prince Gage said, his voice desperate.

"It sounds to me," Drake said, "like he understands the situation better than you do."

"He's my responsibility," Wick replied, ignoring Prince Gage's concerns about him revealing his identity. "I'm not handing him over to anyone for any reason. So, ask what you will, but you aren't taking him."

Drake eyed the sword just below his chin. "And here I'd hoped that as two lords' men, we might come to a reasonable understanding. Your blatant disregard for our claim to him tells me either Merek is correct, and you have no idea who this man is, or you aren't who you say you are."

"Well, then tell me," Wick said, infuriated by the soldier's insinuation. "Who do you think he is?" Prince Gage looked horrified by his request, but Wick wanted answers to whatever possible justification these soldiers thought they had for demanding to be able to seize a prince of Edelmar.

"Who is he?" Merek, the blond soldier, answered with scorn, "He's a rebel thief and a smuggler."

"A rebel!" Wick scoffed. "You think he's a rebel?" He almost laughed in relief. "Well, now I know you have the wrong person." Releasing Drake's tabard, he removed his sword from the soldier's neck. "Whoever you're after, it's not him. He's no rebel. And you can be sure I'd never protect their kind. So you may be on your way. We'll all forgive and forget this misunderstanding." None of the soldiers moved. "I mean it, leave!" Wick said forcefully. "Before you start an actual conflict between Edelmar and Delkara that you don't want to be the ones to have caused."

Backing away from the table, Drake straightened his tabard. "Radnor, you're sure?"

"The proof is on his wrist," the muscular soldier replied.

Wick shook his head in disbelief. Were they truly going to keep going with this nonsense?

"Well, knight of Edelmar?" Drake said. "If you're so certain you know who he is, tell him to take off his vambraces and show us his arms, for the rebel we seek is marked."

"This is ridiculous," Wick answered. "He's no rebel."

"I think it's you who's no knight," Merek spat.

"I agree." Drake drew his sword. "Take them both."

24

As Drake and Merek turned their swords on Sir Wick, the cold panic inside Gage shifted to rage. This problem was his, not Sir Wick's. He wasn't going to let the knight be taken as a supposed rebel because of him. Not if he could help it. But what could he do? He was weaponless, and Radnor was headed his way.

He hurriedly searched around him. The fireplace logs were too far away, the low bench he'd been sitting on was too cumbersome for a surprise attack, and the pegs above him were empty. The pegs. They just might work. But dare he fight back? He drew a swift breath and tried not to let the memory of having a sword slash across his chest stop him.

Fury and fear intermingled inside him. He didn't remember Radnor from the manor, but that the soldier remembered him and had been with Sir Jarret told him plenty. When Radnor was four strides away, Gage drew his arms up in front of his body as if to protect himself from an anticipated blow.

Snorting, Radnor raised his sword's tip as he closed the space between them and reached for Gage's arm. It didn't matter that the soldiers had no intention of killing them. The fear of the pain Gage knew they had no problem inflicting, not to mention what they would likely do to Sir Wick if they thought him a rebel as well, was enough to motivate Gage.

Hearing the clash of Sir Wick fending off a strike from Merek's blade, Gage raised his arms the rest of the way over his head and closed his fingers around the pegs above him. Pulling up and jumping at the same time, he painfully heaved his body upward and slammed his feet against Radnor's chest.

The impact knocked the man backward and gave Gage the space he needed to land crouched and seize a more suitable weapon. His heart pounding, he hauled up the bench he'd been sitting on and raised it like a shield. It was thick and unwieldy but surprisingly light. To his left, the screech of weapons sliding down each other made him shudder. He swallowed but dared not divert his gaze to see how Sir Wick was faring. Snarling in anger, Radnor thrust his sword at him.

Gage jerked the bench higher, and Radnor's blade hacked off a chunk of wood just below his fingers. His stomach lurched. A shield with no handles was not very good protection. But shields were used for more than just defense.

Radnor struck at him again, a low swing aimed at his side. Gage braced the bench, shifted his body, and prepared to act. The blade thudded into the wood. Radnor yanked it free, then flattened the sword against the bench's edge and swept it upward. Gage saw its sharp edge coming for his fingers. Panicking, he did as he had planned and used his full weight to drive the bench into Radnor's body.

Shoving the soldier backward, he succeeded in taking him by surprise, which disengaged his weapon. But the advantage lasted only a moment. Radnor grabbed both sides of the bench and instantly halted Gage's forward motion. Then the muscular soldier braced his feet. Dread rushed through Gage's body.

He was about to be seriously overpowered. His arms trembled. All Radnor had to do was give the bench one hard shove, and he would be flat on his back with the soldier over top of him. An idea entered his head. Keeping his hands locked on the bench, he waited for Radnor to make his move.

Sure enough the soldier shifted and plowed his weight into the wood like a battering ram. Gage instantly twisted out from behind it. With all resistance gone, Radnor flew forward and fell onto the bench, which broke beneath him with a loud snap.

Angered and clearly in pain, Radnor gasped for air. Gage placed a knee on Radnor's back, grabbed the man's sword arm, and attempted to twist it behind him to pry the weapon from his grasp. Radnor was on his stomach and injured, but he was still stronger than Gage.

The sword scraped across the floor as they fought over it. Radnor refused to surrender the weapon and shoved upright. Holding tightly to Radnor's wrist, Gage wrapped his other arm around the man's neck and anchored himself behind Radnor's rising form, so his body would be out of reach of the flailing weapon.

Radnor clawed at Gage's arm around his neck. The man's nails bit into Gage's skin just above his vambrace. Determined to hold on, Gage fought angrily for control of the soldier's sword. Radnor clawed even more fiercely at his arm and struggled to pull his sword hand free.

Gage realized then that Radnor could easily go from using his nails to seizing the dagger at his belt and slicing his arm. He shifted his hold around the man's neck to try to spot the secondary weapon.

Before Gage could locate the man's dagger, Radnor let out a low grunt and toppled forward onto the bench, dragging Gage forward with him. For a moment, sprawled over top of him, Gage thought Radnor was faking it, but when he let go of the soldier's neck, Radnor didn't move. He seized the man's sword. The soldier's fingers easily released its hilt. Gage drew the weapon into his own grasp. Breathing hard, he climbed to his feet.

Drake instantly broke from his and Merek's fight with Sir Wick and headed toward him. Gage spun Radnor's sword in his hand to test its weight and met Drake's gaze with confidence. He finally had a decent weapon back in his hands and was more than willing to use it.

※

IT HAD TAKEN all Wick's focus to keep Merek and Drake from working together to disarm him or back him into a corner. He had drawn his dagger, so he had a blade in each fist, and had kept his feet moving while he blocked and thrust. Despite the armor he and the soldiers wore, they were all disadvantaged by the fact that none of them were wearing helmets or gauntlets. Desperately working to protect himself from their blows, Wick utilized every one of his parries to push the soldiers back and to search for ways to end the fight without killing either man.

He had landed several blows but only on armor. He knew where he needed to strike to disable them, but together the two soldiers had effectively prevented his attacks and kept his weapons in constant motion. Then Drake had said something to Merek and disengaged from the fight.

Sneering, Merek made a hard thrust at Wick and bound their blades together. Then the soldier lunged forward, twisting his sword backward.

Glad for the training he'd had with brothers who rarely fought fair, Wick ducked just in time to avoid getting cracked in the face by the pommel of Merek's weapon. In the next moment their armored bodies were touching, and their arms were tangled together. Having failed to hit him, Merek grabbed Wick's wrist and attempted to twist his sword around Wick's blade and disarm him. With their weapons locked together and Merek too close to see it coming, Wick yanked up his dagger and stabbed the man's underarm through a gap in his armor. Then he brought his knee up into the man's unprotected groin.

Bellowing, the soldier stumbled back and clutched his bleeding arm.

Still holding his dagger, Wick clenched his hand about the hilts of both their swords. He squeezed hard and twisted.

Fingers caught between the three weapons, Merek gasped in pain and dropped to his knees to ease the pressure Wick was applying to his wrist. Sensing when the soldier had had enough, Wick briefly loosened his hold. Merek instantly withdrew his pinched hand, leaving Wick in possession of both blades. He crossed the weapons in front of Merek's neck and looked about for the other two soldiers.

Radnor was on the ground, and Drake was hard pressed fighting Prince Gage. His Highness was landing an impressive volley of thrusts and blows between his parries, but he was unarmored. It would only take one slip for him to be struck down. "Drake," Wick called out. His intention was to seek the man's surrender, but in that moment Prince Gage flicked Drake's blade outward and brought the edge of his own sword against the soldier's cheek.

"Drop your weapon," Prince Gage commanded.

Wick smiled at Drake's startled expression. The man obviously hadn't expected a mere commoner to wield a sword with such skill. "I'd do as he says if I were you," Wick commented.

Drake glanced at his two defeated companions, growled, then released his weapon. The sword clattered to the floor, making the two guests and the innkeeper jump.

"Go," Prince Gage said. "I'll hold them here."

Wick stared at His Highness. Was he insane? There was no way he was leaving him alone to deal with three soldiers. He supposed a loyal servant might offer to hold back an enemy while his master escaped, but still. "I'm not going anywhere without you. We'll deal with them together."

"No, you have to go. Now," Prince Gage answered forcefully.

All the pride Wick had felt watching Prince Gage defeat Drake disappeared. If this was His Highness seizing an opportunity to slip away from him, it wasn't happening. "I'm not leaving you."

Prince Gage's determined expression turned frightened. "This is my problem, not yours."

Realizing then that maybe Prince Gage legitimately was, in a warped way, trying to protect him, Wick attempted to reason with him instead. "Look, we can both get out of here." He glanced about. "We just need a means to make sure no one here raises an alarm until after we're gone."

Prince Gage hesitated but then seemed to come to his senses. "Latham, do you have a windowless room?"

The innkeeper pointed shakily. "First door past the stairs."

25

Glancing back over his shoulder, Gage rode close beside Sir Wick as they trotted toward Nikledon's eastern gate. They didn't dare flee any faster lest their behavior raise suspicion, but the angst of each passing moment quickened Gage's heartbeat and made his skin crawl. He steered Athalos around a cart and barely missed clipping the edge of a fruit seller's stand. Panic consumed him. If they were delayed by some incident and caught now, he was positive neither he nor Sir Wick would ever see freedom again.

Back at the inn they had shoved everyone, including the inn's guests, into a windowless room and used the soldiers' three swords to jam the door closed. Then they had moved a table to further block the door and departed in haste. With no telling how long their makeshift barrier would hold and no other option but to run, they rode for Nikledon's eastern gate.

Gage berated himself as they went. He should have told Sir Wick the night before that he had recognized one of the guards at the gate and that they should stay at a different inn. He also should never have let Sir Wick defend him. He'd foolishly thought that in Delkara it would be him at risk riding with Sir Wick not the other way around.

He yanked Athalos to a stop to avoid crashing into a girl selling eggs and hurriedly apologized to a merchant who had to dodge sideways when he let Athalos burst back into a trot. Catching up with Sir Wick, Gage viewed the eastern gate at the end of the lane. They had to get out of the city. But everything in him panicked at the thought of approaching another of Nikledon's gates where there were other soldiers who could just as easily also have been at the manor like Radnor or part of the guard from the road like Merek. Or worse, they might actually be headed straight for Sir Jarret. He swallowed hard. "Sir Wick."

"What? Are they behind us?" The knight twisted in his saddle.

Gage glanced back as well. "No. I…I just need you to promise me something."

Sir Wick's expression became wary. "What?"

"If we're stopped and questioned at the gate like at the inn, promise me that you'll say nothing on my behalf. And if they move to take me, let them, so that you at least might go free."

Sir Wick stared at him as if he'd gone mad. "What? No. You cannot expect me to let them take you."

"Yes, I can, because I won't have you or my family getting caught up in this. For the honor and protection of the crown of Edelmar, you must do as I ask. Say nothing about who I am, and do nothing to stop them. Promise me, Sir Wick." The knight's jaw set while they rode toward the city gate. "Sir Wick?"

They were already slowing their horses to join the collection of people waiting in line to get through the gate when Sir Wick finally nodded. "I promise you."

Exhaling in fearful relief, Gage turned his attention to the guards. He searched every face for anyone he recognized as he steered Athalos along behind Sir Wick's mount. The knight wove his horse through those waiting in line, directly toward one of the gatemen. Gage wanted to drag him to a stop and ask him what he was doing, but it was too late.

"Guard, clear me a path through this gate," Sir Wick barked, "for I have urgent business that cannot be delayed."

To Gage's amazement, the soldier snapped to attention. "Yes, sir." Turning, the man yelled. "Make way!" Peasants shuffled aside. And with all the guardsmen looking on, the two of them trotted toward the gate without so much as a single question.

His heart thundering in his chest, Gage expected at any moment for someone to shout and for the portcullis to drop in front of them. But instead they passed through the gate's mouth and pounded over the drawbridge on its far side. Three more guards were outside the gate, searching and questioning a line of peasants coming into the city, but none of them even glanced their way.

Relief flooded through Gage but also terror, for he knew the road ahead could be just as treacherous. Sir Wick kicked his mount into a faster speed, and Gage followed. His heartbeats matched the pounding of Athalos's hooves as they tore down the road and away from Nikledon.

They quickly entered the woods and passed the empty fairgrounds. Other than the rutted lane turning into the huge trampled meadow, no evidence of the event remained. Gage felt the familiar twist of anger at Manton.

They came upon the fork in the road a moment later. Last time Gage had traveled left and directly into Sir Jarret's path. The other direction led to Delipp, where he'd watched soldiers raid homes in search of rebels.

"Which way?" Sir Wick asked.

Since the alternative to Delipp was Lyster and Baron Bertram, Gage made up his mind. "Go right."

They did so and galloped along the road for what felt like an hour or two. Listening intently, Gage had heard no evidence of anyone following them. When they reached a patch of forest with fewer tall trees, Sir Wick eased his mount to a walk. Gage slowed Athalos as well and drew long slow breaths. They rode through saplings and shrubbery that pushed close around them. The plants might have overtaken the road entirely if not for the consistent wear of passing hooves and wheels. Birds twittered at them from the brush and burst into the blue sky when they drew near.

Athalos tripped on a downed sapling, and Gage suddenly realized how heavily the horse was breathing. Unrestricted access to grainfields and hay piles with little exercise had not been particularly good for the animal.

"Sorry, fella." He leaned forward to pet Athalos's sweaty neck. At the action, pain stabbed through his shoulder. He hissed and clutched at his wound. The spot where he'd been cut the deepest stung and then ached. He gritted his teeth. He'd felt the same pain when he'd heaved himself up to kick at Radnor. He breathed shallowly.

"Are you alright?"

"I'm fine."

"Really?" Sir Wick said angrily. "Because first you're attacked and almost killed in Delkara, and now soldiers are hunting you who are convinced you're a rebel. Whatever is going on here, it isn't nothing. And you know it, because you're trying to keep your family's name out of it. So tell me, what exactly have you gotten yourself tangled up in?"

Gage swallowed hard. At the moment Sir Wick was his only ally and the closest thing he had to a friend. But how much did he dare tell him? "If I explain, Sir Wick, all it will do is put you in an impossible position."

"I'm already in an impossible position." Frustration filled Sir Wick's voice. "I'm supposed to be protecting you, but I can't do that when I have no idea what's going on."

Gage shook his head. "It's too late for you to protect me, and the longer you try, the more likely it will be that we'll both be arrested. And when that happens, whether true or not, their accusations against you will turn into an actual conviction."

26

Prince Gage's words tugged at Wick's mind like a thought demanding to be finished. Prince Gage hadn't said, "their accusations against *us*," but rather "their accusations against *you*." He'd also said at the inn, *"This is my problem not yours,"* which implied Prince Gage knew what the issue was and that it had already occurred.

Merek had accused Prince Gage of being a rebel thief and smuggler, something Wick knew couldn't be true, but what had Radnor said to Drake when he'd asked if he was sure? *"The proof is on his wrist."*

Wick suddenly considered Prince Gage's bandaged right wrist at the abbey, the vambraces he now wore, and Drake's demand that they be removed.

The hair on Wick's arms stood on end. Could it be? He recalled again what the abbot of Saint Jerome's Abbey had said about Prince Gage, *"It is best if I allow him to choose when and how he reveals what happened to him. Such is not required of my position.... You must learn of it yourself."*

The cold swirling reality of it all settled over Wick. He now understood why the soldiers had questioned his identity as a knight. In their minds there had been no doubt that he was protecting a rebel, which meant to them every word out of his mouth had to be a lie. *"Do your duty,"* Drake had said, *"let us take him."* And Prince Gage had said, *"so that you at least might go free."*

Wick scrubbed his hand over his mouth, trying to suppress the panic he felt. Prince Gage was right; knowing would put him in an impossible position. Because if it was true, by law there were actions required of Wick, actions he was loath to even consider, let alone carry out.

Serving at the ford, he'd seen his share of marked individuals traveling with their masters. He'd also once, as a squire, had to ride with Sir Hedrick to deliver back to her master a marked girl who had been caught attempting to escape over the border. But this? This was so far beyond anything he had ever thought he'd have to deal with as a knight of Edelmar.

For a moment, questions of how Prince Gage could possibly have ended up in such a situation crashed about his mind. He desperately wanted to know everything, but he also didn't want to ask anything, lest a single answer confirm the horrendous possibility. For what then? What was he to do if Prince Gage of Edelmar really was a marked man?

Wick spoke hesitantly. "I think I understand now why you didn't wish to travel back with me to Edelmar. You knew if I found out what those soldiers already know that I'd have to choose between loyalty to you and duty to the law."

Prince Gage looked tortured. "I picked men for my retinue who had never been known to place personal loyalties over duty. You're an honorable knight, Sir Wick. No further suspicion should fall on you because of me."

Air caught in Wick's lungs. He wasn't sure if Prince Gage was suggesting that he turn him in or simply that they divide from each other's company, but neither option was acceptable to him. They were already on the run together. Parting ways would only leave Prince Gage unprotected. And while handing His Highness over to some Delkaran lord might remove suspicion from himself—though Wick doubted it considering he'd just helped lock three soldiers in an inn—what then? Was he supposed to just go back to Edelmar and tell Prince Haaken that he'd delivered his brother to the lords of Delkara as a rebel thief because it was his duty to do so? He shuddered even considering the possibility.

Taking Prince Gage back to Prince Haaken and letting the two of them figure out what to do seemed a far better solution. If nothing else, it would prevent him from returning without Prince Gage and being stuck again in the middle of everyone's questions, the way he'd been when Prince Gage had disappeared from Aro. But could he take him back to Edelmar without violating the laws of both kingdoms? What exactly were his moral and legal obligations?

He thought about what the two kingdoms' laws actually stated about a lord's man encountering someone who was marked. Since Edelmar and Delkara had once been a united kingdom, their legal systems had, in the past, been one and the same. But there were no guarantees that was still the case, which meant he'd have to risk utilizing what he knew and hope it was sufficient to save him in Delkara as well as in Edelmar.

"By law," Wick said slowly and pointedly, "if a lord's man sees that a person is marked and fleeing, he is required to apprehend them and return them to their master." He held Prince Gage's gaze. "But if I have not seen any mark, my duty is to my current orders. Thus, my duty is to conduct you safely to Edelmar."

"I can't let you risk that."

"It's not your choice. I follow my orders, remember?"

"You don't understand," Prince Gage said. "You can't take me back. If it was discovered that you, sent by my brother, helped me escape from Delkara, there's no telling what assumptions would be made or what accusations might result."

Wick shook his head. "Not if there's a legitimate explanation for what was wrongfully done to you, and not if your father brings the matter to light himself and deals with it before it's discovered."

"No! That's exactly what I don't want to happen. Think about it. How would my father even address the issue? It can't be through a claim of innocence. What they did to me is an irreversible punishment based on supposedly indisputable evidence. The only way to approach the wrongfulness of it would be to accuse the Delkaran lords' own men of dealing unjustly with someone they reasonably thought to be a rebel. And if their crime is simply the way they are responding to the rebels, why would King Axel of Edelmar be making an issue of it? And if they asked him, how would he answer?

"I traveled into Delkara as a commoner, Sir Wick. He cannot acknowledge me as his son. If he did, the questions would no longer be about their own men's conduct but about mine. And at that point they could just as easily add 'royal Edelmarian spy' to my charges and turn their accusations upon King Axel of Edelmar. So, no matter what, I cannot bring this to my father's door."

Wick cringed. Prince Gage was right, but there had to be another way. He considered the problem for a long moment. "Those in Delkara think you are indisputably a rebel, so prove them wrong. Prince Haaken is waiting for more information from you before he moves to take Lord Gregory at Veiroot. You clearly know more about the rebels than any of us. You can't solve your problem by going to the lords, so go after those who made it a problem in the first place. Use the rebels you catch in Edelmar to prove to those in Delkara that you aren't one of them."

Prince Gage shook his head. "The risk—"

"The risk is worth it," Wick said, his heartbeat throbbing in his ears. "Prince Haaken needs the information you have to stop those in Edelmar, and you need a way to prove to Delkara you aren't a rebel."

Prince Gage nodded. "You're right."

"Then we ride for Edelmar?" Wick asked.

"Yes, but first, we should visit a chandler shop in Delipp. The owners are friends of Manton's and likely also rebels. They might be able to tell us where we can find Manton."

Wick nodded. "Then we—" He paused, suddenly realizing the pounding he was hearing wasn't just his heart but horses' hooves coming behind them. "They're upon us! We need to move!"

He and Prince Gage kicked their horses into a dead run.

27

A THIN BRANCH caught Gage across the face, stinging his cheek. He ducked the next one, missed a beat, and slammed down in his saddle. The collision jarred his shoulder. Hissing a breath, he threw himself back into Athalos's stride. Laboring to keep up with Sir Wick, he tried to listen for the sound of hooves behind them but couldn't hear anything above the wind and his own heavy breathing.

Fortunately, their horses had the benefit of having just rested, whereas the soldiers probably hadn't slowed their mounts since leaving Nikledon. That gave him and Sir Wick an advantage, if they could keep it.

On and on they galloped, their horses' breathing becoming loud and strained. Still they pushed them to keep going. Gage's struggle wasn't just in keeping Athalos moving though. His own body began to tremble. Twice his legs gave out, and he lost his coordination in matching Athalos's stride. The first time he recovered quickly, but the second time he was jostled to the side and felt himself sliding off Athalos's back. A surge of fear gave him strength enough to heave himself back straight, but he wasn't sure how much longer he would last.

What felt like an hour later, Sir Wick eased his mount to a trot. Gage did the same. A wave of heat instantly swept over him. His head pounding and his wound aching, he leaned forward, bouncing hard. His legs refused to support his weight, and his back spasmed. He pulled Athalos to a walk.

Bent over his saddle's pommel and inhaling air in gasps, Gage hoped Sir Wick would notice him falling behind, because he didn't dare call out to him.

Sir Wick was about twenty paces beyond him before he glanced back and let his mount stumble to a stop. "I think we've outdistanced them, but we should keep moving." The knight looked none the worse for the ride, though his horse's sides were flecked with foam and heaving in and out rapidly.

Gage tried to straighten himself on Athalos but had to hold on to his saddle to keep from sliding off.

Sir Wick eyed him. "Or perhaps it would be wiser to find somewhere we can get out of sight."

Gage only had enough energy to nod.

◈

INSIDE A BARN on the edge of a manor village, Gage slid from Athalos's back. They'd ridden past the village then circled back to the barn so that hopefully people would tell the soldiers they'd seen them ride by. Gage hit the ground. He was lightheaded, and his knees shook. He tried to take a step and had to grab a nearby stall wall to steady himself. Sir Wick stepped in beside him and pulled his arm over his shoulder. "Come on, you need food and rest."

Assisting him across the barn, Sir Wick eased him down into a pile of hay then came back and thrust a leather waterskin into his hands.

Feeling embarrassed and frustrated that he needed the help but also grateful for it, Gage drank, then looked at Sir Wick crouched beside him. "Thank you."

The knight simply nodded, then glanced around at the loose chickens and a donkey tied in the corner. "We should be fine here for a bit. You rest. I'll stand watch."

Too exhausted to protest, Gage lay back and let his eyes drift closed.

The next thing he knew, Sir Wick was gently shaking him awake. The light in the barn had faded. He hurriedly sat up. "How long have I been asleep?"

"Not long," Sir Wick said. "The sun has simply clouded over. Here." The knight handed him the waterskin along with a hunk of hard cheese and dried meat.

Gage gratefully ate and drank. As he did so, he noted that Sir Wick now wore a brown commoner's tunic. "What happened to your surcoat and armor?"

"What I could conceal is underneath. The rest is in my saddlebags. I bought the tunic off a villager. I figured two commoners were less obvious than a knight and servant. I've got good news and bad news. The soldiers didn't find us, but they did ride past. There are about ten of them with Drake and Merek."

Distressed, Gage rose to his feet. "By now they could be waiting for us on the road ahead."

"I don't think so," Sir Wick said. "At this point they don't know we've stopped. They will likely ride to the next village or all the way to Delipp before circling back to look for us."

Gage cringed. The last thing the poor townspeople of Delipp needed was another angry mob of lord's men turning their businesses and homes inside out looking for rebels. Not that they would find the rebels who actually lived there. "What if we turn back and go a different way?"

"I'm not sure that'd be any better. Radnor wasn't riding with them, which means he's probably at the head of a second search party, which is exactly what I'd have done if I was them. I'd have covered every possible direction we might have gone."

Anxiety stirred within Gage. He paced down the barn, his knees, thankfully, now supporting him. "We should have just stayed ahead of them."

"You wouldn't have made it."

He glared at the knight.

Sir Wick shrugged. "At least now we can travel at our own pace, and they're angry which means they probably aren't being cautious. So, we take our time and listen as we go. If I remember correctly, most of this road is through forest, which means we can hide quickly if we need to."

Gage clenched his fingers into fists and was tempted to punch the wall beside him. Here they were, a knight and a prince, running and hiding from soldiers all because of Manton and the rebels. He expelled a heavy breath. "Fine. We do what we must to get to Edelmar, then we stop running and start fighting."

28

AFTER THEIR FIFTH round dodging into the woods to avoid what this time had turned out to be just two merchants on mules, Gage was ready to throttle anyone he knew who was connected to the rebels. He had sap in his hair, scratches on his arms, numerous bug bites, and bruised knees. At least they were still free, but every moment spent trying to stay that way left him feeling that much more powerless. Meanwhile, the day was waning, and he was starting to wonder if they would even make it to Delipp before dark.

Finally, they heard the trickling sound of moving water. It grew louder, and gaps in the trees began to reveal the fields of Delipp cut out of the forest. Mossy, brick-lined ditches running along the road shunted water into the trenches throughout the fields.

"Not far now," Sir Wick said. "Keep your eyes open."

With fields on either side with serfs in them, they had nowhere left to hide.

A group of people rounded the corner ahead. Gage's heart skipped a beat, then eased to a slow pound. They were just peasants, probably heading to their homes. Several carried loaves of bread, another a basket of yarn, one a bucket, and the last a handful of horseshoes.

They were talking amongst themselves in the muggy evening heat and paid little mind to the two of them, which surprised Gage until he remembered Sir Wick no longer wore a knight's livery.

"Seems soldiers is always looking for someone these days," a woman said with disgust.

"Well, at least these ones're more civilized about it," one of the other women commented.

"For now." The man pointed with his horseshoes. "But mark my words, once they've got the scent of blood, they'll tear apart whatever's in their way. I'd guess right now they ain't sure where their prey is, but they must know their faces. Why else haunt the inside of every gate? Probably they're waitin' to catch 'em leaving the city or to snag them when they come in it."

Gage exchanged glances with Sir Wick. The group fell silent before passing them, but their words continued to ring in Gage's ears even after the peasants had disappeared down the road. "We can't go through Delipp," he said.

The knight nodded to the fields. "There might be a trail that circumvents the city. From what I've heard from other guards, there usually are. Peasants create them to avoid the tolls."

Sweating in the sticky heat, Gage glanced up at the darkening sky. "We don't have much daylight left."

"We best start looking for that trail then. If we can make it around the city, there's a small abbey on the far side where Brother Ephraim and I stayed. Hopefully, they'll put us up for the night and feed us." Sir Wick frowned at his packs. "We've little food even for an evening meal. It's a pity I didn't think to buy more supplies last night."

At the mention of food, Gage's stomach grumbled. He turned Athalos off the road toward the edge of one of the fields. "Better to go hungry than to get caught."

※

Wick pointed at a peasant ahead who was gathering rocks into a wagon. "We could ask him if he knows of such a path." He didn't wish to admit defeat, but they had been searching the forest fields surrounding Delipp for the better part of an hour, and the day's light was nearly gone.

Prince Gage sighed. "Do it."

Wick rode up to the wagon. The peasant straightened, holding rocks the size of onions in either hand. "What do you want?"

"A moment's help is all. We're looking for a trail around the city. Do you know of such a thing and where we might find it?"

The man scoffed. "A trail? There's no trail. What you're looking for is not much more than a deer path, but it does go around the city. You won't be able to ride down it though. It's on the other side of the road in the field with the big oak tree. The path starts on the southwest edge. You won't see it until you're right on top of it, and that's in the daylight. You'd do better to wait for morning before attempting it."

Inwardly groaning, Wick nodded. "Thanks." He rode back and pulled his horse close, but not too close, to Prince Gage's mount. "We're probably going to be stuck in the dark either way. The only question is do we go farther tonight or take his advice and wait for morning? I have flint and tinder and a lantern. And I think the more unexpected our travel is, the less likely we are to be found or followed."

※

Gage seriously disliked the idea of pressing down another dark forest path, but it was better than waiting to get caught. Besides, there was confidence in not being alone and in having light.

They had to travel twice along the edge of the field with the oak tree to find the opening to the path. Then it was a matter of dismounting, lighting a lantern, and hoping the trail didn't get any narrower, since they were not about to leave their horses behind.

Keeping track of the well-used path was not difficult, but making progress along it was arduous. Downed trees, which forest animals or a single person on foot could have easily navigated over or around, were abundant, and branches were constantly snagging at them. Insects harassed them, and as the dark continued to close in around them, the sounds of other forest creatures grew louder and closer.

Gage's tunic was damp with sweat, and his stomach gurgled hungrily. He swatted at bugs and shoved around yet one more bush. He was exhausted, in pain, and wanted nothing else than to be far away from Delkara and forests.

"Did you hear that?" Sir Wick asked.

Gage listened but couldn't discern anything new. "Hear what?"

"It sounded like thunder."

Gage thought Sir Wick was hearing his stomach grumbling, but then he too noted the rumble in the distance. "Great, just what we need."

"Maybe a storm will keep the wolves and boars in their dens," Wick said optimistically.

By the time they paused to eat the last of their food, the thunder had grown louder and much closer. Watching the flame of their lantern flicker and dance, Gage realized the wind was also picking up. He had no desire to camp in the woods, but choosing a place to stop was better than being forced to stop because they had no light. "I think maybe we should find somewhere to shelter for the night."

Sir Wick glanced up at the sky as a flash of lightning preceded a snap of thunder. "I was hoping we'd make it through to the abbey, but I think you're right."

Not daring to stray too far off the path, they used the lightning to search for any place that might offer some protection—a rock overhang, a bank of earth, anything they could put at their backs. There was nothing of the like. The trees around them began to stir hard with the winds of the arriving storm, and their lantern's flame danced within its shield, barely keeping grasp of its hemp cord. A sprinkle of rain began to fall.

More lightning lit the forest around them. For a moment every tree, rock, and hollow became visible. Gage spotted a cluster of pines off to their left. Wet darkness rushed back over the forest, and thunder cracked directly above them, making Gage jump. Drawing a breath, he called to Sir Wick. "Over here. There's a patch of thick pines we can shelter beneath."

The best they could do for their horses was to tie the animals to a nearby beech tree. Guarding their lantern from the wind, he and Sir Wick pulled on their cloaks, then stripped the tack off their horses. Ducking low, they dragged their tack and bags under prickly branches into a bed of crunchy pine needles. They settled against the biggest tree's trunk and sat staring out from beneath the pine boughs at the legs of their mounts.

For a while Sir Wick managed to keep the lantern protected with his cloak, but then a strong gust of wind snatched the flame away. Darkness swirled around them, and the rain fell harder. It pelted the ground surrounding the pines and drizzled endlessly through the thrashing branches, slowly drenching the ground. Gage's cloak—too worn to fully keep out the water—began to seep through. Tugging the damp garment closer around his shoulders, he shivered.

His shoulder aching, he shifted his position and felt pine needles prick his legs and water soak into his clothes. He bit his tongue to keep from screaming in exasperation. All he wanted was to be somewhere dry where there was food.

Sir Wick grunted. "Looks like this storm is going to last a while. You might as well get some sleep. I can keep first watch."

"I'll keep watch," Gage said.

"Are you sure?"

Gage angrily wiped at drops of rain trailing down his face. "I'm sure." It wasn't like he was going to fall asleep any time soon. Every bit of his body ached.

"Very well." Sir Wick shifted on the wet ground to lie against his saddle. "Wake me when you're ready to trade."

Gage stared into the forest, listening for any threat. The thrashing of the trees became a rhythmic noise, and the darkness became a numbing void. Gage let his body sink against his own saddle. He lay with one hand holding his cloak closed and the other hand ready to shake Sir Wick awake, since he was the only one with a weapon.

Somewhere nearby a branch cracked. Instantly alert, Gage sat up. A dark form came rushing through the undergrowth toward them. He hollered and grabbed Sir Wick's arm.

29

"Be careful with that!" Rhonalyn snapped. The servant, who had just heaved a trunk up into the back of the wagon, cringed. Instead of shoving the chest the rest of the way forward, as Rhonalyn suspected he'd have done a moment before, he picked it up and gently placed it at the front of the wagon.

Clearly, none of the servants had expected her to be there at dawn overseeing the last of the loading, nor did they have any idea the value of the items within the trunks. Rhonalyn had packed them herself in the privacy of her chambers. They were each full of the items she intended to use to impress King Strephon. "If anything in there is broken, I will hold you responsible."

The color drained from the man's face. "Yes, Your Royal Highness."

Rhonalyn turned, her maroon skirt swirling around her riding boots. "Marshal, don't forget to have my other two personal trunks brought from the hall. And for goodness' sake, make sure everything is covered so that it is not damaged by mud or water on the way."

"I will indeed, Your Royal Highness," the marshal answered.

Rhonalyn inspected the royal guard gathering with their horses, then glanced toward the two kitchen attendants loading a wagon with food freshly packed that morning. Soon they would be ready to depart. They would travel first to Indomitus, then into Delkara. So far, no one except her father knew their route or that Nikledon was their final destination.

She and he had thoroughly discussed the risks of the journey and decided it was best to keep her travel plans secret until she was within her entourage and on the way there. She and her father had also decided that she would travel lightly and swiftly with the best of their best, fifteen knights and twenty men-at-arms of the royal guard.

A seasoned, level-headed warrior named Baron Philip was the guards' commander. His right hand was Sir Nolan, one of Rhonalyn's cousins. Ten years older than her, married, and as dependable as the seasons, Nolan was third eldest son of her father's brother. Also within the company of knights was her cousin Erwyn, the twenty-three-year-old son of her mother's sister. He was as shrewd as Rhonalyn was, though she'd have never admitted that to him. She had entrusted to him the care of the destrier she intended to show off and hopefully trade to Strephon, for Wyn rode well and liked to make an impression.

Many a girl had tried claiming Wyn's affection, but he danced around most of them, and to Rhonalyn's amusement, scared off the rest by loosing his peregrine falcon to hunt in front of them.

Rhonalyn herself owned three falcons, one owl, and an eagle and loved watching them swoop across a field to hammer their prey or dive from the sky to strike in midair. But she had quickly learned she was not like most girls in this regard. Her mother had had no stomach for the hunt, none of her ladies-in-waiting liked hawking, and as it turned out, most men were uncomfortable with the fact that she loved it. But not Wyn, he was not intimidated by her. Growing up, they had spent many a glorious afternoon flying their birds together.

Rhonalyn had always felt a sort of kinship with the fierce, beautiful creatures who did what they were born to do with a skill no one quite understood. Out of all of them, Eagles were her favorite. Adult eagles were unrivaled and almost never killed by another animal.

But everything had a weakness. Even the smallest thieves could raid an eagle's unprotected nest. A lesson Rhonalyn now understood all too well.

She welcomed having their best guardsmen traveling with her. And, if given the chance, she'd happily utilize their force to seize the treacherous vermin raiding her kingdom. But first things first; she needed to arrive in Nikledon with her goods intact and succeed in her business with Strephon.

She had never actually traveled farther into Delkara than Nikor Harbor. Her father hadn't done so in years, and he had never been to Nikledon. He had found her a map of the area and a messenger who had carried letters into Delkara and knew the terrain, but since Rhonalyn did not dare question the man about their journey until they were underway, the unknowns of the trip continued to haunt her.

How long would it take to reach Nikledon? Should they have left earlier? Would they be able to make it there and back on the supplies they were taking?

Financially, she did not want to have to spend their limited coin to replenish supplies in Delkara. She'd rather save it for other possible expenses, like inns. But would there be towns with good inns along the way? Or would she have to sleep in a pitched pavilion? She shuddered at the thought.

Being outdoors after dark was all well and good as long as it was at the top of a tower staring up at the glowing moon or walking along the battlements watching the first stars come awake. But sleeping at ground level with nothing but a pavilion's canvas wall between her and everything beyond was a situation she adamantly sought to avoid.

At the same time, sleeping in some smelly, ramshackle inn was also unacceptable to her in terms of comfort and appearance. She sincerely hoped King Strephon's kingdom was as well off as its bustling harbor suggested and thus able to provide quality accommodations throughout its land.

Rhonalyn swept back inside the castle. "Aisley?"

The child jumped at her voice, then turned and curtsied. "Aye, Princess Rhonalyn?" Aisley had been chatting with the two maidservants who would be accompanying them.

"You placed the last items you needed within your trunk before it was fetched down by the attendants, did you not?"

Dressed in a practical yet pretty blue dress with her blond hair collected back in a silver net, the girl nodded. "Aye, Your Royal Highness. I even have my shoes on." She slid her right foot out from under her gown to reveal her new dark-brown boots.

Rhonalyn couldn't help but smile. "Good. Then we shall have no delays when it is time to mount and ride out."

The girl's eyes widened. "You mean we shall travel on horseback and not stuck in the carriage?" Aisley sounded truly thrilled by the possibility.

"Aye, for at least parts of the journey." Rhonalyn preferred the freedom and control of riding her own mount, but she thought it wise to have the ability to be safely enclosed within a carriage if necessary. A carriage was also more fitting for their arrival in Nikledon.

Aisley clapped her hands and turned delightedly to the maidservants to express her excitement.

Rhonalyn had debated long and hard over which of her ladies-in-waiting to bring with her and had initially intended to leave Aisley behind. But in the end she had chosen Aisley and none of the others, for she realized she did not want King Strephon distracted by her retinue but rather focused solely on her and the business they were meeting to discuss. Still, it was advantageous to have at least one female companion who understood the noblemen's tongue, particularly someone no one would give much thought to, who could mingle and listen to what was being said beyond the negotiation table.

The only problem was that despite how smart and capable Aisley was, she didn't care about the impressions she made on others, was not ambitious, and would smile more at a hound than she would at any person. And though ardently obedient to specific instructions, the girl tended to swiftly and freely take liberties wherever instructions were not clearly defined. This exasperated Rhonalyn to no end, but it also intrigued her, for it was the one area in which the girl showed initiative.

Meanwhile, despite exhibiting no desire for a place at court, when asked to give her observations, Aisley could accurately identify who had legitimate power and who did not in any given setting, which made her ideal as a royal companion. Taming her lack of decorum presented a challenge for this role, but Rhonalyn had been working hard to teach the girl the importance of appearance and propriety, and she was making progress. Thankfully, there would be time on the way to further instruct the child, for there would be little else to occupy them on the journey.

Returning outside, Rhonalyn watched the marshal confirm the last wagon was acceptably covered. Meanwhile, across the castle's courtyard near the royal guard, her father stood speaking with Baron Philip.

Rhonalyn inhaled a slow breath. Her father still had no idea what she planned to offer Strephon. He had, however, given her his permission to solve the problem. Besides, he had failed to mention what he had first tried as a solution. Therefore, they would be even in their deception, except that her actions would accomplish the task, whereas his had only resulted in more loss.

    She felt through her skirt to a hidden pocket and coiled her fingers around one of the remaining coins from her mother's collection. It was her reminder of everything she was striving to attain by meeting with King Strephon. She slid her fingers over the surface of the thick coin. She could feel the outline of the ram's head and knew by heart the Latin words stamped in a circle on its underside. Pressing her hand flat over the gold coin, she smoothed her skirt once more and headed down the castle steps. She would bring prosperity back to her kingdom no matter what.

30

Gage's eyes drifted closed in the daylight, and his head bobbed with Athalos's stride.

"Hey, stay awake." Sir Wick's voice yanked him out of the lulling embrace of his exhaustion.

He groaned, wanting so badly to snap back that sleep was important and that maybe Sir Wick should let him get some, particularly since it was daylight now and there were no badgers around to scare him half to death. But he knew they couldn't afford the delay, so he forced himself back to wakefulness.

Hours earlier they had realized it was morning only because the darkness of the storm had lessened along with its force. Crawling out from under the soggy pine branches, they had saddled their wet mounts and continued working their way miserably along the path through the forest.

Shivering and hungry, they had trekked on and on. The rain stopped, and finally the path met with a wider road. They could not see Delipp, but a scowling trader with a bundle of goods on his boney back told them Delipp was behind them and that they were headed toward Duvall.

Grateful they were going the right direction and that they could ride their horses again, they wearily trotted onward. They'd anticipated at least receiving a meal at the abbey where Sir Wick and Brother

Ephraim had stayed, but the farther they rode the more Gage began to suspect they had somehow traveled past the abbey. Whether by means of the path they had taken or simply because they had missed spotting the trail turning to the abbey, neither of them knew for certain. They had argued briefly and heatedly about it, and Gage had concluded he was not the only one who was grumpy, tired, and hungry. The only good thing about their night in the woods was that they had seen nothing of the soldiers from Nikledon.

Eventually, they came upon a village and sought anyone willing to sell them food. A woman agreed to allow them to purchase the last of her barley bread, but she charged a steep price. Sir Wick attempted to barter with her, but she wouldn't budge, saying food was hard to come by, and she wasn't about to see her children go hungry for the sake of two dirty travelers. So, they paid what she asked, drank water from the village well, and continued on their way, splitting the bread and a handful of peas they had gotten from another villager.

The measly meal blunted the sharpness of Gage's hunger but left his stomach growling and his hands shaky. His clothes were damp and chafing, his wound ached, and his body longed for rest. In his mind everything stolen from him and heaped upon him in the last year intermingled in livid complaints and fierce anger. He directed much of it at Manton, another part at Sir Jarret, and other portions he dumped on himself, God, and everyone in between.

The sun peeked out, but he was too lost in his stewing to notice. Then his exhaustion took over completely, and he started contemplating what it would be like to sleep for a week on a soft, dry bed. That's when Sir Wick's "Stake awake" had yanked him back.

"How much farther do you think?" Gage asked, sounding more cross than he intended.

"I don't know," Sir Wick said dully. "It's past midday, I think, but who knows what time we actually started traveling this morning. Probably we should pick up speed again if we hope to make Duvall before dark."

Gage scrubbed a hand over his face, nodded, and nudged Athalos faster. His body hated the effort it took to sit a trot, but he overrode its protests.

It began to rain again. Hunched beneath their cloaks, they trotted by meadows with sheep and cattle until they came upon a village that Sir Wick said looked familiar. They got a decent meal there, ate it swiftly, and learned it was less than a half day's journey on foot to Duvall.

Back on the road, they alternated their riding speed the rest of the afternoon. It stopped raining, but gray clouds remained overhead. Gage was beginning to wonder how much longer he could keep his chilled body awake when he noted the thinning of the trees ahead and the beginning of fields. He stopped Athalos and stared at the distant walls and busy, curved barbican of Duvall. Hope and fear gripped him.

"I think it's time I change back into my surcoat," Sir Wick said.

Gage's stomach knotted. If soldiers from Nikledon were waiting in the half-moon barbican between Duvall's double gates, they'd be looking for a knight and a commoner. At the same time, regardless of who was at the gate, if they tried to travel as two commoners, they and their bags might be searched and his mark and Sir Wick's armor found. "What if Drake or Radnor are already here? The risk—"

"If the people of Delipp can figure out there are soldiers from Nikledon inside their city, commoners leaving Duvall should be able to tell us the same thing," Sir Wick said. "If the soldiers arrived before us, we will go to Maneo instead."

It was a simple and sensible solution, but still Gage felt uneasy.

They waited in the tree line for travelers from the city to reach them, which didn't take long. They tried several approaches to asking about Nikledon soldiers being in the city. Their questions produced suspicious looks and were answered hurriedly, as if people were afraid the two of them were looking for trouble rather than trying to avoid it. As far as they could learn no soldiers from Nikledon had been seen in the city.

"Duvall to Awnquera it is then," Sir Wick said, then disappeared into the woods to change his clothes. He returned looking again like a knight of the White Fortress.

They left the forest's edge and rode for Duvall's barbican. Gage kept his face angled toward the ground and positioned Athalos close behind Sir Wick's mount. He did not want to be recognized as Gabe or Gage since Duvall was one of the few places in Delkara where people might actually recognize him as Prince Gage of Edelmar.

They merged with others along the road to the gate. Voices chatted and bartered around them. Gage's downturned gaze passed over sets of bare feet, the wares of sellers who had laid out their goods along the roadway, and then the paving stones of the entrance through the barbican's thick walls. Once in the open again, Sir Wick's mount stopped in front of him, and Gage briefly glanced up. They were past the first gate, trapped now within the walled, half-moon area between the barbican and the city's second gate. If anything went wrong, the guards behind them, who'd let them ride unhindered through the first gate, would make sure they couldn't ride back out.

The good news was there were no soldiers in blue-and-green tabards, and the gate ahead was open. Two guardsmen with crossed lances currently blocked the way to it, but they seemed to be letting through all those the other guards sent their way from the line of people waiting with carts, bundles, and animals.

The first time Gage had entered Duvall was in his father's retinue as a child. The royal standard of Edelmar had been conveyed before them by dozens of knights, and every guard and commoner within the area had stood aside for them. He had felt proud and important. Now he just hoped no one glanced at him twice.

"You there, knight," a husky voice called out. "Come forward."

Sir Wick's mount circled the crowd, and Gage kept Athalos close beside the animal's flank.

"You must be the White Fortress knight everyone has been talking about around here."

Gage glanced sharply at the guard, his heart pounding.

"I...don't know what you mean," Sir Wick said.

"Really?" The guard frowned. "They've all been talking about a White Fortress knight who came through here with a monk a few days back. They were headed for some abbey. I figured you were him."

Gage flicked his gaze back down and breathed again.

"Oh." Sir Wick sounded just as relieved. "Yes, that was me."

"Ah, well, I see you aren't returning to Edelmar empty handed."

"No, I'm not."

"He a gift from the abbey or a return?" a different voice asked with amusement. Several of the other soldiers laughed. Gage's skin prickled, and heat filled his face. Being talked about like he was more of a belonging than a person was not an experience he was accustomed to.

"He is none of your business," Sir Wick said sharply.

His tone made Gage's heart pound. The last thing they needed was to make more enemies.

"You're right," the husky-voiced guard said, "but there's no need to take offense. As a knight of the White Fortress surely you know what it is like for men on guard duty. Curiosity and a sense of humor are our only defense against boredom."

Sir Wick's tone eased. "I do know, but daylight is disappearing, and I've orders to attend to and a city yet to cross."

"Well then, we shall not delay you further." The guard raised his voice. "Let the knight through!"

"Thank you." Sir Wick kicked his mount forward.

Hoping the command included him as well, Gage urged Athalos to follow Sir Wick's horse. The two guards of the second gate withdrew their lances and stepped aside.

Head still down and heart racing, Gage heard an angry comment murmured by one of the guard behind them. "Yes, go, guard of the White Fortress, for we'd not wish to delay a knight of Edelmar."

The tone of the man's voice caught Gage's attention, but a moment later, winding through the people and wagons in Duvall's darkening streets, he forgot any thought he had of the guards behind.

31

Shop owners in Duvall were already pulling in their goods and closing up their street level windows. Gage's stomach knotted. What if the gate to the bridge crossing from Duvall to Awnquera was already shut?

He was contemplating this horrid possibility and, in his exhaustion, trying to figure out whether or not they were yet more than halfway across the city, when a herald's voice somewhere nearby yelled, "Make way!"

Gage heard the hoofbeats but couldn't tell which direction they were coming from. "Sir Wick?"

"I hear them." The knight's tone had risen a notch.

"Make way for Baron Hewitt!" the herald hollered. Around them, the people still out and about in the dusk hastened to the sides of the street.

"We have to get out of here," Gage murmured. Alone he might have avoided being noticed, but Sir Wick's surcoat wouldn't be overlooked. And of all the Delkaran lords, Hewitt and his men had seen the most of him as Prince Gage.

"There's an alley just past that building," Sir Wick said, pointing. "Go."

Spotting the opening between shops, Gage swung Athalos into it, but the lane was narrower than it had looked. A second building behind the first jutted out into the space, reducing the distance between the building's walls to barely wide enough for Athalos to pass between them. There wasn't time or room to dismount. Athalos plowed forward, and Gage attempted to pull up his legs.

He managed to get his right foot clear, but his left boot caught hard against the wall. He bit his tongue and twisted his foot up and free. He and Athalos burst out the other side of the alley onto a wider street. He hissed in a breath and lowered his knees from inside his elbows. Two maidens carrying baskets of laundry shook their heads and giggled at him.

Sir Wick scraped out of the alley behind him and exhaled as if he'd held his breath to get through the opening. "That was close," he said.

"You're telling me." Gage wiggled his throbbing ankle to make sure his foot still worked, then glanced back through the alley. Two soldiers passed by the other end, followed by a herald, and then someone in dark colors that did not match Duvall's coat-of-arms. Almost positive it was the blue and green of Nikledon, Gage didn't wait to see more. He urged Athalos away from the opening. "We need to get over that bridge, now."

Sir Wick nodded. "There's the top of the gate's towers over there. If we keep going this direction, we should be able to work our way there."

Three turns and another alley later, they could see ahead through Duvall's gate to the first part of the border bridge. Built before the division of the three kingdoms, the long bridge was constructed of masoned stones that spanned the river via five magnificent arches. Twin towers, gates, and drawbridges secured both ends of it and were manned by gatemen and guards of the respective cities.

Two guards were half in the doorway of one of the towers, lighting torches. The other three guards were standing outside the gate on the bridge. They seemed to be inspecting the drawbridge's chains and arguing over something involving the gate.

Gage was pretty sure he didn't know any of them, but it was hard to be positive in the dim light.

Sir Wick kicked his mount past the two soldiers, who were distracted with their torches, and rode up to the three guards on the drawbridge above the rushing river. Trailing behind him, Gage could see through the archway and down the bridge. The gate on Awnquera's side was already closed. Suddenly feeling lightheaded, he pulled Athalos to a stop. They were too late.

The soldiers Sir Wick spoke with gestured to Awnquera's gate and shook their heads. Gage wanted to scream. The rooftops of Awnquera were in sight, but it wasn't going to matter. He could see Edelmar, but he couldn't get there. His stomach knotted, and exhaustion and fear began to overheat his body.

The bridge had been their best chance, but all they could do now was retreat from it. If Nikledon soldiers were in the city, by the time both gates were open in the morning, it would likely be too late for them to safely cross. They'd be trapped in Duvall. The only possible escape was if they could conceal themselves and find a different way out of the city.

Impatiently, he waited for Sir Wick to ride back and tell him what he already knew, but the knight kept talking with the guards. Gage shifted on Athalos. The last thing they needed was to stay in the open. But still, Sir Wick spoke and pointed forcefully toward Awnquera's gate. Gage debated whether or not to ride forward and fetch the knight. No servant would do such a thing. But how long did he dare wait? Gage clenched his fingers, and Athalos sidestepped beneath him.

Sir Wick handed the guards something, turned in his saddle, and waved for Gage to come. Confused but eager to speak with him, Gage trotted Athalos toward the gate.

A guard stepped in his way, the flame of his torch whooshing. "Where do you think you're going?"

Athalos leapt sideways and tried to bolt back the way they'd come. Gage clenched his legs around the horse's sides and hauled on the reins. Forcing Athalos in a circle, he managed to stop the animal. Breathing hard, he leaned over Athalos's trembling neck.

The guard drew his sword. "I asked you a question."

Pushing himself upright, Gage shakily gestured after Sir Wick, who was astoundingly headed across the bridge toward Awnquera. "I'm...I'm going to Edelmar."

The guard snorted. "To pass through this gate, you must pay a bridge toll and prove that you're a free man." He pointed his sword at him. "Show me your wrists and what's in your purse, and then I'll decide whether to let you go or not. If you've proof you've the right and means to cross this bridge, I'll assume you acted in ignorance and allow you to return in the morning when you can cross. But if I'm right and you've no money, then you and I will have a very different conversation."

The second torch-wielding guard scooped up a spear. Gage's heart raced. He knew he couldn't comply with their request, but he didn't know whether to rush after Sir Wick or flee back into Duvall. Either way would trap him between walls and the guards, but what else could he do?

"Well?" the guard said. "Not so eager anymore, hmm?"

The second guard moved around behind Gage.

Anxiety squeezed the air from Gage's lungs. Dread and exhaustion dismantled the last shreds of hope he'd had of making it back to

Edelmar. His chest and shoulder hurt, and his head ached. He tried to focus on finding some means of saving himself, but it was like he was falling down some dark hole. His sight narrowed, and his hearing took on a ringing hollowness.

"What's going on here?" Sir Wick's voice yanked him back from his descent into darkness. Clutching his saddle, Gage struggled to breathe and clear the haze from his vision.

"That's exactly what I'd like to know," one of the guards Sir Wick had been talking to said as he marched back through the gate.

"This peasant was trying to make a run for it across the bridge," the torch-wielding guard explained.

"This peasant? You mean the servant of this Edelmarian knight who just paid tolls for the both of them to ride to Awnquera?" The older guard's tone of ridicule shifted to a strident rebuke. "Maybe if you were paying more attention while lighting torches you'd have noticed a knight riding through the gate and not just his servant."

The guard scowled. "They still can't go across. Awnquera's gate is closed, and ours is only open because of a warped timber."

"This knight says they'll open Awnquera's gate for him," the old guard replied.

A tendril of hope wove its way back into Gage's body. Why hadn't he thought of that? It was Edelmar after all, and Sir Wick was a border guard.

"He'll not make it through."

"Well, he's made a deal with us. If they don't let him and his servant in, we get to divide their tolls amongst ourselves, and he'll pay again to cross tomorrow when the gate is open."

The torch-wielding guard stepped aside. "Fine, let him attempt it."

Elated and lightheaded, Gage fought to drag in air. This could be the only chance they got to get to Awnquera, particularly if these same guards discovered the following day that he and Sir Wick were wanted by Nikledon soldiers.

Sir Wick spun his mount and rode again through the gate. Gage loosed his reins for Athalos to follow him out onto Duvall's drawbridge and clutched his saddle. The torch-wielding guard eyed him scornfully, and the dark hole threatened to retake Gage. He fought to keep his senses obedient to his command and his body steady, but he could feel the battle carving away at his strength. The harder he fought, the more his body trembled. Feeling both hot and cold, he knew he was pushing himself beyond his limits just as Brother Sholan had warned him against, but at the moment he couldn't afford not to. He had to get to Awnquera.

He vaguely heard the rushing water below and the airy sound of Athalos's hooves thudding across the wood spanning the river. His concentration suddenly spiraled downward, and his sweating body wavered sideways.

He clutched all the tighter to his saddle, but he wasn't sure his hands and legs were even doing what he was telling them to do. His racing heart was all he could fully feel. Even in his growing weariness, he knew the drawbridge had no edges to catch him if he came off Athalos.

The clack of solid rock beneath the animal's feet a moment later reassured him he was at least no longer on the drawbridge, but still there remained ahead the rest of the bridge and Awnquera's closed gate.

He tried to convince his mind not to give up, but even breathing felt like too much work. He let his eyes drift closed. The clip-clop of

Athalos's hooves faded into the sound of the river rushing beneath the bridge.

He felt water surround him chilling him to the bone and squeezing the air from his lungs. He was trying so hard to hold onto Novia and the branch, but he was so tired. He couldn't fight any more. He wanted to save her, but the water was too strong. He needed to let go.

"Gage!" Sir Wick's sharp voice yanked at him. "Stay with me! Do you hear me? We're almost there."

Gage attempted to do as the knight instructed, but he was so very weary.

32

WICK GLANCED BACK at Prince Gage once more, then kicked his horse into a canter. His mount's hooves clattered over the last of the stone bridge and thundered across Awnquera's drawbridge. Reining to a fast stop, Wick threw himself off the animal and pounded a fist against the small wicket door in Awnquera's gate. "Open up!"

He had hoped once they'd left Duvall's guards behind that Prince Gage would revive like he'd done in Nikledon, but His Highness still looked ready to tumble from his horse and seemed to be fighting to breathe. Wick hammered on the gate again.

He swallowed hard. When Prince Haaken had ordered him to ride to Saint Jerome's Abbey to bring Prince Gage back, this was not how he'd pictured returning with him to Edelmar. He kept one eye on His Highness, ready to bolt back to catch him if he started to fall from his horse, and the other eye on the cracks around the wicket gate. So far there was no sign of any light beyond its timbers. He banged harder.

He was too close to see up to the window of the guard tower where he'd earlier spotted a candle burning. Prince Gage's horse thudded slowly forward onto the drawbridge behind him and then stopped. Amazingly, Prince Gage was still on the animal, but there was no telling how much longer that would last. Wick again beat at the door, wishing he could break it down. "Open up!"

Metal scraped, and a patch of light appeared at the top of the wicket door where a window was thrust aside by someone holding a candle. "You there," the porter snapped, "whoever's pounding. It's past dusk. This gate's closed. Go back to Duvall."

The man's voice was the best sound Wick had heard all day. "Listen to me. I am Sir Wick of the White Fortress of Edelmar. I've with me an injured member of His Highness's retinue and urgent news for Prince Haaken."

The porter was silent for a moment before responding. "How do I know you speak the truth?"

"Use your eyes, man! I wear the surcoat of the White Fortress, and my companion is about to topple off his horse. If you need yet further proof, go to the house of Baron Elmon, and fetch His Royal Highness. He can verify who I am and that you have indeed left me standing outside Awnquera's gate!"

"All right already. No need to take my head off. You'd be asking questions too if you had someone pounding on the White Fortress's gate after dusk. Now back up. I'll let you in." The porter closed the window.

Wick led his horse out of the way. A moment later one side of Awnquera's gate swung outward with a low moan. Prince Gage's horse snorted and backed up, causing His Highness's body to sway precariously. Abandoning his own horse, Wick headed for Prince Gage's mount, intending to steady His Highness. The mount laid back its ears. Wick slowed his approach to let the animal get used to him being there, then reached for Prince Gage. The horse's head swung around. Wick leapt backward, barely avoiding its teeth.

"You coming or not?" the porter called. "I'm not leaving this gate open all night."

"Just give me a moment!" Wick yelled back, then turned back to the stupid beast. "Look here, horse, if you won't let me help him, then the least you can do is carry him through the gate without dropping him." He seized his own horse's bridle and led the way into Awnquera.

Prince Gage's horse stayed where he was on the drawbridge.

Growling in frustration, Wick left his mount with the porter and headed back onto the bridge. He was desperate enough to consider spooking the animal through the gate, but he didn't want to risk a sudden movement that might cause Prince Gage to topple out of his saddle. "Gabe, I need you to dismount or get your horse to walk on. You hear me?"

Prince Gage's eyes fluttered open. His body sagged farther forward, and he murmured something too quiet to hear. His horse lumbered forward. Retreating out of its way, Wick watched in amazement as the animal trekked through the gate and stopped beside his own mount in the light of a brazier the porter had just lit. Sighing in relief, Wick followed.

Two guards came running up to the porter. "You signaled?"

"Yes." The porter closed the gate. "I need the two of you to go with this knight to Baron Elmon's manor and confirm that he and this servant are indeed expected there."

"Sir Wick." Prince Gage's voice was barely audible. "I can't… ride…any…farther." His Highness's foot slid from his stirrup, and he leaned all the way forward in his saddle.

Realizing too late what he was doing, Wick lunged forward and intervened in Prince Gage's free-fall descent from his mount by catching him under his arms. He grunted at the weight and stumbled backward. Thankfully, the horse sidestepped and didn't come at him. He dragged Prince Gage away from the animal until he figured he was at a safe distance, then glanced about for help. The two guards hung back. "Well, don't just stand there," Wick snapped, "lend me a hand."

※

THE RATTLE OF a wagon pulled Gage back to wakefulness. His body was hot, his head ached, and his wound felt like it had been ripped open again, but he was pretty sure they were over the border, which was what mattered. "Sir Wick?"

He felt someone shift beside him, then heard the knight's voice. "I'm here. Just rest. We're almost to Baron Elmon's manor."

"Rest," Gage murmured. "Rest is good." He let his head rock again with the wagon's motion.

He was about to drift back to sleep when he heard Sir Wick mutter, "Your brother's going to kill me for bringing you back in this condition."

Too exhausted to move but aware enough to talk, Gage mumbled back, "It'll be me he kills, not you. Besides, I'm fine. Just in need of sleep."

"You're not fine," Sir Wick said. "You're hot to the touch and bleeding through your tunic."

Startled by this news, Gage opened his eyes. In the light of the lantern that Sir Wick held, he could see the knight's concerned gaze. He glanced down at the left side of his chest and noted a red stain saturating his tunic. Beneath it was the stinging pain he'd already been feeling. It hurt, but nothing like when Felix had first cut him. "It's not that bad."

"Well, let's hope your brother agrees because we're turning into the manor now."

Gage glanced past the lantern's light and saw the stone walls and thick tree cover of the courtyard to his uncle's home. The wagon pulled to a stop. There was a hurried rush of voices, people asking questions and receiving explanations, then Haaken's strident tone pushed past all else. "Sir Wick? Where is he?"

The knight held up his lantern. "Here, Your Royal Highness. He is right here."

Torches drew near the wagon. "Gage!" Haaken's voice was startled and angry. "What in heaven's name, Sir Wick?" Haaken hoisted himself up into the wagon.

Gage took in the sight of his brother, barefoot, in an intricate green tunic, no crown on his head, his light-brown hair loose about his shoulders, and his face full of emotion. Even their mother couldn't have looked more concerned than Haaken did at that moment. "Verily, I am all right, Haaken," he said in the noblemen's tongue, attempting to reassure him.

"If you were all right, you would be on a horse, not in the back of a wagon," Haaken replied, glaring at Sir Wick.

"Prithee, do not blame him." Gage's words slurred in his tiredness. "This is not Sir Wick's fault. It was Felix's doing."

"Felix?"

"Aye, he and I fought. I won, and then I lost, and then Athalos killed him."

Confusion and concern filled Haaken's face. "Sir Wick, how long has he been like this?"

Gage rolled his eyes toward Sir Wick. "Tell him I am fine."

The knight stared at him. "Actually, I am not sure that you are."

Gage scowled at him.

Haaken motioned to Sir Wick. "Help me get him inside."

33

Gage woke under a blanket in a soft canopy bed. He blinked at the bright sunlight creating a glowing square across a thick rug splayed on the room's floor. He rolled onto his back. The previous night's events filled his mind. He was in his uncle's home as Prince Gage. He was safe, so long as no one else discovered his secret. At that thought he sat bolt upright and looked down at his wrists. He exhaled in relief. He still wore the plain vambraces Brother Sholan had given him. He touched the leather.

"You were adamant last night that they not be taken off and were too tired to be reasoned with, so we left them on," Haaken explained in the noblemen's tongue.

Gage glanced at where his brother leaned against the wall beside the room's carved door. He did recall telling him forcefully not to remove them while willingly allowing his bloody tunic to be stripped off and his chest wound bandaged again. "How long have I been asleep?"

"About ten hours. You stirred when I entered." Haaken gestured to the end of the bed. "Aunt Mildred found you some clothes. Uncle is about your size, so they are likely his."

Gage tugged the pile toward himself. On top was a long dark-blue tunic with tan trim embroidered with crimson thread. With it was a matching woven belt and a pair of hose. Gage pulled the tunic over his head and was happy to find that the ache of his wound had lessened.

He climbed out of bed to finish dressing, then pulled on his own boots. He rose from doing so, expecting to feel lightheaded but stood steadily on his feet. He adjusted the vambraces on his wrists and smiled at Haaken. "It's amazing what a full night of sleep in a soft bed can do for one's health. I feel better than I have in weeks."

Frowning, Haaken crossed the room toward him. "From the look of that wound, I would think you could use a few more days in bed."

Gage spread his hand over the injury. The blood had come from where the scab at the end of the cut had been scuffed off. "Believe me, I have rested enough. Besides, it's nothing worse now than what I used to receive training with swords."

"Now that it is almost fully healed, you mean?" Haaken said pointedly. "Because by Brother Ephraim's account and the look of that scar, it was clearly a lot worse a week or two ago. Any deeper and you might not have survived."

Knowing he almost hadn't survived, Gage shifted. "Prithee, do you always have to evaluate my injuries?" He spoke teasingly but hoped Haaken would take the hint and back off.

"When they are life-threatening, take place in a neighboring kingdom, and are apparently inflicted by the hand of a wanted man, aye. I would say my assessment is more than fair. Particularly considering you previously claimed your intention was to travel quietly as a buyer and seller of mounts, not as a knight errant."

Gage cringed and held up his hands. "I concede your point. And I promise you I was pursuing my stated intention. Finding Felix and almost getting killed by him was never part of my plan."

"Then it really was Felix who did this to you?"

"Aye. I crossed paths with him accidentally after the fair in Nikledon, and instead of running him through when I had the chance, I chose to bring him to justice." Gage scoffed. "A lot of good it did me. He'd have gotten away too had he not tried to flee on my horse. Athalos threw him and killed him."

"Having met your horse at Einhart and again last night, I am not surprised. In fact, Brother Ephraim's description of the animal was how I was confident it was you they had found in the woods. Your horse is not the sort one can sell or steal."

Gage cringed. "Nay, he is not."

"He also followed you here last night from Awnquera's gate. Uncle's porter and marshal spent a good half hour fighting with him but finally managed to drive him into a pen."

"Was anyone injured?"

"Nay."

Gage exhaled. "Good. Athalos is not a mean animal, just self-protective, which is what Felix failed to take into account. And in truth it was not Athalos throwing him that actually killed him. When Felix fell, he rolled off the edge of a ravine."

"I take it then it is not Felix we should be attempting to find at Veiroot?" Haaken said.

"Nay, but Felix was there, and he boasted to me about a new force he had gathered and sent ahead of him. His exact words were, 'We will bring Edelmar to her knees one way or another.' Thus, prithee, tell me you have not waited until now to take any action. If the rebels have already left Veiroot, I doubt we will find them again until they attack."

"Well, as seems to be your habit of late, your letter was too cryptic for me to confidently interpret it. I didn't know for certain if it was the rebels who were actually at Veiroot or simply Felix and Lady

Natriece and they knew where the rebels were." Haaken shrugged. "But I figured anyone coming and going from Veiroot Fortress could be suspect. Therefore, I decided keeping a distance and allowing people to leave was something that could be used to our advantage."

"What do you mean?"

"Come, I will show you," Haaken said. "But first, let us get you some food, and I would like an explanation of your exploits in Delkara and how you came across Lady Natriece and the traveler, Manton."

Gage nodded. He would tell Haaken all about Manton, just not what had happened after they'd parted ways. Gage touched his right vambrace. Part of him wanted to tell Haaken everything, because he knew Haaken would help. But he also knew how Haaken would react to the news. He had no desire to face that conversation or the legal entanglement that would follow. Besides, he had made their father a promise, and he would keep it. He would inform Haaken of what he needed to know and conceal the rest until he could find the actual thieves responsible and bring them himself to King Strephon of Delkara.

34

Standing with Sir Holbird and Sir Renner, Wick studied a map of the three kingdoms spread across a desk in Baron Elmon's study. Though a decent size room, the study felt crowded as the headquarters for Prince Haaken's campaign against Veiroot.

Near a bookshelf in the corner, Prince Haaken's squire and several knights stood listening to Baron Elmon explain battle tactics while helping thumb through books looking for an account of Veiroot that the baron was positive contained a description of the fortress's layout and back entrance. Meanwhile, Sir Adrian and Sir Jocelyn were seated in chairs on either end of a low table sorting through and arranging parchments with lists of names on them that attendants were bringing to them.

Sir Renner tapped the map in front of Wick where a handful of small metal pins had been placed to represent people. "Prince Haaken had every inn and tavern within this area searched for chessboards," he said in the noblemen's tongue. "They found no games with pieces that opened."

"Which seems odd," Sir Holbird said, pointing at the pins, "considering these are the locations of everyone who has left Veiroot's fortress in the last nine days. So, the question is, if not through chessboards or carrier pigeons, how are they communicating with each other?"

Wick frowned at the map. "Mayhap it is like Prince Gage said, and they are using a smuggler to pass along information and supplies. Or it could be that their orders are prearranged." As he stared at the map thinking about Prince Gage, his gaze drifted to Nikledon.

As the newest source of information in the group, he had spent a good part of the night and morning answering and avoiding questions about what he'd learned from Prince Gage. Part of him was thankful for this because it meant he hadn't yet been sent back to the White Fortress. But at the same time, he'd already twice almost mentioned his and Prince Gage's trouble at the inn in Nikledon, which would have led directly to the reason the soldiers had come looking for them. Of all people, why did it have to be him who knew Prince Gage's secret? He ran his hand down his face.

"Are you all right?"

Startled, he glanced at Sir Renner. "Aye. Just tired."

"Mayhap you should have slept the morning away like Prince Gage," Sir Holbird teased.

"Had I known that was an option, I might have done just that."

"As a knight? Never," Sir Renner said with mock seriousness. "It is only acceptable if you are sick, injured, or dead."

"Well, if there is a next time, regardless of it gaining me sleep or not," Sir Wick said, "I have no doubt me being the one bleeding would be far better for my health."

The two knights laughed, and Sir Holbird nodded. "That is likely true."

༺༻

A SHORT TIME later, Prince Haaken entered the study, followed by Prince Gage. Wick bowed along with everyone else. When he straightened, he was relieved to see Prince Gage looked a far cry better than he had the night before. His face had full color again, his gaze was focused, and his movements were confident.

Watching him, Wick realized he felt a sense of ownership in Prince Gage's well-being and a bond with him that was different and stronger than he'd felt in the past. They'd been united by what they'd gone through to make it safely to Edelmar. But the feelings of protectiveness Wick had toward His Highness were also melded with discomfort and anger, because the journey back wasn't the only thing they shared.

In trying to keep Prince Gage's secret, he'd already come far too close to lying to Prince Haaken and to his fellow knights. By itself a secret wasn't a lie, but maintaining a secret often involved resorting to lies, and lies always came with a cost.

Wick had experienced that over and over at the White Fortress. When someone lied and it was revealed or discovered, it did far worse than just temporarily compromise trust. It altered people's perspectives of the person who had lied and made it difficult for anyone to ever have complete confidence in that person again. That was something Wick now struggled with in regard to Prince Gage, even more so since he was now responsible for keeping his secret. Thanks to His Highness, they both had a fine mess on their hands.

Greeting them each by name, Prince Gage joined Prince Haaken at the desk to view the map and motioned to the pins. "I take it these are those you have tracked leaving Veiroot?"

Prince Haaken nodded. "Uncle had a number of men who knew the area and could blend in well. They were the first group chosen. I sent them with pigeons and supplies. They were to watch and report everything they could find in relation to Lord Gregory, Lady Natriece, and Veiroot that might verify the information you provided.

The second batch of men I sent were ordered to follow anyone leaving Veiroot fortress."

"So, both groups have been collecting information?" Prince Gage asked.

"Aye, the first batch discovered that Lord Gregory is hosting visitors, though they have yet to get a full count of them and have been unable to discern whether or not they are connected to Felix."

"What about those who left the fortress and were followed?"

"There is little known there so far," Prince Haaken said. "My thought in having them followed was if they were—"

"Part of Felix's men, they might lead you to other rebels outside the fortress," Prince Gage finished for his brother.

"Exactly." Prince Haaken pointed to the pins spread across the map. "These are the locations of those who have departed the fortress so far. Those tracking them have been instructed to follow closely and note anyone they come in contact with. Meanwhile, those back at Veiroot have been creating lists of all visitors to Veiroot but also of all Lord Gregory's men. Who are they? What are their jobs at the fortress? How well are they armed? Do they have families outside the fortress? What are their weaknesses? Where do their loyalties lie?"

"What about Lady Natriece?" Prince Gage asked.

"She has not been seen outside the fortress."

"She has not been seen at all?" Prince Gage asked, his voice rising. "Or she has not been seen beyond the fortress walls?"

"Nay," Prince Haaken answered, "she was spotted inside the fortress. One of Uncle's men saw her briefly while he was inside the fortress's yard helping deliver goods with a local merchant. But that is as close as we have gotten to her. So, I doubt she is going to be of help to us. Though according to him, she was moving about the fortress freely. Which brings us back to the question, can she actually be trusted? You are absolutely certain her conversation with you was not anticipated by her or the rebels?"

Wick glanced at Prince Gage along with everyone else in the room.

"Like I said, I approached her, and believe me, she had no idea I was at the fair, let alone that I would seek her out and speak to her." Prince Gage proceeded to tell them about discovering his stolen brooch in a seller's booth and tracing it back to Lady Natriece. He explained how she had thought he was one of Felix's men and about the conversation they'd had as a result.

Sir Holbird shook his head in disbelief. "After stealing a brooch that Felix knew Lady Natriece saw you receive as a tournament prize, he gave it to her as a token of his affection?"

Prince Gage nodded. "That is what she told me."

"What a romantic gesture," Sir Jocelyn remarked sarcastically.

"More like a statement of his power," Baron Elmon commented.

They all turned to look at the baron.

"What do you mean?" Sir Renner asked.

Baron Elmon set aside the book he was holding. "Good men woo a woman with affection, but some men do not possess true affection. They lay claim to a woman instead by force of will. In the end, both types of men might possess a wife, but submission and love are two very different things."

Wick's skin crawled. He didn't have any sisters, unlike most of the other knights present, but he figured if he did and someone like Felix took an interest in her, he'd do whatever it took to keep the man away from her. "You would think her father would have intervened on her behalf." Wick observed.

"If what Natriece told me is true," Prince Gage said, "I doubt Lord Gregory would have risked refusing Felix anything that might have also made the rebels his enemies."

"Her father cowers while she spites Felix by selling the brooch he gave her." Prince Haaken sounded amazed. "Either she is braver than any woman I know, despite the den of vipers surrounding her, or she's lying about her role in all of this."

"Either way," Prince Gage said, "the fact remains, the brooch Felix stole was in her possession at Veiroot."

"I agree. It seems we will not know for certain which side she is on until we are inside Veiroot Fortress. Father has made it clear this campaign is ours and that he will support us however we ask. So tell me, is there anything else we need to know or put in place before we make our move?"

35

Careful to keep her dress away from the ash-covered fire grate, Rhonalyn pressed her skirt against the inn's bed and turned to view her crown. "I think it should be higher."

Kendra, one of her maidservants, adjusted the exquisite piece, while Tess held the looking glass Rhonalyn was using to see herself. The room was the largest private space the village inn had, but it still felt suffocatingly small.

Baron Philip stood outside the room's open door. Rhonalyn addressed him in the noblemen's tongue. "Is everything ready? Shall we arrive in Nikledon on time?"

"Aye, if we depart here within the hour, Your Royal Highness. Nikledon should be in sight shortly after midday."

Motioning for Tess to raise the looking glass once more, Rhonalyn nodded at her reflection and told her stomach to stop doing somersaults. They would be there exactly when she'd planned, providing they had no more issues along the way. A wagon wheel had cracked as they were leaving Indomitus, and one of her guard's horses had thrown a shoe on the way to Dinslage. Thankfully, despite these delays, they had still made decent time across Delkara and would have arrived in Nikledon a day ago. But instead of pushing on and arriving early, Rhonalyn had sought a place to stop outside the city, so they would reach Nikledon when expected and only after she had effectively prepared herself and her entourage. "The carriage and wagons are washed?" she asked Baron Philip.

"They were taken care of last night."

"And the men?"

"All bathed with fresh uniforms, clean boots, polished armor, and gleaming weaponry. Just as you requested."

She had only herself left then. She touched the gold-and-diamond crown in her brown hair, then let her hand trail from it to her neck where three strands of gold chain were joined by clusters of amethysts and diamonds. The strands matched her earrings and the gilded embroidery of her dark-purple dress.

Having already seen to Aisley's hair and dress, she'd sent the girl out of the room to make more space. She could only hope the child was staying clean. Smoothing her hands down her skirt, she turned to the baron. "Let us depart then."

Leaving her maids to pack up the last of her things, she followed Baron Philip out of the inn. Her men's tents had been taken down. The wagons were fully loaded—all except for where the last of her trunks would go—and her carriage stood at the ready in the sunlight. Surrounding her, the royal guard tarried with their mounts at hand. In their midst, Aisley stood stroking the nose of the white palfrey she had been riding. To Rhonalyn's satisfaction, she looked very much like a lady in her long-sleeved pale pink dress with her blond hair braided in a crown.

"Your Royal Highness." Baron Philip held out his hand to help her into the carriage.

Rhonalyn took his offer and let her voice float on the wind. "Lady Aisley, it is time to depart."

Turning, the child burst into a run toward her, then blanched at Rhonalyn's frown and slid to a stop. The child recomposed herself and crossed to the carriage in a more lady-like stroll. Baron Philip coughed on a laugh. Rhonalyn looked heavenward and climbed into the carriage.

❦

Another tree branch scraped the side of the carriage, and Rhonalyn turned her fingers into claws. Couldn't King Strephon manage to keep his roads trimmed? She supposed maybe they had been and just grew too fast. They didn't have much tree cover in Keric.

Shoving her irritation away, she returned her focus to Aisley's reading. They had started a new book when they'd left the inn that morning and were now a third of the way through it. The girl struggled to sound out a longer word. Rhonalyn gave her a moment, then supplied the word and its meaning.

Aisley repeated it to herself as Rhonalyn had instructed her to do and then continued through the text.

A short time later there was a tap on the outside of the carriage. "Your Royal Highness, Nikledon is in sight," Baron Philip said.

Rhonalyn pulled back the carriage's curtains. They were passing a large meadow beside the road. Ahead through the trees she could see the city's towers.

"Will the guard unfurl their banners now?" Aisley whispered to Kendra in the commoners' tongue.

Kendra smiled. "That and blow their trumpets."

"They brought trumpets?"

Baron Philip chuckled from where he rode beside them. "Aye, little lady. Her Royal Highness shall be announced in proper Keric style."

Rhonalyn dropped the curtains back in place. She was curious to see Nikledon and its surrounding area, but she preferred to preserve an air of mystery about herself until after meeting with King Strephon. "You will keep silent from here, Lady Aisley."

The child nodded seriously. A moment later though, Aisley's face shone with delight as the resounding announcement of the trumpets filled the carriage.

A company of horsemen thundered toward them soon after, armor jangling. Baron Philip and Sir Nolan exchanged greetings with them. They were King Strephon's knights, come to escort them to the baron of Nikledon's manor.

Rhonalyn's stomach clenched. What would King Strephon be like? Could she really negotiate a deal with him when she knew so little about him? She shoved her clammy fingers under the edge of her skirt. She'd have to. As the future queen of Keric, she couldn't afford to be intimidated by him. She would negotiate with him just as she would anyone else.

Besides, she was just as powerful and important as he was. And if she could not succeed in this way, she would find another way. Failure only came in quitting, something she had no intention of doing.

Distant voices called excitedly in the commoners' tongue. People—likely the serfs out in the fields—were asking each other whose knights and carriage were passing.

Her arrival had caused a stir.

Her knights once more announced her with trumpets. A moment later the carriage pulled to a stop. Rhonalyn lifted her chin and smoothed her skirt.

When Baron Philip opened the carriage door, she placed her hand in his and glided out into the daylight. Flanked by her knights, she stood within the walls of a well-maintained red-roofed manor. Numerous white-washed buildings surrounded the large stone house, which had a broad face and a huge square tower rising from within it.

In front of the house, over a dozen men-at-arms stood at attention. They created a line of blue-and-green tabards behind a lord and lady.

"I present daughter and heir to His Royal Majesty, King Bryant, Her Royal Highness, Princess Rhonalyn of Keric!" Rhonalyn's herald announced in his rich voice. Everyone bowed.

"Baron Selwin and Baroness Juliana of Nikledon bid you welcome, Your Royal Highness," the lord and lady's herald proclaimed.

Dressed in velvet, the baron had decent looks but expressed nothing upon his face, whereas his wife, an exotic-looking beauty, gushed her pleasure.

Rhonalyn glided forward to greet them and in so doing allowed space for Baron Philip to assist Aisley and her maids out of the carriage. "My thanks for your hospitality, Baron Selwin and Baroness Juliana. Prithee, accept this token of my appreciation for your generosity in hosting myself and my retinue." She gestured to Sir Nolan. The knight presented the baron and baroness with a barrel of salt and a small chest containing a beautifully crafted agate saltcellar in a fixture of gold and silver. Meanwhile, Rhonalyn silently repeated their names to herself so that she would remember them later.

"Your Royal Highness." Baron Selwin bowed once more. "His Royal Majesty, King Strephon, sends his apology that he could not be here when you arrived. He had unexpected business to attend to and will return as soon as he can."

"This is an inconvenience, we know, Your Royal Highness," Baroness Juliana added, "but a delay that will mayhap serve you well. It allows you time to take refreshment and rest if you wish." She waved her hand toward the house. "You have no doubt had enough of the outdoors. Prithee, allow me to show you inside."

Though more than a little annoyed that Strephon was not present but grateful for the baroness's womanly intuition, Rhonalyn kept her smile gracious. "Thank you, Lady Juliana."

⁂

Rhonalyn watched Aisley excitedly explore the chamber where they would sleep for the next few days. It was a spacious and elegantly decorated room that claimed the entire third floor of the manor's square tower. Her maidservants had already unpacked most of her things while she had been occupied below being served refreshments by Lady Juliana.

"Princess Rhonalyn, look at the view," Aisley said in awe as she held back the thick curtain, so Rhonalyn could see out.

The lush green of the land around the manor drew Rhonalyn to the window. Trees of all kinds grew between the manor's open fields and the edge of the city of Nikledon. A river flowed beside the manor, disappearing through an arch in the city's wall.

Curiously, Rhonalyn glanced down into the manor's yard. Her wagons were already unloaded and tucked against the side of what she was certain had to be a stable. Sir Erwyn was brushing down the destrier outside the building while servants drifted around him completing various chores.

"Look, horsemen are coming from the city." Aisley pointed. "Do you think it is King Strephon's retinue?"

Rhonalyn observed the party of horsemen galloping along the road. They swept past thick fields being weeded by serfs and then slowed as they approached the manor's gate. Three groups of two knights each filed through the opening, followed by a single tall rider, then the rest entered, again in groups of two. They spread out into the manor's yard, but Rhonalyn kept her eye on the single rider as he dismounted.

No feathers plumed his helmet, no cape adorned his shoulders, and no caparison covered his mount, but a servant immediately took his horse. The rider pulled off his helmet to reveal dark-blond hair. One of his guards reached out to receive his helmet. The man stripped off his gauntlets next, glanced at the prancing destrier Sir Erwyn held, then headed for the manor's main house. Baron Selwin met him halfway there, bowed, then fell in step beside him.

"Well, Lady Aisley, is King Strephon below or not?"

"He must be," the girl answered.

"Why?"

"Because the baron bowed to the man who just arrived, and the man did not bow back."

Rhonalyn nodded her approval of the child's observation. King Strephon had indeed arrived, though it was not exactly the kingly entrance she had expected. And now she must decide. Should she descend immediately to meet him or wait to be summoned?

Making a surprise entrance within her own castle where she knew the terrain had simply been a matter of timing. Here she might wander about and come upon him accidentally or not at all. She didn't like the thought of being summoned by him any better, but the idea of him having to seek her out and await her arrival did hold a certain appeal. She made her decision. Better to wait and capitalize on making an entrance where she would have his full attention.

36

Rhonalyn stood in the center of her room, forcing herself not to pace. Her maidservants had redone her hair, brushed out her dress, and were now fidgeting at the edges of the room. Meanwhile, Aisley looked bored to tears. Rhonalyn spoke. "Aisley, you may read aloud more from the book we started this morning."

The child's shoulders slumped as she rose to comply, but just then a knock sounded at the door, followed by Baron Philip's voice. "Your Royal Highness, King Strephon of Delkara sends his welcome and invites you to meet with him before the evening meal."

Rhonalyn sighed in relief and motioned. "Tess."

The maidservant hurried to unbolt the door.

Baron Philip bowed along with Sir Nolan.

Burying her vexation at Strephon, Rhonalyn allowed the weight of her necklace and crown, the smoothness of her skirt, and the gentle clinking of her dangling diamond-and-amethyst earrings to sooth her emotions. She was more than ready. "See me to him."

Baron Philip led the way through the manor house. As they went, they acquired six more of her guard and were met by Baron Selwin. He showed them to a doorway flanked by two royal knights whose bucklers and red tabards bore the coat-of-arms of Delkara—the crowned golden lion with one paw resting upon the top edge of a shield and the other paw resting upon the hilt of a sword.

The baron reached out and opened the door, swinging it aside for them. Sir Nolan stepped forward, but Rhonalyn held up her hand. She would not be preceded as if she were in need of protection. In one fluid motion she skimmed through the doorway and into the solar. Three more royal knights shifted to face her and bowed. Beyond them at the back of the room was the rider she had seen arrive almost an hour ago.

Clearly, he had put the time to good use. He now looked like a king. A high gold crown rested in his dark-blond hair, and from his tall shoulders was draped a mantle trimmed with soft white ermine fur. A twisting chain clasped the mantle across a multi-layered tunic accompanied by a jeweled gold belt and an equally ornamented dagger. His close-cut beard, angular jawline, and flawless skin made his features look neither old nor young. His eyes, which seemed full of thoughts and ideas, met hers.

Her herald announced her. Sliding her right foot behind her left ankle, Rhonalyn briefly broke her gaze from Strephon's. The edge of her skirt heaped momentarily upon the floor, then unfurled. She lifted her eyes back to his.

He did not bow in return, but she didn't mind, for his lips curved delightfully upward. "It is a pleasure to finally meet you, Princess Rhonalyn. I know seeking your acquaintance now leaves us with a rather inconvenient amount of time before the evening meal. And doubtless the easiest course of action would have been for me to allow our introduction to take place over food, but I confess, I was too intrigued for patience."

His smile was enchanting. Reminding herself why she'd come, Rhonalyn suppressed the flutter in her stomach and kept her voice casual. "The paths of our two kingdoms have long run parallel. It is past time they intersected."

"Verily," Strephon said, "and on that score, you and I have much to discuss." His gaze flicked over her shoulder. She could feel her men crowding in behind her. His vivid eyes returned to her face. "What say you? Shall we converse about the futures of our kingdoms now or after the evening meal?"

That he would grant her the decision was surprising and flattering. "Time is a precious resource, but you offer it to me without hesitation."

"Indeed, I do." His eyes held pleasure. "I think you will find there are many advantages to being my friend, Princess Rhonalyn."

She felt a blush creep into her cheeks but did not lower her gaze lest she give him ground before they'd even begun negotiations. "As you said, we have much to discuss. I suggest, therefore, that we proceed directly to business."

"Business before food it is." Strephon glanced at his knights and commented with amusement, "She strikes a hard bargain already."

The knights chuckled.

Annoyed with his backhanded compliment, Rhonalyn considered a retort about how women's ability to prioritize business over their stomachs was how food made it upon men's tables, but she thought better of it. Her silence would politely accept his compliment, whereas a remark would likely weaken her position and reveal her dislike for being contrasted with a man.

Strephon gestured to where a trio of curved chairs encircled a table. "Shall we sit?"

"Indeed, but mayhap first the room should be made a bit less crowded."

"Well, it was you who brought a whole retinue," he teased.

She feigned indignation. "How was I to know we were meeting in the solar and not the main hall?"

He frowned. "Here I thought it fitting for our business."

"It is," Rhonalyn quickly answered, "and once the abundance of my audience is diminished, it will no doubt serve us well." She turned. "Baron Philip, you and your men may depart. Leave only Sir Nolan with me, and see to it that the first of my trunks is brought here."

"As you wish, Your Royal Highness."

Strephon motioned for Baron Selwin to stay but dismissed his two knights with a swish of his fingers.

Both groups bowed and departed. In the quiet that followed, she and Strephon settled in chairs at opposite sides of the table. The third chair stayed empty. She knew Sir Nolan would not sit in it, and apparently Baron Selwin felt the same. The baron took a position about two strides behind Strephon, and Rhonalyn could feel Sir Nolan's presence just behind her right shoulder.

She lifted her chin, her earrings clinking, and focused her gaze on Strephon. "For years Nikor Harbor has divided our two kingdoms. I wish to see that change."

Strephon scoffed. "As I see it, Nikor Harbor is the only thing that has united our two kingdoms."

"United, you say?" Rhonalyn wanted to say that of course that's how he felt about it, being the harbor's owner, but it was not at all how those in Keric felt. Instead, she waited for Strephon's response, hoping to gain more information.

"Mayhap united is the wrong word," Strephon answered. "But it is the one place our two kingdoms interact and profit from each other. The division you speak of between our two kingdoms is a choice Keric made, not one that Delkara sought."

Thankful he had led right to the heart of the matter, Rhonalyn nodded. "You are correct. Due to what has taken place in the past, many in Keric have long considered Delkara an unworthy trading partner. But I am not of the past. I am the future of Keric."

Strephon quoted her own words from her letter. "Change is necessary for a kingdom to prosper."

She nodded.

A knock sounded at the door. Strephon motioned to Baron Selwin. The baron headed that way, and a moment later, two of Rhonalyn's men shuffled inside. They set the trunk she had asked for beside her, then hurried out of the room.

Rhonalyn turned her gaze from the trunk back to Strephon. "Change is necessary, but the question is, what change will prosper my kingdom? As you have pointed out, it is Keric that has long made the choice to reject Delkara as a trading partner. I could just as easily uphold this tradition and find change elsewhere, but instead I am here to make you a proposition. For, I believe leaders should be judged by their own merits, not shunned for their predecessors' choices. Therefore, this is the offer I make to you. Do away with the prejudice created by requiring a harbor toll of Keric, and in return I promise you trade between our two kingdoms."

Strephon's eyebrows lifted. "A bold ask."

"Nay, a bold offer."

"Mayhap," he said, "but how can I be sure you are truly able to deliver on this offer?"

"I have with me trade items from Keric. In respect to what has been, and in promise of what will be, I am willing to pay you the current price of the harbor toll using items of trade. Additionally, I am willing to guarantee that a certain amount of trade will take place between our two kingdoms yearly going forward. If that trade amount is not met, we will again owe the harbor toll."

"You have my interest." Strephon nodded at the trunk. "Show me the trade items you have brought."

37

"Clearly, I am a jouster, not a climber," Gage said to seven shadowy forms as he sat down in the darkness to rest beside the manor's wall.

"Nay," Haaken teased from within the midst of the six others. "'Tis probably just all the food Aunt Mildred has been feeding you."

The others chuckled, and Gage appreciated Haaken's deflection from the real reason. On the surface his wound was healing, but bearing weight was still painful.

"Had any of us thought to bring gloves, I think we all might do better attempting this," Sir Wick commented.

"Verily, for I already have at least three rope burns." Sir Jocelyn held out his arms as if in the dark they could actually see the state of his hands.

"What are you complaining about?" Sir Renner said accusingly. "You actually made it to the top on your first try."

They all laughed, for it was true. Sir Jocelyn had easily succeeded at what had brought them out there in the dark.

Having spent the last several days discussing and outlining their strategy for how to approach and deal with those at Veiroot, they had decided on a plan. People were chosen, and their paths of approach were charted. Knowing it was advisable to have a backup plan or two, they had also established two additional means of gaining support within the fortress in case of trouble.

The second of these two plans required having a small force available to scale the fortress's wall if those of their own inside the fortress were cut off from the gate. Since bringing siege equipment up the mountain wasn't feasible, anyone scaling the wall would have to do so with simple ropes, something their uncle had pointed out would require men comfortable with heights, skilled at quickly climbing in armor, and good with weapons. He assured them he had such men. This, however, had spurred the question at the evening meal of how quickly any of them could climb a wall. They had trekked out into the dark after eating to race each other.

Pressing his hand to his wound, Gage watched the others. For the last several days he had been happy and safe. It had even felt like old times. But now that they had actually established a plan, one that they intended to set in motion the following day, thoughts and fears bombarded him.

Sir Renner's dark form approached the manor's wall and seized the line Sir Jocelyn had just left dangling. Gage stood up to watch. The knight placed one foot against the wall and attempted another swift climb. At about head height, his left foot slipped. His body struck the wall. The knight grunted, hung by the rope for a second, then dropped to the ground with a thud. "Ow!"

Commiserative laughter followed.

"Prince Haaken, may I try?" a young voice asked.

It was Haaken's squire. Without a moment's hesitation, Haaken gave the boy permission. Gage clenched his teeth. Joel's thin silhouette took hold of the rope, and his dark form began to climb the wall.

The higher the boy got, the more apprehension Gage felt. Joel drew close to the top, and the others called their encouragement. Gage silently pleaded with him not to fall. Visible against the lighter darkness of the sky, Joel braced himself using the rope and then reached his free arm up over the wall. Gage held his breath. After several moments of twisting and scuffing, the boy squirmed onto the top of the wall. Turning around, Joel waved down at them. "I made it!"

The others cheered, but Gage felt sick to his stomach. He headed away from the group. Once his stomach had ceased threatening to expel its contents, he returned to his quarters, his mind churning.

A half hour or so later, Haaken came tromping in, his face flushed with laughter. "Gage, there you are. You should have seen it. Joel had this idea to take a rope and—"

"I do not want to hear it," Gage said from where he sat at the end of his bed.

The merriment on Haaken's face disappeared. "What is amiss with you?"

Gage rose to his feet and stilled his shaking hands by pressing them against his legs. "Taking Veiroot is not like some jovial hunt or summer picnic, Haaken."

"I know that." Haaken's expression turned serious. "Why else do you think I would spend so much time carefully planning the endeavor?"

Visualizing Joel on the top of the wall and someone running him through with a sword and pushing him off, Gage felt his stomach tighten. All it would take was one wrong word or trusting the wrong person at Veiroot, and the element of surprise would be gone. They could plan for a hundred possibilities, but the only certainty in his mind was that if a rebel drew a sword or arrow upon any of them, it would be to kill. As such, any of them walking into Veiroot Fortress felt like utter insanity. "Planning is one thing," he said, trying to keep his voice steady, "but when was the last time you led others into a battle where people were actually trying to kill you?"

Haaken's jaw set. "Never. But that does not mean—"

"Exactly. Never." Gage's insides trembled as he held Haaken's gaze. "You are not prepared to take on the rebels." He pointed at the door. "And neither are any of them. 'Tis not worth the risk."

"They are knights and soldiers, and they have been preparing their whole lives for battle. Besides, you were the one who brought the rebels' location to me, remember? And not only is it our duty to stop them, but from what I have seen, you want them caught as much as I do. So, do not tell me taking this fight to them is not worth the risk."

"Of course I want them stopped," Gage replied, "but if in pursuing that goal good people are led to their deaths, will we really be preventing the rebels from killing others or just causing it ourselves?"

Haaken stared at him like he was despicable. "That is what you are worried about? Lord Gregory is a traitor to the crown, and you said it yourself, the rebels will only grow stronger. They are not going away. Think it through, Gage. If we do not risk standing against them now, who might they go after next?" Pacing away from him, Haaken continued. "What if it's not a well-armed lord they attack but a lord's wife and children? Right now we have a choice to pursue them expecting a fight, and, aye, some of us might be injured or even killed while choosing to prevent them from doing harm to anyone else. Or we could stand back, not risk *our* lives, and let the rebels plot against people who will have no idea how or when they might be coming. You tell me, which choice is right, and which is wrong?"

Gage's face was hot, and his heartbeat rocked his body. He knew exactly how he was supposed to answer, but everything in him screamed the opposite. His knees were trembling so hard he had to sit down again on his bed. Breathing slowly, he tried to calm the panic inside.

Haaken paused in front of him. "Look, I know you almost died fighting Felix in Delkara, but you are not alone this time. I tell you, we can do this. We will take the rebels at Veiroot, and we will stop them."

Gage wanted to believe that, but he was alone and dealing with things Haaken didn't even know about.

Haaken spoke with annoyance. "That is mayhap the fifteenth time I have seen you do that."

Gage glanced up. "Do what?"

"That." Haaken pointed at Gage's lap.

Gage looked down at where he had absently wrapped his left hand over the vambrace on his right wrist. He swiftly separated his hands, his heart racing. "'Tis nothing."

"Gage, you have never liked wearing vambraces. Yet upon your arrival from the abbey, you adamantly insisted those you are wearing not be removed, and as far as I can tell you have not taken them off since. Yet clearly they are annoying you. You have been constantly fiddling with them, and every time your knight sees you do so, he squirms. Why are you wearing them?"

Gage's heart hammered in his chest. He couldn't think of any way to explain them away. "If I choose to wear vambraces, that is my business, not yours. You may be crown prince, but I do not have to answer to you for every decision I make."

Haaken's expression held concern. "Then I am right. They do mean something."

Gage felt like a force was squeezing the air from his lungs. "Prithee, Haaken, just leave it alone."

"You told your knight, but you will not tell me?"

Gage's stomach dropped. "I did not tell Sir Wick. And prithee for my sake and for your own, do not seek to know."

Haaken's expression held both hurt and anger. "You and I used to have no secrets from each other, but it seems like that is all we have between us these days."

Guilt joined the anxiety that was battering Gage's body. He clenched his teeth. He would not be made into the enemy. "I have told you everything that I can. And having heard what I had to say about my experiences with the rebels, you should understand my concerns about Veiroot. Any commoner out there could be allied with them and pose a threat that we may not see coming."

"Nay," Haaken said, "what I understand is that this whole plan rests on information you provided. And what I discover is that you are now concerned about acting upon that information and are concealing things from me."

Gage growled in frustration. "I am simply trying to protect you and everyone else who is part of this."

Disappointment filled Haaken's face, and disgust reigned in his voice. "You know, over the last few days I thought I really did have you back. But I was wrong. You cannot figure out whether it is better to go after the rebels or just leave them alone because it is not honor or protectiveness driving you but fear. You are running scared."

"What do you know?" Leaping to his feet, Gage stormed to the far side of the room. A tapestry of a lord jubilantly entering a city hung in front of him. With his knees shaking, he stared at the woven image and wished he'd never returned to Edelmar. But Haaken wasn't finished.

"Listen to me, Gage," he said in an even more berating tone, "on your own or as a leader, you will never make good decisions when you are consumed by fear. Fear will always tell you that any risk is not worth doing what is right. There should be no question in your mind between standing aside and letting evil kill at whim versus standing between evil and the innocent."

Haaken's words pierced a part of Gage's soul that had not been breached since Allard's death. He felt a burst of decimating pain, then the cold surge of a powerful emotion. Gage allowed its strength to pour into every part of his being. He had been the one attacked by the rebels, not Haaken, and he had been the one who had lost men. He would not be called a coward for feeling the way he did.

He turned and hurled his questions at Haaken like javelins. "How is doing what is right worth losing the one thing none of us can regain? Tell me, why should anyone give their life to save someone else's? I say let people protect themselves. Then if they fail, they fail for themselves alone. For, why is it right to ask others to sacrifice life and limb for the sake of someone else?"

"It is right," Haaken snapped, "because being willing to lay down one's life for the sake of someone else is what God asks of us and what He did for us. It is the greatest expression of love we can make, and that is exactly what Allard did for you."

Startled by the comparison and infuriated by it, Gage screamed back, "Aye, but I did not ask him to! And I did not want him to!"

"It was his choice!"

"Nay! It was his choice to help me. Not to die." Gage drew a shuddering breath. "He should have stayed hidden and not come to my rescue."

"Then you would be dead instead of him."

"Nay! We both would have lived. God did not care if Allard died, but He would have made sure I lived."

"What are you talking about?" Haaken sounded genuinely bewildered by Gage's words.

Gage's eyes burned as he replied. "Novia died. Allard died. Bardon died. But I lived. Again and again, I live. God took no action to save any of them, but He blatantly intervenes to keep me alive. He picks people, Haaken, and He chooses times to act and times not to. That is neither love nor justice." Gage swallowed before continuing. "You talk about doing what is right and standing against evil despite the risk." He shook his head. "But even though it would cost God nothing, He does not do it. Countless times He neither stops the evil nor helps the good. Therefore, tell me why He should have the right to ask any of us to risk our lives to pursue something He has not and will not do Himself. God is not worth it. The risk is not worth it. None of it is worth it."

Haaken looked irate. "You are accusing God of not standing against evil? How do you not count what Jesus did on the cross once and for all to stop evil?"

"I know what He did!" Gage screamed. "But what good is heavenly justice when He, who could prevent evil here and now, stands back and lets people be harmed and killed every day? You call His action of dying for us loving, but I call His inaction here and now despicable. He has every ability to do something to prevent the lives lost and the pain caused, but He does nothing. And for that I want nothing to do with Him."

A look of deep concern swept over Haaken's face. "You cannot mean that. Prithee, tell me you do not mean that."

Gage balled his fists.

Haaken looked appalled. "Gage, God cares about every person, and He is not standing idly by in the face of evil."

"Prove it."

Haaken hesitated.

"You cannot," Gage said.

"I can." Haaken sounded desperate. "We are part of that proof. What God asks us to do on His behalf is evidence of what He desires and who He is. 'Overcome evil with good.' 'Do unto others as you would have them do unto you.' 'See that no one renders evil for evil to anyone, but always pursue what is good both for yourselves and for all.' These are the things God asks of us because these are the things He desires. He does care."

"Right, a God who could speak one word and stop every evil instead sends people who cannot even help themselves to do what He desires." Gage shook his head. "Mayhap that works for you as proof that He cares, but it does not work for me."

"Oh, because God answers to you, does He? He does not do things the way you want, therefore, you reject Him? Is that how you serve a king?"

Infuriated, Gage was tempted to turn and rip the tapestry off the wall. "Nay, I refuse to serve God because He is not true to who He claims to be. He says one thing and does another. I do not know why you do not have a problem with that too."

"Mayhap because that is not at all what I see." Haaken threw his hand upward. "I see a God who keeps His promises, who never lies, and who sacrificed Himself to prove His love for the world."

Disgust filled Gage's being. "You can choose to see God however you wish, but do not tell me that I should believe that sacrificing anything for Him is worth it. You can love Him, you can serve Him, and you can be willing to die for Him. And mayhap at the end of the day, He will actually answer all your prayers. But I am no fool for counting the cost and being cautious because in my experience it is my own efforts, not God's love, that will keep those around me safe."

Haaken's jaw clenched. "Clearly, you do not know God the way I do."

With fury burning through his inhibition, Gage gathered together all the angry thoughts that had been stacking up inside him. "Nay, of course you know God in a way I do not and could not. Of course you understand who He is and align with Him perfectly, because you have always been so much better than me. You see everything the right way. You always choose the right things. You trust the right people." Bitterness edged into his voice. "Which I guess would explain why you are safe from ever knowing God the way I do."

Haaken's fingers closed into fists. "That is not fair, Gage. I am far from perfect, just like you."

"Nay, you know what is unfair?" Gage asked. "What is unfair is that being a prince has always been easy for you. You fit the role you were born into. You thrive under the responsibility of leading, and you never fail to measure up to the royal standard. You do not have to be afraid of what people think of you or of the circumstances you face. Because you live as the favored one of God and man."

"And you do not? Is that it?" Haaken's voice became loud and determined. "We each make our own decisions, Gage. That is on us, not anyone else. I am who I am not because I'm perfect but because no matter what happens I submit to and serve God. And you are who you are because you have submitted to fear."

Gage jutted a finger back at him. "Nay! You are who you are because you are the pride and joy of Edelmar, and Father and Mother are always proud of you. Because, unlike me—your scared, pathetic, younger brother—you are capable of being calm, brave, level-headed, and trustworthy no matter the risks. Meanwhile, no matter how hard I try, I will always be found wanting."

Haaken looked stunned and responded strongly, "That is not true. I have failed in numerous endeavors, and you have excelled in many."

"Name two where I have succeeded."

"Well, jousting and..." Haaken's forehead furrowed.

"And what?" Gage snarled. "Try a little harder, big brother, and maybe you can come up with one more."

"Stop this!" Haaken's voice turned pleading. "This is not you."

Gage felt both lost and empowered by Haaken's words. "You think you know who I am? Well, you do not. You never have! You have always been too busy being Edelmar's perfect crown prince to realize I am not like you, Haaken. And no matter how much pressure you apply or how many times you tell me to fix myself, I will never be you."

"It is not trying to be me that is your problem," Haaken said. "Nay, your problem is you do not know how to be you. You clearly despise yourself and your life, and yet instead of dealing with that, you would rather blame others. But hating me and God and everyone else will not solve your life. So, grow up, and before God and man, own who you are and seek whatever forgiveness you need. Because honestly, God is the only one who can help you."

Panic wrapped around Gage's chest. He clenched his shaking hands into fists and shoved away the truth in what Haaken had said. "Nay, what I despise, Haaken, is you recklessly risking people's lives while acting like I am a coward because I do not wish to do the same."

"Despise me if you want," Haaken responded with calm scorn, "but at the end of the day at least I can live with myself."

Enraged by his brother's words, Gage screamed and rushed at him. He plowed into Haaken's chest and landed a punch to his ribs, then pulled back to swing at his face. Haaken grabbed Gage's arm, but in the effort of trying to shove him off, tripped on the rug behind him. Elbows out and feet flying, they crashed onto the floor together. Mostly on top, Gage wrestled his arm free and pummeled Haaken twice more in the chest. Haaken caught him in the chin with his elbow, then kneed him in the stomach.

Grunting, Gage rose up and swung at Haaken's face. Haaken heaved them both sideways. Locked together they rolled across the rug, both raining blows where they could. It was then that Gage realized Haaken was softening his punches. Irate, he struck Haaken hard in the ribs, then hit him in the mouth.

"Enough of this!" Haaken slammed a fist into Gage's wounded shoulder. Gasping in pain, Gage recoiled. Haaken scrambled away, kicking him as he went. "You happy now?"

Too angry to see straight, Gage clutched his shoulder and screamed, "Get out!"

Haaken rose to his feet, his chest heaving. "Have it your way!" Turning on his heel, he stormed out of the room, slamming the door behind him.

The thud rattled a candlestick on the other side of the room, but once that sound died there was left only an empty loneliness. Curling into a ball in the middle of the rug, Gage exhaled a shuddering breath and began to sob. He cried for Allard, and for Novia, and for all the stupid things he had just said to Haaken. He cried because he *was* a coward. He cried because he was in pain and because he needed help but had probably just destroyed the one chance he had of getting it.

Once he finally cried himself out, he thought about Haaken's comment about his motivation not being honorable or protective, and he got angry all over again. There was no strength left to his fury, but it still raged through him. His insides churned with the jumble of emotions from their argument. He seethed about Haaken's comments and spit insults across the empty room. But instead of making himself feel better or justified, he eventually just felt that much more ashamed.

He did hate himself. The acknowledgment shifted his anger away from Haaken, and for a time he steeped in self-loathing. But even that could not expend the abundance of rage inside him. He wanted to be free from all of it.

A thought entered his mind. He could run again. He had money buried outside of Aro. He could retrieve it, choose a new identity, go to Ivenyhan, get on a ship, and leave the three kingdoms forever. Once he had disembarked on some other shore, his mark wouldn't matter anymore, and he would be free of the mess he had made of his life.

The thought held so much appeal. Athalos was in the yard. He could be on his way to Aro before anyone even knew he was gone. He would not have to face Haaken or deal with Veiroot. He could just go. His thoughts churned bitterly. After all, wasn't running scared how he made his decisions?

Other thoughts rose up against his plan. His mark might be found out by a ship's captain. He might simply get himself in worse trouble somewhere else. And he could not deceive himself this time; he knew leaving Edelmar permanently would impact more than just him.

He thought of Prince Thayer of Delkara, who had perished at sea, and his Uncle Elmon's comments at the feast at Nardell about the event. *"T'was a tragic day. All three kingdoms mourned Delkara's loss, and King Maurice was never the same."* Gage rolled onto his back on the rug and heard Haaken's words echo in his head. *"You tell me, which choice is right, and which is wrong?"*

Gage's anger churned in his stomach. It was his choice. He could leave. The temptation played in his mind, tugging at him.

Staring up at the ceiling with his wound aching, he was reminded of all the days he had spent on his back at Saint Jerome's Abbey and exactly how he had gotten himself there.

38

WITH A CANDLE in hand, Wick entered the manor's study and headed for the desk where Baron Elmon had said he'd left the book containing information about Veiroot. Wick had wanted to reread a section of it.

He had just reached the map-covered desk when he noticed a form sitting on the floor next to the fireplace. Head bowed and arms folded over his raised knees, Prince Haaken's clothes were unmistakable. Wick started. "Your Royal Highness!"

Sniffing, Prince Haaken lifted his head. "Sir Wick?"

Horrified that he had barged into such a private moment, Wick backed away. "I beg your pardon. I did not know you were in here." He turned toward the door. His tunic caught one of the maps and dragged it off the desk. Hurriedly, he retrieved it, shoved it back in place, and headed once more for the door.

"Wait, Sir Wick." Prince Haaken's voice sounded strained.

Pausing in his hasty retreat, Wick cringed. "Aye, Your Royal Highness."

Prince Haaken sighed. "Do you think it is possible that there are people God favors more than others?"

Not at all sure what to make of his question or what context to place it in, Wick repeated it. "People God favors more?"

"Aye," Prince Haaken said, "like specific people God watches out for while others He lets things happen to and does not protect?"

Wick frowned, wondering how Prince Haaken had gone from laughing with them in the courtyard to sitting alone contemplating such a question. Ditching his curiosity, he instead considered how to answer. As the youngest of seven brothers and a border guard, it was not the first time he'd thought about God's favor, but he wasn't sure he should give his actual thoughts on the matter. "I suppose," he said cautiously, "it would depend on how you look at God's favor."

"Go on," Prince Haaken said.

Wick nervously looked down at the flickering flame of his candle. "Well, it seems like there are those people that, no matter what they do or how hard they try, bad things just keep happening to them." He glanced at where Prince Haaken sat in the dark. Feeling awkward standing over him, Wick sank to the floor as he continued. "But is that because they are not favored by God? Or is it just because that is the way life sometimes works? Or is it because Satan is angry that they are favored by God? I mean, when I look at the story of Job, it seems like making that distinction can be difficult. Job was definitely favored by God, but God allowed some terrible things to happen to him."

"I suppose you are right," Prince Haaken said. "We assume God's favor will match our ideals of a good life here, like having ease, wealth, and happiness, which are definitely blessings God can give us, but they are not things He promises us here on earth. There are certain favorable things God does promise us though when we live in accordance with Him. He promises to provide for our needs and give us the benefits of His presence in our lives, which, like Paul says in Galatians, allows us to experience and express God's love, joy, patience, and all the rest of His gifts."

Not exactly sure how that was relevant but not about to interrupt, Wick remained silent.

Prince Haaken looked over at him as if he'd just found the answer he had been seeking. "When we have God with us as His Holy Spirit, we have what we need to respond well and rightly regardless of our circumstances. That is God's favor toward us. Not that our circumstances are necessarily changed, but rather that we are changed in making the choice to access God's mindset toward the situation rather than our own."

In hearing Prince Haaken's thoughts, it occurred to Wick how often in situations he did not seek to respond out of God's Spirit, even though it was available to him. He relied far more readily upon himself and his own wisdom, which if he was honest, was often influenced by his own fear or pride. He wondered how different his approach to life might be if he always sought God's mindset over his own.

Wick knew that him making choices by God's principles spared him the consequences of the bad decisions he would've made without God in his life, but Haaken's words took living a Christian life a lot further than that. The concept that God's favor may not mean protection but rather giving people what they needed to respond well to hard things was not one that Wick was particularly comfortable with either. He thought about all the people he knew who served God and yet had faced things like illness, decimated crops, burnt-down homes, terrible marriages, and children dying. It made sense in light of Job and what Prince Haaken was saying, but it didn't really make sense to him in light of who God was.

Prince Haaken's surprised voice cut through his thoughts. "You do not agree?"

Mortified that he had let his opinion slip onto his face, Wick answered swiftly. "Nay, I agree…"

"But?"

Wick swallowed hard. "It is just that...there are those who believe and follow God faithfully who suffer in ways that seem..." He trailed off again, searching for the right words to describe what he meant and wishing he had just kept his face blank and his mouth shut. It wasn't as if he believed God hated those people or did not care about them. But it did feel like the bad things they faced were to an inordinate degree considering God claimed to be loving and had the ability to make their lives easier. "I do not know. I suppose it just seems like their lives lack the sorts of blessings one might expect to receive when serving an all-powerful King."

"You mean it kind of feels like their King is failing to be what He promised to be?"

Wick shifted uncomfortably, both because he had never thought of God as failing in anything and because he was talking to a future king. "Mayhap."

"I guess then the question comes back to what exactly has God promised us." Prince Haaken's forehead furrowed.

Wick stared through his candle. "He promises us life and protection."

"But not here," Prince Haaken said. "We think having a happy existence on earth is what is important. But it is the redemption and salvation from our sin-filled lives to an eternal holy existence beyond this life that God has promised us. They can kill the body but not the soul. God says, in following Him as our King, we will be hated here on earth and suffer persecution for His name's sake, which was definitely true of His prophets and the apostles. Even Mary, Jesus's mother, who was called highly favored by God, had to flee her homeland and watch her firstborn son be crucified."

Wick's insides squirmed at these thoughts, and he shifted on the floor. "In other words, God's favor and love is, as you said, definitely not about guaranteeing earthly comfort or protection."

Prince Haaken's gaze drifted past him as if lost in thought. "Nay, it is not, which is likely what bothers him so much."

Wick wondered who Prince Haaken meant but was too bothered by the concept himself to ask. Prince Haaken continued absently. "He is misunderstanding God's love and intentions because his only focus is on here and now." Prince Haaken looked back at Wick. "He thinks God does not care because He is not fixing earthly problems. But that is like wanting a king, who knows a castle is going to be invaded by an enemy and ultimately destroyed, to make sure the castle's soldiers have good food, that their commander is treating them well, and that their beds are comfortable and free of fleas. Does he care about these things? Of course. But are they what matter? Or is the true need for the king to be handing out weapons to fight the invading enemy and explaining a way to escape the castle's destruction?"

Wick felt his own perspective on humanity's difficulties reorient in response to Prince Haaken's words. "God is not failing us or abandoning us to the perils of earth. He has and is rescued us from them."

"Exactly," Prince Haaken said. "Therefore, accepting and following Him as our king and being faithful to do whatever He asks of us is ultimately what is most important." Prince Haaken continued more slowly, as if considering his own words. "For some of us that might mean being like Job, who remained committed to God despite everything else being taken away, or it might mean being like King Solomon, who asked God for wisdom and was given wealth as well so that God's supremacy would be known." Prince Haaken sighed and threw up his hand. "Which brings us back to the question, why does God choose some people to have it easier than others?"

"You know," Wick said cautiously, "I used to think being a prince was so much easier than being a bottom-rung knight or a peasant, but the more I have seen, the more I think that everyone has hard things in their lives. We just each experience difficulties in our own ways."

Prince Haaken looked at him thoughtfully. "You are probably right. And had I not taken offense at his words, I might have realized sooner what was beneath them. Thank you for your help, Sir Wick."

"Um, you are welcome," Wick answered awkwardly, "though I am not sure what I did."

"You helped me to see what I was missing, and now I can go set right what I got wrong." Rising, Prince Haaken grunted and pressed his hand to his ribs.

"Are you all right?" Wick asked, swiftly climbing to his own feet.

"Aye." Prince Haaken chuckled ruefully. "Though mayhap I might be wise to put on armor before I try talking to him again."

"Him?" Wick stiffened. "Someone did this to you?"

"Gage and I got into an argument."

"And he hit you?"

Prince Haaken's voice turned reproving. "What are you, our mother?"

Wick backed up a step. "I did not mean it like that. I just—"

"You what? Are shocked to hear the princes of Edelmar are so immature as to attempt to settle their disputes using their fists? Well, apparently we are. Not our finest hour, clearly." Prince Haaken frowned. "Believe it or not, usually mine and Gage's mock fights are a show of affection."

"I take it those fights do not usually result in bruised ribs?"

"Nay, but I may have deserved that. I said some things I probably owe him an apology for, even yet tonight. Along with setting straight his misperceptions about me and God, even if he does not wish to hear them."

"Should I fetch a field marshal to accompany you?" Wick asked, only half joking.

Prince Haaken chuckled. "Nay, but if you hear anything breaking, send Sir Renner."

Wick nodded.

39

Having retrieved the book, Wick had figured he would settle in his room to read it, but after his conversation with Prince Haaken, he couldn't concentrate. He headed instead toward the manor hall intending to join Squire Joel, Sir Holbird, and Sir Adrian in a game of cards. He came around a corner on his way there and found himself face to face with Prince Haaken. Having not expected to cross paths with His Royal Highness again that night, let alone so quickly, he was about to joke about running into him again when he noted the panicked look on the prince's face. "What is the matter?" he asked.

"Gage is not in his room, and I cannot find him anywhere."

Wick's heart sank into his stomach. "You do not think that he would—" He cut himself off and shook his head. "He would not leave. He is determined to take down the rebels."

"Nay, he is afraid of risking people's lives by going to Veiroot. That is why we were arguing."

Wick felt like he'd just swallowed rocks. "Is his horse in the yard?"

"I am headed there now."

Wick matched his stride to Prince Haaken's. Frustration surged through him as he considered the very real possibility that Prince Gage might actually have left. "I tell you, if he slipped away again, I am going to kill him," he muttered the words without thinking. He bit his tongue and glanced at Prince Haaken. "Figuratively speaking, of course, Your Royal Highness."

"He's my brother," Prince Haaken growled. "I get to kill him first."

They checked the yard and found Prince Gage's horse still penned there. Relieved but still not at ease, they returned to the manor hall and were starting a second search inside when they turned a corner and found Baron Elmon talking with Prince Gage at the end of a corridor just outside the baron's private chambers.

"Gage, we have been looking everywhere for you."

Baron Elmon glanced between the two brothers and laid his hand on Prince Gage's shoulder. "The two of you have much to discuss." The baron then gestured to Wick. "Come, Sir Wick. Let us leave them to it."

Wick obediently walked away with the baron, but before turning the corner, he glanced back to make sure the two were not about to break into a brawl. The brothers were standing opposite each other, neither one saying a word.

"Do not fear for them," Baron Elmon said. "They will work things out. They always do."

Wick wished he had the baron's confidence.

◎✕◎

Gage swallowed, not knowing exactly how to say what he wanted to say. A long moment of awkward silence stretched between them, then Haaken motioned to the end of the corridor where a bench sat under a metal shield displaying Elmon's coat-of-arms. "Will you join me?"

Gage drew a steadying breath. "Aye, here and at Veiroot." He saw the surprise on Haaken's face and continued. "Forgive me for my earlier words. I said things I should not have and that I did not mean.

I agree it would be wrong to stand aside and let the evil the rebels are doing continue. Despite the risk of going to Veiroot, 'tis the right thing to do and the best way to keep people safe. And Uncle assures me the plan is solid. As you know, I have made a lot of dumb, fearful decisions of late, but I do not want this to be one of them."

"Gage," Haaken sank onto the bench, "I too owe you an apology for things that I said and for things I should have said a long time ago." The gloss of tears in Haaken's eyes caught Gage off guard.

He stared at his brother. "I do not understand what you mean."

"Mayhap because you do not know me as well as you think you do. I do not trek ahead without fear, Gage. I am just as terrified of messing up as you are. And I have messed up before. You and Novia were my responsibility, and I almost lost both of you. Had you died that day too, I do not know what I would have done. I still regret that because I did not want to accept that she was gone, I carried her back first and left you shivering by the edge of the river. Had I brought you first, you may not have gotten so sick afterward. I remember watching Novia's casket being buried and fearing that I might still lose you too."

Pain tightened in Gage's chest.

Haaken wiped his hand swiftly across his face to catch his tears. "The truth is, if you hadn't jumped into the river after her, I would have never known what happened to her. So, thank you for risking your life to save her."

Gage felt hot tears spill from his own eyes. "But I did not save her."

"Nay, but you tried. And I understand why you do not want to risk losing anyone again. I am sorry for what I said earlier about how you are making your decisions. I had not realized how you felt about God. That changes so much about how you view life here."

Gage gritted his teeth. "God could have saved her, Haaken."

"I know, but He chose not to."

Gage blinked back more tears. "Why?"

"There are probably a hundred reasons. But I believe it was because God chose to answer Novia's prayer."

"What?" Gage wasn't sure he'd heard Haaken correctly. "What do you mean?"

"At Novia's funeral her mother gave me a letter Novia had written and had intended to give to me. In it Novia wrote that her most ardent prayer was that I would know God like she did and that I would serve Him with all my heart. Novia's delight for life and passion for God was something I very much admired, but until her death I had no desire or interest in seeking out a relationship with God."

Surprised by Haaken's words and reminded of how Novia had been, Gage pictured her, just hours before her death, a smile on her face and a crown of daisies in her auburn hair. He choked on tears and dropped onto the bench beside Haaken. "She did love life and God."

Haaken nodded. "God was always the first thing on her mind, and you and her, you two were always talking about Him. You would say something like, 'Did you see that bird, Novia? Why do you think God made it with so many colors?' And she would answer, 'I think because He likes to surprise us and make us smile.'"

Gage nodded through a tearful laugh. "Aye, she would."

"Do you remember that time when the three of us were sprawled in the grass under that big beech tree? You and I were seeing how far we could throw beechnuts up into the tree, and Novia was staring up at the sky. And she said that—"

"That she could not wait to see what heaven was like. Because if this was what a broken world looked like then heaven had to be spectacular."

Haaken nodded. "We were all young, and thanks to our parents, we were sheltered from how ugly the world can truly be. I did not see the evil and sin in others then, nor did I recognize it in myself. To me, at that point life was simply full of promise and opportunities. I knew God's moral standard, and in my opinion, I was doing a great job measuring up. I figured God would be pleased with me the same way everyone else was regardless of whether or not I actually cared about Him." Haaken looked ashamed. "Verily, you were right about who I was. I knew all the right things to do and say to look good, and I thought a lot of myself. I was confident in my ability to be crown prince and accomplish whatever was placed before me. And I assumed I did not need God.

"Then Novia died, and I realized two things. No matter how confident, good, or determined we are, life is fleeting, and we have no power to change that. The other thing was that I had no idea how to handle my life not going the way I wanted it to. I read Novia's letter, and words that I would have just disregarded had she still been alive became words I could not ignore."

Haaken smiled tearfully. "You know that irresistible joy she always seemed to emanate? Well, with her gone, my life was completely devoid of joy. I was in agony, and I had no idea how to find my way out of it. She had something that I did not have and had never had. Even though she had lost people she loved, she possessed a delight for life that I could not fathom after her death. Thus, I wanted, nay, I needed, to understand God. Because if He was why she had been able to have no fear of death and have joy despite loss, then I needed Him too."

Gage had never thought about Novia within the context of her own loss. Novia's older brother had died when she was seven, and though she had often talked about him and shown grief at him no longer being present, she had also continued to embrace life and those around her.

"Gage, you said you will not serve a God who can prevent evil yet lets people be harmed and killed. I know what God allows can seem unloving and unjust from our perspective. A loving God would protect and help the good people and stop the bad things and bad people, right? But who is good and who is bad? We see ourselves and the people we care about as the good people, but if we are honest, we have all at one time or another, by our thoughts, actions, and inactions, caused harm to ourselves and others. To one degree or another we all have evil in us. Thus, none of us are devoid of what we want stopped.

"Therefore the truth of the matter is, if God put an end to evil here and now like you want, not one of us would still be breathing. Rather, God is continually and lovingly intervening for each of us by withholding His complete judgment of evil for the time being and giving us all grace upon grace to live despite the sin every last one of us commits.

"Novia's death was not the result of God doing nothing. He had already given her the best and most loving things He could: His presence and His redemption. With His presence, she fought against the evil here and showed others His means of rescue. And because of God's redemption, she did not die that day, she simply got to depart this broken world and get to heaven sooner than we expected. We each have our allotted time here, not as a right but as a gift, a chance to either align with evil or accept God's salvation from it. Thus, the existence of evil should not be our accusation against God but rather our motivation to run to Him.

"So, do not hate God for allowing the losses that compel us to seek answers about life and death or for His being patient and gracious toward those of us who have thought we did not need Him.

"I should have told you long ago how Novia's death brought about God's work and grace in my life. If I had, you may have seen her death and God very differently. And I am sorry that I made you feel like you needed to measure up to my standard or that I had somehow accomplished what you had not. Verily, I am constantly seeking God's help to overcome my fears, to make the right decisions, and not to walk away when my responsibilities feel overwhelming. Really, we are not that different, you and I. We both need God's help to live and to lead."

Gage looked down at his wrists. "Mayhap God's grace is that He does offer redemption from sin instead of death, but what if I want to live but do not want to lead? Am I allowed to choose a different path than what He has determined for me? Or will God use some means to punish me until I do what He wants? Are we His slaves?"

When his question was met by silence, he glanced up at Haaken. His brother looked conflicted, but he finally spoke. "The day you asked our father if he would give his permission for you to leave Einhart and travel as a commoner, he wished to deny your request. It was not his desire for you to leave, but he allowed you the choice." Haaken exhaled deeply. "It was his way of expressing God's heart toward you. God would rather that you choose what is right than be forced into it. Does that mean He will not correct or punish you if you disobey Him? Nay, but it does mean His heart toward you is one of a loving Father, and that, if He is directing you on a certain path, it is not for your harm but for your good. Therefore, I suggest you ask God what path He desires for you."

At Haaken's words, Gage's emotions ran in a hundred different directions. He didn't want to ask. He was petrified to know. It was a responsibility he didn't want, a life he couldn't fathom, and a weight he absolutely knew he could not carry. So many fears, so much panic, so strong a desire to simply run clutched him that he could no longer sit still. He shifted to rise.

"Gage." Haaken caught his arm.

Gage sank back onto the bench, his penned-up emotions rising into his voice. "I cannot, Haaken. I cannot trust God."

Haaken's steady gaze held his. "You doubt God's trustworthiness, but are you sure you can trust yourself?"

Gage glared at him. "What is that supposed to mean?"

Haaken raised his hands. "I am not criticizing you. I am only saying that you have your experience, but in my experience even when God does not do what I would have wanted, I can still trust that what He does is for the right reasons and for good, not evil. But when following myself, I have no such confidence. I can, and have, easily lied to myself about my goal and my motivation in doing something. So, I ask you, are you sure it is better to trust yourself?"

Gage leaned his head back against the wall. "I do not know." The moment the words were out of his mouth, he heard Prior Joseph's response in his head, *"Then you are of the lost who has yet to have the veil of blindness removed from his eyes. Seek, and you will find. Knock, and the door will be opened to you."* Sighing, Gage sat forward and looked at Haaken. "I appreciate everything you have said, and I wish I could tell you that you have completely changed my mind. But the truth is, I am not yet where you are."

The gloss returned to Haaken's eyes, and when he answered, Gage heard a strain in his voice. "I wish you were, but I understand. You have to make your own choice."

"Do you still want me at Veiroot?" Gage asked.

"Of course I do. Who else would I send with Sir Wick and Sir Holbird to secure the back entrance to Veiroot Fortress? Not only do you know well how to travel without being noticed, you have actually seen the tunnel, unlike either of them."

"There are others who would be just as capable of making their way up the mountain, locating the entrance, and signaling with a hunting horn when they find it."

"I agree, but I want you. Can you handle that?"

Gage smiled. "Aye, I can handle that."

Haaken nodded. "Good, then we both best get some sleep before the morrow."

40

Wick wasn't thrilled about the part of their orders that required wearing commoners' clothing, particularly knowing what he knew about Prince Gage, but he was not about to object. He was part of the campaign, and for that he was grateful.

Baron Elmon's servants for the last several days had been attending to all the details for their departure. Thus, there was a spread of food, supplies, weapons, and packs already awaiting them in the hall. Anything else required would be collected on their way.

A number of Baron Elmon's men had also already been sent out disguised as travelers and merchants, which meant there was a good collection of commoners' clothes and items. With an already full pack, Wick added to his tunic a rough belt, a short knife, a straw hat, and a small satchel that he could keep his more personal belongings in, such as his tools for lock picking. He'd brought the tools with him when he'd left the White Fortress and was glad, for they might come in handy at the back entrance of Veiroot Fortress.

In addition to food, clothes, and normal items of travel, he also selected a wool blanket, a lantern that could handle weather, and a pot for cooking over an open fire, just in case. Then he reluctantly folded and left his cloak from the White Fortress and selected instead a plain commoners' cloak, under which he could conceal his sword.

His arms full, he headed out into the manor's courtyard, which was just as busy with activity as the hall inside. Prince Gage, dressed in similar attire, though with vambraces and a felt hat, was across the way saddling his horse in its pen. Meanwhile near the stable, Baron Elmon's and Prince Haaken's men-at-arms were also preparing to depart.

Wick found his bay tied in a line of horses near the manor's front gate. The animals were the mounts of Prince Haaken's knights. Sir Renner tightened a last tie on his horse's gear and headed back toward the manor house. Meanwhile Sir Jocelyn had just begun loading his saddlebags onto his horse. "Is not your ride one of the mules back by the stable?" Sir Jocelyn teased over his shoulder as Wick approached.

Wick nudged his hat up so that he could see better over his armload of supplies. "Prithee, tell me you are joking."

Sir Jocelyn laughed. "Aye." He pointed to Wick's horse. "Though it does look like someone thought ahead and switched out your tack."

Wick frowned at the worn, basic saddle and bridle. Definitely not the way he had pictured himself riding after the rebels. He dumped his cloak, bags, weapon, and blanket beside his horse and began tying things onto his saddle. "Have you seen Sir Holbird yet?"

Sir Jocelyn smirked. "Dressed as a commoner? Nay, not yet."

The dinging bell of the manor's gate caused Wick to glance over his shoulder. Baron Elmon's porter broke away from chatting with another servant and hurried toward the sound. A moment later when Wick switched sides of his horse, he noticed the porter standing in the gate speaking with someone outside. It was obviously not someone who belonged at the manor, for they were not let in. Wick returned his focus to the task at hand. He was glad the saddle's ties, despite being old, were still sturdy. He used them to bind his cloak and sword against his saddlebag while ensuring the weapon was concealed and would not rub on his horse's flank.

The porter hurried around the line of horses and headed toward the manor house. He'd left the gate closed behind him. Wick figured the porter was likely going to pass on whatever news he had just received. Thinking about news, he was reminded of when he'd received Prince Gage's letter and marveled at the chain of events that had followed and led to him being about to ride against Veiroot. He tied his blanket around and over his sword's hilt.

The porter returned from the manor house, followed by Baron Elmon, Prince Haaken, and Sir Renner. The four of them crossed the yard and paused before the gate. The porter swung it open, allowing inside a knight and eight soldiers trailing their horses. The soldiers wore the blue-and-green tabards of Nikledon. Wick's heart dropped into his stomach, and his blood turned to ice. It couldn't be a coincidence. He searched the soldier's ranks. Sure enough, he recognized two of them. Panic assaulted him. How had Drake and Merek tracked them there?

He glanced across the courtyard, desperately hoping Prince Gage had noticed the activity at the gate and had gotten out of sight. His heart sank. No such luck. Prince Gage had finished loading his horse and was conversing with one of Baron Elmon's servants outside the animal's pen. Wick glanced back toward the soldiers, praying that by some miracle they had not yet spotted Prince Gage, and he could still warn him.

"Your Royal Highness and Baron," the Nikledon knight said with a deep bow to Prince Haaken and Baron Elmon, "forgive the intrusion. We are seeking a commoner who came from Duvall. The gateman at Awnquera's entrance said he was brought from the gate by wagon to this manor. And from what my men have observed of this manor's gate over the last several days, he has not left since. We have—"

"That's him there speaking with the other servant," Drake said, pointing across the manor's yard.

Prince Haaken and Baron Elmon looked in the direction Drake pointed. By the description of their arrival, Wick figured the two of them had to know the knight was talking about Prince Gage, but unlike Wick they didn't know why the soldiers were seeking His Highness. And since neither he or Prince Gage had said anything about their troubles at Nikledon, no one had thought anything of letting the soldiers inside the manor.

"The man in the felt hat?" Prince Haaken asked. "What is your business with him?"

"It is a legal matter," the knight answered, "one more easily explained with him present."

Prince Haaken frowned but nodded. "Very well. Sir Renner, fetch him here."

Sir Renner headed across the courtyard toward Prince Gage, who was still oblivious to what was taking place at the gate. Wick wanted desperately to yell at Prince Gage, to tell him to run, to escape, to do anything but stand there, but it was too late. If Prince Gage tried to flee now, the soldiers of Nikledon would go after him. And if that happened, Wick had no doubt that all hell would break loose in the manor.

Concealed among the horses, he watched in dread as Sir Renner approached His Highness. The knight must have said something because Prince Gage turned at the last moment. Wick saw him take in Sir Renner, then those at the gate. Horror widened Prince Gage's eyes, and his body stiffened. For a moment Wick thought he might actually bolt, but in the next second His Highness's rigid posture went slack, and his chin lowered.

Sir Renner seized Prince Gage's arm. From his hold Wick knew it wasn't to keep Prince Gage from fleeing but to keep him upright. The two exchanged words, but at the sudden look of intensity that flashed back into Prince Gage's expression, Wick had a feeling what was being said was probably something similar to what Prince Gage had begged of him at Nikledon's gate. *"For the honor and protection of the crown of Edelmar, you must do as I ask. Say nothing about who I am, and do nothing to stop them. Promise me."*

Wick's stomach twisted. After everything they had gone through to get back to Awnquera, he could not believe it had all come to this. He wanted to do something, anything, but there was nothing he could do without being spotted and also accused of being a rebel or, worse, it being discovered he was a true Edelmarian knight who had helped a marked man. No, there was nothing he could do, and no one else knew to do anything.

With a look of tormented acceptance, Prince Gage lifted his arm out of Sir Renner's grasp and walked stiffly ahead of him to where the baron, Prince Haaken, and the soldiers awaited him.

41

"Your Royal Highness. Baron Elmon." Gage bowed low to his brother and uncle and caught Haaken's gaze as he lifted his head. His heart pounding, he silently implored Haaken to treat him as nothing but a servant. Sir Renner stepped up beside Haaken and murmured in his ear. Gage dropped his gaze to the ground. He knew no matter what happened next he would be utterly humiliated, but most of all, he feared Haaken would ignore his request and say something that would irreparably join the two of them together in a disgrace that would destroy Haaken along with him. Sir Renner stepped away. Gage swallowed hard and spoke in the commoners' tongue. "You wished to see me?"

There was a subtle twinge in Haaken's voice as he too spoke in the commoners' tongue. "Yes, these men say you are involved in a legal matter." Haaken glanced toward the knight from Nikledon. "A matter for which I am still awaiting an explanation."

"Have him remove his vambraces," the knight said, "and you'll have your answer."

Gage couldn't breathe. He wished to heaven and earth they had caught him in Nikledon instead.

Haaken's command came out with an airy tremor, as if he too was struggling to breathe. "You heard the man. Take off your vambraces."

Gage knew refusing to comply would only drag out the situation and his humiliation. So, with his heart throbbing in his ears and his hands cold, he turned over his left wrist, loosed, and stripped off that vambrace. He let it fall to the ground. Then he unlaced his right vambrace and let it too fall. The consequences of his stupidity were his and his alone to bear. He turned his hand over, revealing the flail and crossbow seared in an X above his hand.

He heard his uncle's sharp intake of breath. Thankfully, that was the only sound Elmon made. Haaken's response was more controlled, though it was like the intense control of someone trying desperately to hold onto a crumbling ledge. "Aye, I see the issue. I take it this is Delkaran?"

"It is," the knight said, "and by the laws of Delkara and Edelmar we have legal right to take—"

"I know what the laws say," Haaken said sharply.

Gage cringed. He could hear the shock and confusion in Haaken's voice. He lifted his eyes to catch his brother's gaze, imploring him not to let his response give them both away. There was utter turmoil beneath the angry look on Haaken's face. "Of what crime is he accused?"

"He's a rebel thief."

"That cannot be," Elmon said. "He must have been confused with someone else."

"It's no mistake," Merek said coldly. "I was there to witness it."

Haaken's jaw clenched. "Well, if that is the case, then allow me to pay restitution to the Delkaran lord from whom he is accused of stealing, and I will deal with him myself and save you the trouble."

Despite the genuine anger in Haaken's voice and how mortified Gage felt being in such a position, gratitude flowed through his soul. Haaken paying restitution on his behalf was a wonderful solution.

The knight shook his head. "Your offer, Your Royal Highness, is generous but unacceptable. I have strict orders to bring him to whom he is marked."

Gage's heart sunk into the pit of his stomach, and a shiver of fear ran down his spine. They had tracked him across half of Delkara and into Edelmar to get their hands on him. Of course they had no intention of letting Haaken have him.

"Very well," Haaken said with a hint of frustration, "then tell me to which lord you are going that I might speak with him myself about this matter."

"We are not at liberty to disclose where we are going for safety reasons on the road. You understand, I am sure. But if you are determined to know, you can send a pigeon with us. I will see to it that a name is sent back to you."

Haaken turned toward Sir Renner, who nodded. "I will see to it at once."

While Sir Renner hurried away, the knight from Nikledon handed Drake a rope and motioned to Gage. "Bind him."

Gage's stomach lurched.

"Wait." Haaken's voice was strained yet forcefully quiet. "Do me one favor. Leave here with him free, and bind him once you are on the road. I would rather every man watching assume he has been sent on a mission with you rather than wonder what he has done and why I would allow you to take him. For if they knew why you had come for him, they would want justice done here and now."

The knight smiled tolerantly and nodded. "I understand."

Haaken spoke then to Gage as if in threat. "When I come, I will make sure you face justice."

Gage swallowed hard at Haaken's words. He felt grateful for the promise Haaken was making and the shred of dignity his brother had just given him. Despite the circumstances, he would depart as a commoner returning to Delkara instead of a prince of Edelmar arrested in front of his uncle's house and an entire royal retinue. But when the soldiers closed in around him, it was not gratitude he felt but pure panic that spread through every fiber of his being.

He wanted to beg Haaken to do whatever was necessary to prevent the soldiers from taking him, but instead he clenched his teeth and swallowed the cry threatening to burst from his lips. He could not ask Haaken to break one law let alone the half dozen it would take to rescue him from the soldiers' clutches. Their claim to him could not be legally overridden by anyone except the mark's owner. The moment Sir Jarret had pinned him against the wall of the smithy, he had known that, but somehow he had convinced himself he could be free in Edelmar.

Sir Renner returned with a pigeon in a small basket and handed it to the knight. The knight signaled his men to depart. Gage drew a shuddering breath and forced his knees not to buckle as he was escorted out the manor's gate. He'd spent countless hours at Saint Jerome's Abbey anticipating and fearing the moment Delkaran soldiers came for him, but never once had he imagined it would happen like this. He glanced back but couldn't see past his escorts.

A moment later, with fear and shame overwhelming him and his captors surrounding him, he heard the creak of hinges and the thud of the manor's gate closing behind him. The next thing he knew, Drake was approaching him with a rope. Gage worked quickly to wall away every bit of himself that cared about anything or anyone, for caring now would only make the situation so much worse. Towering over him, Drake disarmed him, then drew his hands together. Drake wound the end of the cord over and under Gage's wrists in a swift tether, which he then drew as tight as the knot in Gage's stomach.

Leaving him standing there bound, Drake uncoiled the rest of the rope and handed its end to the already mounted knight. The knight secured the line to his saddle and urged his horse into motion. The rope went taut, tugging Gage forward by his wrists. With a hollow numbness growing in his chest, Gage trailed behind the knight's mount.

42

The moment the gate was closed, Wick hurried from between the horses and toward Prince Haaken. His Royal Highness's shoulders had slumped, and his eyes were pressed closed. "I cannot believe I just let them take him."

"You had no choice," Sir Renner said. "Legally, there was nothing you could do, and he knew that."

Prince Haaken opened his eyes, his face full of misery. "Aye, but now they have him and what am I to do?"

Baron Elmon still looked and sounded shocked. "How could this have even happened? Why would he not have sought aid before it came to…came to that?"

Wick approached, feeling like the lone survivor of a battle that, until then, none of them had known existed. "I may be able to shed some light on that."

"You!" Prince Haaken said. "I knew you knew more than you were saying. Why did you not speak earlier?"

Wick cringed. "For the same reason you did not tell those soldiers his title. Prince Gage is innocent, but those soldiers are convinced they are in the right, and they have the law on their side. Currently, nothing can change that."

"Nothing yet." Prince Haaken thrust a finger against Wick's chest. "But you are going to help me solve that. Do you understand me?"

Staring into Prince Haaken's furious gaze, Wick nodded. His heart was racing with the same anger. "Believe me, I do. And from what I know, the answers lie with Manton."

Prince Haaken took a breath. "Then it would seem my mission is unaltered, but yours has been, Sir Wick. I do not wish to rely on a pigeon to know where my brother is. I want you to go after the soldiers and ride with them to wherever they are going."

Wick shook his head. If he went after the soldiers, they would arrest him on sight. "Your Royal Highness, prithee, I am willing to do anything to help, but I am not the right person to send. I—"

"You are the perfect person. You have been to Delkara recently and have spent the most time with my brother. Sir Renner will accompany you. You will see to my brother's safety."

"Aye, Your Royal Highness, but that is not the—"

"Sir Wick, the two of you must catch up with them to ride with them. There is no time to waste. Find them and stay with them. They cannot refuse the two of you joining them. You will have your orders, and they will have theirs."

"I understand, but—"

"Prince Haaken," Sir Renner interrupted, "I do not think we will be able to—

"To what?" Prince Haaken cast a challenging look at Sir Renner, then back at Wick. "I am trusting the two of you to get me the answers needed to make sure my brother receives justice. Is that somehow unclear?"

Feeling the same way he had at Aro when Prince Gage had ordered him, against his better judgment, to depart without him, Wick shook his head. "Nay, Your Royal Highness."

Sir Renner also shook his head.

"Good. Then get moving before you lose them, and take Gage's mount with you. There is no need for my brother to walk all the way to Delkara."

Beginning to regret having ever left the White Fortress in the first place, Wick opened his mouth to try once more to explain, but Prince Haaken turned to the Baron Elmon and began a hurried conversation with him. Drawing a breath, Wick spoke to Sir Renner instead. "If I do what he asks, it will not end well. They know what I look like, and they think me a rebel as well."

Sir Renner frowned. "What are you talking about?"

"The Nikledon soldiers," Wick said, lowering his voice. "His Highness and I crossed paths with them earlier and under less than ideal circumstances. That is why I cannot go. If we come upon them on the road together, I guarantee you, they will seize me as a rebel."

"That will not be a problem," Sir Renner said. "We are not going to join them on the road."

Wick stared at him. "But Prince Haaken's orders—"

"Prince Haaken just lost a family member in an event he has not yet had the chance to grasp logically. His orders need to be taken for their intention, not their exact words. Those Delkaran soldiers would never let us join them. We need to know where they are going, and it is best not to ask for something that you know will be refused. Therefore, we will not seek to ride with them, but we will follow them at a distance."

Wick exhaled and nodded.

Sir Renner motioned to the fenced enclosure where Prince Gage's brown beast stood. "We will still need to take his horse with us. I will grab your mount and mine. See what you can do with the animal."

While Sir Renner hurried away, Wick frowned and headed for the pen. He climbed cautiously through the bars and tried twice to approach Prince Gage's horse. Both times the animal backed away. The third time Wick reached for its reins, the creature laid back its ears.

Sir Renner rode up, and Wick ducked out of the pen to take his own horse from the knight. He nodded back to Prince Gage's horse. "It will not even let me get near it. Do you think it will come of its own accord if I open the gate?"

"It has followed him before. It may be worth a try."

Wick swung the fence open. Sure enough, the horse meandered out of the pen and headed for the manor's gate.

Sir Renner rode alongside the creature and looped a lead line through its reins. He kept going then as if he hadn't done anything at all and left the line slack.

Wick nodded in admiration. "Well done."

"Well, at least now it looks like it belongs with us," Sir Renner said.

Wick quickly mounted his own horse and was about to catch up to the knight when Prince Haaken called out to him. "Sir Wick, wait!" Hurrying up to him, Prince Haaken held out a thick leather-wrapped, book-shaped item. "When you can, give this to Gage for me. Tell him—" Prince Haaken's voice caught. "Tell him that her prayer for me is my prayer for him."

Figuring the words would mean something more to Prince Gage, Wick took the item and placed it in his saddlebag. "I will, Your Royal Highness."

"Thank you," Prince Haaken said. "Porter, open the gate!"

43

Rhonalyn strolled along the shaded top floor of the manor's tower. The wind played with her hair and caused the flowers of the potted plants set at intervals along the parapet to twist in the breeze.

The top of the tower was a beautiful spot with cushioned benches and elaborate lanterns tucked within a hanging garden. The baroness had shown it to her on the first night of her stay. Since then Rhonalyn had visited the spot every day, for it was the perfect place to seize a quiet moment.

She paused to look out over the green land before her. Her mission had been a success. She and Strephon had finalized their negotiations that morning. Over the last several days, he had tried to drive a hard bargain, but she had held her own. For access to Nikor Harbor and freedom from the harbor toll in the future, she had paid in a promise, a trunk's worth of goods, and a king's destrier. A royal document outlining the terms of their new deal was signed, sealed, and in Baron Philip's possession.

Rhonalyn laid her hand against her skirt and felt through to the coin tucked in the hidden pocket underneath. She smiled. Her mother would have been proud of her, for her mother had often proclaimed, *"My princess is just as capable as any prince."*

The fact these words were spoken because Rhonalyn's father had wanted a son had never been lost on Rhonalyn, but that knowledge had also never dampened the pleasure she derived from her mother's adoration. And her father had indeed eventually learned to accept her, though his acceptance had its limits, and she would no doubt have a lot of explaining to do when she returned.

Already she had noticed looks from several of the men in her guard. They were not pleased with her decision to open trade with Delkara, but despite their dislike for her choice, they would not voice their opinions aloud. Her father, on the other hand, would have no qualms about telling her exactly what he thought. But the deed was done for the benefit of all Keric. And not only had she negotiated it to their advantage, she had proven to herself that she was indeed just as capable as a prince, even a king.

"Your Royal Highness, King Strephon," Sir Nolan announced from the top of the tower stairs.

"You looked rather pleased with yourself. Should I be offended?" Strephon asked lightly from where he stood waiting beside Sir Nolan. "Did I agree in the midst of your hard bargaining to that which I could have had for a better price?" he continued in an amused tone.

Dipping a curtsy, Rhonalyn changed the topic by accusing him teasingly. "Do you always sneak up on people?"

"Mayhap." He grinned a boyish smile that made her laugh.

She motioned for Sir Nolan to let Delkara's king pass and glanced back out over Strephon's land. "I have been enjoying the view from up here."

He came to join her. "It is pretty, but it is not as impressive as the view from Ithera."

"Your castle?"

"Aye, there is nothing like it." He leaned against one of the columns supporting the roof.

"Are you there very often?"

"Nay, but when I am, I throw grand feasts."

Rhonalyn laughed. "Of course you do."

"Well, is that not what a castle's great hall is for?"

She laughed again. "I suppose it is."

His eyes trailed over her face.

Suddenly uncomfortable with the intensity of his gaze, she turned away and touched her sapphire necklace, certain she was blushing. "Do not stare at me so."

He shook his head. "You are such a princess."

"Excuse me?"

He chuckled. "You cannot help but give orders."

She opened her mouth to argue but then realized doing so would prove his point.

He smirked.

She pressed her lips together, striving to conceal her amusement.

Reaching out, Strephon plucked a flower from one of the plants in front of him. "You, Princess Rhonalyn, are smart, beautiful, and ambitious. Clearly, you meant what you said in your letter about bringing prosperity to your kingdom by pursuing new ways of doing things." His voice changed. "I am curious though, have all your efforts in this regard been successful?"

Since Rhonalyn's current endeavor was her only full-fledged attempt, she shifted but answered confidently. "Aye, so far."

"And what of opposition to these changes? I assume in coming here to offer Delkara trade and breaking a tradition Keric has held for years, you have faced your share of resistance."

"I am the future queen of Keric. What opposition or resistance arises does not and will not prevent me from pursuing and gaining what I know is best for my kingdom."

"Your confidence in your title is something I once shared, particularly when I first began to rule." Looking troubled, Strephon gazed at the horizon. "But recently, I have begun to realize people do not always choose a logical course of action when resisting change." He turned back to her. "I have spent the last four years striving to improve the lives of my people, but instead of respect and loyalty, I have a group of commoners who have taken to attacking and stealing from my barons and their men. They claim I and my lords have betrayed their trust and that this gives them the right to steal and kill as they please."

His description sounded far too familiar. She clenched her fingers. Clearly, the group that Lord Tenebris and the sheriff of Asper had encountered were not just roaming Keric.

"This group," she asked carefully, trying to sound curious rather than surprised that these well-armed commoners were also terrorizing Delkara, "you have not been able to stop them?"

Strephon heaved a sigh of frustration. "Honestly, catching them has been far more difficult than anticipated. They attack when least expected and are continually fleeing into the cliffs of Nikor. Once in the cliffs, they somehow always find ways to elude us. I have wondered on occasion if they pass all the way through and take refuge in Keric."

At his words, Rhonalyn realized it might actually be a good idea to acknowledge their mutual troubles with the group and thereby remove any question as to their loyalties, but she also decided there was no need to mention that the member they'd caught briefly had claimed to be from Keric. "Nay, they are not taking refuge among us," she said, "for we too have had trouble with a group of thieves who attack and then use the cliffs as a means of retreat during pursuit. We assumed, like you, that they were possibly passing all the way through the cliffs and into Delkara."

Strephon's fingers closed around the flower he was holding. "Perhaps they are doing both. Until this point our two kingdoms have communicated very little. Thus, this group could easily be attacking you and retreating into Delkara and then attacking us and retreating into Keric. As long as they came in and out from the cliffs at different points, they could easily travel as they pleased without anyone being the wiser."

Rhonalyn felt her anger toward the outlaws deepen, for there was an infuriating ingenuity in the possibilities of such a strategy. "You are right. They could be doing exactly that."

"Do you have among your people anyone who is familiar with the cliffs?" Strephon asked.

Rhonalyn recalled the old sheepherder Kalev's tales about the sounds of the crag's lost souls and wondered now if the sounds were actually those coming and going through the cliffs. For obviously, there were ways to pass through since these commoners were clearly doing so. She thought of her mother's stolen coins and closed her fingers around the gold piece pocketed under her skirt. "Nay, I know of no one who knows the cliffs well. But I will find someone who does, even if I have to search all of Keric."

"I have sought for a guide myself but found none," Strephon said. "Mayhap if we unite our efforts, we can help each other drive these fiends out of the cliffs and into the open where we can lay hands on them."

He had Rhonalyn's full attention. "What do you propose?"

44

Awnquera and Duvall were busy with morning foot and cart traffic. Gage kept his head and gaze down, but there was no avoiding the feel of people's eyes staring at him, nor could he ignore the sight of their feet slowing on the street or pausing in doorways. He tried to block out their murmured comments and whispered questions, but he was so afraid of being recognized, even dressed as a commoner, that he found himself instead listening intently to every word spoken. As it turned out, no one cared who he was. Their interest was in what he had done, which made his face burn even hotter.

The slow progression they made through both cities in sight of everyone felt like an emotional gauntlet, forcing him to endure his shame and humiliation over and over again. Leaving the cities behind for empty land and forest felt like a welcome reprieve, until he realized no people meant the soldiers' horses could move more quickly.

Where the pace had been agonizingly slow, now he struggled to keep up. The ropes dug into his wrists more than once before he managed to find a way to effectively alternate between long strides and a quick burst of speed to maintain slack.

It wasn't long though before he began to tire. He stumbled a step, and immediately he had to run to keep from being yanked off his feet. He heard a snicker behind him. "Is it just me or is his dance beginning to lack its previous grace?" one of the soldiers behind him asked. Other soldiers chuckled.

Gage wasn't sure if the man was trying to barb him or to inform the knight, but regardless the distraction made him miss his footing once more.

"He's getting lazy is all," Merek said.

Cold anger wrapped around Gage's chest. He bit his tongue and concentrated on staying upright. Fifty paces later he tripped again, this time on a tree root, and fell onto his knees. He scrambled up and just managed to avoid the rope hauling him forward onto his face. The rush of fear created by the thought of being dragged kept his legs moving for a good while after that.

Damp with sweat and breathing heavily, he jogged to gain ground as the knight's horse started up a hill. Made up of rocks and sand, the loose incline slid beneath the horse's hooves. Struggling as well, Gage's foot caught on the edge of a rock. His ankle twisted, and he landed hard on his forearms and knees. He scrambled up the sandy slope, grabbed the trailing rope, and used it to pull himself back to his feet. Glad the horses coming behind him hadn't trampled him, he trudged onward, his legs trembling.

The more exhausted he became, the more he began to misstep and fall. With his knees and arms bloody and bruised and his shoulder aching, he eventually got to the point where he wondered if it would be easier to just let himself be dragged. Utterly fatigued, he took four more steps, tripped on a tuft of grass, and sprawled headlong onto the road. He swiftly seized the rope in his pulsing fingers and curled his body, waiting for it to tighten and for the ground to tear at him. But the line did not go taut. He drew a shuddering breath and lifted his head. He was lying behind the back legs of the knight's horse. The animal had paused to drink from a stream. Blood was pounding so hard in Gage's head that he hadn't heard the flowing water.

He didn't want to move, but his parched tongue begged him to rise to his knees. He crawled gingerly around the knight's horse, reached the stream's rocky edge, and used his trembling hands to scoop up the cool water.

He brought his fingers to his lips, only to have the rope tugged by the knight and the liquid sloshed from his hands. Gritting his teeth, he dipped his hands and tried again to drink, but again his hands were pulled away from his mouth, spilling the water. A waterskin hit the ground beside him. "Fill it and return it to me," the knight said. "Then you may drink."

Gage considered his options. He could fill the skin and drink out of it himself, hurl it back at the knight, or maybe act like he was going to fill it but instead use the rope, which the knight still had in his hand, to attempt to jerk the knight off his horse. Gage was making up his mind when a boot set against his back and kicked him face-first into the water.

Though not a large stream, it was deep enough to soak him instantly. His heart raced as he struggled to use his bound hands to thrust his mouth and nose out of its depths. Someone splashed in beside him and shoved his head farther under.

As he fought the person's hold, panic and memories mingled inside him. Heaving upward with his fists, he managed to surface briefly. He inhaled half water and half air. He tried to cough the water out of his lungs, but his face was resubmerged. Then just as suddenly the same hands hauled him out and dumped him onto dry ground. On his knees, Gage coughed and heaved water, every bit of him shaking.

Drake walked away from him. "Next time, do as you're told."

45

Wick fidgeted on his horse. "Are you absolutely positive there's nothing in its hoof?" he asked in the commoners' tongue.

"I'm positive." Sir Renner set down his mount's foot and checked the animal's knee once more.

They had had no difficulty entering Delkara as a knight and servant and had trailed the soldiers down the same road that Wick and Gage had come from—the road leading to Delipp and beyond that to Nikledon. Less than an hour into the forest though, Sir Renner's horse had come up lame with no apparent cause.

Having exhausted all explanations and solutions, Sir Renner tried walking beside the animal, but every step seemed to make the creature worse. It could barely hobble down the road even at a painstakingly slow pace.

Too frustrated to have any sympathy for the animal, Wick tightened his hands on his own horse's reins. "Sir Renner, they are long out of sight. What if they turn off on some side path and head to a manor that we might never find?"

"We need to catch up, I know, but we will need speed to do so. I am loath to leave the animal behind, but," Sir Renner nodded toward Prince Gage's dark-brown beast, whose lead line was now in Wick's grasp, "we do have another mount."

Wick shook his head. "He won't let you ride him."

"What other choice do we have?"

Wick's own horse could not carry both of them, at least not at the speed or distance they might possibly need to travel. Therefore, attempting to utilize Prince Gage's horse really did seem to be their only option.

Sir Renner walked calmly toward the animal. The creature eyed Sir Renner but stayed still. The knight reached out to touch the horse's shoulder. It flicked its ears and sidestepped out of his reach. "It's alright," Sir Renner murmured. "I won't hurt you." He tried instead to simply touch the animal's saddle. The horse's ears flattened fully, and it flung its head around to bite at Sir Renner. The lead line Wick held snapped tight.

He kept his grip on it, determined to protect Sir Renner and not lose the animal. The horse squealed. Throwing its head, it tried to spin the opposite direction and run. It hit the end of the lead once more, and Wick put his full weight into pulling the animal back around so that it could not break free.

The moment he did, he realized he'd made a mistake. The horse's eyes rolled white, and it exploded off the ground. It threw a front foot at him, then lashed both back legs at Sir Renner. Its hooves connected with Sir Renner's lower body, sending the knight crashing backward.

Mortified, Wick hollered at the horse and threw the lead line at it. The animal bolted down the road, leaving Wick breathing hard and Sir Renner sprawled on his back. Swinging down off his mount, Wick hurried to Sir Renner. "Are you alright?" he asked as he helped the knight up.

Sir Renner rose on his left leg and tried to put weight on his right. He hissed and clenched his teeth, "Apparently not. He got me pretty good." The knight limped a step, then leaned over breathing heavily. "I'm afraid it wouldn't matter now even if I could get on that horse. I wouldn't be able to ride at speed." Sir Renner looked up at him, pain pinching his expression. "I'm sorry, but you're going to have to go on without me."

Apprehension rose within Wick. "If I'm spotted, I'll end up bound right beside Prince Gage, and I'll be no good to anyone."

"Then don't get spotted. Just find out where they're taking him, then come back to Awnquera."

Wick nodded shakily. He would not forsake Prince Gage or return to Prince Haaken empty handed. "I'll do my best. But can you even walk?"

"About as well as my horse. She and I will hobble back to Duvall."

"What if you cannot make it to the city?"

"I have a weapon and supplies enough to last me two days. I'll manage. Go, and take this. You may need it." The knight quickly loosed something from his belt. He passed a small weighty drawstring purse to Wick. Coins clinked together inside it.

Wick closed his fingers around the purse and then swung back up onto his horse. "Be safe, Sir Renner."

"Same to you, and Godspeed."

46

As Wick rode, his determination dwindled into fear and frustration. He had no idea how far the soldiers were ahead; therefore, he could not just race along, lest he round a corner and run straight into them. To make matters worse, despite the creature's clear dislike of him, Prince Gage's horse had decided to trail along with him, which made concealment impossible.

Thus, though he could move at speed along straight sections, he was stuck riding the curving portions of road with extreme caution. This took time he did not have and made him that much more anxious to find Prince Gage.

His thoughts and complaints churned. Why did Sir Renner's horse have to come up lame? Why did the Nikledon soldiers have to find Prince Gage at Awnquera? And why was he the one sent on this mission? It felt like every opportunity that came his way—like being a member of a royal retinue or going after the rebels at Veiroot—brought with it one calamity or another. He was starting to think that when it came to God's favor in his life, he was definitely more of a Job than a Solomon.

Prince Gage's predicament came to mind, and Wick amended his thoughts. His woes were not nearly as bad as His Highness's. However, that he might still share in Prince Gage's fate, brought him right back to stewing about his own adversities. The more he thought about the trajectory of his current existence the more upset he became. This was, after all, the third time his life had been uprooted and thrown into chaos because of Prince Gage. Why couldn't His Highness become someone else's problem? Why did it have to be him sent to make sure justice was done, as if that were even possible at this point?

He was a capable knight, and if not for Prince Gage, he'd have had a solid future ahead of him. And now he might not even have any future as a knight if he got caught by the soldiers. He had spent his life following orders and doing what was right before God and man, and this was where his faithfulness had led. The coins Sir Renner had given him came to mind, and he thought bitterly about how he could decide, as Prince Gage had done, to simply abandon his position and take off to wherever he pleased as some random commoner.

Not that that choice had actually played out well for His Highness. It was also the reason Wick struggled to have any respect for him. Sighing, he kicked his horse into a gallop down a straight section, then slowed to round another corner. The path was indented with hoof marks, but there was no sight of the Nikledon soldiers or Prince Gage.

Wick thought again about Job and how, no matter what happened, Job remained faithful. He knew he too would stay faithful and stick to his search, but he couldn't help feeling angry about having to do so. Grudgingly, he kicked his horse once more into a gallop and was reminded of what Prince Haaken had said about choosing to respond to situations out of God's mindset, not his own.

It should have been easy to ask God for a correct perspective on the situation, but Wick felt justified in being upset. He had done everything right, and yet this was his reward. He reined his mount back to a walk to steer it up a curving sandy hill and heard the hoofbeats of Prince Gage's mount pound up behind him.

He had to talk himself out of turning around and screaming at the animal, which made him abruptly aware of just how angry he was. He drew a deep breath and exhaled it in a brief prayer. "God, help me." He continued praying, at first just venting his woes, but then he transitioned to sincerely asking God to exchange his fear for peace, his anger for faithfulness, and his indecision for wisdom. As he prayed he felt the chaos inside him begin to ease.

Encountering more empty road ahead, he sighed. "God, you know what I have been sent to accomplish and what You ask of me. Prithee, help me to succeed in this endeavor and to forgive Prince Gage."

As the words came from his mouth, he noticed a glimmer of red in a sandy patch on the road. He saw another spot in the grass about twenty paces farther on. He feared he would find more but saw nothing else as he continued on. Then he came to a stream. There at the edge of the water on the rocks were definite smears of blood.

The whole area around the stream was trampled with hoof marks and boot prints. Sir Wick figured it had to be from the party of soldiers, which meant the blood was almost undoubtedly Prince Gage's. A righteous indignation reawakened Wick's loyalty and his protective zeal.

⁂

WICK SPENT THE next two hours sickeningly and angrily following an intermittent trail of blood and drag marks. He wished more than anything that he had his own men and could overtake the soldiers and put a stop to what they were doing.

Suddenly, he came upon the outer edge of the village that he and Prince Gage had paused in for a meal only a handful of days before. He was about to ride through it when he spotted a collection of horses and riders outside the village tavern. There was no mistaking the colors displayed on the mounts' tack nor the tall frame of Drake amidst the riders. Pulling his mount into the trees, Wick searched quickly for Prince Gage but did not see him among them. The way the soldiers were milling about, he wasn't sure if they were arriving or leaving.

Dismounting, Wick led his horse deeper into the trees. Prince Gage's horse, which had been trailing about twelve horse lengths behind him, stopped on the road and dropped its head to graze. Hoping the animal would not be spotted but not daring to make a commotion by trying to shoo it into the woods, Wick tied his own horse out of sight and crept forward. He stilled when he reached a spot where he could once more see the tavern.

Merek and three others headed inside while Drake and the knight stood out front talking with an armed man in a dark leather tunic. Wick again searched for any sign of Prince Gage but found none. Had they already stopped at a lord's manor? Could it be he'd missed his chance to find him? The blood trail said otherwise, but maybe it wasn't Prince Gage's. Wick's thoughts and fears ran rampant. He squeezed closed his eyes. "God, what do I do?"

A thought entered his mind. If the soldiers had arrived with a prisoner in tow, the villagers would have noticed. All he had to do was ask the right person, without being seen by the soldiers. Wick waited for what felt like an hour for Drake and the knight to finish talking and head into the tavern. Then he cautiously made his way into the village.

With his hat pulled low, he approached a man repairing a croft fence near the road. "Wonder where that lot's coming from," he said in the commoners' tongue.

The man glanced up at him, then over at the tavern. "Who's to know. They come and go as they please. They'll eat and no doubt be on their way again to wherever they are headed." He grunted and scooped up his hammer.

"You get a glimpse of the prisoner they had with them?" Wick asked in between the man's pounding swings.

The man paused. "I did. Won't last the day if you ask me. Looked dead on his feet already."

Wick flinched but forced his voice to remain steady. "Is he in the tavern with them? I can't imagine his presence will make for merry drinking among the common folk."

"Nah, two of 'em dragged him off toward the manor. My guess is they locked him in the undercroft of the old grain barn. Didn't look capable of slipping his ropes to me, but no doubt they figured it was better to put the likes of him under lock and key while they take their time at the tavern."

"The likes of him?"

The man squinted up at him and nodded. "A rebel. Least that's what I suspect, considering the way they're treating him."

Wick shoved down his emotions. "Well, good day to you."

The man grunted and went back to mending his fence.

Trying to look like he actually had business in the village, Wick strolled off down the lane until he was out of sight. Then he carefully returned to his horse and stood in the woods debating his course of action. The man's words about Prince Gage haunted him. Having seen the blood and drag marks on the road, Wick knew what had likely occurred during a good part of the morning. Worse yet, he knew the condition Prince Gage had been in while previously crossing Delkara to Edelmar. He had barely made it riding. Could he make it walking?

"Won't last the day if you ask me."

"I am trusting the two of you to get me the answers needed to make sure my brother receives justice."

To receive justice, Prince Gage needed to be alive. The fact that the soldiers had no issue causing him harm was deeply concerning. Usually, marked individuals were treated decently since their value was in their ability to work. The soldiers' blatant disregard for Prince Gage's well-being opened the very real possibility that they felt no need to make sure he arrived alive.

Unable to approach the soldiers and challenge their actions, and without the time to take the issue to Delkara's king or to Prince Haaken, Wick wondered what he was to do.

The drag marks and blood filled his mind. Legally and morally, lords' men were not permitted to torture a prisoner, but that was essentially what they were doing. The purpose of the law was to punish evildoers and to aid those who did good. Neither of which was taking place here, nor would it take place since Prince Gage had been falsely accused and convicted. He thought of Sir Renner's words: *"Prince Haaken's orders need to be taken for their intention not their exact words."* In this case, did the law also need to be taken for its intention and not its exact words? The soldiers had rightful custody of Prince Gage, but they were using their lawful power over a prisoner in an abusive and illegal manner. The heart of the law was to make sure justice prevailed, which required just punishment of criminals and rightful actions from those in authority.

Wick could not strip the soldiers of the power they were misusing, but he could prevent them from continuing to abuse it. He could remove Prince Gage from their custody. Doing so would be just, but since there was no time to appeal to a higher authority for permission, it would be perceived as unlawful. Fear coursed through him. Dare he take such action? He thought of Prince Haaken's words about seeking

God's mindset. As he had done earlier on the road, he prayed earnestly. "Lord God, prithee show me what You would have me do."

47

UTTERLY SPENT, GAGE lay in the dirt in a dim stall-like enclosure. Drake and the knight had half carried, half dragged him down an earthen ramp into the cavernous underbelly of a barn. The undercroft had an open space for equipment, four normal stalls, and an enclosed stall with a hinged people door. It was in this they had dumped him, locking the door behind them.

His hands had been cut free from the rope, but his fingers were still numb. The rest of his body stung with scrapes and cuts, and he was so exhausted that he hadn't bothered moving from where he had crumpled. On the road all he had been able to concentrate on was staying upright, but now his thoughts wandered. After his late-night conversation with Haaken in Awnquera, he'd actually started to think that perhaps God was not who he had thought He was. He had even begun to embrace Haaken's words about God actually caring about him. But those words rang hollow now, leaving an ache in the part of him that had, for the first time in years, wanted to believe that God had not and would not abandon him.

But abandoned and betrayed was exactly how he felt. At the tavern the knight had taken out the pigeon Haaken had sent. Thinking this meant they had arrived at where they were taking him, Gage had felt hope stir inside him. The knight held the bird in his hand, then he broke its neck and passed it to one of the soldiers. "Should make a fine meal, don't you think?" The soldiers laughed, and the embers of hope that had burned inside Gage turned to ash.

It was as if God had no regard at all for the fact he had just begun to believe in His goodness again. For what good God did such things? What God would save him from death in a clear act of intervention and see him returned safely to Edelmar, only to do nothing to stop him from then being dragged through misery upon misery? It didn't matter what Haaken said or thought; God couldn't be trusted.

Burying his face in his arms, Gage wept tears of bitter anger and screamed inside his head. "Stay away from me, God. You do not care about me, and I want nothing to do with You. Do you hear me?"

The lock on the stall's door rattled. Fear and dread shot through every fiber of Gage's being. He couldn't bear the thought of having to get to his feet yet, let alone trying to walk farther. Why couldn't the soldiers have gotten drunk and stayed at the tavern for the rest of the day?

The rattling continued. Apparently, they were drunk. He cringed at each clink and waited in agony for the door to open. Finally, it did. Someone approached him. Gage fantasized about springing up, overpowering the person, and sprinting away, but he couldn't even motivate himself to lift his head. Squeezing his eyes closed, he anticipated being ordered to rise, knowing he couldn't, and being struck for not doing so.

When a hand touched his arm, he flinched.

"Gage."

Surprise and fear snapped his eyes open. "Sir Wick!" Had they caught him too?

"Thank God, you're conscious," Sir Wick said in the commoners' tongue. "Can you rise? We need to go, quickly, if possible."

Gage stared at Sir Wick, then at the open door behind him. "How did you—" he was going to say, "find me," but Sir Wick answered before he could finish.

"I picked the lock, which I tell you is no easy task while panicking about the possibilities of getting caught."

For a moment, hope rekindled inside Gage. "Are there others with you?"

"No. So, if you don't mind, can we run now and talk later?"

Despair once more darkened Gage's world. "Run?" He shook his head. "I can't even rise. And they will be back any moment. You need to leave, Sir Wick, before they catch you too. Go, while you still can."

Sir Wick muttered, "It's a little late for that."

Unable to handle the thought of watching Sir Wick beaten into submission like he had been, Gage struggled to put force into his voice. "No, it's not too late. Not if you leave before they know you were ever here. Just close the door, and go."

"I won't, nor can I," Sir Wick said. "I have orders to make sure you stay alive and see justice. So, like it or not, your life and mine are intertwined. And I don't care that you have some idiotic notion that me leaving you here to whatever these soldiers do to you next is somehow better for either of us, because you're wrong. What happens to you matters to me, to God, to your family, and to a lot of people. So, stop making decisions for others like you're the only one who cares or has the right to do so. Refusing to let others take a risk to help you isn't selfless; it's selfish. Now, help me help you!"

Gage winced. Sir Wick was right. He wanted to believe that if he could just keep people from trying to help him, they would not get hurt because of him, but it was the same lie he'd held onto during the months after the ambush when he'd told himself his departure was better for everyone. He'd wanted to keep his problems to himself, which hadn't seemed like a selfish choice, but because of it, people had searched for him and feared for him. And now here was Sir Wick once again risking getting caught because of him.

Unfortunately, Gage's willingness to change his position and accept the knight's help didn't make his body capable of doing so. "Sir Wick, for your sake, I wish I could, but at the moment I can't even stand up on my own. I'd get us both caught before we could even make it off this manor."

"You don't have to help me get you off the manor, just out the door and into a wheelbarrow I borrowed. I couldn't sneak the horses in here, and me dragging you out of here was sure to be noticed, so a wheelbarrow with straw in it seemed like the best alternative."

Gage reached out his hand to Sir Wick. "Then why are we still talking?"

✥

HIS HEART POUNDING with relief and fear, Wick strained to steer the wheelbarrow. He trundled it along a section of ground between two strip fields high with grain. Sweat trickled down his bent back, and his hands began to cramp holding onto the wooden handles. He loosed his deathlike grip and tried to look like he was truly just transporting a simple load of straw, but the more ground he crossed, the more Prince Gage's weight made it difficult to maintain the illusion. Thankfully, many of the manor's workers were occupied with sheep shearing on the other side of the manor. The few serfs coming and going glanced his way as he struggled past, but none of them stared for long or called out to question him. He trekked onward, yearning with every breath for the safety of the woods.

The closer he drew, the more the possibility of getting caught screamed inside him. His heart thundering, he prayed. "God, help us make it."

He didn't know how often new people worked on the manor, but he was pretty sure the moment the soldiers' prisoner was discovered missing, someone would put two and two together. Stressing over this, he hit a bump and had to put his full weight into one handle of the wheelbarrow to keep from dumping Prince Gage into a field. The wood creaked loudly and threatened to break on him. He held his breath. The handle held, and he managed to balance out the weight once more. He exhaled and told himself to be more careful, or it wouldn't be people's assumptions that gave them away.

Grunting at the effort, he shoved the wheelbarrow onward, thankful Prince Gage wasn't the well-fed, muscular jouster he'd been a year and a half ago.

"Hey!" a serf yelled. Wick's heart flinched and began to race even harder. Were they calling to him? Did he dare look back, or should he just pretend he hadn't heard?

"What?" someone answered in return.

"Bring that shovel when you come."

Wick breathed again and in four strides trundled his load into the forest's embrace. He twisted and turned around trees until he could no longer see anyone through the leaves, then eagerly lowered the wheelbarrow to the ground. Wiping the perspiration from his face, he sighed. "You can come out. We're in the woods. It will be easier to continue on foot from here."

The pile of straw stirred, and Prince Gage emerged. Wick winced seeing him in full light. The chaff stuck to the sticky smears of blood trailing from his bruises and scrapes, and his mark was plainly visible. Prince Gage tried to rise from the wheelbarrow but couldn't manage to do so. Wick caught him around the waist. "Here." Hooking Prince Gage's arm over his shoulder, Wick pulled him up and helped him through the woods.

"What now?" Prince Gage asked, his body trembling in Wick's grasp.

"We get to the horses, and we get out of here."

"I can't go back to Edelmar."

"I know." Wick expected to feel resentment rise up inside him at the acknowledgment, but it didn't come. Instead, all he felt was determination. "We're going to get you justice."

"How?"

Wick turned sideways, so they could maneuver together under a low branch. "Why don't we start by you telling me everything you know."

As they made their way through the woods, both sweating buckets, Prince Gage haltingly told him about Manton, what he'd discovered about his smuggling after speaking with Lady Natriece, his swift departure from the fair, Sir Jarret finding the gold in his saddlebags, the unidentifiable entourage of soldiers with Felix, and the rebels' attack.

"Alright," Wick said, "so all we need to do is track down Manton, get the names of the real thieves from him, apprehend them, and bring them to whoever's mark that is." Wick sighed. "Except we have no idea where to find Manton, we're not equipped to apprehend anyone, we don't know whose mark it is, and we don't have the gold."

"Now you know why I told you to leave me in the cell."

Wick clenched his jaw. "We just need a better plan, that's all. Any ideas?"

"No," Prince Gage said. "But I do know a way we might be able to track down Manton."

"Really?"

"We'll need to go to Delipp."

"Delipp." Wick puffed out a breath and tried to sound hopeful. "Well, it's closer than Legan and likely not the direction the soldiers will look first."

48

Riding to Delipp was not as difficult as Gage had feared it would be. Rest, food, and drink had helped, and despite keeping a constant vigil for any soldiers, they were able to cover ground at a decent pace. Still, they didn't reach the city until after dark. With the city gates closed, they camped in the woods. But unlike their last night outside of Delipp, this time the weather was clear. And because he'd loaded Athalos before the soldiers had come, Gage not only had clean clothes, replacement vambraces, a dagger, an extra knife for his boot, and water to wash up, he also had a thick cloak, a blanket, cookware, and plenty of food.

The following morning after they'd both changed their appearances as much as they could, they cautiously made their way back along irrigated fields and up to the city gate. The guards there were minimal, lax, and seemed to only be collecting tolls. Convinced there were no Nikledon soldiers present, he and Sir Wick risked seeking entrance.

Less than a quarter hour later, Gage passed under the big trees in Delipp's square. The overflowing water basin with its nymph and hippocampus trickled on one end of the square while the church rose up on the other. Watching the people around him doing business, Gage could not help but think about the last time he'd been there.

Sir Wick nodded toward the door to the chandler's shop. "Is that the place?"

"Yes. Wait here for me." Gage crossed the open ground and entered the shop. The sweet smell of beeswax greeted him. He inhaled the scent and waited for his eyes to adjust to the shop's dim interior. He could hear a scraping sound at the back of the shop. Circling a low-hanging line of golden candles, he spotted Evan cleaning the edges of his wax vat. "Evan."

The old man looked up. "Gabe!" A smile burst over his face. "It's good to see you." Glancing past him, Evan's smile faded into a frown. "Manton isn't with you?"

"No, but he's why I'm here. Have you seen him lately?"

"He came here after the fair asking the same thing about you. Said you left the grounds in a hurry without mentioning where you were going."

"I did, and I owe him an explanation. But first I need to find him. Do you know where he might be?"

"Well, I haven't seen him for a while." Evan scratched the gray stubble on his jawline. "You might try looking for him at Dinslage though."

The city name drew to Gage's mind the faces of Manton's two friends he'd met at the fair. "Isn't that where Arron and Michael are from?"

Evan seemed surprised he knew those names. "It is."

"Do you know where in Dinslage I could find them? If Manton passed through there, they might be the ones who can tell me where he was headed next."

Nodding at his words, it took Evan a moment to respond. "Try Murk Tavern."

"Murk Tavern. I'll do that. Thank you."

Gage stepped back out into the sunlit square feeling uneasy. He couldn't be sure how much the old man knew about the fair or if it was even safe to follow his instructions. Truth be told though, he wasn't even sure how much Manton knew. They could think he still had the coins, which would perhaps explain why Evan was willing to help him. Or was he helping him?

"I take it from your expression," Sir Wick said, "that the conversation didn't go as well as hoped."

Gage glanced back at the chandler's shop. "Depends on if we dare trust an old man who's probably a rebel and who may or may not trust me."

"Have we any alternative?"

"No."

"Well, then where are we headed?"

"Murk Tavern in Dinslage."

Sir Wick snorted. "If that doesn't sound like the perfect place for an ambush, I don't know what does."

Gage swung onto Athalos. "Exactly. So, we keep both eyes open and weapons at hand."

※

"W‍ELL, AT LEAST we know the tavern exists," Gage said to Sir Wick a day later as they worked their way along yet another street in Dinslage looking for it.

They had been told by a potter a quarter hour earlier that Murk Tavern was a well-known establishment in the center of the south side of the city, but Dinslage was sprawling.

Having obviously outgrown itself multiple times and in no particular regard, the city's buildings and shops towered in varying degrees of crowdedness across a broad stretch of uneven land. Portions of what had clearly at one point been the city's ramparts could be seen at intervals, but it was as if the city had clawed through its own walls to seize more ground. While navigating, one encountered a variety of strange sights from broad streets cut off by random chunks of wall, guard towers being used for businesses, and city gates that opened into people's vegetable gardens.

The exuberance and disorderliness of the city's layout was quite opposite from the city's atmosphere, which felt withdrawn and self-contained, almost as if, despite lacking effective fortification, there was a clear warning toward outsiders that they were noticed and being watched. Since travelers could access the city from just about any direction, Gage was at first at a loss to identify what created this feeling. The local people were reserved but didn't seem overly observant or hostile and went about their business with the general clamor of city life. It wasn't until he started noticing the silent watchmen everywhere that the feeling made sense. Apparently, Dinslage's guard functioned inside the city instead of on the city's rim.

He had spotted the first yellow-clothed guard tucked inside a one-man tower on a street corner and another up on a balcony watching those below. Then he'd noticed them on the move as well. One rode along a side street. Two others spoke with a shopkeeper. Their presence throughout the city made them feel more like that of an occupying force than guardians of the city's residents.

That he and Sir Wick had come to Dinslage in search of rebels told Gage the lord of Dinslage was wise to display such a raw blade. Yet at the same time, his previous experiences with Delkaran soldiers made it hard not to feel unnerved.

"You're seeing them too, aren't you?" Sir Wick said.

Gage nodded. "Two are coming this way."

"Just pretend they aren't there."

"Easier said than done," Gage muttered. He knew Sir Wick was right. If they acted like they belonged, they probably wouldn't have any issues, but his heart rate still increased as the guards neared.

It was only once they were past and he could breathe again that he realized, in his and Sir Wick's winding journey up one lane and through to another, they had somehow ended up back on a street they'd previously been down.

Begrudgingly they asked a second time for directions. Finally they found Murk Tavern three streets down and one row over. The shop next door to it had half a dozen outdoor fires in use preserving meat. The smoldering green wood filled the whole area with a heavily scented haze. Gage's stomach growled at the smell.

"Well, dare we venture inside?" Sir Wick asked over the crackle of the fires, the tavern's drifting music, and the general din of the busy street.

Viewing the tavern's broad door and two grime-coated windows partially lit by the setting sun, Gage thought about the way he and Manton had always come and gone from such places. "I say you go first and find somewhere to sit. I'll come in after you. If I see any familiar faces, I'll either approach them or sit by myself, leaving you to watch my back. But if I enter and don't see anyone I recognize, I'll come sit with you, and we'll figure out what to do next."

49

Wick entered the tavern and inwardly cringed as he noted among its patrons a group of soldiers. Thankfully, they were from Dinslage. Their serious expressions and yellow uniforms with black boar's heads above crossed boar spears kept them segregated from the tavern's sea of laughing faces and un-dyed tunics.

Purchasing something to eat and drink, Wick slid into a spot where his back was to a wall but in a central enough location to see almost everyone in the tavern. In front of him, two lively gittern players plucked their instruments with quills while a third minstrel blew heartily on a shawm. Beyond the musicians, three tables of games were surrounded by a number of patrons. Wick heard dice being rolled at one along with the howls of the success and failure of the rollers. Around the other two tables men sat opposite each other at draughts, chess, and mancala boards.

Prince Gage entered the tavern and tarried by the door, his eyes roaming the room. Wick glanced back at his food, then at the soldiers. They were plenty occupied with their drinks.

A moment later, Prince Gage approached and gestured to the empty bench beside Wick. "May I?"

Wick shrugged, keeping his eyes on the game tables.

"I recognize no one," Prince Gage murmured. "But maybe if we wait, someone will show up?"

"Maybe," Wick said, "or maybe our answer is already here. See the chessboard across the room? It looks a lot like the ones Manton was purchasing from Brit Carver of Dulcis."

Prince Gage stiffened. "Then maybe we should go play some chess and see if any of the pieces open."

"We could, but if we find a message within one of the pieces what are the chances we'll actually understand it?"

"I take it you have a better idea?"

Wick nodded. "If we keep an eye on the game, maybe we can spot someone who comes for the message."

"In other words, sit here and be patient?"

Wick chuckled at the annoyance in Prince Gage's voice. "It's a useful skill."

For a long while they chatted on and off as they watched those coming and going from the game tables, but they saw nothing out of the ordinary. Wick was about to admit that perhaps they should check out the chess pieces to be sure it even was one of Manton's boards when a newcomer approached the chess table.

The man hovered behind one of the players but seemed to simply be there to watch. The player he stood behind captured a new piece and set it alongside the board. Wick sighed. "I think maybe we—" He didn't finish, for just then the man he'd been observing leaned forward, placed his hand beside the board, and said something to the player. When the newcomer withdrew his hand and straightened, the player's newly captured piece was gone.

"He has a bishop."

"The player on the left?" Prince Gage asked.

"No, the man who just leaned over the table."

"Oh, well the player on the left just twisted open a different piece under the table."

Having missed the other player's actions while distracted by the newcomer, Wick attempted to keep an eye on both. "Which one do we follow?"

"I say whichever one leaves first," Prince Gage answered, "for we can't exactly ask questions of either of them here in the tavern."

The man with the bishop moved a short distance away from the table and turned to face the wall. Meanwhile, the player on the left casually noted those around him, then tipped his hand in his lap to see whatever he had withdrawn from the piece. Being across the room, Wick could see his movements under the table, but could only tell what he was doing because he knew what he was looking for. Otherwise he would have just assumed the player was fiddling with a piece while concentrating on the game.

The newcomer with the bishop returned to the table and again leaned over the player's shoulder. When he pulled away, the bishop was back on the table, and a moment later, the man headed for the door.

Prince Gage shifted. "Time to go."

Wick nodded. "You leave first. I'll follow."

50

Rhonalyn's maids had just begun unlacing her traveling dress when a knock sounded on the door of her room on the inn's third floor. "Your Royal Highness, are you feeling well?"

Pulled from thoughts about her and Strephon's plan to clear the cliffs, Rhonalyn frowned at Baron Philip's question. She motioned for Kendra to leave off loosening her dress and open the door. They were staying at the same inn in Dinslage they'd used on their way to Nikledon. Unlike most of the other inns she'd found in Delkara, this one actually had a room suited for her use. It consisted of half the inn's third floor, had a large four-poster bed, a decent feather mattress, quality linens, thick curtains, a trundle bed, and a well-stocked fireplace.

Baron Philip bowed quickly. "Forgive my intrusion. I just wanted to confirm you are feeling well."

"Of course, I am well," Rhonalyn answered, then noted the worry creasing his face. Unease crawled through her. "Why do you ask?"

The baron switched to the commoners' tongue as his gaze searched the room. "And Lady Aisley and your maids? They're all feeling well?"

The two maids nodded, and Rhonalyn glanced at Aisley, who was sitting on the floor by the fire with a book Baroness Juliana had given her. The girl's eyes lifted from reading. "I'm fine."

"Good. I'm glad." Baron Philip looked relieved but still concerned.

Rhonalyn eyed him. "What is going on?" she asked in the noblemen's tongue.

He hesitated before answering. "Several of the guard are ill. I think probably due to something they ate."

"How ill?"

"I am hopeful they will be fine by morning."

The nervous edge to his voice seized Rhonalyn's attention. "How many of them?"

He shifted. "Three quarters."

"Three quarters!" Rhonalyn's stomach rolled, and she wondered if she really was well after all. "How did this happen?"

"I am not sure, but I intend to find out."

"Let me know the moment you do."

Baron Phillip bowed. "Aye, Your Royal Highness."

※

Despite being on foot, the tavern's patron moved swiftly through Dinslage in the descending dusk. Gage and Sir Wick trailed the man along one street after another, through a portion of wall, and out the southern side of the city. The man cut across a narrow meadow where cows, a herd of sheep, and a few goats grazed. For a moment Gage thought they would lose him in the woods, but just on the edge of the tree line the man turned and headed toward what looked like a barn.

Choosing a different trajectory in case the man looked back, Gage steered Athalos onto a path that curved along the outer edge of the meadow toward the same tree line but a ways to the right of the stone-and-wood building. The man they were following headed around the back of the barn and out of sight.

Gage urged Athalos into a trot. At the point the path they were on reached the trees, it divided into multiple trails. One branched west, another continued as a footpath straight into the woods, and the third turned east. The westward route was clearly more heavily traveled. What veered eastward along the forest's edge toward the barn did not look to be an actual road but was wide enough to be one. Gage could see along it to the back of the barn where several mounts stood tied. He was just about to suggest they work their way that direction, when the man they'd followed exited the barn, swung up onto one of these mounts, and rode down the eastward forest trail.

Gage's heartbeat quickened at what he saw.

"Aren't we going to follow him?" Sir Wick asked.

"No," Gage growled.

"Why not?"

He jutted his chin toward the back of the barn. "Because that's Nigel, Manton's mule tied with the other mount."

"You're sure?"

"I'm positive. I traveled with the animal for months and tacked it on more than one occasion. I'd know it and its load anywhere. See the bag with the dark leather strings and the light colored patch? That's Manton's game bag."

"Do you think he's inside?"

Gage clenched his jaw. "Only one way to find out."

51

Rhonalyn paced from the canopy bed to the door, then back to where Tess still waited to assist her in undressing. She was no longer interested in preparing for bed. She was too busy worrying about what was to be done if the men were still ill by morning.

"Do you think the guards will be all right?" Aisley asked. When Rhonalyn didn't respond, she repeated her question in the commoners' tongue.

"I'm sure they'll be fine," Kendra answered quietly.

"I didn't notice any of them looking sick when we arrived."

Rhonalyn considered the child's observation. "No, you're right. They all looked well."

"It's been several hours since we arrived," Tess said. "If more than one of them is suddenly feeling unwell it is likely something they ate."

Rhonalyn located her mother's coin beneath her skirt and closed her fingers around it. She'd been too preoccupied that day to notice what her men were eating, and she'd taken her evening meal in her room with her maids, so she had no way of knowing if her guard had all shared the same dish or not. Bad food or poison seemed the most likely suspects, and both could be deadly, though the intentionality of one over the other was far more concerning. It was a miracle she, her maids, and Aisley were all fine. She continued pacing.

Something hit the floor in the hall outside her room with a heavy thud. She frowned in that direction. Had one of her two door guards fallen over? A knock sounded. Rhonalyn exhaled. Apparently, they were fine. The knock sounded again. "Your Royal Highness?"

She didn't recognize the voice and assumed this meant her normal guard was probably part of those sick. She nodded, and Kendra lifted the bar on the door. Rather than one of her uniformed guards, two cloaked men and a woman in common clothes entered and bowed.

Rhonalyn stiffened. "What is the meaning of this? Who are you? Guards!"

The woman, probably twice her age, with weary features but bright green eyes, stretched out her hand. "Please, Your Royal Highness, hear us out. We have come to seek an audience with you."

"Well, I don't give an audience to people who come after dark and barge into my private chambers." Rhonalyn opened her mouth to yell once more for those who should have been right outside her door.

"Don't." The first of the two men flipped back his cloak and raised a loaded crossbow. "Don't call out again."

Rhonalyn's breath caught in her throat. Tess gasped, and Aisley whimpered. Kendra, on the other hand, grabbed a fire poker and swung it at the man. The other cloaked figure, a large man with red hair, closed his arms around her and wrestled the tool out of her grasp. Kendra clawed at him and would have screamed, but he clamped his hand over her mouth. Muffled, she struggled against him.

A cold shudder traveled down Rhonalyn's spine. She met the gaze of the man with the crossbow and tried to sound braver than she felt. "What do you want?" His eyes held hers as his work-worn hands kept the weapon steady.

"Forgive my husband. This is not the way we wished this to go." The green-eyed woman placed her hand on the man's darkly tanned arm. He frowned at his wife but lowered the crossbow a bit. "We really do need an audience with you," the woman continued, "but you must come with us for that to happen." She stepped forward.

Rhonalyn backed away. "I'm not going anywhere with you." The fact that no one had answered her earlier cry settled over her like a suffocating avalanche. "Where is my guard? What have you done to them?"

With an annoyed grunt, the husband spoke over his shoulder. "Bring them inside, and bolt the door." Two more commoners dragged her two guards bound and gagged into the room.

Rhonalyn gasped in dismay. "Wyn!" Other than looking outraged at being tied up, her cousin and his fellow guardsman appeared unharmed. Anger and fear surged through Rhonalyn. "How dare—"

"Don't lecture us." The man leveled his crossbow at her once more. "We're doing what we must. Now, you decide. Will you heed our request and come with us, or should we take you by force?"

"I'm not leaving this room."

"Are your people's lives valuable to you?" the woman asked.

"Of course they are!" Rhonalyn said, frightened by the possible threat in her words.

"Good, then come and hear us out, because we value their lives as well. We're not here to do harm to you or them. That's why your men are sick and not dead and why we didn't kill these two outside your door."

Rhonalyn's stomach clenched. "It was you who made my men sick!"

"They are alive," the husband said with a growl. "Whether they stay that way or not is up to you."

The woman sighed. "Please, come with us willingly, and no further pain or harm need come of any of this. I promise you. You will be back here and on your way again in the morning as if we were never here."

Rhonalyn had no idea if she could trust their promises, but the state of her guards told her they were quite capable of carrying out their threats and would no doubt take her from the inn regardless of her desires. Trembling, she nodded slowly. "I will come."

"Good, then we have a deal. But this little one will come with us to make sure you keep your end of it." The woman crossed the room and drew Aisley to her feet. The girl squeaked like a mouse caught by a cat. The woman shushed her, and Aisley went instantly silent.

The man with the crossbow motioned to the three other commoners. "Bind her two maids to keep them quiet, then make sure the servants' backstair is still clear."

52

Sword in hand, Wick crouched beside Prince Gage next to the barn's stone base. The sounds of nightfall were stirring to life around them when they heard a gruff, nervous voice inside the barn. "When you finish saddling that one, can you get these reins unknotted?"

"I'll see to it," a laid-back voice replied.

"We were supposed to have them ready to go before dark."

"They'll be ready in plenty of time."

Wick glanced at Prince Gage. The look on his face in the swiftly fading light told Wick that at least one of the voices was familiar. Prince Gage rose to his feet and headed for the barn door. All pretense of stealth or caution was gone from his posture.

Wick hesitated for only a moment, then raced after him. Wisdom told him to snatch His Highness back and force him to create a plan rather than acting recklessly, but it was too late for that.

Prince Gage shoved through the door and entered the barn like he owned it. Wick eased in after him, glad for the lanterns that lit the place. Flickering light fell through slatted walls on either side of the large doorway and over heaps of hay piled between the building's support posts. On the east end of the barn three horses stood tied to posts while two more horses stomped beside a hay wain parked at the west end of the building. A stocky, bald man, who must have heard them enter, came around the horses by the hay wain. He pulled a knife and eyed them. Meanwhile, a tall fellow with light-brown hair and a scraggly beard was bent over tightening a cinch on one of the three other horses.

Wick didn't have to wonder who was who. Prince Gage aimed straight for the light-haired man. "Manton!"

The stocky man hesitated, apparently unsure if they represented a threat or not. Manton snapped upright. "Gabriel! What in heaven's name are you doing here?"

Prince Gage punched him. The blow knocked Manton flat on his back between the horses. "What am I doing here? I'll tell you what I am doing here. I'm here for answers. Where did those gold coins come from? And who stole them?"

Manton sat up rubbing his jaw. His surprise was gone, and his voice held idle annoyance. "Oh, so now you want answers?" Manton shoved to his feet. "You know, if you'd waited like you said you were going to, you wouldn't have even known those coins existed." Dusting himself off, Manton shrugged. "Besides, why are you so mad? You're the one who ended up with them."

Wick cringed. Wrong answer. He closed his eyes but still heard the thud. Opening his eyes, he watched Manton stagger and straighten. Blood trickled from Manton's nose, and an awakened vengefulness entered his eyes. "What is your problem?" he bellowed.

"You are!" Prince Gage swung at him once more, and Manton delivered his own quick blow.

Wick figured it was time to intervene, but he wasn't the only one who had come to that conclusion. The stocky, bald rebel headed for Prince Gage as well. Wick stepped in his way and pointed his sword at the man. "Stay back." The rebel's knife flashed, knocking Wick's blade aside and opening a path for the man to plow full-speed into him. Tangled up with the man, Wick crashed backward into a large hay pile with the rebel on top of him. He fought to free himself, but the more he struggled, the deeper he sank in the hay. Past the man's bald head, he saw Prince Gage's and Manton's fistfight grow in fury. He struggled harder to untangle himself from his adversary. The rebel held his sword hand pinned, but Wick got his left fist free and nailed the man low in the ribs.

Growling, the rebel tried to strike at him with his knife. Wick caught the man's wrist, suspending the blade above his chest. Eyes locked with his, the rebel continued to drive the weapon downward with unrelenting force. The pressure of holding it back began to build against Wick. His arm shook. He stared at the knife's slowly lowering tip. If he didn't do something, he was sure the blade would end up buried in his chest.

Gathering his strength, Wick threw his full weight sideways. The knife jammed into the hay beside his shoulder, and the rebel's bulk descended with it into the fodder. Squirming backward to gain space between them, Wick pulled up his feet and booted the man in the stomach. The force of his kick wrenched the man's fingers off his sword arm and sent the rebel rolling down the hay. Inhaling sharply, Wick swept his sword back up and into motion.

The rebel scrambled out of the hay pile. Wick followed him, breathing hard and driving him backward. Keeping his focus on his rival but also needing to know if Prince Gage was all right, he flicked his gaze toward the thuds and grunts across the barn.

Despite the intensity at which Prince Gage and his past traveling companion were punching, dodging, and scrambling about the hay, neither had drawn a weapon. Wick's own attacker retreated down the side of the hay wain past the tied horses.

Wick advanced, hoping to corner him against the wagon and the back of the barn. The rebel dodged between the wall and the hay wain's back wheels and crawled beneath its flat surface. Following him would have put Wick at an equal disadvantage on his hands and knees, and circling it while guessing where the man would come out was a mistake his brothers had often made while chasing him as a boy. Instead, Wick heaved himself on top of the hay wain. The flat wooden surface rocked and creaked beneath his feet. Becoming motionless, Wick waited for the rebel to emerge from beneath it.

⚘

Gage had no desire to draw his dagger and turn his and Manton's fight into a trial by combat. The only problem was, Manton was swiftly proving himself the more adept at dodging and using his fists. In his rage Gage had been convinced he could beat Manton without needing a weapon, but his stinging lip, aching shoulder, and bruised ribs told him he needed to rethink his approach.

His fingers clenched and his eyes locked on Manton, he kept his feet moving. Manton circled with him, no longer appearing annoyed but simply focused, as if their fight was just a task he was determined to finish.

Regretting having not used his moment of surprise to immediately apprehend Manton, Gage mapped his next steps more carefully. The numerous chess games he had played with Manton had taught him a lot about Manton's strategies. But the way the fight was going, he figured he'd only have one attempt to utilize what he knew.

He swung a punch. It went wide, leaving him exposed. He swiftly retreated, running into a post as he did. Manton took swift advantage of his inability to back away and closed the distance between them. Manton's first punch collided with Gage's bruised arms, and the second caught him in the side.

Groaning and ducking, Gage splayed his left hand in front of his face and lowered his right arm as if in defeat. With his head tipped down, he saw exactly what he expected, Manton drawing a knife. He grabbed Manton's wrist and, drawing his own dagger, pressed its tip into Manton's side. "Drop it."

The disbelief on Manton's face diverged into a look of admiration. "Well played." He loosened his fingers, and Gage took the knife from him. "You know," Manton said, "there's no need for you and I to be enemies. We can work this out."

"We are enemies. You're a criminal."

"No, I'm not," Manton said with conviction. "I'm someone who is helping people stand against the injustices and wrongs taking place against them. The lords in Delkara are abusing their power and stealing what has rightfully belonged to the common people for generations. A return to reasonable labor requirements and fair taxes is all we're asking for, but the lords refuse to listen. People in Delkara are starving, Gabe, and not because there isn't food to be had but because the ruling class is taking it in taxes and selling it off to fill their own coffers. Therefore, the way I see it, our efforts are a just restoration of goods from the lords back to the people."

"Don't spin your lies to me," Gage said in disgust. "These wrongs you speak of are nothing but tales told to justify attacking and stealing from whatever lords you choose to target."

Frustration entered Manton's voice. "You know that's not true. You saw what took place at Delipp and at the fair."

"No!" Gage said. "What I saw were lords responding to attacks made against them. And what I know is what I witnessed in Edelmar when the retinue of a nobleman who had done nothing to deserve it was attacked by your rebel friends. I was there. I heard them spout the same lies to justify stealing from him and killing those who got in their way, both noble and common alike." Gage blinked back the stinging heat in his eyes. "So don't you dare tell me that your rebel cause is just or honorable. You and every last one of your companions deserve to be hanged."

Manton looked confused. "This attack you witnessed was in Edelmar?"

"Yes."

Manton shook his head. "That's not possible. We've never taken action against anyone in Edelmar. If a lord was attacked there, it wasn't our doing."

"Don't try to manipulate me, Manton. I'm not buying your lies any more. You were traveling in Edelmar when I met you and deceiving me even then. You and your kind clearly cross the border, and even if you really thought that what you've just said is true, there's no way you could possibly know everyone your rebel companions have or haven't attacked."

"No, listen to me!" Manton sounded and looked shaken. "Yes, we travel to Edelmar, because for those of us who can get there, it's a safe place to retreat to and sell what we've taken from the lords of Delkara. Risking losing our safety on that side of the border by attacking anyone in Edelmar would be absolutely foolish on our part. We're already waging a war in Delkara that we're ill equipped to win. We've every motivation to not bring the wrath of any other kingdom down on ourselves."

"You say that, but I've heard you speak against the injustices in Edelmar."

"Of course you have. Why would I not, considering where I come from? But what happens in Edelmar is nothing compared to what's taking place here in Delkara. Here we're fighting against the tyranny of the lords for the sake of our people's very lives."

"And that's supposed to convince me that you actually—"

"Watch your back!"

At Sir Wick's shout, Gage spun around. With a knife in hand, the bald rebel scrambled off the ground near the hay wain and ran at him. Clutching Manton's knife and his own dagger, Gage prepared to defend himself. The hay wain rocked crazily as Sir Wick leapt from it. The knight hit the ground and dove at the man's legs. The bald rebel slammed into the ground with Sir Wick's arm wrapped around his ankles. Sword still in hand, Sir Wick scrambled forward and pinned the man down.

Trembling in anger, Gage turned on Manton. He pressed him backward with both blades, one at Manton's neck and the other at his stomach. "Stop just moving your mouth, and tell me who stole those gold coins and from which lord!"

"And then what?" Manton asked.

"Then I'll make sure justice is done."

"Justice?" Manton shook his head. "If you think turning over those coins and those who took them to a Delkaran lord will result in fair judgment, you're a fool. The courts of Delkara no longer know justice. All you will do is get good men killed. You'll risk the lives of the few people brave enough to ask the same things you asked for in Edelmar, when you demanded back the money for every person at that rat-infested inn. Gabe, you believe as we do, that no commoner should be mistreated simply because they lack a voice and that those in positions of authority should be held accountable for what they do and don't do with their power."

Gage's stomach twisted at the realization that this was how he had been perceived. "No! I don't believe as you do. You're murderers and thieves."

"You still don't get it," Manton said. "Those gold coins were taken from soldiers coming back from Lemar. The same soldiers who the day before delivered to Lemar six wagons full of Delkaran food. They made a profit selling those goods while those who worked to produce them are starving."

"Yet your rebel friends stole the gold and not the food," Gage said.

"Believe me, they'd have taken the produce and grain, but we didn't know about it being transported to Lemar until after the wagons were already gone. Stealing the profit they returned with at least helps put food back in our people's mouths."

"Which lord was the gold taken from?"

Manton shrugged. "I never asked."

Offended further that it didn't even matter to him which lord they'd stolen from, Gage shook his head. "Then you're the one who's a fool. Tell me the names of the rebels who stole the gold and where I can find them."

"You won't find them," Manton said.

"I found you, didn't I?"

Manton paused and frowned. "Yes, you did. How did you manage that?"

"It was Evan who pointed us to Dinslage, but it was Nigel who gave you away."

"Nigel? Well, I'm not sure whether to be impressed or baffled."

Gage glared. "Stop wasting my time and answer my questions."

Manton smiled and tipped his head. "I could, but that'd defeat the purpose."

"Gabe?" The serious warning in Sir Wick's voice drew Gage's attention. Sir Wick's empty hands were raised, and he was easing his knee off the other rebel's back.

A man advanced into the barn's lantern light holding a crossbow with a bolt aimed for Sir Wick's chest. The same gut-wrenching fear that the Blue Crow and his archers had caused when they'd stepped from the woods filled Gage. "You too," the man said, jutting his chin at him. "Drop the blades and back away from him."

This time Gage didn't question whether or not their threat would be carried out. He tossed both weapons and stepped away from Manton.

Manton bent to retrieve the knives. "Your timing couldn't have been better."

"Really?" the crossbow man said sharply. "Because to me it looks like we've been discovered and are probably even now being surrounded."

A bulky, red-haired man stepped into the light behind the first man. "We figured they'd find us in the city, not here. How long do we have?"

53

Rhonalyn pulled Aisley close beside her in the shadows inside the barn door. The concealment of the dark commoners' cloaks she and the girl had been forced to wear from the inn suddenly felt like protection. Rhonalyn had no idea who the two strangers were who had paused their captors' hurried rush into the barn or why they might be surrounding them, but she was grateful for every moment's delay that increased the possibility of her guard finding them.

The lanky commoner with shoulder-length brown hair shoved the knives into his belt. "Relax. They're not soldiers. This is Gabriel, a past acquaintance. He recognized my mule and came to settle a misunderstanding between us."

The green-eyed woman stayed beside Rhonalyn and Aisley while the two other men advanced into the barn. "Gabriel?" the woman's husband said. "As in Gabe, your traveling companion, in whose bag you stored the goods you were charged with transporting?"

His accusation was met with annoyance. "Yes, that Gabe."

"Does he still have those goods?" the large red-haired man asked.

"No," Gabe replied, "and even if I did, I wouldn't hand it over to the likes of you."

"We don't have time for this," the woman commented. "We've got other business to attend to."

"She's right," her husband said. "You two, deal with them. The rest of you get mounted."

Pulling Aisley back into her grasp, the woman gestured for Rhonalyn to move ahead of her toward a trio of horses.

Trembling inside, Rhonalyn walked rigidly forward, trying to appear composed and powerful despite the panic consuming her. What did "deal with them" mean? Were they going to kill the two men? And what about her and Aisley? Her stomach, which was already twisted in knots, rolled. Bile rose up her throat and into her mouth. She didn't believe these people just wanted to talk to her. They had to want something. She swallowed hard.

The lanky commoner untied a lead line from one of the horse's bridles and sliced it in half. Rhonalyn told herself not to watch, but she couldn't help herself. Her gaze followed him to the two men. Gabe stared back at her. He appeared aghast. Then his expression turned into a look of extreme anger. Rhonalyn was used to her presence causing adoration and intimidation but never fury. Frightened even further, she slowed her approach to the horses.

She actually felt relieved when the lanky commoner and his bald comrade seized Gabe's arms. They pulled him to where they could bind his hands around behind a post. He twisted against them. "Tell me, is this the just rebellion you spoke of, Manton? Kidnapping nobility? Who are they? Which lords' daughters?" He wrenched against the post. "What are you going to do with them?"

Realizing he wasn't furious at her but on her behalf, Rhonalyn felt her stomach roll once more and her skin turn hot.

"Despite how this looks," Manton said as he moved to tie up Gabe's companion, "we're not monsters. We don't intend to harm them or the two of you."

"For some strange reason," Gabe said with vehemence, "I don't believe you."

"We need to move," the man with the crossbow said as he climbed onto one of the mounts by the hay wain.

The man's wife nudged Rhonalyn and pointed to a horse whose reins were still tied to a post. "Get on."

Rhonalyn glanced back at Gabe. His expression told her not to obey, but when the man who'd subdued Kendra headed for her, she figured she didn't have any choice. She swept herself up into the saddle, thankful to at least be in a riding dress and not one of the full-skirted, royal gowns she'd worn at Nikledon.

The green-eyed woman directed Aisley onto the next horse. Mute, pale, and compliant as a ceramic doll, the child did as she was told. The woman swung up behind the girl. The red-haired man handed the woman her reins. He pulled loose Rhonalyn's reins next but held onto them as he mounted his own horse.

With no control of her animal, Rhonalyn gripped her mount's mane. She wanted to dismount, but she knew with a sickening stir in her stomach that she'd probably just end up back in the saddle and tied to it if she did.

Manton and his bald comrade handed out the lanterns, then threw open the barn's large door. The group urged their horses out into the semidarkness of a night half lit by the rising moon. Rhonalyn's horse jostled into a trot in their midst. Scared out of her mind, she glanced over at Aisley then back toward the barn but could no longer see Gabe or his companion.

54

The moment the rebels left, Wick twisted his hands in the rope. He growled in frustration. Manton had done his job well. A scuffling sound and a grunt came from Prince Gage. Wick squinted toward him in the dark. "What are you doing over there?"

Prince Gage's answer came as if through gritted teeth. "Getting hold of the knife I keep in my boot."

"You still have a knife?" Wick exhaled. "Thank God. Here I thought we'd be stuck here half the night trying to struggle out of these ropes." Already the hoofbeats of the rebel's horses were fading eastward.

A grunt of success came from Prince Gage, and a few moments later Wick felt His Highness behind him cutting him free. The rope popped loose, and Wick pulled his hands forward. It took him only a moment to locate his sword on the ground. "What now?" he asked, sweeping the weapon into his grasp. He knew exactly what he wanted to do, but he wasn't sure which version of Prince Gage was beside him, the one who ran away after being attacked or the one who barged into barns and audaciously jousted against the toughest knights in Edelmar.

"We go after them," Prince Gage answered.

Wick nodded. "I like that plan."

They ran for their horses, tucked in the darkness of the forest opposite the barn. Wick yanked his reins loose and grabbed onto his saddle. A rush of hooves coming from Dinslage pounded toward the barn. Wick froze in place. A large company of armored horsemen, carrying torches, swords, spears, and lanterns, drew to a stop outside the building. At the front of the group were three soldiers in yellow tabards with boars' heads above crossed spears, but none of the rest of the riders wore any visible colors, insignias, or coat-of-arms.

"You're sure this is where they came?" the foremost rider asked above the stir of the group.

"I'm sure," one of the Dinslage soldiers answered.

"Well, it looks deserted now. Check the barn."

"Empty." someone answered a moment later.

"There! Down the path that direction." A rider pointed eastward. "Their lantern light can still be seen."

"Then we're not too late. You three," the leader commanded, "return to your lord and report that she has indeed been taken by the rebels." The three Dinslage soldiers immediately turned their mounts and took off for the city. Wick felt relieved. Stopping the rebels was no longer just in their hands.

"Are we to bring her back then?" a rider next to the leader asked in the noblemen's tongue.

"Nay," the leader answered also in the nobleman's tongue, "but this way when she and her young companion turn up dead it will be assumed those who stole her are the ones responsible." Twisting in his saddle, the man switched back to the commoners' tongue. "Put out all but the lanterns. We ride to overtake them. Leave no witnesses, and take no prisoners."

The relief Wick had felt turned into alarm. Releasing his saddle, he turned to try to find Prince Gage.

His Highness seized his arm, holding Wick still, and raised a finger to his lips.

It felt like an eternity to Gage that the riders tarried in front of the barn. The group had well-made armor and an abundance of weapons. They were a force he'd have been thrilled to have going after the rebels, except that the last time he'd seen such a group he'd been chained to a wagon in their custody.

Even that knowledge hadn't prepared him though for the man's words about the women. Their lives were in danger, but the soldiers weren't riding to help them. They were riding to make sure they didn't come back. Their intention was to kill them along with the rebels, but why?

Who were the women? And who did these soldiers serve that they dared to kill nobles and blatantly disregard justice? Sir Jarret's actions in branding him came to mind. He recalled as well the unidentified soldiers with Felix and how they had laughed at him when he'd told them Felix was a traitor to Delkara and responsible for the murders of more than one lord's man.

Gage's mind spun. Felix's response to his accusation suddenly fell into a new light. *"You think I helped plan today's ambush? You've tracked me halfway across Delkara and gotten yourself captured and branded a rebel thief, but still you don't know."* Was this what he'd missed? That the soldiers with Felix that day were also traitors and murderers?

But traitors to who? Lady Natriece had said of Felix, *"He himself answers to someone, but I do not know who."* And Sir Jarret had claimed to serve a Delkaran lord, but could that be true? And if it was, why would they kill commoners and nobles?

He thought about his own ambush and then about Manton's claim. *"Risking losing our safety on that side of the border by attacking anyone in Edelmar would be absolutely foolish on our part. We're already* waging a war in Delkara that we're ill equipped to win. We've every motivation to not bring the wrath of any other kingdom down on ourselves."

A stark contrast to Felix's boast, *"I've gathered a new force of men. We will bring Edelmar to her knees."*

Bardon and Allard hadn't been killed by Manton's rebels. The reality of that sunk into Gage's thoughts with relief, confusion, and fear. By their own admission, the rebel commoners had still attacked lords and soldiers in Delkara and currently held two noblewomen hostage. They were not innocent, but regardless of why they had taken the two noblewomen or who the women were, it was completely unjust for the soldiers to murder any of them and even more so for them to blame the noblewomen's deaths on the rebels. The thought of it all made Gage sick.

Everything in him wanted to stop the soldiers, but he and Sir Wick were armor-less, almost weaponless, and looked like commoners. It was one thing for them to go up against rebels who had a crossbow and a few knives. It was a completely different matter for them to try to stop a military force. They'd get killed and probably wouldn't even slow down the soldiers.

A wave of extreme fear coursed through him along with a suffocating feeling of helplessness. It was the same helplessness that had lived inside him ever since being ambushed and watching Allard die. Agony twisted in Gage's stomach. More people were about to be murdered, and he couldn't do anything to stop it.

He closed his eyes and screamed inwardly. *God, this is wrong! Everything about it is wrong. And I can't prevent it, but You can! So do something!*

The soldiers took off down the eastern trail. Gage released Sir Wick's arm and held his breath, but nothing happened. No fire rained from heaven, no horses dropped dead, and no angels stood in their path. Gage stood there with his heart shuddering in grief and anger.

Sir Wick swung up onto his horse. "You coming or not?" the knight asked.

Gage looked up at him and said in despair. "Coming where?"

"After them."

"They're an army. We don't stand a chance."

"Maybe, and maybe not. But the ones who definitely don't stand a chance are those two women if we do nothing."

"I admire your courage, Sir Wick, but did you see the weapons those soldiers were carrying? What can we do against them?"

"With God on our side, we can fight."

"With what weapons?" Gage asked. "We'll die in their midst, accomplishing nothing, and you know it."

"I know it sounds crazy," Sir Wick said, "but I think we were brought here to save those two women."

Gage sighed. "I want to help them just as much as you do, but there's no way we can."

"No, we can't, but I think with God's help we can."

Gage groaned and shook his head.

"Just hear me," Sir Wick said. "I don't believe it's some random coincidence that so many things happened to bring you and me here at the exact moment to hear those two speaking in the noblemen's tongue. We could have been in Veiroot. You could be serving in some lord's fields. Or we could still have been tied up in that barn and found by the soldiers. But we weren't. We were right here. We met those women, and we know what those soldiers intend to do. And right now it's like there's a hand on my back pressing me forward and a compulsion inside me from God that we are supposed to go after them and save them."

Gage stood there trying to form some answer to the insanity of Sir Wick's words, but instead he heard Haaken's voice in his head. *"Gage, God cares about every person, and He is not standing idly by in the face of evil. What He asks us to do on His behalf is evidence of what He desires and who He is."*

Gage dug his fingers into his hair and inwardly cried out. "God, I want to believe that You care, and I want to make the right decision, but I am so afraid that if we go, we will not be enough and You will not show up to help us." He thought about how when he'd been alone in the cell in the barn's undercroft he'd been sure God had abandoned him, but then moments later Sir Wick had come. He hadn't been able to see the help that God had already sent, but that hadn't meant it wasn't there.

He lowered his hands and considered what it would mean to trust. He cringed. Waiting for God to show up hadn't been painless. A thought flew at him. *Don't go, and order Sir Wick to stay as well.*

The suggestion promised protection, but the moment it entered Gage's mind, chaos, fear, and darkness followed it. He knew the voice, and for the first time he also knew it was evil. He rejected it with everything in him. He would not use his power to force someone else to his will, and he was not going to let his fear twist him again into the kind of person who walked away and abandoned the people in his life who needed him.

Drawing a breath, he looked at the empty barn and the moonlit road. Allard and Bardon were gone. He couldn't change that, but he could do everything possible to save the people who were alive and currently at risk. If that meant riding after the soldiers, trusting that God had a plan and would help them, then so be it.

He mounted Athalos and nodded to Sir Wick. "We ride, and may God preserve us both."

Exuberant determination filled Sir Wick's voice. "Verily!"

Within moments they were tearing through the shadows of the moonlit trail following the distant lantern light of the soldiers. Athalos was more than happy to be racing after them, and Gage felt the horse's strides contact with the ground in sync with the furious beating of his heart. He breathed out a prayer. "God, I am still running scared, but I think at least this time I am running in the right direction. So prithee, help us. What are we to do when we catch up to the soldiers?"

His conversation with Haaken about seeking the back entrance to Veiroot Fortress and signaling when he found it came to mind.

55

Rhonalyn wasn't sure where she thought the commoners would take them, but a meadow loud with crickets and lit by four big fires was not what she'd expected. The commoners brought their horses to a stop between the fires and dismounted. Having wished the whole ride there that she could escape her horse, Rhonalyn found herself suddenly wanting to stay on the animal.

Burning wood crackled and sent glowing specks into the air. With the fires' heat on either side of her, the cool of the evening air at her back, and raw fear within her, Rhonalyn sweated and shivered at the same time. She glanced at Aisley. The child clung to her own horse and shook her head at the woman's gesture for her to get down.

Rhonalyn figured the girl would be pulled off the animal, but the woman's attention turned to movement along the edges of the meadow. Over twenty commoners began to slip into the light of the fires. Four individuals—a spry-looking old fellow, a large-boned man with a limp and a staff, a gray-haired woman, and a scar-faced young man—approached. Rhonalyn swallowed. Every commoner present bore a weapon of one form or another, everything from longbows hooked across their chests to cudgels tied to their belts.

The man with the limp spoke, his voice deep and placid. "Your Royal Highness, thank you for coming." He and his three companions bowed to her. Surprised, Rhonalyn blinked and stared as every commoner in the meadow bowed to her.

Still frightened but feeling slightly less afraid of being killed by them, Rhonalyn answered. "What choice did I have? I was brought here against my will."

"Please accept our sincere apologies for our methods." Leaning forward on his staff, the man motioned to all in the meadow. "We also had no choice. Had we attempted to speak with you any other way, the Delkaran lords would've stopped us. They don't wish you to hear the evils we can tell you of them. Many times before now we've considered bringing their wrongs forward and asking for help, but we've not done so since traditionally Keric has strictly chosen to have nothing to do with Delkara. When we learned that you'd met with King Strephon at Nikledon and made a deal with him, we knew we must attempt to speak with you ourselves."

Rhonalyn had feared even back in Dinslage that these people might be the very attackers she and Strephon had made plans to drive from the cliffs. Now she was certain of it. And here she was at their mercy. She cringed. She dare not tell them she and Strephon had become allies against them.

Their clear desire for information though was somewhat steadying to her. It meant she might be able to approach the situation more like a negotiation. Not exactly an easy mindset to hold considering her current position, but she knew what they wanted and, therefore, had an element of leverage she could apply.

Gaining accurate information from someone was always simpler if the person gave the information willingly. No doubt this was why the commoners were feigning respect for her and requesting her aid. She decided to test her supposition. "Why should I listen to you or trust you when still you keep me captive?" She nodded to her horse's reins, which were held by the red-haired commoner.

The spokesman and the old woman turned to the other two standing with them as if discussing the matter.

Rhonalyn held her breath. If they agreed with her, then there was hope, but if they disagreed, she had a feeling she and Aisley were as good as dead regardless of what information she did or did not give to them.

Agonizing moments passed, then the spokesman squared his shoulders and turned back to face her. "You are right. If we're asking you to trust us, we must also—"

The blast of a hunting horn cut off his words.

Rhonalyn assumed the long, loud call was a signal from one of their own people, but their sudden looks of confusion and fear said otherwise. Murmurs arose, weapons were drawn, and the commoners who'd brought her swiftly remounted their horses.

"Depart for the Joined Oak," the spry-looking old fellow said to the red-haired man. "We'll regather there."

The words had only just left his mouth when a company of horsemen charged into the meadow. Their helmets, armor, and weapons gleamed in the firelight.

Cries of warning rang out. Arrows and bolts flew at the soldiers from every direction. The clank of metal tips hitting armor filled the meadow. One soldier fell. Three horses went down, taking their riders with them and stumbling a fourth horse. The rest of the riders kept coming. Soldiers on foot poured from the woods as well.

The commoners scattered. Rhonalyn's horse was yanked into motion by the red-headed man while the woman with Aisley kicked her mount the opposite direction, but the soldiers were already in their midst.

In front of Rhonalyn, a hurled spear impaled the red-headed man leading her horse. He fell from his mount. Rhonalyn screamed and tried to kick her horse onward, but its reins were caught under the dead man's body.

The soldier who had just killed him turned his horse, drew his sword, and came at her. She shrieked and cowered as he pounded toward her, his weapon raised. A dark horse plowed into her attacker's mount from the side. The impact toppled the soldier and his horse and landed the dark horse on top of them in a sprawling stop that sent its armor-less rider flying over its head.

The soldier scrambled away from the two struggling animals and climbed to his feet. His features were hidden by his helmet, but there was no mistaking his intent. Sword in hand, he once more came at her. Panic filled Rhonalyn.

※

Gage galloped into the meadow behind Sir Wick. He veered Athalos toward a spear jutting from the ground beside a horse that had been taken down by the rebels' volley of arrows. He leaned over and snatched the weapon out of the ground. With it in hand, he raced into the chaos.

The hunting horn had at least warned the commoners they were not alone. It had also prevented the soldiers from quietly encircling the meadow, something they had been in the midst of doing when he and Sir Wick had caught up with them. Even so, the warning seemed to have come too late. In every direction commoners were engaged with the soldiers in a life-and-death battle that wouldn't last long.

Gage spotted the little noble girl on a horse with the common woman seated behind her. Two soldiers had them trapped near one of the fires. Sir Wick was already galloping to their aid, and Gage followed. The knight swung his sword. It clanged into the back of the closest soldier's helmet. The rider fell forward in his saddle. Gage prepared to thwack him off his horse with his spear, but a woman's scream from the opposite side of the meadow rent the air.

His heart jolting, Gage swerved Athalos in that direction, searching amid the fighting and flames for a woman's form. Coming instead upon a soldier on horseback leaning down about to slash at the back of a fleeing commoner, Gage angled Athalos and swung his spear like a cudgel into the back legs of the soldier's horse. The animal leapt forward, dumping the soldier. Racing onward, Gage galloped Athalos around a sword-versus-staff fight and past Nigel, who stood alone in the middle of the meadow. Then he saw the noblewoman.

Two horses were tangled together in front of her mount, and a soldier on foot was coming at her with a sword. Gage knew he wouldn't get to her in time. He raised his spear. He'd never been much good at throwing weapons, but it was better than doing nothing. Just as he prepared to heave the long shaft, Manton stumbled out of the grass behind the soldier and leapt onto his back.

Manton struggled to take the soldier down, and Gage would have come to his aid, but farther down the meadow a second soldier yanked his spear free from an old man's body, leveled it, and spurred his mount toward the noblewoman's back.

His heart racing, Gage kicked Athalos into a gallop toward the rider. Tightening his fingers on his own spear, he couched the weapon across Athalos's neck and leaned into the animal's strides. The soldier was already halfway to the woman. The beat of Athalos's hooves pounded through Gage's body. Exhaling, he clenched his legs tight and took aim at the man's armored side.

The soldier was so focused on the noblewoman through the slit in his helmet that, miraculously, he failed to notice Gage coming at him until it was too late for him to adequately re-aim his weapon.

Gage's spear slammed into the man's side. Unlike a tournament lance, the weapon didn't just ram the soldier off his horse. Instead, it pierced the man's armor and jolted painfully in Gage's bare hand. The unbroken shaft hit Gage's own chest and flipped up to crack into his chin as the man's falling weight rotated the weapon up and over the side of his horse. Gage tipped backward to keep from being unhorsed by the shaft and galloped onward.

He managed to right himself a moment later and spun Athalos back around. Breathing hard and again weaponless but thankful to be alive, he again raced Athalos toward the noblewoman. In light of the fire and the moon, he saw Manton struggle to his feet above the soldier he'd been fighting.

Gage slid Athalos to a stop. The noblewoman looked like she was about to be sick but otherwise seemed unharmed. Manton yanked a knife from a gap in the soldier's armor and stumbled toward his fallen red-headed comrade.

Gage urged Athalos closer. "Manton."

Cutting swiftly at something, Manton straightened and thrust the woman's reins and a lantern at him. "Gabe, get her out of here. Take her somewhere safe. Go!"

Gage met Manton's fierce, grief-filled gaze, then grabbed the reins and the lantern.

56

Wick had reached the second soldier just as the man seized the bridle of the little girl's and the woman's horse. He hacked at the soldier's arm. It dented the man's armor and did what Wick hoped it would. It shifted his attention.

Hollering, the soldier turned and thrust at him. Wick parried the blow. The soldier swung again, even harder. This time Wick diverted the power of the soldier's blade upward and tried to stab at the man's exposed armpit. The soldier jammed his elbow down, and Wick's sword skimmed harmlessly across his plate armor.

Growling, the soldier came at him with fierce strength. For a moment it was all Wick could do just to ward off the swift series of thrusts and strikes. He survived the onslaught by long-practiced skill fueled by extreme apprehension.

Unable to take a blow to his unarmored person, Wick couldn't afford to attempt the riskier offensive maneuvers that might actually have injured the soldier and ended the fight. Instead he was too busy protecting himself and keeping the man occupied. He considered his effort a success though because their battle allowed the common woman time to throw herself and the noble girl off their horse. On the ground, the two of them scrambled toward the woods.

Wick deflected another of the soldier's strikes but misjudged his parry by a finger's breadth. The sting of the man's blade bit into his arm. He gritted his teeth and warded off a slash at his stomach. Then he made his own aggressive strike. Since he couldn't protect his back and was positive the soldier would kill him if he tried to flee, he figured he was in a fight to the death.

A moment later, with swords clashing, they turned their horses too close to the fire. Wick's mount sidestepped to avoid the flames, but the soldier leaned out to stab at him anyway. The overextension meant that the soldier's sword lacked strength as it came at Wick and that his hand was within Wick's reach. Had the man been firmly seated in his saddle, neither would have mattered, but as it was, the combination gave Wick the perfect opportunity.

Knocking the man's blade aside, Wick seized the soldier's wrist and yanked hard toward himself. The soldier fell forward, right off his horse. He hit the ground helmet first and did not rise. With a rush of triumph and relief, Wick drew a breath but then spotted another soldier on foot headed toward the little girl. She was still a stone's throw from the tree line and completely unprotected.

He kicked his horse into a gallop and raced toward the child who looked terrified. "Your ladyship," he called as he thundered toward her. "You won't outrun them on foot! Give me your hand." Slowing his horse, he reached down for her.

Glancing toward the soldier coming at her, she grabbed Wick's arm. He drew her upward and rode onward leaning the opposite direction as she scrambled behind him. There wasn't much space with his saddlebags, but as he kicked his mount back into a gallop, her small body pressed against his back and her arms wrapped around his sides.

Dodging his horse around a soldier on horseback, Wick searched for Prince Gage. He spotted him on the opposite edge of the meadow with the noblewoman and Manton. "Hold on back there!" he said as he cut between two fires and raced toward them.

"Your friend is coming with the little girl," Manton said. "Now, go!"

Gage glanced at the noblewoman. She wavered forward and looked the same way he'd felt after witnessing his first battle. "Manton, I don't think she's going to stay on!"

Manton looked at the woman, then at the meadow. Gage followed his gaze. At least three other soldiers were already headed toward them. Cursing, Manton grabbed the reins of the noblewoman's horse from Gage and swung himself up behind her. With one arm wrapped around her and the other holding the reins, Manton kicked the horse into motion. "Get to the woods!"

Clutching the lantern, Gage drove Athalos swiftly into the trees. Manton followed with the noblewoman, and Sir Wick and the little girl pounded behind him. "They're coming fast!" Sir Wick warned.

"Go straight for a hundred paces, then veer left," Manton instructed. "There should be a game trail."

Between the lantern's light and the moon, Gage managed to steer Athalos at a fast trot around big trees and low branches while ignoring the underbrush and small trees slapping at him. The others followed on Athalos's heels, weaving fast and hard through the woods.

Gage tried to go straight, but with no way to orient himself he had no idea what direction he was taking them. He heard a yell and the sound of horses following them.

"Left," Manton said.

Gage turned that way and spotted the well-worn game trail. He angled onto it and kicked Athalos back into a gallop. He heard Manton and Sir Wick do the same behind him.

They flew along the trail, down a hill, through a creek, and around the edge of a bluff. The moment they were on the bluff's far side, Manton instructed. "Turn off the trail just ahead, and go down the incline. The moment we reach the bottom, blow out the lantern."

Hoping Manton knew what he was doing, Gage drew Athalos to a walk, found a gap in the trees, and turned. The ground angled swiftly under Athalos's feet. Gage leaned back in his saddle and was glad there were fewer trees on the slope. Steering carefully, he led the way to the flat ground at the bottom and stopped Athalos. As the others joined him, he heard the pounding of hooves coming around the bluff above them. He swiftly opened the lantern and blew it out. Then he prayed to God that the soldiers would simply ride past.

The soldiers' horses pummeled down the trail, their tack and weapons jangling. Gage held his breath. The two foremost riders galloped past the turn they had made and on down the game trail. A moment later, five other riders did the same. All of them continued full speed along the curving forest trail, obviously assuming their prey was still somewhere ahead.

Gage watched until their lights disappeared from sight. He then exhaled slowly.

"What now?" Sir Wick asked from the darkness.

"We get out of here before they come back," Manton replied. "The moment they realize we're not in front of them, they'll turn around and search this whole area." Manton dismounted, leaving the noblewoman's dark form alone on her horse. "Thankfully, I know a few things about these woods, which hopefully they don't. This way." Leading the noblewoman's horse, Manton headed into the black embrace of the trees, straight out from the hill they had just come down.

With little choice but to follow, Gage urged Athalos after Manton. Sir Wick rode close behind him. It was rough going, even though Manton was clearly choosing the largest openings he could find through the trees. Gage tried not to let the branches that caught on him and Athalos whip backward into Sir Wick's face, but he was having a hard enough time seeing and avoiding them himself.

It seemed no one else could either, for they cracked and twisted their way through the woods with so much noise that Gage was sure the soldiers back at the clearing would hear them. Somewhere off to their left a stick cracked loudly. Gage felt the hair on his arms rise. He stared hard in that direction. The moonlight exposed patches of ground between the trees, but otherwise nothing but black tree trunks and groping branches filled the shadows surrounding them.

Gage ducked through the next set of trees, and a spider's web caught him across the face and neck. The sticky strands of the web clung to his skin. In the next moment he felt something scurry down his cheek. He dropped Athalos's reins and smashed the thing. Just then a bird screeched somewhere nearby.

"Can't he light the lantern again?" a small, frightened voice asked behind him. "I don't like the dark."

"None of us do, little one, but right now it's keeping us safe," Sir Wick said. "And personally I'd mind it a little less if your fingernails weren't digging into my sides."

"Sorry."

Ahead of Gage, the noblewoman spoke for the first time. "Where are you taking us?"

"Somewhere safe," Manton answered.

"My guard is in Dinslage. I want to go back to Dinslage." The authority in her words didn't match the tremor in her voice.

"If you do, you'll end up killed by those soldiers. Now shush," Manton said, "I need to concentrate. I've never tried to find his place from this direction before."

With Manton trekking in front of them, they wandered wearily through the dark woods for what felt like forever. Twice Manton stopped and adjusted their course.

The third time he did so, Gage rubbed at his tired eyes. "Are you sure you know where you're going?"

"Yes, it's just over this rise." With the noblewoman's horse in tow, Manton headed up a lightly wooded hill toward a rocky outcropping that shone brightly in the moonlight. He led them through the rocks and then down a trail that curved back into the trees again. The sound of gurgling water burst to life to their left, and suddenly they were stopped in front of what Gage was pretty sure was a woodsman's hut.

Manton knocked on the door.

"Who's there?" a disgruntled voice called out.

"It's me, Manton."

The door swung open, revealing the light of a candle held by a squinting man with long hair and thick limbs. "What are you doing in these parts at this hour?"

"Trying to avoid soldiers." Manton answered.

The man shook his head. "Leave it to you." He held his candle higher and eyed the rest of them. "How many are you?"

"Five."

"Well, see to your horses, then come inside."

Exhausted and trusting that Manton knew what he was doing, Gage swung off Athalos. Sir Wick followed and helped the little girl down as well. The noblewoman was the last to dismount. She hit the ground but stood clutching her horse like she was afraid to let go. Gage knew the feeling. He glanced back the way they'd come and wished he could promise her and himself that all would be well, but the night was far from over.

Discussion Questions

1. Do you think the monks would have believed Gage had he told them the whole truth immediately? How did his concealment of the truth actually make the monks that much more suspicious of him?

2. Have you ever been afraid to tell someone the truth not knowing how they would respond? The truth has a way of coming out eventually. Have you ever had someone conceal something from you? How did you feel when the truth was revealed?

3. The monks thought Gage a thief and a liar, yet how did they treat him? Tending to him and praying for him took time and effort. Why did they choose to do these things regardless of thinking him a thief?

4. Do you treat every person you encounter with dignity and care even if they may not be a nice or good person? How did the monks care and grace toward Gage communicate God's heart?

5. What is it that Princess Rhonalyn values most? How does what she values impact the way she treats the people around her?

6. Have you ever placed more value on looking good and being the one in control than on caring well for the people around you?

7. Rhonalyn seems confident and capable as a ruler, but where does her confidence come from? What would happen if she did not have the security of a castle and people to order about? In what are you placing your trust?

8. Gage chose for years to believe that God did not exist. Why does he want to believe this? God intervened to save Gage, and

this makes Gage angry. What is it that Gage has assumed God's intervention means?

9. Brother Sholan is expecting that Gage is either a follower of God or a nonbeliever, but Gage defines himself as a believer in God but as someone who does not love God and who does not want to serve God. Why is this concerning to Brother Sholan? (Read James 2:14-20)

10. Are we saved by works? How about by faith? What if we're doing good works but not as a means of serving God? Gage has been following the principles of Christianity but not because he wishes to obey or honor God. What if now Gage does works to appease God, but has no faith in who God says He is? (Even the demons believe God exists, but they reject Him as their King) Why are both faith and works important? What does our faith and our works together reveal about our heart toward God?

11. Gage has lost so much; how has he let that change him? Have you ever felt like you were the only one you could trust? How did your distrust affect your choices? Where you able to live well in community or did your distrust leave you isolated?

12. Gage wants to protect the people around him but doesn't take into account what they want. How could he do a better job of helping others and of letting other people help him?

13. Gage's actions after the ambush majorly impacted Sir Wick's life. How did Wick cope with being sent back to the White Fortress? What kind of decisions did he make in regard to how he would respond to what was being said and assumed about him?

14. Have you ever been betrayed by someone who promised you things and then walked out on those promises? Were you able to forgive them and make healthy choices going forward?

15. Gage fears that he will not be enough to save the people around him. What is the difference between being responsible for our own actions and being responsible for everything that happens?

16. When Gage and Haaken talk about wanting God to stop evil, Haaken points out that if God put a stop to evil here and now it would mean the end of every person. How does this concept change your perspective of God's grace toward us all?

17. Haaken acknowledges that for a long time he didn't recognize his need to be saved from the evil in his own life. Have you ever seen yourself as the good person and others as the evil people? How might recognizing the evil in yourself change the way you respond to other people in your life who still need to understand God's grace toward them?

18. How does Haaken deal with what Gage has chosen to believe about God? Have you ever gotten mad at someone because of their beliefs rather than asking more questions to understand why they believe what they do? Haaken chose to go away and process what Gage said and then come back and apologize. How did that change the way Gage thought about God?

19. Rhonalyn is annoyed that her father's pride is getting in the way of renegotiating the harbor's toll, but what is it that is motivating her to want to re-negotiate the toll?

20. Rhonalyn cares a lot about title and position. How does the status of the people around her impact how she views them and responds to them?

21. Do you let the position someone holds change the way you respond to them? Have you ever treated someone younger than you as less important or less significant than yourself? Or have you yourself ever been treated as less valuable? Is a person's value

in their age, gender, title, etc., or is the value of every person the same, no matter who they are?

22. Have you ever let your own or someone else's power and status influence your decision making? Can you think of any modern position, job, or education title that prompts us to allow people additional influence in our lives?

23. We're told in Scripture to obey and submit to governing authorities for the praise of those who do good and the punishment of those who do evil. (1Peter 2:13-15) Is there a place for doing what Sir Wick did and overriding the authority of people who are using their power to do evil instead of good?

24. What changed Gage's mind when it came to helping the two noblewomen? Truth spoken into our lives sometimes takes awhile to make a difference. Have you ever had words of truth from your past come to mind just when you needed them? Have you ever spoken truth to someone else and wondered if those words would ever make a difference?

25. God does not completely protect Prince Gage; instead God uses Gage's injuries and encounters to bring about a greater purpose. Have you ever wondered why God has allowed something hard in your life? Have you gotten the chance to look back at any of those moments later on and been able to see how God used them to accomplish something good?

LIKE GAGE, YOU will probably have some hard experiences in your life. So know that God is who He says He is, that He has not abandoned you, and that God still loves you even when hard things happen to you, because God always has a purpose for what He allows.

Acknowledgements

I WANT TO thank my mother, Eileen Hoffman, for encouraging me to pursue my fiction writing and for being a part of so much of my journey as a writer. I am hugely blessed that she and my family stand with me as I navigate writing, publishing, and selling.

This book had a lot of concepts that were challenging to communicate well, and my gratitude goes to all of you who listened to me process what God placed on my heart for this book and who all helped me brainstorm how to write those messages. My beta readers especially were hugely helpful in identifying were those messages were being hindered and how to fix those scenes. All of you helped make this book so much better!

My heartfelt "Thank You!" to everyone who helped during this project, particularly Eileen Hoffman, BriAnn Beck, Rachael Lofgren, Katie Briggs, Victor Michlik, Gabriela Michlik, Colton Anderson, Oren Printy, Kate Damn, Nancy Bjorkman, Patricia Mueller, Betty Arntds, Kevin Miller, Elena Karoumpali, and everyone at my publisher.

"Listen to advice and accept instruction, that you may gain wisdom in the future." Proverbs 19:20

Books by Given Hoffman

Contemporary Suspense
The Eighth Ransom

Medieval Action/Adventure
The Tournament's Price
The Rebel's Mark
The Healer's Secret

Nonfiction
The Voices of the Pioneers: Homeschooling in Minnesota

Visit GivenHoffman.com to learn more.

www.ingramcontent.com/pod-product-compliance
Lightning Source LLC
LaVergne TN
LVHW040731250326
834688LV00031B/250